THE FEAST OF THE INNOCENTS

These pages are dedicated to the author's parents, with deep gratitude for their love and encouragement, and to the famed philosopher and author of *Caleb Williams* and *Mandeville*, the esteemed Mr. William Godwin.

I am that dark, that disinherited,
That all dishonored Prince of Aquitaine,
The Star upon my scutcheon long hath fled;
A black sun on my hite doth yet remain!
Oh, thou that didst console me not in vain,
Within the Tomb, among the midnight dead,
Show me Italian seas, and blossoms wed,
The rose, the wine-leaf, and the golden grain.

Say, am I Love or Phoebus? Have I been
Or Lusignan or Biron? By a queen
Caressed within the Mermaid's haunt I lay,
And twice I crossed the unpermitted stream,
And touched an Orpheus' lute as in a dream,
Sighs of a Saint, and laughter of a Fay!

—Gérard de Nerval, "El Desdichado" (trans. Andrew Lang)

Cast of Principal Characters

Cyrus Plainstaff – A young man of dubious parentage, straitened means, and desperate circumstances who has traveled from London to the moors of Scotland in hopes of escaping the relentless doom that has haunted his steps ever since the death of his father.

Squire Toby Wadham – A friend of the Gosselins with a penchant for gambling and a love for London politics and playhouses.

Mrs. Leaske – A housekeeper in the service of His Lordship the 34th Earl of Lauderness.

Lord Andrew Ebenezer Montrose – The 34th Earl of Lauderness and four times widowed Lord Montrose has a fondness for marriage, the gaming table, and the tender ministrations of his housekeeper.

Childermass – A young chimney sweeper with pale, sharp features, a marble eye, and a taste for chivalric tales, hidden passages, and discarded thumbscrews.

Dagworth – The keeper of the priory's kennels, Master Dagworth divides his time between encouraging his hounds to love the taste of fox blood and sparring with Master Childermass.

Feversham – Melancholic and indolent by nature, the Master of Horses often finds himself either the butt of Dagworth's jests or the observer of his frequent quarrels.

Lord Withing Gosselin – The young grandson of Sir Robert Gosselin whose high spirits and charming affability seem only matched by the mysterious pall of doom that seems, at odd times, to haunt his moods and which only the stupor of liquor can drive away.

Clarice Abelin – The niece of Reverend Abelin. Her chief vices? Curiosity and Childermass.

Lady Mariah Gosselin – The cousin of Withing Gosselin. Are her suspicions of Childermass well-founded or misplaced?

Sir Robert Gosselin – The lord of the Priory and grandfather to young Withing.

Reverend Hugo Abelin – The household chaplain; uncle to Clarice Abelin; a man of few words and many secrets.

The Marquis Antoine St. Aubert – If the kind reader will be patient, the Marquis will have the pleasure of describing himself to you in the thirteenth chapter of this volume.

Shipwash – The intrepid head of a wassailing troupe of men known as The Worshipful Company of Grocers; the one-time opponent of a Scottish witch and her wicked sons.

Volume I

Chapter One: In which Cyrus comes to Houndswick and dreams.

In the winter of 1665, a stranger came to Houndswick.

Twilight had settled its royal purple upon the distant hills and valleys of Annandale County, darkening the rising mists that surrounded the haggard Scottish mountains and heathlands like the great shadow of a storm. A few stars twinkled in the pitchy darkness but, like the moon, their cold brilliance was often obscured by the grey, gauzy clouds that passed across the sky. As faint as this light was, the silvery shafts that fell illumined the shades of roiling mist so that they shone with a dim, amphibious light.

The swinging lantern of a watchman sent its wavering, solicitous beam down a Houndswick alley as the young man stopped before an inn, shaking off the snow that had settled on his shoulders. He looked behind him, the constant notion of a half-heard, following footstep riding him like an unshakeable weight. The innkeeper, who was standing beside his porch, a clear glass of scotch in his hand, noticed this look. His smile when the young man looked up was in an empty, emotionless register.

"Looking for a place to stay," he stated.

"Yes."

They went inside. The storm lantern that stood upon a nearby table shone upon a ledger filled with the scrawls of travellers.

"Your name?"

"Cyrus Plainstaff," the young man said.

The innkeeper bit the nib of his pen and looked more speculatively at his guest. The traveller, a young man of nineteen years, was clothed in drab leather and jerkin with a face that seemed at first glance to be cut of the same severe cloth. However, this first impression was soon proven on closer examination to be largely the combined effects of anxious care and fatigue; the thin lips held in them more wariness than disapproval and the large, dark eyes were more expressive of a melancholic nature than a dour distemper. With his cropped, dark hair, his unadorned loose-sleeved white shirt, and the immoderate sparkle of peculiar fire that often lit the gloom of his countenance, he had all the appearance of either a fanatic or a poet. After considering the curious name that he had given, the innkeeper began to wonder whether he was not one of those tiresome Fifth Monarchy men or, worse, some Covenanter with John Calvin and Foxe buzzing incessantly in his brain amid confused ideas of revolution and Scottish independence.

"Tell me," he began slowly. "Where do you hail from?"

"Essex County, sir," was the prompt reply.

"And what brings you so far north, young Englishman?"

Cyrus thought back to the miles of highway and heathland that he had travelled in the last week.

"Please," he said. "I am very tired."

The innkeeper shrugged. "Of course. But you must understand, most people who stop to sample my hospitality usually are. You are hardly an exception, lad."

"I am here to look for work."

"Good, good. Though Houndswick is a peculiar place to go looking for it."

"I have had a peculiarly difficult time finding work everywhere else."

"Too bad." The innkeeper unhooked a brass key from his belt and gave it to the young man. "I doubt that Houndswick will serve you any better."

As Cyrus began to ascend the stairs, the innkeeper called out, "I don't play the host to thieves or cutthroats. If you're looking for trouble, find another man to burden."

He kept an eye on the stranger until he had disappeared up the landing, the lantern on the table throwing a tremulous shadow across the painting that hung at his back. With a sigh, he turned to watch the quivering of its possessed valleys, while lifting the glass of scotch again to his lips.

***

That night, Cyrus dreamt of a horror that had happened to him the previous night during his journeying, when he had stood in the middle of a valley heathland, several miles from Houndswick and far from his Essex home. The night air had been very still. There was not a shudder of wind about the land, nor even the faint rustle of some nocturnal beast amongst the thickets: only the silent mists that left their dewy fingers upon the rough rocks and the high, grey grasses of the moors.

That was when he had heard it: the rising, unrestrained laughter of humor given over to madness, of a hilarity that sounded to the startled and horrified hearer to contain in it as much agony as amusement. It rose like the rippling black waters of some abysmal font and then grew until, like the foaming breakers of the sea rushing headlong to murder themselves upon the jagged rocks, it died away and ceased with a finality as abrupt as its commencement. Cyrus had stood there, shaking fully as much as the laugher himself must have done when given over to the throes of his humor.

It was evident that whoever this person might be, only a madman could have uttered such a cry – however, there was something in that ecstatic laugh that had held the nearly human quality of despair and that humanity, lonely as Cyrus was, filled him for the first time with a desperate hope, like that of a drowning man who clutches at the hand held out to him above the surf, little caring whether it is the hand of his dearest friend or cruelest enemy: knowing only that it is a living, human hand.

"Whoever you are," he cried. "Show your face!"

As he uttered this last word, his voice broke but he kept his eyes steadily in the direction of the eastern heaths and forests, knowing that whoever his potential companion might be, that last ghastly laugh had risen from this direction. The silence that filled the interlude after the young man's plea seemed to intimate something almost like pity, though the traveller could not be certain whether it was merely his own wearied imagination that suggested this or not. But, like the brightening of the cold moon's rays as it emerges from behind a wreath of pale cloud, the traveller felt something change in the immediate atmosphere that surrounded him; but this change, like added moonlight, lent little warmth to his precarious position, only a new sense of mystery. He scanned the mountainous ridges that reared above him, glistening with the frost of December snow, but saw no sign of movement there nor upon the path ahead or behind.

For some reason, however, his wandering eyes lingered particularly upon a patch of dead weeds and grasses that surrounded a tall old tree whose wide, dark trunk and extended branches shadowed the eastern portion of the valley over which it dominated. So tall was this ancient growth that its upper branches managed to catch the last faint rays of the dying sun so that the twining, leafless limbs seemed at first like crimson-dabbled hands extended in idolatrous supplication to the Moon. But on second glance, the bent of those boughs seemed less worshipful and more covetous, as though their trembling in the wind was provoked less by reverence and more by a terrible longing that seemed only restrained by the physical limitations of the upmost branches which, for all their looming height, could only barely touch the silver rim of the Moon with their dark fingertips. Yet something in the faint, chill breath of wind that swept westward past the tree and brushed the traveller's own face carried with it a patient promise as though to say, Thou art above me and I can but watch thee now – but there will come a time this night when thou shalt be lowered into my arms and then thou shalt surely be mine. Cyrus colored slightly at the dark lust that his imagination had so powerfully conjured, but he could not forbear looking at that tree with the same fascination that he would have felt had he looked into a wide and blossoming maw.

***

There had been something in that tree, he remembered; something that had climbed the coiled branches with the ease that a man ascends a treacherous staircase, perilous to strangers but grown familiar to him through the practice of long custom. Up and up, from thick and sturdy branches to frail and bending boughs, the thing rose with a lightness and ease that convinced the traveller for a moment that he was looking upon a monkey or some other such creature – until the thing, having reached the topmost precarious branch of the tree, turned its face towards him. The moonlight at its back blanched the wind-blown hair to a color as white as the dead grasses that grew about the base of the tree, but the lingering rays of the setting sun lit up the eyes so that they burned like two blood-colored jewels in a face otherwise shadowed. Cyrus realized with a jolt, then, that it was a man.

It is peculiar how a series of impressions, howsoever imaginative and fanciful they may be, can so quickly revise a man's opinion on something. Cyrus, so desperate before for companionship that he had cried for help from a thing whose very laughter had frozen his heart, when at last confronted with a fellow human who more than probably was the personage whom he had implored aid from, was suddenly desirous of one thing only: to flee this terrible valley. At that moment it appeared that the man in the tree, who had been scanning the valley for the person who had so desperately called to him for help, at last settled his gaze upon the traveller. Then, with the same alacrity that had informed his ascent up the tree, he began to descend to the ground with the evident intention of running to the youth's assistance.

The young man's nerves had borne a great many terrors that night without fully snapping, but the impression that this sight had upon him was more than he could bear. Without another thought, he took to his heels and began to run down the road as though the Devil himself were after him rather than the peculiar, red-eyed stranger in the tree. He was not at all sure, or even interested, in the direction that his flight took him, but continued to run, his ears attentive to any sound that might indicate the pursuit of the stranger. In spite of his terror, he ventured as he fled to turn his head back and see if he was yet alone –

***

– only to find that his dream had shifted and now stood him upon the porch of the Houndswick chapel. He had passed it for the first time only several hours before in his waking life, and the grey stones and glass windows of its making uprose in his imagination with an added grandeur, swelling it to ten times its original proportion. In the center of its sanctuary, flourishing between the pulpit and before the pews, was the tree that Cyrus had dreamt of earlier in the field. There was a bloated contour to its spreading limbs that made his eye linger long and fascinatedly upon it before lowering to the congregation.

Shadows milled in driftwood motions around the sinewy structure of the tree. Cyrus felt himself begin to shake, all his nerves writhing. Someone took his hand. He turned, teeth chattering, but could not see who held him. He could only hear a voice close by his ear that whispered for him to open his eyes.

"Oh God – it's too horrible – I must come awake, I must – "

It was his own voice, but he did not recognize it; his own tongue, but he did not feel it move. He came awake with a start in the morning sunlight, his own face pale and bloodless.

Chapter Two: In which Cyrus meets with a peculiar procession.

The innkeeper was enjoying a smoke on the porch of his inn when Cyrus emerged at last.

"You'll be wanting a bit of breakfast?" the man gestured with his pipe to the back door of the kitchen.

Cyrus nodded and the two of them stepped inside the scullery. The man poured him a glass of milk and set a slice of honeyed cake on the table. "Are you *really* looking for work here in Houndswick, then?"

"Yes." Cyrus sipped at his milk. "Really and truly."

The innkeeper shook his head, breathed a wreath of smoke out, looked at Cyrus with a kind of dead calm.

"Sleep well last night, lad?"

Cyrus started. "Why do you ask?"

"Well, I looked in on you last night – " The man smiled as Cyrus stared. "—and you appeared quite restless."

"I see that privacy and hospitality don't go hand in hand around these parts."

"I'm a careful man, as I'm sure you've noticed."

"Well, if you must know, I didn't sleep well."

"It would have surprised me if you had, young man."

"You don't seem to have a very high opinion of your own establishment," Cyrus observed.

"No, no, it's not that," the innkeeper replied.

"You didn't lend me a haunted old room, did you?" After his dream last night, Cyrus's question was only half in jest.

The innkeeper's smile returned, his ancient eyes observing the confusion in Cyrus's face.

"No," he said. "I slept poorly myself as well." He drew on his pipe. "What sort of job are you looking to find, Master Plainstaff?"

"I was a shepherd in Essex."

The innkeeper looked out the window and Cyrus followed his gaze by instinct. There was nothing to be seen save a few passing carriages, the lower floor of a tenement across the street, windows bright with candles, and a slight snatch of early morning sky that shone wanly above the distant church steeple.

"Not many shepherds out there, are there?"

Cyrus did not bother to reply.

"Well?" the innkeeper turned to look at him. "Looks like the market's freed up just for you, hasn't it, lad?"

Thanking the man for his hospitality, Cyrus stood and left the scullery, leaving the innkeeper to watch his departure with a silent smile.

***

Cyrus felt the stale draft of the scullery door as it closed behind him, shutting out the innkeeper's enigmatic humor and any further words of advice or probing questions. There would be no more knowledge to be gained from that quarter – not if he himself did not prove equally forthcoming to his host. It was easy to see that the man did not fully trust either Cyrus or the bland reason that he had given for choosing Houndswick as a harbor. But Cyrus felt no reason to dispel the dead, calm question in the innkeeper's gaze. The light of enthusiasm or pity that would replace that questioning look could presage disaster. Let them all think of him as merely a mysterious stranger. The moment that anyone came to learn the true reason behind his flight could very well be his last.

There was a definite drift in the moving current of townsfolk and Cyrus allowed himself to be pulled along, looking out for any passing cart of sheep's wool, any sign of a fellow shepherd or shepherd's boy. A merchant elbowed past him, still following the general momentum of the crowd. Cyrus lost his footing and would have fallen beneath the press, had someone not caught him by the shoulders and waited for him to regain his balance before releasing him. In that long moment, Cyrus had time to notice the fingers gauntleted in leather that held him so tightly and caught a black, scorched scent that dankly filled his senses.

He half-turned, then, to look at his rescuer, a young man close to the same age as himself. At first, he believed it to be a trick of the light that caused the young man's eye to seem fixed and motionless, like the sightless gaze of some marble angel. Yet he was startled when the stranger happened to turn his face askance, allowing Cyrus to glimpse his other eye, its pale luminance settling upon him with a look of questioning curiosity that was undoubtedly quick and alive. It was only after a long moment that Cyrus realized that this uncanny effect was produced because the young man had a marble eye.

"Are you a stranger? I have not seen your face before," the chimney sweeper said.

Before Cyrus could reply, a distant murmur of thunder drew his attention away from the strange young man's interrogation. Towards the east, where the sun rose against a dark massing of clouds, they saw a drawn platform pulled by two horses and flanked by four men wearing the dark, hooded garments of executioners. Their prisoner stood upon the platform, tied to a stake of wood, his head drooped against his chest as though he were drowsing. When the rain began to fall steadily, the horses began instinctually to fall into step with its blurred and beating rhythm.

***

Alan started awake at the touch of raindrops upon his face. An hour ago, when they had awakened him in his cell and brought him out to the back of the prison, when they had stood him in the cart and tied him to the stake, the ropes had felt unbearably tight, the more so because he was already having difficulty catching his breath, finding it hard to think of what was about to happen to him without beginning to faint and weep abjectly. The guards only watched him and smiled.

When he left the grounds of the prison and began his winding journey through Houndswick's streets to the gallows, he was met with the usual horde that awaits any condemned man. The guards allowed him to accept their offerings of bitter ale and he drank until the ropes felt like friendly arms and the silhouette of the scaffold looked as soft and indistinct as a dream. The tears that had run across his face were dried and a comforting warmth stole over him. By the time he had reached the place where Cyrus and the one-eyed chimney sweeper caught sight of him, he was barely conscious.

When the rain began, however, he stirred and a sense of dull horror began to animate him. The guards were obliged to support him on either side to prevent him from falling once they unbound him. He felt as though he were being led along the steps of an old, obscene waltz that he had seen many times but never been obliged to dance. A girl from the crowd was laughing at his tardiness, saying that he was slower than a reluctant bride at the altar, prompting some jokester to coarsely whistle out a wedding march.

When he finally reached the center of the scaffold and had a clearer view of the noose, his legs buckled. Naturally, the guards were ready for him. Their hands had carried every sort of man to that dangling circle of rope: the ones who swooned, the ones who cursed, the ones who wept. Usually bets were made the night beforehand, as to which sort of prisoner they would have on their hands the following morning. So far, Alan had disappointed all the more exaggerated predictions. He would, apparently, simply allow himself to be led to the noose without any response more enthusiastic or objectionable than a slight, awed trembling.

The crowd was growing restless. Somewhere in that sea of eyes beneath him, he caught the look of bewildered pity on the face of Cyrus and the glint of marble in the face of the one-eyed young man. Of all the faces, those two were the only ones untouched by either the tincture of malice or of coarse amusement. In Cyrus's face, there was only sympathy; in the marble-eyed young man's countenance, curiosity. Under one, he felt a martyr; under the other, a player in some exalted, ritual masque. Both were roles that Alan preferred to that of mere murderer. He felt dreamlike again, restored to his original state of unreality.

Then, as they put the stiff noose around his throat, an idea occurred to him. A moment of blindingly brilliant improvisation, with a simplicity that stunned him, a certain surety that it would dazzle his audience. His lips parted and he saw their faces grow pale as some of them realized what it was that he was about to say.

"The shadow of Houndswick," he whispered, knowing that no matter how lowly he spoke, that they could all hear him in that hush. "The dead ones. Let me speak their names and then – then I call on you, my fellow townsmen, to spare me."

The thunder behind the mountains mingled with the crowd's murmured, hungering assent.

Chapter Three: In which Alan trades one kind of fate for another.

Cyrus had been looking all this while for a passage in the sea of human bodies that surrounded him; some egress of flesh that would allow him to escape the coming, gruesome spectacle of the prisoner's hanging. The young man with the marble eye left off the careful attention that he had been paying to the scaffold and, noticing Cyrus's discomfort, pushed his long chimney sweeper's broom, dusty with soot and cobwebs, through the crowd, making way for Cyrus. Surprised at this second act of sympathy, Cyrus saw his pointing finger and followed his direction without thinking, only to find himself even closer to the stage of the scaffold than before. He looked back at the chimney sweeper, horrified by this consequence of his misunderstanding, but could catch no glimpse of him past the heads of those who surrounded him. Now he stood so close to that wooden platform that, as the executioners took their places on either side of the condemned sacrifice, his own body trembled in tandem with every footfall.

But at that moment, Alan whispered those words that sounded to Cyrus so mysterious and yet seemed to be understood by every Houndswick citizen to which they were addressed and he saw the guards lift the noose clear of the prisoner's neck and stand back, waiting for him to speak. And this is what he heard:

"John, Thomas, William, Robert, Nicholas, Julian, Francis, Henry, Christopher…"

Alan recited the names with a shaky look of expectancy and at every name, the crowd seemed to breathe differently. The recitation had the sound of a litany about it; Cyrus felt as though with each name, some particular image and tale was awakened in the minds of the listeners – an image that he, the uninitiated, could not himself see.

"Will they never be avenged?" cried Alan. He was very pale. "Why must we silently accept these horrors and do nothing to prevent them?"

The hangmen looked at one another, uneasy. Cyrus, being a stranger, had no idea what the condemned young man was speaking of, but his words had evidently animated the crowd. They began to press closer to the scaffold – one woman threw an iron spoon at a guard, while another shouted, "Shall we lose all our young men, then? Let him not be hung!"

A few others shouted, “Spare him! He honored the names of the slain! Spare him!”

“No one may protect him as he leaves Houndswick,” one of the guards shouted above the crowd, now seething in a fearful frenzy, as Alan clambered from the platform. A woman, it looked to Cyrus like the very woman who had earlier mocked his tardiness, gave the ropes that bound his wrists a deft cut with the edge of a blade. The hangmen, seeing that they had lost utter control over the crowd and their prisoner, gave up the morning as a loss.

“If he departs with his life,” said one, “then he will have done so by his own cunning. But let him not return to Houndswick ever again. For he is a murderer, even though you fools have grown so preciously fond of his carcass.”

Cyrus watched, bewildered, as the crowd about him began, murmuring, to disperse. He could not understand what he had seen; could not account for the mysterious pall and then fury that had descended upon that gathering, much less understand what had happened to cause them to clamor so violently for the release of the condemned man upon hearing those strange, spoken names.

The rain now fell upon the desolate stones of a deserted courtyard. Cyrus pulled the collar of his coat up close to his throat and left the eerie openness of that space. It was time to search out an employer, not an answer to this mystery. Otherwise, he would be forced upon the road again – and the winter was growing no warmer.

***

What was his crime? Alan himself hardly recalled it, in the pale frenzy that he felt as he ran back to the churchwarden’s cottage in which he had lived all his life. He was looking for all the money that he had in the world, anything to help him survive the next several weeks as he fled to look for work elsewhere. It was more than mere sympathy that he had seen in Cyrus’s eyes; on some unspoken level, he had recognized the look of the fugitive and known that it was to be his future as well.

As he entered the parlor, he glanced at the gilded brass clock over the hearth. He had little above a half an hour to leave Houndswick and stand a fighting chance of keeping his life. The guards would be after him again soon, but he was more fearful of a certain superstition that had hung over the town for the past year: that to even whisper *those names,* to acknowledge the horribleness of their deaths, was in and of itself a death sentence. The last one to recite those names that Alan had spoken on the scaffold, a girl of the tavern named Abigail, had died within that very hour. They had found her on her mother's porch, stabbed seven times through the heart. Her fate had been kinder than what had befallen the young men who had committed the same offense before her. *They* had all died exactly like those whose names they had dared to speak.

Shaking, Alan tried to put the memory of those silent corpses out of his head, fumbling for the floorboard under which he had hidden his savings. Once he found the purse, he stowed it away in his pocket. As he straightened, he momentarily caught a glimpse of himself in a nearby mirror: a dark-haired young man of twenty with eyes that favored his mother's own deep grey. For a brief second, he imagined a smattering of blood covering his face like crimson freckles, just like the night before his arrest: that night when he had stood over the body of Alice's brother and realized that he had killed a man whose sole mistake had been to interrupt him. Something stirred behind him and he started, pale again, imagining that he had seen the murdered man smiling at his back. There was no one.

He looked once more around that room that he would never see again.

It was when he reached the front door that he saw the man again, standing in the shadow of an adjoining room, watching him. Alan reflexively stumbled back, his mind telling him that he was already finished, his body too afraid to accept this. His hand was fumbling for the pistol that hung mounted on the wall. When the first four shots did nothing but rip a few holes in the man's coat, he put it to his own head.

"God forgive me," he whispered. He envisioned at once the explosion of his own blood on the wall behind him and the image of Alice's brother at his feet, sprawling in a pool of blood.

Before he could pull the trigger, however, he felt something like a pricking sting touch the side of his throat. A spreading warmth enveloped him. Then the gun was slipping from his hand and he was falling back into someone else's arms, feeling his awful closeness, smelling the salted scent of blood, like the smell of the blood that his own hand had drawn. He tried to speak to the nightmare, but his tongue could form no supplication. Whatever poison had been injected into his throat had left him wonderfully lax and unresponsive: he could feel with his body, but he could not command it.

A part of him feared and knew that he was in the hands of the Houndswick horror. Another part of him, though, thought that he was caught by his own victim, his mind babbling away its own nightmare, how once there had been a young man named Alan Hamish and how he had loved a girl named Alice and one night had meant to have her, but her brother had decided to surprise them together in the attic and before he knew it, Alan had an axe in his hand and was laying into the girl's brother and that Alan was meant to hang for this, but somehow thanks to the fickle kindness of the mob he had escaped home with his life, but you see, his victim hadn't really died…it was like those men buried in collapsed caves and tunnels for days, whose bodies begin to alter and break down, feeding on their own substance in order to survive…well, buried far into the ground, couched among maggots, what else could a body do but grow and squeeze itself into the slimy skin of a blind, stinging worm itself, urging its way in squeezing motions up and clear of the ground to find Alan out, to paralyze him with the maggot stinger that had poked like a growth from its stomach…

It was a testimony to how desperately afraid the young man was of his coming fate, that this gruesome fantasy that now surfaced and flickered across the landscape of his imagination was actually of some comfort to him.

But at the same time, his mind started to hysterically recite back those names that he had spoken on the scaffold and with each name, an image broke like a fork of lightning into the darkness of his stricken mind: John, fingers bitten off, lying facedown in the snow; Thomas, twisted body skewered with silver pikes to a barn wall; William, pressed beneath a pile of stones a mile from the outskirts of town…and not a drop of blood in any of their bodies. Not even a butchered spill.

As the poison began to take effect, Alan's body began to twitch and convulse, his hands brushing the face of the person who held him from behind. The skin of that unseen countenance was smooth and as his head fell back, he felt beneath the masculine garments of his captor the shape of a breast. He closed his eyes, his heart still beating in mute panic. The two were talking, the man in the shadows and the woman in men's clothes who held him, but he could not make out what they were saying; they were muffled and indistinct, like voices overheard while half-asleep. Occasionally, the woman would chafe his wrists and cheeks and make some laughing remark.

At last, the man came forward and lifted Alan by the feet, the woman holding him by the shoulders. Together they carried him back into the parlor, towards the sopha. His mind was crying "*no, no, no*" and the poison must have been fading somewhat, for the woman whispered in his ear "*shhhhh*" which must have meant that his tongue, at least, was working again, if only feebly. She kissed his ear as they lowered him to the sopha. He felt as though he were in the hands of two doting but firm parents preparing him for the village surgeon who would soon arrive, cluck his tongue, and force Alan to drink some foul-tasting medicine. The homeliness of the image made his stomach turn. Then his sickness gave way to darkness and he fell into a deep, strange sleep.

He awoke some time later in candlelight, in a chamber that he did not recognize, his muscles still straining against the poison that held them paralyzed. The most that he could do was move his tongue, and twitch a finger.

Across the cushioned back of the couch, he saw five long creases extending from where a hand gripped the couch above his head. He raised his eyes. The face that looked steadily down at him was veiled in a mottled cloth of black. The lower half of the veil twitched slightly: the motion of a licking tongue.

Chapter Four: In which Cyrus encounters a most unusual mode of transportation.

There were no farmers looking for shepherds to guard their livestock – or at least, no shepherd that looked like a wanderer like Cyrus. The old men listened to his offer of work carefully and then shook their heads, glancing back towards their houses as though embarrassed to even countenance such a proposition.

By evening, he was fairly exhausted. At the last farmhouse at which he stopped, its owner, a Master Angus Macpherson, offered him a stoup of brown ale and suggested with a sympathetic look that he might want to try his luck farther north.

"I hate to continue on, so close to the start of winter," Cyrus admitted.

"How long have you been travelling and looking for work, lad?"

"For close to a month now, all the way up from Essex."

Angus whistled. "What brings an Essex man to the border, I wonder?"

"I've had no luck finding work in England, so – "

"So you ran out of road and found yourself in Scotland." The man chuckled, but there was a humorless, disbelieving look in his eyes. "God help you for finding Houndswick."

"Yes," Cyrus agreed, looking down from the hill on which they stood. "It is an odd town. Perhaps the oddest I've passed through this month past."

"Now why would you say that?"

"That hanging earlier this morning, for one thing. Why did the mob demand that they release that prisoner for reciting those names, do you know?"

"Oh, I know," said Angus. "And pray to God that you remain as ignorant as you are now."

Cyrus sighed. "I don't find this reticence at all humorous, sir."

"Do I look like a man with a sense of humor?"

Cyrus thanked him for the ale and departed. He knew that the man was not entirely satisfied with Cyrus's own terse explanation for what had brought him all the way from southern England to southern Scotland. Perhaps Houndswick, with all its air of compulsory silence and mystery, suited him well after all. A town that could give no answers could hardly afford to ask questions.

He looked below at the glitter of streetlamps, the abandoned scaffold, the spire of the meeting house. So wrapped was Cyrus in his own thoughts, the purpose behind his own coming, and the strange sight of Alan's flight, that he did not hear the sound of horses' hooves at his back, nor see the beams cast by two carriage lights, moving like twin torches held aloft by invisible racers. For a moment, he felt a shock of pain as the vehicle struck him, his right leg afire with an unexpected agony. Before he could cry aloud or react in any way, however, his body went into shock and chose to let itself slip into the merciful oblivion of a faint.

***

"Come out of it, come out of it, my sluggish lad! You were very lucky to have escaped with a bruised ankle rather than a broken crown, but I fancy you're still well enough to speak." The distant sound of a man's voice, light and faintly lisped, as well as the slimy application of something that felt like a wettened handkerchief managed to rouse Cyrus from his momentary faint. He opened his eyes and blinked in the harsh light of the torch that hung from a hook at the front of the vehicle.

"There, there now," the voice now altered from a tone of imperious command to one of relief as Cyrus shifted his gaze towards the face that hovered above his own. In the uncertain light, he could only make out the long, loose-jowled face that nodded from a neck, the slender length of which reminded the youth rather unpleasantly of a serpent.

"Now, lad, why don't you tell me what you were doing under the wheels of my carriage at this time of night – and what had so absorbed your interest that you failed, if I may be so bold as to burden a suffering invalid with blame, you *failed* to notice the rather conspicuous bulk of my oncoming equipage?"

Cyrus blinked at the face of the stranger and tried to right himself upon his elbows, only to cry out in pain. The man made a clucking sound of sympathy.

"Now," said the owner of the mysterious carriage. "Rather than lie here in the cold, why do we not unravel the mystery of your incaution within the relatively comfortable interior of my carriage – that is, if you have no objection to accepting the hospitality of the man who so effectively injured you?"

"Thank you, sir," Cyrus said through gritted teeth and, taking the man's proffered hand, entered the curtained confines of the coach. What other choice did he have?

"Why don't you tell me what your name is, against the possibility of your falling unconscious before we arrive at the apothecary's?" the stranger asked solicitously.

"Plainstaff, sir – Cyrus Plainstaff," the young traveller replied.

"Squire Toby Wadham at your service, then, Master Plainstaff," the long-necked gentleman said, proffering his hand for a friendly shake.

A candle burned upon a low, wooden shelf that lined the inside of one of the coach doors and in its flickering light, Cyrus could clearly see the claret-colored velvet of the Squire's coat as well as the tightly curled grey locks of his periwig, flowing past his shoulders and down to his breast. The gold-lining of the tri-cornered hat that sat upon his knee as well as the diamond-edged watch that sparkled from a chain hanging across his waistcoat bespoke his wealth even more eloquently than the plump, silken purse that hung from his belt. The white powder and rouge that colored his dimpled, long-jowled face put Cyrus in mind of the fashionable cavaliers that he had seen so often frequenting London's streets and playhouses when he had had occasion to visit that city as a child.

Squire Toby, his painted lips now pursed in silent thought, likewise examined the young stranger that serendipity had literally thrown into his path, observing with some consternation that this Cyrus Plainstaff could not have been more his opposite if the gods had deliberately fashioned a man to counter him in every aspect imaginable. The Squire had never seen so sober or dismal-looking a youth in all his life. He began to regret maiming the young man even more vigorously.

"Tell me," he began slowly. "Where do you hail from?"

"Essex County, sir," was the prompt reply.

Then he is a good English lad at least, the Squire thought with some relief.

"And what are your opinions on our good King Charles II's choice of advisors?" he continued a bit more nervously, moving on to politics.

However, rather than replying, Cyrus abruptly asked, "Sir, forgive my curiosity, but whither are we going? I fear...that I can hardly follow you. I must have pulled a muscle out of joint when you struck me with your coach."

It was true; Cyrus's ankle was swelling and there was little remedy for such an injury save bandages of ice water and rest. Fingering the chain of his watch, wiping his perspiring fingers again and again upon his silken kerchief, the Squire seemed the picture of agitation to such an extent that common politeness required Cyrus to enquire as to the cause of this sudden violent attack of emotion.

"Nothing of importance, I assure you," he said. "Only I do hope that we arrive by midnight. Artemas!" This last shout was directed to the coachman. "Can you not accelerate our speed by a fraction, my good man?"

Artemas called something back, but his voice was lost in the howling winter's wind that swept past the coach and sent a flock of withered leaves billowing into the confines of the carriage. The Squire was unconscious of this inconvenience, however, and after sidling to a corner of his seat nearest the windows, managed the astonishing feat of poking his head out of one of these apertures and twisting his serpentine throat around the side so that he could gain a better view of the direction in which they were travelling at such an undesirably slow pace.

Though he had not the fortune of possessing so formidable a neck as the Squire's, Cyrus was able to command a tolerable view of the road and prospect ahead of the coach from the vantage point of his own window. At first, he saw and felt only the pale, faintly warm fog that swept over the heath like the gentle waves of some white sea, drifting and billowing in the night wind and casting mottled, moving shadows against the rolling hills. However, he soon discerned their return to Houndswick in the ragged line of spires and chimneys that rose against the evening sky like the spears of a standing army. The town's rooftops huddled in a soldierly cluster about the taller peak of a steeple belonging to a church set in the center of the town, the moonlight illuminating its stained-glass windows so that they shed the pictures of warring angels and serpentine devils upon the cobbled streets. As Squire Toby's coach entered the precincts of Houndswick, Cyrus saw the drunkards and dandies that milled about the streets, passing the porch of the church on their way to the alehouse, and began to wonder what appointment his new, nervous companion was bound for.

Some faraway belltower struck the hour and out of instinct, the young man marked off the distant peals and counted twelve.

"Midnight exactly," the Squire said, his fingers prying the ruffled lace about his long throat in order to loosen its strangling hold somewhat.

"Artemas – draw our coach to a stop, will you? Master Plainstaff and I can find our way to Hart Street ourselves. God's blood, but I am terribly late already."

As the carriage came to a halt in the middle of the cobbled street, Squire Toby clambered out and helped the bewildered Cyrus to his feet, half-supporting the limping youth against his shoulder while examining the nearby streets with the aid of his gold-rimmed quizzing glass.

"I am sorry to delay you, my boy – now where could that blasted steeplehouse be? – but I am afraid that before our acquaintance, an appointment of pressing urgency – and here is West Lane! – demanded and still demands my most immediate attention. Come, come now, none of that!" he cried as Cyrus, faint with the agony of his swollen foot, began to lean against the damp wall of a brothel to catch his breath. "You're a strong enough lad, I can tell, and can surely walk the short distance to Hart Street!"

Cyrus protested that he would rather be left in the square than trotted even the short distance to Hart Street.

"Nonsense!" the Squire returned, disgusted. "Never let it be said that Squire Toby Wadham left an injured man in the street to look after himself when Fate so unequivocally threw him into his path and when common charity itself revolts at the very idea."

And so, amid Cyrus's feeble groans and weak protestations, the Squire half-supported and half-dragged the sufferer down numerous cobbled lanes and beneath the sagging porches of tall, leaning houses, hardly slackening his pace except occasionally to peer down an alley with his quizzing glass as though to gain a better sense of direction. In spite of the sharp, dizzying pain in his foot, Cyrus was sufficiently curious of his surroundings to notice that though the buildings that lined the street that they presently traversed all cast their long straight shadows upon the paved walk, one building in particular cast a peculiarly slanted pool of black that appeared to thwart all the other shadows that fell in its path, sending them into crosshatches that in turn redounded into confused patterns of darkness.

It was before this crooked, leaning tenement that Squire Toby's steps at last paused and, as Cyrus grasped his shoulder with trembling fingers in order to steady himself and relieve his swollen ankle of its pain somewhat, the Squire raised his eyes and quizzing glass towards an upper window of the apartment with a keen and searching look. Cyrus looked up as well and noticed that this window, though bleared with grime, was softly illuminated by the golden light of a candle, the flame of which was raised once, twice, and thrice in greeting to the Squire who, in reply, doffed his plumed hat and waved it aloft four times with a measured deliberation. A long silence ensued, broken only by the faint call of a reveler from some distant tavern and the answering laughter of his comrades, echoing like the mirth of some faraway, phantom troupe. Something in that half-heard sound of human joy, swallowed so suddenly in the melancholic silence of the night, caused the sharp prickle of tears to blind young Cyrus for a moment. Though he could not say why, he felt a sense of danger and darkness here and he began to wonder with a morbid listlessness as to whether he would survive to even appreciate an apothecary by morning.

Chapter Five: In which Cyrus finds himself a witness to a clandestine appointment, and notices a curious tower upon the horizon.

The tortured creaking of the door before which they stood recalled his mind from the shadowed perils of the past and future to those of the present, as the low voice of a woman uttered the Squire's name.

"Yes, Mrs. Leaske, it is I," the Squire said. "And this is a friend of mine. Now will you be so good as to take us upstairs immediately? I believe that your master is expecting me."

"His Lordship was expecting you a good half hour ago," the woman replied. "And I heard him swearing up and down by four and twenty devils and saints that he'd have your beating heart upon his mantle for causing him and his companions to wait so long whilst you took your precious time in coming."

In spite of his white powder and rouge, Cyrus saw the Squire pale visibly at this statement. However, whatever had motivated his visit in the first place still remained as powerful a provocation as before, for he brandished his quizzing glass before his eyes as though it were a visor and again demanded to be taken to Mrs. Leaske's master.

As the door widened to admit them both, the moonlight fell upon the owner of the voice and Cyrus was startled to behold the face that accompanied it. It was a round face, with cheeks as smooth as marble and highlighted with two spots of rouge, lips as thin as a piece of red thread, and framed by a mist of white hair that shadowed the two eyes which glistened like the twin black beads of a doll's eyes. These eyes were by custom of a dullish, leaden hue, but as Cyrus continued to gaze upon Mrs. Leaske in fascination, he found that occasionally they would come alive with a feverish light that would last as momentarily as a marsh fire before giving way again to their former somnolence.

There were no candles lit in that vast lower floor of the tenement save the taper that Mrs. Leaske herself held and its wan light only faintly revealed the cloth-covered bulks of furniture that surrounded them, their white shapes seeming to stretch endlessly in every direction of that empty expanse. The Squire, his voice instinctively lowered to a whisper, enquired as to whether

Mrs. Leaske's employer meant to abandon his present residence in the near future?

"Aye," Mrs. Leaske replied, her doll-like eyes glowing for a fraction of a second. "His Lordship desires to repair to his ancestral estate close by but not within Houndswick and, once an arrangement with his uncle is settled, will repair there are soon as possible."

Her thin, blood-red lips closed with a peculiar fastness after this last remark and Squire Toby, realizing that further enquiry would be fruitless, followed her without another word. She led them to the dark foot of a spiral staircase, the narrowness of which appeared fully equal to its height, encompassing at least seven floors in its towering ascent. Somehow, the Squire managed the difficult task of easing himself up those treacherous stairs while at the same time assisting the limping Cyrus up as well, who all the while protested that he would be happy enough to remain on the lower floor.

"Heaven forbid," the Squire returned under his breath. "That I should leave an invalid to wait upon himself in the dark when His Lordship will surely be supplied with spirits and victuals that would restore you to your health, somewhat."

Cyrus suspected that a consideration of His Lordship's remarks concerning the possible value of the Squire's beating heart as an ornament for his mantelpiece might be a stronger motivation for the latter's sudden desire for companionship, but kept this notion to himself.

"Does your master have a wife or children, madam?" he asked Mrs. Leaske.

She paused in her ascent, her small, black eyes darting instantly upon the youth's face. "What should make you fancy such a thing?" she asked, her high, emotionless voice making a sharp contrast to the gleam that leapt for a moment in her gaze.

"Only..." Cyrus paused, a bit embarrassed at his own inquisitiveness. "It seems peculiar for such a large apartment to be inhabited by two persons alone."

Mrs. Leaske's lips, if possible, compressed even further and the Squire hastily interposed: "What my young friend means to ask is whether the Earl is not lonely living here by himself without the company of a wife or child? Of course," he added with a light, false laugh. "He does not mean to pry into His Lordship's private affairs."

Their guide seemed somewhat appeased by this conciliatory explanation and replied that His Lordship was a widower and widowed not once, but thrice.

"As you may imagine," Mrs. Leaske said. "The subject of marital bliss is a sensitive one to His Lordship and I am sure that he would prefer it to be avoided altogether."

Both Cyrus and Squire Toby bowed submission to this last order and the rest of the steep, twisting ascent to the seventh floor was conducted in a silence broken only by the smart click of the Squire's heels and the indistinct murmur of voices and footsteps echoing from some chamber far above their heads.

***

"His Lordship is entertaining several guests at the moment," Mrs. Leaske said in a low voice as she paused before a certain chamber situated upon the seventh floor, the door of which was currently closed. "I suggest that you knock – after all, he is already expecting you."

The housekeeper departed then, leaving the Squire to give the chamber door a nervous rap or two whilst stroking his long neck with fingers that shook ever so slightly. A moment or two passed – then the door opened, a flood of candlelight spilled across the hallway before them, and a merry, ringing voice cried, "Squire Toby Wadham! Why, I thought that a highway brigand had waylaid you and that we should never have the pleasure of your company. And who is this charming young stranger by your side?"

Both the Squire and Cyrus could only reply with expressions of blinking stupefaction. For Cyrus, the shock was all the more severe: he had never encountered Squire Toby's friend and the contrast between the forbidding image that he had already conjured in his imagination with the reality of the handsome, green-eyed gentleman before him was startling. For Squire Toby, who had met the Earl upon one occasion alone formerly, the peculiar nature of His Lordship's varying moods seemed all the more confirmed in his mind.

"Well, come in, come in!" the Earl insisted, beckoning them in with a wave of a fair, long-fingered hand. "But will you not introduce me, good Squire, to your friend?"

His voice lost nothing of its former friendliness, but a sharp, searching fire seemed kindled in those deep hazel eyes as though only one more added pinch of tender was needed to set them blazing. The Squire, catching this look, hastily said, "Only a friend I met upon the highway – a Master Cyrus Plainstaff." An awkward pause ensued in which the Earl's gaze swept over Cyrus as though weighing his qualities by some mysterious measuring stick and determining whether these qualities matched the Squire's brief account. Anxious to break the awful silence, Squire Toby added, "Master Plainstaff, allow me to introduce you to His Lordship Andrew Ebenezer Montrose, the 34th Earl of Lauderness."

Cyrus, keenly embarrassed by the obvious suspicion in Montrose's eyes, bowed deeply and attempted to mask his irritation at the Squire for putting him in this position in the first place by maintaining an expression of mask-like gravity. Mercifully, he could not see the blush that had spread over his customarily colorless cheeks; the Earl perceived it, however, and a somewhat gratified smile returned to his lips. Returning Cyrus' bow with an elegant nod, Montrose prayed that he seat himself by the window and help himself to as much brandy as he so desired, before turning his attention fully upon the Squire.

"Are you certain that you wish to begin a new hand with me?" the Earl enquired, his eyes fixed upon the Squire's face with that genial look so habitual to him. "You know as well as I that you lost a handsome sum to me yesternight and I should think very lowly of myself if I were to sacrifice so noble a friendship upon the altar of avarice."

The Squire's rouge-colored cheeks turned a sickly shade of white, causing him to appear vaguely apoplectic, but he replied in a hoarse voice, "My Lord, I do not believe that our acquaintance has been of such a duration that I would term it as a friendship, though you in your generosity seem ready enough to do so. Furthermore, you have already ruined me and the game that I wish to play with you tonight is the last attempt of a man who must topple tonight either upon the side of poverty or riches – believe me, if I possessed another choice, I would have snatched at it rather than come here to wrangle once again with you."

The tenderness in Montrose's eyes altered to a look that suggested a peculiar appetite that has been gladly whetted but he replied softly, "Good Squire Toby, you astonish me. While I had thought that you would slink off to your London bankers and ask His Majesty for a pension, you come to *me*," here he pointed a lily-white finger towards his breast, "to *me* and courageously demand to fight another night against your plunderer in defiance of Lady Luck and, indeed, all customary notions of common-sense. But as it happens, I myself am rather embarrassed financially and am dubious as to whether such a game would be at all wise from my own standpoint."

Squire Toby fidgeted in agony with his silken collar, not knowing altogether what to say, while Montrose continued, "However, I believe that I must be as much of a fool as you, my friend – if I may still term you so? – because I feel that I could not turn down your challenge without appearing not only a coward before these gentlemen," he glanced towards the silent assembly of gamers who sat about a round table in the center of the room, "But a coward before my own conscience as well."

"With all respect, my Lord," the Squire murmured nervously. "Are you indeed in possession of this last object?"

Montrose blinked with a look of delighted injury at this insinuation and returned, "That, my dear fellow, must be determined once this night has passed and it is discovered which one of us is still the lord and which the pauper. Come, come now," he continued, beckoning towards the table. "Sit yourself down and let us, without further ado, commence your ruination."

***

The moon was sinking low upon the horizon as Cyrus, his eyes turning from the gaming table to the window by which he sat, gazed upon the town below and the moors and forests that lay beyond. He had not bothered to indulge in more than a taste of the rust-colored liquid in the decanter set before him, but this sip had been enough to pervade his mouth with a bittersweet flavor that no amount of swallowing seemed to clear away. Glancing back towards the gaming table, he noticed that Montrose was sipping at yet another glass of the heady brandy and Cyrus could not help but wonder at what jaded tongue could tolerate so deep a dose of so strong a spirit. Montrose, noticing Cyrus's gaze fixed upon him, returned the look with a charming tilt of his chin before returning his attention to the Squire, who was busily wiping the perspiration from his neck whilst squinting at the cards that he had been dealt.

The candlelight in that chamber was so bright that when Cyrus glanced back towards the window, he could not see beyond its golden reflection upon the panes. However, as his eyes gradually adjusted to the darkness outside, he began to notice objects in the distance that he had not been privy to before, such as the rising darkness of the lowland hills and the skeletal branches of trees. Unconsciously, his eyes began to wander as though in search of that horrible tree with the laughing figure that he had beheld and later dreamt of in that forsaken valley several nights ago. Unsurprisingly, however, he could not distinguish a landmark that could, for all he knew, be situated in a direction wholly opposite to the one which the Earl's tenement faced.

A golden gleam in the distance, barely larger than a star, shone from somewhere amid the trees and caught Cyrus's eye so that he gazed at it in silent fascination, wondering what its source could be. It seemed to hang aloft, like a lost star without a constellation, but as Cyrus continued to gaze upon it, he began to make out the faint point of a spire and the grey outline of a stone wall. He realized then that he looked not upon a transfixed star but rather upon the candle of some distant chamber that stood as high and aloof as Montrose's tenement, gleaming back with the same motionless light as the lantern that stood upon the table beside the youth. Prompted by an impulse that even he did not fully understand, Cyrus lifted this lantern high with his eyes fixed upon the light in the distance. At first, nothing happened: but what an awed wonder seized upon his soul when at length he spied the faraway gleam rise and fall itself in silent reply! Setting the lantern down again upon the table, the youth ventured to turn his eyes back upon the gaming table and in a voice that barely concealed his curiosity, enquired:

"My Lord, what are those towers that stand off in the distance?"

Montrose's eyes flickered slightly at the question as he turned his attention from his cards to the inquisitive Cyrus: "Towers? Oh, you must mean those gloomy spires off in the forest. Why, those belong to Laughlin Priory."

"Do you know the persons who dwell there now?" Cyrus asked.

"Indeed I do," Montrose replied, giving him a curious, quizzical look. "I dare say, in fact, that I am one of the few who can claim to have any knowledge of them. The Gosselins, at least as long as I have known them, have always kept to themselves."

Chapter Six: In which we learn who held the other lamp.

For a moment, let us return to the events of the morning, only looking at them through another's eye.

When Alan ran through the crowd towards the churchwarden's cottage, and while the mob was beginning to disperse and Cyrus to look for work, the hangmen remained at the scaffold, taking down the rope, nodding farewell to the chaplain and the guards, and shaking their heads in bemusement over the peculiar turn-of-events that had left them empty-handed and corpseless.

"Tell me, sirs, do you know in which direction he went?"

The hangmen looked down from their midmorning flasks of liquor and cloth-wrapped loafs of bread to see the same one-eyed chimney sweeper who had steadied Cyrus when he had almost fallen in the midst of the mob.

"Oh, come now, Master Childermass, you don't really think that we'll help you help that murdering boy, now, do you? That really wouldn't be fair, would it, even to your way of thinking?"

"Come up here and help us finish off this ale like a good lad. He'll be out of Houndswick before nightfall and some other hangman's problem."

Childermass gave a sigh and looked about, as though any moment he expected the fugitive to reappear like a tardy actor from some imagined stage right or stage left.

"There, you see, you've already broken the law by looking for him. Come up here before we clap you in irons, haul you up here, and force some ale down your throat ourselves."

They spoke with a kind of friendly malice, their eyes twinkling and their hands resting on their muskets. Their moods had been somewhat soured by the bullying mob and the botched execution and the last thing they wanted was another show of disobedience.

"I hope you won't take our insistence the wrong way, Master Childermass," one of the hangmen, an Allerton and customarily a fishmongerer by trade, said as they helped him up the platform. "It's only that we've had to suffer such a disappointment. You understand."

Childermass met an expression that had caused many condemned girls and impressionable young men to fall into hysterics and said, "As it happens, I came into town to buy a few pounds of salmon off you."

"Well, come to me in an hour and I'll see what I can do for you, my lad. For Laughlin Priory's kitchens, I imagine?"

"Of course."

"I'd be curious to know what they do up in your Priory. Been a while since there's been a hanging, which of course means that it's been a while since any of us three have seen the inside of the place. A pity."

Childermass looked at their wistful faces and said, "You understand, I only work there."

"Oblige us some day by offending Lord Gosselin or speaking ill against the King and then we'll have the doubled pleasure of hanging you and seeing the inner sanctuary again. We would be eternally in your debt."

Childermass sat at the base of the upright gallows post, in the shadow of the crossbeam. While he ate the proffered bread and washed it down with ale, he felt intensely aware of the distant black towers that rose above the trees and the grey stretch of moorland at his back. He felt the same shudder that he had felt when Allerton had mentioned the Priory earlier and a peculiar smile touched his lips.

Allerton, still harping on his earlier theme, remarked, "Well, isn't that why everyone comes to our little shows? As a kind of rehearsal? I suppose everyone knows that he either deserves or will one day get a hanging. You, Master Childermass, now you've never missed a hanging in your life. Do you not like my theory? Don't you feel that you deserve the drop a little?"

"Come now, you know I can't keep up with you gentlemen when you start philosophizing."

Childermass was no longer really listening to their prattle; had the hangmen bothered to notice, they would have sensed the distance in his voice. They would have looked at his face and seen in that motionless eye the gaze that never moves but is still somehow always searching. He was searching out Alan, but also something more than him: for a darkness that seemed inhuman, shapeless, an impossibility. A noonday shadow on a cloudless day.

Allerton put a hand on his shoulder and the chimney sweeper turned to look at the hangman. The single pale eye of Childermass was now suddenly vacant and transfixed like a slack, panting mouth: his train of darkness interrupted.

***

As soon as he was able to get free of them, Childermass left the hangmen for the Houndswick marketplace, wandering wherever he willed, trying to collect his thoughts. It was apparent that Alan was already out of Houndswick, already either fled or spirited away by the shadow that had swallowed the names of the murdered that he had recited on the scaffold. Childermass had still not quite resolved whether this recitation was a stroke of genius or madness on the young man's part. On the one hand, it hardly seemed a wise trade to exchange a relatively quick execution for a possibly tortuous death. On the other hand, Childermass himself had always harbored a profound fear of strangulation, far beyond any ordinary aversion.

Still warm-throated from Allerton's ale, he chose to debate his next course of action in a nearby tavern. No sooner had he seated himself at a table, than he felt a hand drop upon his shoulder and, turning, found two men behind him.

"Why, Master Chimney, what a pleasure to find you here."

He gestured with his broom to two other chairs. "Please, make yourselves comfortable," he offered in a rather arch and lordly way. He knew these two well, for they also worked within the walls of Laughlin Priory.

"Oh, I'll do just that without your suggestion, have no fear, but thank you all the same," said one of them, taking up a cup and drinking deeply from it before pouring a generous amount of the liquor into a saucer at his feet, from which a large-bodied mongrel began to lap eagerly. This man, Dagworth by name, was the Master of Hounds in the Priory, the menial whose task it was to oversee the kennels of the Priory's lord as well as to keep the hounds well-disciplined and trained for the hunt. With close-set mud-brown eyes, shoulders broad and hunched like a wolfhound's, and teeth that often bared into the savage smile of a panting cur, no man ever looked more the part for his profession. His clothes were made of jerkin and were the soft green and brown dyes of the forest as were his high, leathern boots which reached to his knees, the left boot of which sheathed a long dirk which he had now procured and was busily scraping against the splintered wood of the table before him.

The other man, Feversham, watched Dagworth work with his knife before turning his gloomy, somnolent eye upon Childermass. This Feversham, with his high, noble forehead and his long, grey locks would have appeared the opposite of this Dagworth in terms of station, were it not for the worn quality of his woolen garments and the smell of horse and hay that permeated the air about him. Moreover, there was a peculiar weakness that lay in the vague, sad curve of his lips, a strange irresolution that stood in that eye as it shifted from the bestial merriment of Dagworth's glance to the steady, savage humor in Childermass's pale-eyed gaze. The cruel turn of Dagworth's humor did not agree with Feversham's sense of propriety at all, but something in his stolid constitution could not help but feel that it must be this Dagworth's right, by virtue of his superior age and strength, to lord it over Childermass and that it would be quite improper for Feversham to intervene, as a result, on behalf of the chimney sweeper. Also, if there was a gloating pleasure that Dagworth took in goading the young man, there was a fell and patient cruelty that stood in Childermass's bright gaze like an enthralling deformity. The magnetic hatred that seemed to vibrate so tangibly between the two as well as the energy that they possessed and that he so palpably lacked thus made the cautious Feversham all the more reluctant to step between them lest, like a hand of peace held between two snarling curs, he find himself savaged by both their fangs.

Already Dagworth was leaning forward as Childermass swallowed another mouthful of liquor and saying, "Watching the condemned man get the rope, eh? You must have been ever so disappointed when the crowd let him live."

"If I *was* curious to see a man hang, then I am hardly such a prodigy."

"Every man is curious, to be sure, to be sure," Dagworth said. "But not every man is so monstrously curious as thou art, my pretty."

"Leave off, you two," Feversham suggested.

"What is so monstrous about my curiosity, pray?" asked Childermass, leaning forward smilingly.

"You tell me, Master Chimney." Dagworth pinched his cheek. "I'm not the one who our Lordship has decided to keep shackled every night like a mad dog, am I?"

Dagworth must have then seen the look of distress that crossed Childermass's countenance.

"There, there," he said. "You *know* it's for your own good, lad, don't you?"

Childermass only blessed him with a poisonous little smile.

***

That night, as Childermass waited in the darkness of one of the Priory's upper towers, he looked out a window towards the glittering windows and lamps of Houndswick and thought back on Alan's trembling recitation of those forbidden names and wondered what was happening to Alan now. He tried to conjure his last memory of the young man's face, but the image was corrupted by another that threatened to supplant it – the look of relief on a stranger's face whom he had seen for a moment in the crowd that morning. The chimney sweeper frowned, trying to place the memory. It quivered before his silent, searching curiosity and just at the moment when he felt that he was close to remembering Cyrus's face, a movement of light in the distance caught his attention. He looked and saw, far across in a Houndswick tenement, the golden light of a distant lantern rise and fall. Enchanted with curiosity, he imitated the motion with his own light.

When Feversham came to chain him to bed for the night, Childermass was still attempting to determine which tenement in Houndswick had held the moving light. As he followed the ostler, he suddenly realized that he knew, though the knowledge left him even more baffled than he had been before.

"There is a stranger there," he mused. "Of that I'm certain."

It was a testimony to the chimney sweeper's general fatigue that he failed to discern a connection between his earlier, half-recalled memory of the strange young man that he had met the morning before and this new and silent communication that he had so raptly received.

Chapter Seven: In which a game is concluded, a fortune won and lost, and Cyrus Plainstaff meets Alan again.

Someone called for more brandy.

"Mrs. Leaske!" Montrose called, his voice sounding stifled in the narrow little room. Instantly, the door opened and the thin-lipped housekeeper approached his side. "Would you be good enough to bring up some more brandy for the parched gentleman?"

When Mrs. Leaske departed, he added, while stroking the wrinkles out of his laced cuffs: "She really is much more of a mother than a housekeeper to me – why, she remained with me through all three of my late dearly beloveds and would have been the nurse to my pretty little children, had I ever had the chance to father any."

As he uttered these last words with a peculiar laugh, the door opened and the housekeeper returned, her steps clicking softly upon the wooden floorboards as she came to stand behind Montrose, a tall, glistening decanter in her hand. His Lordship turned in his chair to take it from her, setting it in the center of the table for his comrades to silently fill their glasses. A low-lidded look of languor veiled his deep emerald eyes for a moment as he watched them and a faint smile touched his lips as he saw Cyrus, oblivious to the replenished store of wine, still gazing off towards the dark line of the distant horizon. For a moment, the Earl of Lauderness tilted his handsome, fox-like face back to meet the gaze of the silent housekeeper behind him, his smile mirrored by her own thin lips, before his gaze at last settled softly upon the sweating gentleman that sat across from him.

"Dear Squire – I say, good Toby – will you not show us your cards at last?" As Squire Toby met Montrose's tender gaze, His Lordship added, "Pray, do not be modest – they cannot be worse than the hand I hold, I assure you."

"I thank you for your assurance, my Lord," Squire Toby said, so lowly that his lisp was almost lost. "I only wish that I could share in your gift of foresight."

Montrose's left brow rose slightly with a look of surprised concern.

"Come, come," said he, his mouth twisted awry with the look of a light-hearted skeptic. "May we not be the judges of that?"

Cyrus had been somewhat drowsing in his chair, but the sound of raised voices had roused him awake once more, his sprained ankle seeming all the more painfully alive and sore after the slight respite of oblivion that had deadened its ache. Weariness weighed upon his limbs and his eyelids, he longed for sleep, and yet now that he was awake again, the edges of the chair upon which he sat tortured him with their sharpness and the spirit of oppressive expectancy that had settled upon the room rendered any chance of sleep utterly futile.

Squire Toby, his long, powdered face now seeming moist and oily in the lamplight, parted his painted lips as though to speak whilst turning hunted eyes upon the countenances of the rest of that company. A flash of lightning brightened the chamber for a brief moment, casting its white luminance upon a varied assortment of faces: a lean man in a long, cobalt-colored coat who sat next to Montrose, another of stockier build who leaned by the hearth smoking a fragrant weed from a pipe cut of black wood, and a third seated next to the first man, his face hidden in the shadow of his hooded cloak. Save for the third, whose features were hooded by his cloak and who seemed to have fallen into an inebriated stupor, their eyes held neither sympathy nor enmity. Only, as the lean man in the blue coat stroked his jutting chin slowly with a long thumb and forefinger and his companion by the fireplace exhaled a heady cloud of smoke, a glance of mutual interest and amusement seemed to pass between them like a private joke and they watched the Squire with a cold, jolly sort of mesmerism. Cyrus alone met his gaze with a bleary look of sympathy, but the rest of the room remained pregnant with an atmosphere of gloating watchfulness.

The Squire let a sigh, at last, pass his lips; then, without a word, he let fall the cards that had before remained clutched within his hand. Montrose leaned forward whilst the man in the blue coat and the man by the hearth darkened the table with their own two shadows as they turned their bright, avid gazes upon what had been the Squire's hand.

A long silence passed. When Montrose at last brought his eyes up and met the Squire's gaze, he saw that the corner of the man's painted mouth was trembling ever so slightly and that a high, hectic color had risen ascendant in his cheeks, overwhelming even the generous daubs of crimson that already bloomed there.

"You see, my lord," said Squire Toby Wadham humbly. "As I do not share in your oracular gift of prophecy, you must forgive my timorous apprehensions. Now," he cleared his throat. "May I assume that my former debts have been satisfactorily annulled?"

A startlingly brilliant smile like the flash of a pistol butt and a genial tilt of the head, were the Squire's first replies from the once wealthy, now ruined 34th Earl of Lauderness. Then, swift as an executioner's axe, Montrose's fist came crashing down upon the table, sending the cards scattering like a cloud of frightened pigeons while, without a word, his other hand descended upon the hilt of the rapier that hung from a belt at his side.

However, Squire Toby, with an alacrity that one would not have expected from a man of his indecisive disposition, had leapt to his feet, reached the door, and was already halfway down the spiraling staircase that led to the front door of the Earl of Lauderness's apartment by the time Montrose had drawn his blade. For a time, they listened to the distant clattering of his footsteps before the thunderous slam of the front door heralded the return of silence. All the while, Montrose's face remained grey and bland of all else but fury – but at this last sound, he suddenly lifted his gaze towards his companions and burst into a high, amused laugh. The two men followed suit and the room resounded with a curiously constrained sort of merriment.

During the short interim in which these proceedings had taken place, Cyrus Plainstaff had remained fixed in his seat, listening to the Squire's flight with a sense of mounting disquiet. Now, left alone in the dubious company of the Earl of Lauderness and his men, the young man attempted to rise from his seat – a difficult maneuver, in view of his swollen ankle – and said in as casual a voice as his jangled nerves could summon, "I suppose I ought to depart as well, my Lord, in light of my friend's – "

"Your *friend?*" Montrose's soft voice cut in with all the smooth abruptness of an oiled knife cutting through silk as he tilted his head in the direction of the hapless Cyrus. "And pray, Master Plainstaff, how came you to be acquainted with Squire Toby Wadham?"

With the bright eyes of Montrose's men intent upon him, Cyrus replied, "Only this evening, my Lord – you see, I was on my way to Edinburgh and meant to stop in this town for a night's worth of rest when – "

"Edinburgh," murmured one of the Earl's friends. "Now I wonder, lad, what business brings you there?"

Cyrus had gone pale, far paler than he would have wished under those eyes. Their gazes seemed to search out some proof of weakness or deception in him. Again, turning with an imploring helplessness to Montrose, he said, "To meet a friend – sir, you must believe me. It was to meet a friend." He was not used to lying, but he hoped that desperation lent him an air of truth.

"A friend?" Montrose returned softly. "Oh, of course – like the Squire, I presume. Who is this other friend – a physician?" His gaze ran the length of Cyrus's injured leg before returning again to the young man's face. "Are you quite certain you cannot rise? It could be a trifling bruise that troubles you – or it could, perhaps, be nothing at all." A twinkling look now danced in his eyes as he took Cyrus by the hand and forced him to his feet.

"God in Heaven, my lord, I – " Cyrus could utter no further assurance of his veracity, but a gasp of pain as, white-faced, he clung to Montrose's arm for support. The intensity of his agony was such that for a moment, he felt that he might lose consciousness altogether.

While he struggled for breath, however, he saw Montrose's gaze warm with a sudden look of sympathy and the Earl cried, as though affected with the tenderest of sentiments, "Why, you are injured after all!" He glanced up at his companions with a look that they greeted with shadowed, covert smiles. "Come, come," now pressing Cyrus back into his chair. "It is out of the question that you depart alone in such a pitiable condition."

"My only wish is to depart, my lord," Cyrus whispered. "In any condition."

"I will take no offense at such a remark – I am certain that it is agony that makes you speak so ungently." Montrose regarded him with a pitying affability. "Now, tell me, Master Plainstaff. Did you watch the proceedings of our game with any sort of attention?"

"With some, my lord," Cyrus replied wearily.

Montrose was not to be put off, however. "Then perhaps you noticed the peculiar fashion in which your friend the Squire held his cards and often adjusted the lace at his right wrist while moving his other hand towards the deck? A gesture which, in fact, he repeated several times this evening?"

"I did not, my lord," Cyrus said, his eyes lowering from Montrose's gaze. The last thing he wished was to be involved in this vicious dispute.

"Then I tell you that I saw him do so myself," Montrose suddenly spat. "And I swear to you, Plainstaff, if it be your desire to make a fool of me as your cheating Squire thought to, I shall crush you as I will him. Do you believe me?"

Cyrus, feeling less fear than the wary apprehension that a man feels when he must tread carefully by the lair of a mad cur lest he arouse it, only nodded slightly. Somewhat appeased, Montrose leaned back and, as though apologetic, continued in a softer tone, "But of course, I was a fool to even ask such a question of you. I can see in an instant that you are too innocent a lad to notice or even think of what such a gesture could mean and, considering that the Squire was your friend, why it is only to be expected that such an act would not have alarmed you. Is it not so?" He gave Cyrus one of those charming, wistful smiles of his; the young man managed to return it somewhat half-heartedly. "Then let us forget the entire affair for the moment. Tell me, Master Plainstaff, have you ever played a hand yourself?"

"No, my lord – nor am I eager to begin," Cyrus assured him.

"A fine notion!" Montrose returned. "Why, if every man who viewed a game gone sour entertained such a view, a meager sporting indeed would there be for a merry company upon a winter's night."

"But how grateful their wallets would be after the company dispersed," Cyrus reminded him.

Montrose fixed upon him a penetrating look similar to the one with which he had greeted the young man when first they had met. Then, with a curious smile, he returned, "Ah, yes – you would have us singing psalms through our noses and reading aloud reforming pamphlets on government policy." Cyrus blushed, but Montrose hastened on as though uninterested for the nonce in this peculiar avenue of attack: "But what better communion can jovial fellows enjoy than a leathern bottle and a deck of cards? Such sporting could make friends of mortal enemies, I'd warrant."

"Or, in sooth, enemies of friends," said Cyrus. "For whatsoever you, my lord, and Squire Wadham were at the beginning of this evening, the two of you are now mortal foes, are you not?"

"Cleverly put," Montrose replied. "But, then, what indeed are you and old Toby? He claimed you as his acquaintance during our introductions, did he not? And you arrived in his company as a friend? And yet here you are – quite, quite alone."

Cyrus felt a sudden coldness come over him and made no reply.

"I confess," Montrose continued. "That I have made a study of you, Master Plainstaff, all the evening and have made little headway in my researches. You are clearly no close or highborn friend of the Squire's – I do not discount his cowardice, of course, but I do not believe that he would have possessed the nerve to abandon a man of nobility." He clucked his tongue with a look of cloying cruelty: "Yes, I fear that the Squire is a bit prejudiced in that way. Therefore, I must conclude that you are of the lower classes. Your accent bespeaks an Essex man, yet here you are in Scotland, miles away from your place of origin. Tell me, Master Plainstaff – what are you?"

"A tradesman," the youth replied steadily. "As my father was before I buried him a month ago. And my purpose here in your precious Scotland, my lord, is to find employment as there is none for me in Essex. Does this satisfy you?"

Montrose's eyes flashed with a ruthless delight at this fiery response. "Tell me, are you at all interested in politics, Master Plainstaff?"

"You are the second man to have asked me that tonight. Again, no."

"I ask only because I have heard it rumored that the men of Essex are fonder of psalm-singing and revolutions than they are of card playing – or of their King, for that matter."

"That is treasonous, my lord," Cyrus returned.

"Of course!" Montrose agreed. "But that never stops them. Your righteous indignation on the part of the Crown, however, is gratifying. Soon you will gratify me still more by assuring me that you will be attending the execution held tomorrow in the town square, I suppose."

Cyrus's expression of pale enquiry revealed his ignorance of this event and Montrose elaborated: "Some fellow by the name of Ezekiel Lamentations Rayne, I believe an Essex man like yourself, is to be hung at dawn on account of his having stirred up a number of the Scottish Covenanters in the region against the Crown. They say as well that he used to be a Roundhead during Old Cromwell's time, I believe, and so ought to be hung merely on principle anyhow."

Cyrus sat very still and rigid in his chair, unable to remove his gaze from the Earl's laughing eyes.

"I suppose that if a man put in a good word for the poor wretch," Montrose continued, "He might escape with merely a stand at the whipping post. But, as it is..." He sighed heartily and his words trailed off as he took a sip from his glass, then dabbed at his lips with the edge of his napkin with a faint moue of distaste. "I fear the wine has gone warm."

"Couldn't you put in a word for him, my lord?" Cyrus burst out.

Montrose regarded the melancholic plea in the young man's eyes with a look of astonishment. "I? But – why?" His affectation of surprise soon relaxed into a smile. "Or are you no longer the King's man, Master Plainstaff?" As Cyrus, his lips tight and wan, made no reply, Montrose continued, "Then be assured, my good Puritan, that Ezekiel Lamentations Rayne will not be hung tomorrow at dawn precisely because there is no Ezekiel Lamentations Rayne. Tell me, Master Plainstaff, how did you like my pretty tale? It did not affect you too deeply, did it?"

"What is it precisely that you wish of me, my lord?" Cyrus said, his voice grave and low now with a seething hatred.

"I only wish you to play a single hand with me," Montrose said.

"But why? You know that I loathe the very idea."

"Yes, and I am sorry for that. But as things stand, I cannot very well allow you to leave without providing some sort of recompense for the injury that your 'friend' – " he smiled at the word, "that your friend Squire Wadham dealt me. I little care how much money you have upon you, so long as I have a chance at it." He paused to drink deeply of his wine before continuing, "Allow me to be frank with you, Master Plainstaff, as you have – though rather reluctantly – been so frank with me. When I meet a man like Squire Toby Wadham, the first thing that strikes me is how pitiable a fellow he would have been had he not been born a gentleman. His lack of courage and decision might serve him well enough in palaces and parlors, but would hardly keep him alive for above an hour in an alley tavern in London. The transient fortunes of a card game are the crucibles that test a man for his weaknesses and strengths and I fear that Squire Wadham, though he may have conquered me for the moment, is hardly the best subject for study in such a trial. Likewise, you may be a lowborn merchant's son, but you've a caution and reticence about you that I should like to see tested against my own virtues and vices. Perhaps you shall conquer – who can tell? And so, if you do not object, I should like very much for us to begin."

There was a honeyed appeal in the Earl's words that, mingled with the moonlight from the window that now silvered his hair, somewhat softened his appearance. But another glamour seemed at once to fall upon him as he turned his face slightly away from his guest and began to pour another draught of wine for himself. The long, lean shadows of night traced their lineaments upon his high brow and full lips and drew their own portrait of the soul behind those features: the roses in his cheeks seemed the sickened arbor blooms upon a churchyard gate; the green of his eyes, when lit by the lightning, took on the same glittering gleam as two flashing, razor-edged flecks of glass; and, as he turned towards Cyrus with a faint smile, the wine that stained his voluptuous lips held the grisly likeness of blood. All about him, the softness and amiability that had so distinguished him seemed to fall away to be replaced with a sharp and lithe quality that, for all its blooming vigor, seemed but a veil to hide the tilted head and whetted hunger of the born predator.

"If you had not been born a gentleman, my lord," said Cyrus, his eyes taking their shuddering leave from the Earl's visage and moving in a sidelong fashion towards the door. "You would have been the cleverest, craftiest master thief in all of London's East End, I do declare – much more of a success than those fools they sing of in the broadsides."

Montrose accepted this dubious compliment with a smiling nod of agreement.

"I am afraid, however," Cyrus continued, "That I am not of a mind to play a hand with a high-born gentleman – nor with any other thief, if you take my meaning, my lord."

Montrose moistened the end of his finger and began to trace the rim of his empty wine glass so that an eerie humming filled the room. Then, of a sudden, he seized the fragile glass and dashed it against the floor. Withdrawing the rapier that hung at his side, he advanced towards Cyrus with a trembling implacability that made him seem less a man than an embodied fury. Cyrus, already by this time resigned to the fact that he would probably not survive this night, regarded the approach of the mad lord and his own imminent skewering with a sensation bordering on relief.

"Can you," Montrose whispered, his handsome face shining with the cold sweat of rage. "Can you tell me, Master Plainstaff, why I should not run you through this very moment?"

Before Cyrus could find the courage to reply, the door to that chamber opened and Mrs. Leaske looked in.

"My Lord," she said. "There are men here to see you."

He hesitated and then said, still looking at Cyrus, "What kind of men?"

"The sort that you cannot afford to ignore, I'm afraid. The town militia."

***

A man stood by the wall of the tenement's back lot, holding a lantern and dropping its light upon the pale shape that lay at his feet. Even before he had drawn close enough to see what it was, Montrose was already stumbling back and averting his eyes. Cyrus, who had taken the opportunity to limp out of Montrose's apartment as well, now found himself seized forcibly by the shoulders and held in front of the distraught lord as a kind of bodily screen. The man that held the lantern looked briefly into Cyrus's eyes, then earthward again at what his light had uncovered.

It was Alan, Alan without a doubt, Alan's hair that caught the light in moving glints of red and gold, Alan's wrists that had been tied upon the scaffold and that now lay in two separate black pools of blood, Alan's mouth that now smiled in the lamplight as many of the same eyes that had gazed at him as he stood before the noose now gazed at the spectacle of his pale and silent body.

Someone murmured something about the lad having made a poor exchange after all, though he didn't look as bad as some of the others. The lantern-bearer set his lamp down and lifted the body slightly. Alan's shirtfront was stiff with blood and bile; for the first time, they noticed the soft and shining coils and lumps of intestines and lungs, scattered by the wall. As the corpse was raised, the smiling lips fell open, obscenely slack, and they saw that the lower jaw had been broken: the throat had not apparently been wide enough to accommodate whatever had decided to pull the young man's guts out along that avenue, leaving it ravaged by an upheaval of stomach acid, raw and ragged as though worked at by verminous teeth. The smell that rose from those open lips was unimaginably vile. They found most of Alan's teeth scattered about the place, like sharp pearls from a broken chain.

Some time, a long while ago, Montrose had released his grip on Cyrus's shoulder. The young man balanced for several minutes on nerves and the sheer, invisible thread of dumbstruck curiosity. Then sickness overcame him and he felt the threads loosen and fall away.

Chapter Eight: In which the Master of Hounds and the Master of Horses discuss a topic of which they are not overly fond while Childermass himself enjoys a good night's sleep.

Somewhere in his mind's eye like a dim afterimage, like the gleaming spheres of light that appear behind closed lids after one has looked too intently on the sun, Cyrus saw the black towers of the Priory. They flared and pressed against his vision the way that they had done when he saw them outside Montrose's window, his senses bridling and buckling beneath their shadow, until his consciousness melted into them.

The rain began to fall steadily, wetting Cyrus's cheeks, dampening the livid flesh of the dead Alan, and making the streets shine darkly in the light of porch lanterns. And this same rain, a mile away, sent its sheets to cover the black towers of the Priory, drawing rivulets down the stone walls, like trailing fingers.

Feversham was standing within the open doorway of one of the Priory's many kitchen entranceways, gazing at the rain and wondering whether his horses were cold. He looked towards the stables, at their oaken walls darkening in the storm, and gave a slight shiver.

"You're letting the winter in, Master Horse," Dagworth remarked at his back. Feversham could feel the dank nose of one of the man's hounds sniffing at his heels, its paw tentatively touching the back of his leg.

The ostler reached down to stroke the creature's head before turning indoors, saying, "Forgive me, Master Dagworth. I was only thinking of something that Childermass said before I chained him up for the night."

"And what might that be?" Dagworth asked, with that peculiar sneer that came to his lips whenever the subject of Childermass was raised.

"He said that he suspected another death in the village would soon reach our ears." Feversham shook his head, poured himself a beaker of ale.

"Oh, damn his eye," said Dagworth. "And to hell with that infected tongue of his. You *do* realize, don't you, Master Ostler, that our chimney sweeper has been saying poisonous little things of that sort for the last year?"

The shadows in the kitchen were restless. Feversham's eye caught one that moved like Childermass, with the same casual, coiled motion. It was as though he could see the absent chimney sweeper standing there in the chilly air, blowing on his fingers, leaning into a corner of the wall, his pale, living eye burning with a look of peculiar enthusiasm.

"Damn him," said Dagworth. "Him and all his lucky guesses."

Feversham finished off his draught and said, "Well, enough of Childermass. We must ready this place. Our Lordship's grandson will be here by dawn."

"Has it really already been a year since he left us?" Dagworth asked.

"Aye, and if you wish to keep your post, you will keep silent about the village deaths," Feversham said dryly. "Our Lordship's express wish is that his Christmas should remain untroubled."

***

Once he had been wont to sleep in a different chamber at the far eastern end of the hall, but that was before the last December and the last Feast of the Holy Innocents.

That night, Childermass's curiosity had surpassed his sense of judgment or self-preservation. He had crept into the depths of the Priory, to see something newly buried.

Childermass warmed at the thought, feeling again a sense of shame and excitement at the memory. At some point in the midst of his looking, he had turned about only to discover Feversham and Dagworth watching him, their twin faces as eloquent as two hangman's nooses. And after that, he had slept with shackles locked about his wrists.

Childermass leaned his cheek softly against his chains and marked the distant peal of a Houndswick belltower as it tolled the flying hours, pausing at last upon the first hour. The harshness of his punishment inspired a sense of bewildered awe and curiosity in his heart that overcame whatever sense of oppression he might have felt every night when the Master of Horses, with his dour, mournful countenance, came to shackle him to bed. Night after night he dwelt upon it in silence, his wrists throbbing with the dull ache of iron against flesh while his mind, alive and active, turned from one bewildering series of questions to another. Yet no explanation could satisfy – no excuse of wanton brutality on the part of his overlords could justify. In

Feversham were none of the cruder, crueler strains of human emotion present as they were in Dagworth – and yet he had sanctioned this punishment as readily as the Master of Hounds had done. "It is necessary," he had said. "And moreover, for thy own welfare and good, my lad."

Another soul might have revolted at the implacability and humiliation of this sentence – but it was not so with Childermass. His was a spirit that was, first and foremost, of a curious and analytical bent; the thwarting of this curiosity only inspired a new strain of wondering thought and teasing speculation as to the welfare and good that were meant him by these chains. True, he resented them – it would be impossible not to, for they constrained him from a freer exercise and gratification of this curiosity. But his resentment was mingled with something of a cynical complacency as well. The chimney sweeper had never harbored any desire to escape from Laughlin Priory. Nor did he believe that even if he had entertained such a hope, that he would have been successful or wise in the undertaking of it. There was nothing of worth for him in the outside world – and, indeed, even if there were, it could only be of use to him if it might serve as a means of constraining and forcing whatever secrets there were that these nightly chains were meant to protect and preserve him from. The ancient walls, the massy stones, the aloof, grey chimneys, and ruined domes – these were North, South, East, and West to Childermass and beyond them, his compass would go no farther. This was the mute and indomitable universe and he its lowliest servant, captive before its will. Would it ever be thus?

Eventually he fell asleep and eventually he dreamed. In his dream, he went to a tower window and ascertained with a fevered eye the exact spot in distant Houndswick in which he had glimpsed the answering flash of Cyrus's lantern from Montrose's casement. Some strange intimation told him that this wordless communication presaged something more, something greater. Like the godless Lycaeon who sought in his bloody way to be sure of whether the wandering Zeus was truly a god or not and was transformed into a ravening wolf for his trouble, Childermass stood transfigured by his own curiosity beneath the moonlight: his eyes – both the marble one and its living companion – turning to fixed, livid spheres and his smile glittering like a host of raised knives as he lifted his exultant gaze to Heaven.

But let us take our leave of Master Childermass now as he falls into the darkness of his dreams and take up the thread of the unfortunate Cyrus's narrative once more.

Chapter Nine: In which Cyrus is rescued by a lord and finds his search for employment postponed indefinitely.

The first thing that he felt was someone's hands, someone lifting him by the shoulders, and he remembered that moment earlier in the morning – himself falling in the throng before the scaffold, the one-eyed chimney sweeper catching him and asking him what he was doing there. Cyrus could see Childermass's lips move and heard him say again, "I have not seen your face before." The statement no longer seemed impertinent or sinister; it seemed sorrowful and solacing, a breath of something foreign and familiar from some forgotten homeland. Cyrus came awake with a shudder, his face still pressed against the cobbled street. The body of Alan was gone – they must have taken it away to the church for burial.

"Hello there?" A stranger's voice awoke him from his dark reverie. "Are you all right? Montrose said that you might still be out here."

Cyrus's eyes opened; he passed a bemused hand over his face, wet with rain.

"Montrose?" he murmured.

"Yes, that's right. I was in that room with you and his companions, falling half in and out of sleep, while he was trying to cajole you into playing cards with him. I'm afraid that I eventually napped and missed which of you won the game. Wine always does make me so sleepy."

"I refused to game with him. And he almost killed me."

"Yes, undoubtedly. I hope the two of you got along. He's a good friend of my family's."

Cyrus gave a despairing half-groan at this admission. The youth appeared to take no notice, busily attempting to find and hail a passing carriage. The streets were damp and deserted. Cyrus wondered absent-mindedly what hour it was.

"I'm sorry I don't have a carriage of my own," the stranger called over his shoulder. "But I was only dropped off here by my stagecoach an hour or so ago and was in the midst of finding another to take me the final mile to my home when I saw you."

Cyrus had been considering the benefits and drawbacks of accepting the hospitality of a friend of the Earl of Lauderness's and had swiftly come to a decision.

"Please, I beg you, just leave me here," he implored. "I will find my own way back to my lodgings, I assure—"

He was interrupted by the approaching clatter of hooves and saw, emerging out of the rain-swept mist, none other than the carriage of Squire Toby Wadham himself.

"Why, lad, you escaped!" he cried from the open window. "Come, jump inside, jump inside – a man could drown in this gale! Lord Withing Gosselin, good heavens, is that you? How long has it been since you left us for Oxford – a year?"

Cyrus was assisted by both the Squire and his rescuer, who was apparently someone named Lord Withing, into the interior of the coach and soon the three of them were driving down the cobbled lanes of Houndswick with a speed that would have put a four-horse buggy to shame. A few rivulets of rainwater trickled from behind the curtained windows, staining the rich velvet of the coach's lining, but otherwise they were dry and warm for the present.

"A fine coach you have for yourself, Squire," Cyrus remarked.

"Why, thank you, my boy," Squire Toby beamed.

"But I do not think that it drives quite as fast as its master did this evening when he departed from the Earl of Lauderness's company," the young man finished rather sourly.

"You misunderstand me completely, Master Plainstaff," Squire Toby returned. "I was waiting for you all this long night and refused to depart, even when Artemas advised me that you were most certainly murdered by now. But, Lord Gosselin – what in Heaven's name are you doing here in Houndswick, particularly at this hour?"

The person to whom this last enquiry was directed had by this time lifted the hood from his face and was busily rubbing his eyes at Cyrus.

"Why, whatever is the matter?" he asked, seeing Cyrus's expression of surprise. "Toby," he added. "You aren't going home, are you? I am sure that my grandfather would enjoy having your company at the Priory, if you drive us there."

"You're barely fourteen years old," Cyrus said at last.

“That is true,” Lord Gosselin acquiesced. “It is not my fault that my wise and cynical features belie my youth.”

“I fear that they do not,” said Cyrus. “And your family is probably wondering where on earth you are on a night like this.”

“Oh – well, I won’t keep them in suspense for long.” In spite of his woolen, plaid coat and muffler, the boy shivered. “Is that a broken leg that you have?”

“Only a sprained ankle – but painful nonetheless. You’re not going to test it like your friend Montrose did, are you?”

The boy blinked again. “Grandfather was right – ever since I’ve been to Oxford, I have suffered a lapse in my manners. Please, allow me to introduce myself properly and directly. I am Lord Withing Gosselin.”

With a grudging smile, Cyrus took the boy’s hand and shook it, replying, “I am Cyrus Plainstaff.”

“I like that much better than my own name,” Withing said. “At least you aren’t named after some rake who Queen Elizabeth winked at.” The boy yawned heavily, as indeed he had been doing since the beginning of their short acquaintance. “Do you mind if I go to sleep? I oughtn’t to have stayed up so late, but I didn’t wish to go home yet.”

And, with these words, he nestled his head against the velvet wall of the coach and instantly fell fast asleep.

***

They soon passed out of Houndswick and into the hilly lowlands, their road bordered at times by unkempt hedges, broken fences, and other signs of human life long since abandoned. The worst of the tempest had long since blown over and now a gentle rain fell upon the heath, drenching the tall grasses and trees with a chill curtain of white mist whilst the wind bore in its path an added fog that swept past the forlorn, hilltop cottages and pastures like windborne wraiths.

Cyrus had courted sleep several times during the last hour but had at length ceased, being plagued with dreams that offered less rest than wakefulness. Withing was still lost to sleep and the Squire had joined him as well, his lips loose and parted with the gentle breathing of oblivious slumber. Alone with his thoughts, Cyrus had only the desolate landscapes that passed without his window to occupy his attention – but, for the long-faced, sober youth, their silent beauty was company enough. The hilltops, sometimes crowned with a thatch-roofed hovel or with an abandoned circle of Druidic stones from the time of Rome's ancient empery, appealed to his melancholic frame of mind, for even in their desolation there was a proud forlornness about them that aroused within Cyrus's heart an odd mingling of pity and fear. Oddly, the sight of these landscapes put him in mind of the stranger within the treetops that he had met on that lonely road to Houndswick several evenings before; he wondered whether the being who had so frightened him might be akin to the ancient, gaunt-faced farmers who stood upon their doorsteps and watched the Squire's carriage pass by, their faces as hard and motionless as the granite of the mountain tops upon which they lived. Then he thought of the stranger's laughter and, shuddering, dismissed the idea from his musings altogether.

The trend of these thoughts, unusually morbid even for a gloomy mind such as Cyrus's, caused him to recollect past scenes from his home in Essex – a home that he knew that he must never return to. This thought, coupled with his other anxieties and fears, caused a tear to cloud his gaze for a brief moment even as he spied the golden edge of dawn creeping at last upon the edge of the grey horizon.

"Why, what is it, Cyrus?" Withing's low whisper brought Cyrus's attention to the boy who sat across from him, now blinking a little less sleepily than before.

"Nothing at all," Cyrus returned with a faint smile.

"I seem to remember you telling Montrose of your father's death a month ago," said Withing suddenly. "I am awfully sorry."

Cyrus's smile grew a good deal warmer, though a little more sorrowful as well, at these words. "Thank you – my lord? I must confess," he added with a look of wry apology. "It sits rather ill on my tongue to yoke a lad barely old enough to drive a lamb to market with such a weighty title."

"Then why don't we leave such formalities to Squire Toby?" Withing suggested. "Come – I'm hungry and we've a good few minutes left in this coach before we arrive at Laughlin."

"Then you live in Laughlin Priory?" Cyrus asked, a strange thrill of curiosity running through his heart as he uttered the name.

Withing nodded as he unpacked the contents of his small satchel and parceled out generous helpings of cheese and crackers for Cyrus and himself. "Ever since I was born there."

“It must be a grand thing to live in a priory,” Cyrus could not help but remark.

“I love the place,” Withing said with his usual frank simplicity. “But like you, my own father went to his grave close to a year ago and, ever since, I have been rather glad to get away as often as I can. And yet,” he added, as though thinking better of a sentiment too hastily formed, “The odd thing is that whenever I am away, I’ve no other thought in my head but how soon it will be until I can come home again. Oh, look!” Neglecting the crackers and cheese precariously seated upon his lap, the boy leaned out the window and pointed: “There it is!”

The rain had ceased and against the horizon, now paling rapidly with the approach of dawn, a sloping hill stood in stark prominence against the flat expanse of heathland and forests surrounding it. Like a frozen cataract of moss-covered boulders and gnarled vines, the hillside curved upwards and at its summit, like a towering outgrowth of ancient granite rather than a manmade edifice, there stood the Priory. The sun’s dim rays, though still low upon the horizon, emanated from behind the main wall of the chapel and through the three bare windows – once ornamented with stained glass – situated close to its arched roof so that a faint golden luminance shone from them like the gleaming of three eyes. A few thin, haggard trees shadowed the grey walls of the Priory, but save for these the structure stood solitary and aloof in its lonely elevation. Time had not weathered those stones to a shapeless and blunted ghost of their former glory – rather, the harsh extremities of wind and rain appeared to have lent something of their own stern, stark qualities to the venerable pile so that it melded easily with the wilderness in which it was situated. Just as when he had first spied the towers of the Priory from Montrose’s tenement window, Cyrus felt the stirrings of an exalted and shuddering awe as his gaze continued to follow in the direction of Withing’s pointing finger.

“I fear that this is where I must take my leave of you two young gentlemen,” Squire Toby declared. “Lord Withing, as much as I should like to pay my respects to your grandfather Sir Robert Gosselin, this evening has been far too eventful for me and I should like to remain quietly at home for the remainder of the day, if you don’t mind.”

“Of course,” Withing replied. “Master Plainstaff and I can make it on our own, can’t we, Cyrus? Once we reach the Priory, we can send Dagworth or Childermass – whoever happens to be about – to fetch Doctor Erskine for your foot."

Cyrus gratefully concurred with this last proposition and, once the Squire had called for Artemas to halt the coach, the two of them took their leave of him and proceeded to ascend the steep, hillside path that led to the Priory alone. In the interim, Cyrus managed at last to learn the reason for Withing's otherwise inexplicable presence at Montrose's private card game.

"Andrew Montrose was a good friend of my father's and is still on good terms with Sir Robert Gosselin, my grandfather, as well," Withing explained. "My travelling coach had arrived in Houndswick far earlier than I expected, so I decided to pay him a little visit."

"Does he know that you took pity on me?"

"I don't exactly know – but I am glad for your sake that he didn't pay much heed to you after your swoon. Montrose, as I am sure you've noticed, is not as suspicious of a fellow carouser as he is of a killjoy such as yourself."

Cyrus frowned. "Would he have truly slain me for such a trifling thing? And does he visit the Priory often?"

"A solid 'yes' to both," Withing replied.

Something in the levity of Withing's manner suggested to Cyrus that the boy was wholly ignorant of the dreadful cause of Cyrus's swoon. He was about to ask Withing how much Montrose had told him of Alan's grisly corpse – or indeed whether Montrose had told him at all – when the young lord suddenly pointed to two figures standing beneath the iron grating of the Priory's courtyard gate and whispered, "Come, let's hasten!"

Cyrus limped along until the two of them reached the gate.

"My lord!" one of the men, a lank, rather sad-faced fellow, cried. "You were not expected 'till ten! We have nothing prepared for your arrival at all. And who, pray, is this stranger?"

"Cyrus Plainstaff," Withing replied. "And Cyrus, this is Master Feversham," he gestured towards the long-faced man. "He is our chief groom. And this is Master Dagworth," he pointed to the hulking, broad-shouldered man who stood beside Feversham, "the keeper of our kennels." He hesitated and looked about. "Is Childermass not here?"

"Nay, my lord," Feversham shook his head. "We set him to work cleaning the hearth and chimney in your chamber and methinks he hath been busy at this task since the break of dawn. But may we not fetch you some breakfast in the kitchen?"

"Not if I've a say in the matter!" Dagworth suddenly burst out. "Your Lordship, you've always been a bright lad and I think you'll understand why I'd rather not traipse into the Priory just yet. Why, if your grandfather finds us caught so unprepared for your arrival, early or no, he'll have us turned out of doors just as quickly as you came in!"

Feversham frowned at Dagworth's free way of speaking, but Withing nodded in agreement. "Cyrus and I can stay out here on the hillside until the three of you are ready."

"And I shall bring you some sort of repast in the meantime," Feversham offered.

Once the two servants had departed, Withing sat down upon the grass and Cyrus settled beside him, the two of them admiring in silence the wan morning light as it played upon the ancient stonework of the Priory and the wild arbors that surrounded it.

"I shall be glad for breakfast, at least," Withing remarked. "I haven't tasted a morsel since the middle of yesterday – well, save for the cheese and bread that we already enjoyed this morning."

Cyrus was acutely aware himself of his own increasing hunger. However, once he leaned back upon the dewy grasses of the hill, he found himself seized with a sudden, light-headed drowsiness. As a result, as soon as his head touched the earthy, dank-smelling dirt and grasses that surrounded them, he fell instantly asleep: and for the first time in many days, as though he lay upon enchanted ground, his slumber mercifully remained untroubled with dreams.

***

It seemed that the space of a century had passed before Cyrus awakened from his slumbering to the sound of voices about him. He stumbled to his feet hastily but found himself still too full of sleep to sensibly distinguish what it was that was being discussed. The morning light had grown more golden and pronounced since his last moment of wakefulness, though the heavy cerulean clouds that marred the eastern horizon often obscured the full strength of its rays. He saw that close beside him, Withing was conversing with Feversham, the latter of whom was nodding and interposing a few remarks in a voice too low for Cyrus to comprehend. Seeing that he had at last awakened, Withing hastened to Cyrus's side and informed him that everything was in order for their entrance into the Priory.

"What's more," Withing added. "Childermass went into the village and fetched one of Doctor Erskine's assistants and so once you have met my grandfather, you can go upstairs and he will see about your foot."

Cyrus, rather dizzied by all this information, professed his profound gratitude for this service which had been delayed far too long already. "Who is Childermass?" he asked as they followed Feversham beneath the arch of the chapel and into the courtyard.

"Childermass? Why, he is the Master of the Chimneys here at the Priory – the one who cleans them of soot, chases the rats out, that sort of thing. Other than that, he performs all sorts of odd jobs for Feversham and Dagworth. I like him very much and so shall you. He is the subtlest when it comes to finding a fix for almost any broken contraption. I ploughed a hole into my rowing boat last summer and was certain that it had been made useless, but Childermass patched it up in no time with only a few bits of tar and wood and it floated like a swan. Fear not – you will meet him presently."

Cyrus listened to Withing cheerfully prattle away, wondering at the curious series of events that had all led, with a peculiar inevitability, now to his introduction into the house of a family utterly strange to him. His friendly young guide, with his glowing complexion and starry eyes would have seemed the very image of coddled nobility were it not for an odd hint of desperation that Cyrus thought that he occasionally sensed even in the boy's bright, cheerful prattle as though somehow he loathed to pass the courtyard of the Priory in utter silence. Cyrus at last dismissed this impression as a result of his own rather morbid imagination, but he could not help wondering at the barely perceptible shudder that convulsed Withing's shoulders as they both passed at last into the warm darkness of the Priory's western cloister.

Feversham now led them down a long hallway, illumined only by a few narrow windows set at odd intervals in the wall. Through these windows, Cyrus saw that the rising sun had now been somewhat usurped by a cloud, so that the pale morning light battled with the premature dusk for dominance of the heavens. Paintings, their frames gilded with gold and dust, ornamented the wall as well and Cyrus supposed that their subjects must be the past members of the Gosselin family. The painted eyes of the portraits seemed to follow their progress with the transfixing look of a corpse whose eyes have not yet been mercifully closed and he was rather glad when they at length passed out of that hallway and into the comparatively bright space of the parlor.

Two figures stood by a high, oak banister at the foot of a staircase, one of them the man Dagworth and the other a stranger. As Withing entered, Dagworth touched his forehead in a gruff token of respect while the stranger beside him delivered a courtly bow to both Withing and Cyrus. This stranger was a gaunt young man clothed all in black with high, haggard cheeks and lank, flaxen hair that blanched nearly white in the candlelight of the chandelier overhead, leaning upon a fan-like broom and watching them both with a silent interest that seemed to belie the deference that he had appeared to pay them a moment ago. When he caught Cyrus's eye, and when Cyrus himself saw the glint of marble in his other socket, the two instantly recognized one another from their original meeting at Alan's execution and a look of mutual, silent surprise passed between them at this unexpected reunion.

"Childermass at your service, my lords," said he, his voice, heavy with the lilting tongue of Scotland, reverberating in the high-ceilinged parlor with an eerie music while the distant sound of thunder outside the priory's walls mingled with his last words. He looked at Cyrus and said, "May I not unburden you of your coat, Master Plainstaff?"

"Methinks that it is still too chilly in here for that yet," Cyrus replied. "But thank you, Master Childermass."

The chimney sweep inclined his head with a deference born out of long habit. "I am sorry for the cold – His Lordship Sir Robert Gosselin has not been out of his chamber for many days and with coal so scarce, a hearth has not warmed this part of the priory for some time. I hope that the fire that I kindled in your own chamber will chase some of the chill away." Adding as an afterthought, "I might also fetch you a flagon of ale or a cup of fresh tea, if it would please you."

Cyrus, not used at all to this sort of pampering, appeared profoundly embarrassed and stammered out another expression of gratitude. Childermass responded with a nod before withdrawing to take his place again beside Dagworth, wondering whether he had said something out of turn to cause such a flustered response in the newcomer.

At that moment, a door leading to an adjoining chamber to the parlor opened and two young women entered. One woman, her hair bound into a long golden braid and her own age closer to Cyrus's years than the age of the younger Withing, embraced him closely and then, catching sight of Cyrus, enquired with a demure smile, "A friend from Oxford?"

"No – a friend I met when visiting Montrose," Withing replied. "Cousin, this is Master Cyrus Plainstaff and Cyrus, this is my cousin Lady Mariah Gosselin."

Cyrus accepted the young woman's proffered hand with a kiss, whilst Withing – warming to his self-appointed occupation as chief herald – continued, "And this is Miss Clarice Abelin, the niece of our resident chaplain – who also is about somewhere at the moment."

A dark-haired young woman dressed in a white dress of embroidered muslin gave Cyrus a shy curtsey while he bowed with an equal amount of embarrassment.

"I fear that we receive so few visitors here that our servants are often far more civil than us," she said, her eyes innocently happening to move in Childermass's direction, whilst he returned her gaze with a look of cold, humorless curiosity. "Would you like Dagworth or Childermass to show you to your room now?"

"Even before I have been introduced to my grandson's newest young friend?" All heads turned to behold the approach of an ancient gentleman who, half-supported by a gnarled staff, stood in the doorway of the parlor with a weary smile of welcome.

"Grandfather!" Withing cried, rushing upon the old man and embracing him. "I thought that you would never emerge!"

"Stop, stop, boy, you'll pull my beard out by its roots! Yes, your doddering grandfather managed not to lose himself amongst the mazy corridors of the Priory's western wing on his journey to the parlor to greet his only grandson. Now, wilt thou kindly tell me who this stranger whom you have brought into our home might be and what he is to you?"

"This is Cyrus Plainstaff – and Cyrus, this is my grandfather Sir Robert Gosselin. Cyrus was attending a card game the other night at which I also was present and I managed to rescue him after Lord Montrose left him out in the street in a swoon, after attempting to dispatch him with a rapier."

"Then you merely allowed Montrose the satisfaction of leaving him with an injured foot?" the old man queried with a bewildered frown.

"That was Squire Toby Wadham's doing," Cyrus put in.

"Dear me, you have had a rather odd introduction to the local aristocracy, Master Plainstaff, I must say," said Sir Robert Gosselin. "Childermass, do take this young gentleman upstairs to whatever chamber it is that Withing has had you prepare for him and after a physician has ministered to him, we shall see about dinner."

Cyrus bowed his thanks and Childermass, gesturing with his broom towards the wide staircase, led the way to the second floor of the Priory with Cyrus limping behind.

Chapter Ten: In which Cyrus is the guest at a rather unusual meal.

The physician's assistant was a kind, portly fellow who, after binding Cyrus's swollen foot with strips of white cloth soaked in ice water, advised the invalid that rest would be his best remedy and then departed without further ado. Childermass had stood silently by the entire time, watching the proceedings with a face as expressionless as the stone wall by which he leaned. Once the apothecary left the chamber, however, he came to life once more and, solicitously turning down the linen sheets and helping Cyrus out of his coat, once more repeated his offer of cold ale or warm tea to the sufferer.

Cyrus was beginning to feel a little sorry for the odd lad who seemed, in his own rather aloof manner, obliged and willing to please. Or perhaps, Cyrus thought, this was the usual way that nobles expected to be ministered upon and the chimney sweep was simply performing a role that he had filled for many lords before. It was difficult, however, for the Puritan lad – unused as he was to such attentions – to treat them with an appropriately dismissive attitude and thus, when Childermass held out the proffered jug of ale, Cyrus said without even thinking, "My stomach's still a bit too sour for anything yet – but drink of it yourself, Master Childermass."

The chimney sweep's living eye narrowed with a look of surprise, but he replied obediently, "If you wish, Master Plainstaff."

Cyrus was stunned by this reply as well as by his embarrassed recollection of his own role as an esteemed guest of the Gosselins in the Priory. Hastily, he said, "Forgive me – I didn't mean that you *must* – only if you wish to."

Childermass, his pale, pinched countenance for the first time warming with a look of humor, filled a wooden cup with the liquor and, tipping it in Cyrus's direction said, "God save you, sir," before emptying the cup as though it held water.

Cyrus in the meantime was wondering whether it would be considered inelegant of him if he rested in bed for the next several hours and, little knowing what else to do, asked Childermass what he believed was next expected of him by his hosts.

"Faith, sir, considering the apothecary's instructions, I should think it ill of anyone to expect you to wander about the Priory and I am certain that His Lordship Sir Robert Gosselin would be of the same opinion. If it will ease your mind, I shall repeat what the apothecary said to Lord Withing and tell him that you would prefer to follow his instructions immediately."

Cyrus thanked Childermass for his kindliness and, after undressing, collapsed into bed and almost instantly fell asleep, so profound was his exhaustion. Childermass stood by for a few minutes, stirring the logs in the hearth with the end of a birch branch so that the flames leapt with a merrier dancing, before at last turning upon his heel and departing from that chamber with the noiseless, sideways movement of a winding serpent.

***

Cyrus had meant to rest only for a few hours, but when next he awoke, the lengthening shadows that fell athwart the floor of his chamber told that far more time had passed than he had expected. A cold sheen of perspiration dampened his forehead and he tried to recall the dreaming terror that had awakened him so violently, but at last gave up the pursuit as hopeless. Rising from the bed with difficulty, he looked about the darkened chamber and, seeing his coat hanging from his bedpost, put his hand into the inside pocket, withdrawing two books. One was a small, leather-covered copy of the Holy Scriptures; the other was a battered notebook with pages full of notes in his own long, precise handwriting. Cyrus paused for a moment in thought – then stowed both volumes beneath his pillow. It was a poor place for hiding anything, but he felt that it would do in a pinch and that at least it was more secure a refuge than his old coat.

After washing his face and hands with a basin of ice water and a cloth draped over a low table by his bed, Cyrus took leave of his chamber and began to look about for Withing – or, for that matter, any inhabitant of the Priory. The staircase, parlor, and hallways through which he passed were alike deserted and, through the crystalline glass of the high, arched windows he saw only the rain and windswept moors without. Behind two heavy oaken doors, however, he overheard the faint murmur of voices, and after knocking for politeness' sake, he let himself in.

"Cyrus! I feared that you would sleep through dinner and was just going to have Feversham bring you something once you awoke." Withing's voice echoed airily in the vast expanse of the great hall in which Cyrus now found himself in as, with a gesture of his fork, the young lord beckoned for him to sit at the table. As though he moved in a dream, Cyrus slowly crossed the room and moved in the direction of the empty chair that Withing had indicated, his eyes wandering about with a measure of awed curiosity that the reader must forgive, considering the scene that presented itself before our young hero's eyes.

Conceive of a vast space lit only by hanging cressets and the wan evening light that filtered in through the windows – once the nave of the Priory's chapel and now a twilit world of bare, massy columns, vaulted rafters, and carven angels and saints lost to shadows and dust. The stone floor was strewn with hay upon which half a dozen immense, black-coated curs lay, either sleeping or watching for when Dagworth, who stood above them several feet from the dining table, would let fall a grease-soaked loaf or a partridge bone. From far above, the scent of burning tallow drifted down from the suspended chandeliers that Childermass, standing at the feet of a headless marble angel, lit with the end of a high, flaming pole while Feversham emerged from the shadows of the cloister, bearing in his hands a fresh platter from the kitchens. Tapestries, most of them depicting scenes from the Last Judgment, veiled the lowest and widest of the windows, rising and blowing with the wind and sheltering the nave somewhat from the elements while a few narrow windows provided a view of the brooding sky above. With such a scene before him, it is little wonder that Cyrus's eyes grew starry with the look of a man who wanders within a vision, so solemn and so ethereally melancholic was the spacious setting through which he passed as he approached the table. He found himself noticing for the first time the traces of a thinly-veiled sorrow and apprehension in the features of the two ladies, even as they met his gaze with welcoming smiles, but he could not detect the source of their disquiet.

"Will you not try the partridge?" said Withing. "It is delightful."

Cyrus tried to return the boy's cheerful smile, still troubled by the atmosphere of disquiet that seemed so tangibly to hang over the little company. "Where is Sir Robert Gosselin, if I might ask?"

"He pleaded an indisposition of the stomach, sir," Feversham replied from somewhere behind him. "And apologized that he could not share a meal with you tonight."

Clarice Abelin opened her mouth for a moment as though she were about to speak, but then bit her lower lip and remained silent.

"Did you know, Cousin," Withing continued to Mariah. "That they are opening a playhouse in Shrewsfield, but a mile or so from here? Why, if they can assemble an acting troupe worthy enough to recite a little Dryden or Shakespeare, we may not have to take the coach to Edinburgh to find some entertainment so often."

Mariah nodded with a half-smile, but her eyes lowered to the table with a gaze that ill-reflected the contentment that she sought to feign. Withing, his high spirits swiftly wearing thin, said while casting his gaze about helplessly from the servants to the two girls, "Come now, what is wrong? I pray, one of you tell me – these melancholic spirits begin to make me think that my homecoming was not so joyfully anticipated by the two of you as it was by me."

As soon as the words passed from his lips, he turned pale with shame at their harsh import and fell silent and morose himself. Feversham and Dagworth exchanged glances but said not a word whilst Childermass, having accomplished his task of lighting the pendulous tapers, now sat at the feet of one of the disfigured marble saints, his own gaze fixed intently upon that unhappy company.

Suddenly, Clarice spoke, her words spilling forth in a tone of tearful denial: "Oh, Withing, if you only knew how long Mariah and I have counted the days until you returned – how awful these last several months have been without you, you would never think so lowly of us. Ah, God, if you had any knowledge of the hideous things that have happened since – "

"Hold your tongue, girl!" Feversham cried, his voice unexpectedly harsh. "Or will you disobey His Lordship Sir Robert Gosselin's orders?"

"But he must know some day, mustn't he?" Her eyes now moved pleadingly from Feversham's sad, dour face to Dagworth's brutish countenance. "Why must we keep it from him even now?"

Feversham did not reply directly to her, instead saying, "Methinks, Master Childermass, that Miss Clarice Abelin would prefer to dine within her own chamber before another melancholic spell affects her and Dr. Erskine's services are needed. Would you see the young lady to her chamber?"

Childermass rose with a silent nod of assent and, taking the girl's hand, began to conduct her from the great hall and towards a shadowed doorway that gave out to a corridor leading elsewhere.

This sight was regarded by the three remaining members of that company with a silent horror made all the more profound by the mystery that lay behind it. It was Cyrus who was first to break this silence, crying, "Good Childermass, stay – surely there is no need for all of this!"

"Silence, Master Plainstaff," Feversham interrupted. "And be seated. Or would you too disobey His Lordship's command? Recall that you are his guest here."

This last rebuke was enough to silence Cyrus from another outburst. Though Clarice's intimation had awakened his own horrible memory of what he had seen outside Montrose's tenement, he could not afford to be a wandering outcast. And so he held his tongue and burned with the injustice and mystery of the situation.

"But what is it that my grandfather does not wish me to know?" Withing asked, his gaze clouded with apprehension.

"It is nothing of importance, Cousin," Mariah returned, taking his hand with a faint, strained smile. "Come, now, finish your dinner. It is your first supper here in Laughlin for many months, you know."

Unsurprisingly, the rest of that meal was thenceforth conducted in utter silence.

Chapter Eleven: In which Cyrus is introduced to a few of the Priory's late residents, a meeting is held, and an earlier mystery deepens.

Soon after dinner, Mariah retreated to her chamber complaining of a feverish head and leaving Cyrus and Withing alone to their own devises. Light conversation was still out of the question after the grim atmosphere that the unfortunate Clarice's departing words had left in their wake. Even the merry-minded Withing seemed to have absorbed some of this morose mood for, though his tongue waxed no less volubly, the subject of his discourse diverged markedly from the realm of local playhouses. After having fortified himself upon several successive chalices of wine, the lad abruptly rose unsteadily from the table and beckoned for Cyrus to follow him, whilst Dagworth, Childermass, and Feversham silently took the silver platters up and departed from the great hall. Cyrus, feeling dizzy himself though not from inebriation, followed the young lord beneath the high columns and through a door that led into an alcove, lit by a single taper standing upon a low table. Cyrus's eyes wandered upwards to the cobwebbed, vaulted rafters, dwelling with amazement upon the singular state of disuse to which the place had been abandoned. Even the ornately framed paintings and mirrors that hung upon the walls and encompassed them on either side were overlaid with so thick a layer of dust that, as Cyrus leaned close to make a more minute inspection of one particular portrait, the very motion of his presence caused a cloud of grey motes to float about him.

"I used to call this the Looking Glass Cloister," Withing said, his voice taking on the soft drawl of intoxication as he took up the candlestick and allowed its light to play upon each of the portraits in turn. "That's Sir Etienne du Laughlin." He paused before the painting of a gentleman dressed in knightly armor and wearing a crimson tunic. "He built this place back in 1069 and lived here for a time until he mysteriously disappeared several years later."

"Disappeared? But was he never found again?"

"Oh, he was," Withing replied. "Ten years after his disappearance, they found him one day wandering down a corridor of the western wing, as haggard as an old man and claiming that he had been gone but a mere afternoon. From what the chronicles say, he had gone quite mad and could only repeat something about having met his doom upon the thirteenth of May. He died several days later and is buried somewhere beneath the Priory."

"Poor fellow," Cyrus murmured, gazing now with a chilled awe upon the noble, sorrowful face and haunted eyes of the knight. "But who was this lady?" He pointed to the portrait of a gentlewoman attired in the white ruff and pearls characteristic of an Elizabethan.

"That's Lady Letitia Gosselin," said Withing. "She was the sister of Sir Henry Gosselin, the first of the Gosselins to live in the Priory when King Henry V made a present of it to him. If I remember the tales correctly, she was poisoned by her jealous sister who was later burned alive in the fireplace of the great hall as punishment for the murder."

"You cannot mean the great hall in which we last dined?" Cyrus asked.

"The very one," Withing nodded, oblivious to the sudden consternation in his new friend's countenance. "But you oughtn't to be afraid of Lady Letitia – according to all the old legends, she is something like the guardian spirit of the Priory and she has only appeared to residents in order to do them some good turn or warn them of impending evil."

"Do you truly believe all this?" Cyrus enquired, unable to discern whether the gleam in Withing's eye was derived from humor or liquor.

"I cannot say as though I think upon them enough to believe or disbelieve them. But they make pretty tales, don't they?"

The reflections cast by the cracked, splintering mirrors upon the walls, coupled with the painted eyes of the portraits, often gave Cyrus the oddest sensation that the two of them were being watched closely. His gaze happened then to fall upon a black veil that covered a large portion of the wall and, drawing closer, he said, "What is this meant to hide?"

"Oh, the black veil," Withing said. "You mustn't look behind the black veil, you know."

As he spoke, the boy nearly dropped the candlestick and Cyrus, as much for the sake of the Priory's threadbare rugs as for his own peace of mind, extricated the taper from Withing's inebriated fingers and advanced towards the veil in question. Lifting it by its ebon fringe, he looked full upon what it was that lay behind – and the next instant stumbled back, overcome with a horror and loathing beyond description. His face white as a sheet, he faltered, "Who – who – ?"

“I told you not to look behind the black veil,” Withing said, shaking his head mournfully. “But now that you have – ”

He drew aside the funereal curtain himself and allowed the candlelight to fall upon the sight that had so appalled Cyrus.

Stretched out upon a bier behind a wall of glass and clothed in a robe of black silk lay a corpse. The lips were shriveled back so that only the teeth were visible of the mouth and the grisly traces of the worm were discernable in the livid features of the face and hands – the rest of that awful shape was hidden in the sumptuous folds of its graveclothes.

“What means this?” Cyrus demanded, dismayed as much by Withing’s unperturbed attitude as by the presence of the loathsome object itself.

“I confess, I can understand your agitation. It does look awfully lifelike – or rather, the opposite: particularly in this light.”

“What are you saying?”

“I believe this fine ornament was fashioned for the Priory by the brother of my grandfather Sir Robert Gosselin, Stephen Gosselin. Some said that he had this model of himself fashioned in wax in order to serve as a reminder of his own mortality. Every Good Friday, he would approach this hallway with a retinue of his relations and servants, draw aside the veil, and gaze upon the decaying effigy for an hour while some chaplain in his service sang the requiem for the dead. Then, he would depart and the veil would remain drawn for one year more until the next Good Friday. They say that on his deadbed, he murmured, ‘O, my brethren, and shall I now at last behold what lies behind the black veil?’”

“What a sorrowful thing,” said Cyrus. “That a pious man should be so shackled by a contemplation of the body’s mortality rather than the soul’s eternal life.”

“But that’s the peculiar thing,” Withing said. “All the records say that he was a man with a ‘goodlie fear and knowledge of the Gospell’ but that, for all that, he often said that he wasn’t sure but that he wouldn’t have preferred to inhabit his old body, with all its old hungers and thirsts, rather than trade them for whatever it was that St. Paul prattled on about to the Corinthians.”

“Methinks, then, that this was as much a penance of horror as well as of mortification for him.”

Withing nodded and drew the veil over the morbid effigy before glancing up at a portrait that hung not far above it. “My father, Luke Gosselin,” he said. “He died a year ago.”

Cyrus turned his gaze up to the face in the painting. It possessed much of the same qualities of nobility tinged with sorrow that he had perceived in the portrait of Sir Etienne du Laughlin.

"I wish that Father was still alive," said Withing. "He would have known what it was that Clarice wished to tell us. He always knew how to put things right." He turned his eyes upon Cyrus and, for the first time, Cyrus noticed in that golden, youthful face the growing flush and brightened eyes of a habitual drunkard. "It was my hope that when I returned here, that things would be different. But I suppose a year's time could hardly make a difference. Shall nothing ever be the same again?"

Cyrus, in his hesitant, awkward way, murmured what words of comfort that he could to ease his young host's mind. To his dismay, this merely encouraged an onslaught of maudlin tearfulness in the inebriated Withing, who murmured his thanks with an exaggeratedly formal bow before promptly collapsing against Cyrus in a dead stupor.

Fortunately at that moment, Dagworth, Childermass, and Feversham – appearing like three ministering wraiths – happened to wander down the other end of the Looking Glass Cloister and, noting Cyrus's embarrassing predicament, offered to take the unconscious Withing up to his room and lead the Puritan to his own chamber as well. This offer Cyrus gladly accepted and, in the wake of the three silent domestics, found his way to his chamber once again.

***

Childermass, his silhouette dark against the leaping flames of the fireplace, sits with his knees drawn up against his breast and lazily inspects the polished gleam of his switchblade, making a merry music with its scraping edge whilst sharpening it upon the hearthstones. Dagworth looms above him with a flagon of ale in his hand, his face chapped and ruddy from his proximity to the fire, flanked on all sides by his black curs, whilst Feversham continues to finish his supper in silence at the table, his breath misting in the gathering darkness of the Great Hall.

Several hours had passed since the events last recounted took place. Night had fallen and the first evening stars had begun to emerge from behind the bank of clouds overhead, shining their cold light through the narrow windows above the nave. The tapestries that veiled the lower windows rose and fell with the breath of the night wind, sending their woven demons and saints billowing in outstretched ripples towards the torches that framed them on either side. The marble statues that stood like sentinels beneath the row of stone columns on either side of the chapel cast the shadows of wingless cherubs and headless angels upon the dirt floor of the hall, giving the illusion that the place was full of an invisible throng of deformed spirits. Yet were one to look upwards as Childermass did at that moment from his place at the blazing hearth, to gaze upon the broken statues as they raised their swords and wings to the vaulted ceiling above, an impression of awe as well as melancholy would have been the paramount emotions provoked by such a view: and, indeed, the atmosphere of fallen nobility that pervaded that lonely place proved more effective in exciting a perception of grandeur than the more polished manors of London's upper crust could ever have done. Even Childermass's stern countenance and thin, dour smile softened into something like appreciation as he contemplated this decaying beauty, before he lowered his gaze and once more set about polishing his knife, himself becoming a shadow of the brooding atmosphere that he had so thrillingly surveyed.

"Her Ladyship Mariah Gosselin wishes me to begin readying her favorite hound Penny for the hunt," Dagworth remarked at last. "She said, 'Master Dagworth, there's not another in this castle that I'd trust with my precious creature but you, so see that you have his coat brushed to a gleam for the outing.' Of course, I bowed low and, 'Certainly,' says I, 'you may depend upon your Penny to look the finest of all the hounds upon that day.' And let me tell you, but this very afternoon she approached me and – "

"Sir she said, sir she said," sang Childermass in a mocking, humorless chant.

"Shut your trap, Master Chimney," snarled Dagworth in reply. "I'd like to see you try and curry favor with Her Ladyship – indeed I would. It isn't long before humans grow a bit uncomfortable in the company of devils, if you take my meaning – and ladies do have such soft, sensitive hearts."

"Silence, the both of you!" Feversham said. "Or have neither of you any respect for your offices? Think of what His Lordship would think if he heard such banter!"

And Childermass and Dagworth, though with their deadly hatred not the least bit abated, both exchanged humorous glances before Dagworth rioted in raucous laughter and Childermass, who rarely laughed, allowed himself a ghastly smile.

Presently Feversham rose from his repast and, taking a torch, beckoned for the other two to follow. They accompanied him without a murmur as though from long habit as he led them down several corridors and up a flight of stairs until they reached a certain door made of ornately carven oak. Feversham rapped his knuckles upon this door several times before a muffled voice called for them to enter.

The three of them entered the chamber, its dark confines lit only by the moonlight that filtered in through the crimson stained-glass of a small window and the burning of a single taper that stood upon a chest by the foot of a canopied bed. Two figures already stood within as though awaiting their arrival: the stooped silhouette of Sir Robert Gosselin and a gentleman attired in the black robes and white collar of a cleric.

"I have asked Reverend Abelin to be present," said Robert Gosselin. "For it is he who told me that you, Feversham, wished to inform me of something."

The long-faced ostler stepped forward and, after bowing low, replied, "Aye, my lord – as you desired, we have made no mention of the events of the last year to your grandson. However," he paused. "Miss Clarice Abelin was nearly on the verge of relating those tales and indeed, the secrecy that you desired would have been entirely destroyed, had it not been for my own timely intervention. With Childermass's help, I should add."

"My niece is an impetuous child," Reverend Abelin allowed, his voice deep and rich with a rueful regret as he turned towards Sir Robert. "You say that Childermass was responsible, too, for preserving Withing from such harmful and sorrowful knowledge?"

"Yes, reverend sir," replied Feversham.

The Reverend, the middle finger of his left hand glimmering with a black-jeweled ring, beckoned for the chimney sweep to step forward. Childermass did so, his gleaming eye settling first upon Sir Robert and then upon Reverend Abelin whilst his mouth retained that curiously hard, wry quality that caused him to look as though he were smiling even when his mood was at its most humorless.

"Were I to send Feversham or Dagworth as spies upon my niece, their presence would be noticed in a trice, for rarely are they seen outside the stables or the kennels. But you…you are everywhere and nowhere, in every public or private chamber that contains a chimney, always wandering about to perform odd tasks that fall upon no one else's shoulders. If you were to keep your eye upon her, it is doubtful that your presence would be noticed any more than the passing glance of some stray creature. Therefore, I wish you to continue in the good work that you have done for us today. Watch my niece and see that she does not let fall more from her lips than is prudent. Shall you do this for His Lordship?"

"Recall also," said Sir Robert, "That the fetters that bind you every night may just as well do the same during the day, if you are found to have no care for the welfare of my grandson or this house. It has never sat easily upon my breast that I must punish a youth so harshly and I hope that your service in this matter shall assure me that you possess within your heart a true fealty to this Priory, to my grandson, and to myself. In spite of your…impious curiosity."

Childermass bowed. "It shall, my lord."

"Then hence from here," said Reverend Abelin. "Our business with you is done."

Once the chimney sweep had departed, Sir Robert's haggard features relaxed into a weary look of relief. "Would that I possessed a spy to set upon *him*," he murmured.

"You have nothing to fear from Childermass, my lord," said Feversham. "He has a cunning look about him to be sure, but he has neither the resources nor the inclination to trouble you."

"Aye, though a cruel and wicked devil he is," Dagworth said with a gloating leer, warming to his favorite topic. "If it does strike your Lordship's fancy to keep him chained up a day or so, I'll gladly lend a hand in it."

Reverend Abelin then spoke, his voice still in the same grave, modulated tone: "This Cyrus Plainstaff whom Withing brought home with him – do any of you know who he may be? I myself have not yet had the opportunity to meet him as I remained in my study all of this evening."

Both domestics shook their heads.

"It is of no matter," said Sir Robert quietly. "Our business is not to fill this Priory with discord and suspicion. I only hope – I only hope to avert whatever horror it was that befell my poor son."

"My lord," said Reverend Abelin. "It is the desire of us all that whatever evil it was that befell Luke Gosselin and still plagues Houndswick shall never again enter this house. In that mission, methinks thou hast the full cooperation of us all. As for Master Childermass, the task he has been given ought to afford him enough honest occupation to rein in his malicious curiosity."

Dismissed, Feversham and Dagworth departed from Sir Robert's chamber and Reverend Abelin, after exchanging a few words in private with His Lordship, followed in their wake. Only the shadow of Childermass still darkened the floor close by the chamber door, his ear pressed against the wall where he had been standing hidden in the shadows absorbing every word uttered by his superiors. As motionless as one of the Priory's marble angels, he stood there in the darkness – stood there with a half-smile deforming the still sobriety of his visage, like a dash of red upon a slate of white, listening and waiting, listening and waiting.

***

Presently, Childermass stirred himself free of his reverie and wandered down the hall, intending to enjoy a private repast with the rather lavish amount of scraps that he had gathered from various tables throughout the course of the day. It was not that he would not have been well fed had he chosen to share his dinner with the rest of the domestics in the lower floors of the Priory; rather, it was his own peculiar preference to dine alone.

Whistling a jolly tune under his breath, the hollow echoing of which haunted the low, oaken rafters of the hallway, the chimney sweep continued on until he reached the head of the staircase that led downstairs to the main parlor in which young Cyrus had first been introduced to the main residents of the Priory. Just as he was about to descend, however, he was arrested in his action by the distant sound of a groan from somewhere behind him. He paused, less out of alarm than curiosity, and turned in the direction of the plaintive sound, straining his ears to their utmost. As he had hoped, the sound was repeated – yet this time with an increase in volume that left the chimney sweep in no doubt of its source. Hastening towards a certain chamber door, Childermass put his ear to it in order to discern whether he could make out the sound of a footfall; hearing nothing, he turned the doorknob and, without a moment's hesitation, let himself in.

There was no candle lit in that chamber, but Childermass could see well enough by the moonlight that streamed in through the casement. He soon realized that the sufferer whom he had overheard was none other than the

Priory's new guest, Cyrus Plainstaff. The young man was still groaning in his sleep as though even then under the assault of some invisible enemy. Again and again, he struggled to call out the name of some being whom he sought to placate, but as though his tongue were impeded by some similarly indiscernible force, all that he could manage were a few heartrending groans. Instinctively, Childermass hastened to the side of the bed and managed to wrest the sleeper wholly out of whatever tormenting vision he had succumbed to with a few swift, violent shakes. Cyrus's eyes flew open and, pale and shaken, he seized the chimney sweep by the shoulders and whispered, "Father?" Then, seeing the look of astonishment upon his rescuer's face, he sat up instantly and cried, "Childermass? What are you doing here?"

"I heard you cry out in your sleep, sir," Childermass replied. "And thought to awaken you, lest you do yourself an injury." As he spoke, he watched keenly as Cyrus felt about for a candle and lit it, noting that the youth's hand still trembled as though he were still in the throes of his vision.

"That was good of you, Childermass," Cyrus said at last.

"And were you troubled by a nightmare, sir?"

"That I was," Cyrus shuddered. "Do you suffer from such things often yourself?"

"I should think that every man does at some time, sir," Childermass replied. "I have heard that the thing to do is to contemplate such terrors for a long while as our philosophical men do until it becomes more a thing of tedium than terror."

"Is this what you do?" Cyrus muttered, though his weary mind seemed already forgetful of the chimney sweep's presence.

"Well, that's the trouble, sir," said Childermass. "You see, I can never remember what it was that I dreamt once I wake. But you," he added. "You've at least a chance."

Cyrus turned to meet the chimney sweep's pale, inquisitive eye and Childermass smiled at the look of dawning anxiety upon the young man's countenance. Unable to bear the suspense, Cyrus asked him what he meant by this enigmatic statement.

"You called for your father – or do you not remember?" the chimney sweep queried.

Cyrus remained silent for a time and then, at last, gave a nod of assent.

“Was it your father whom you were terrified of – or for?” Childermass asked.

Cyrus gazed with a repulsed sort of mesmerism upon the pallid brilliance of his questioner’s single living eye. He could not decide which it was that held his gaze more: the look of cold intrigue that seemed to emanate from that eye, or the shifting, ethereal quality of its hue. It seemed at one moment to reflect the ivory color of moonlight, then the wavering flicker of the candle, and then to gleam with a pallid fire all its own. All the while, in spite of this uncanny impression, there was an intensity in the chimney sweeper’s gaze that held him as surely as the imprisoning grasp of some irresistible, adamantine hand. Unable to match that intensity, Cyrus’s eyes faltered beneath its scrutiny and he felt his heart quail before an alien soul that he himself did not comprehend and yet somehow feared. In spite of all this, however, he kept enough of his wits about him so that he managed to remain silent in spite of the subtle pressure of the chimney sweep’s expectant eye.

Childermass himself was profoundly affected by the new guest’s response. The aura of secrecy that had hovered about this Master Plainstaff ever since he had entered the Priory increased considerably in the chimney sweep’s estimation, consequently raising the stakes of their interaction to more than a mere game of curiosity. What was he afraid of? What had it to do with his father? And why was he so desperately fearful of revealing even the cause of his fear?

“Why don’t you light a fire in here, Master Childermass?” Cyrus at last said. “I would like some light in this room and…it seems peculiar to carry on a conversation in the darkness like this.”

Childermass rose from the bedside and obeyed this order without a word, disappointed by what he perceived as a sudden and direct rebuff to his inquiries. Once he had brought a merry blaze leaping in the hearth, he turned upon his heel with the intention of departing the chamber – however, the voice of Cyrus recalled him.

“Childermass – I know full well that after that last nightmare of mine, sleep will not come easily to me. If it is no trouble to you, would you stay and tell me something of the Priory? Withing told me a little, but not enough to satisfy my curiosity. Are there any pleasant tales that you know of?”

“Faith, not I,” said Childermass. “I know nothing of this Priory, sir, excepting what little was told me as a boy. But I would gladly play upon my whistle for you, if it is simple amusement that you wish and if that would serve your turn as well." Cyrus nodded and so the chimney sweep sat upon the edge of the chest at the foot of the bed and began, without further preamble, to withdraw a long, silver pipe from his breast pocket and set it to his lips.

The first melody that the chimney sweeper breathed forth was a slow air, so soft that it seemed to drift lightly about the chamber and settle with a sweet delight upon the listener's ear, like morning dew upon a windowpane. Yet almost as soon as its elusive melody had been caught, the tune suddenly shifted to a lustier, more sprightly rhythm, like the tune that might be whistled by a ploughboy as he wends his way to his rosy-cheeked mistress beneath the shade of a singing lark's nest. Cyrus could not but marvel at the skillful dexterity with which Childermass played, each musical scene following the other in a marvelous succession of images that fairly dizzied the mind with both delight and awe. There were ancient, familiar ballads, intertwined with subtle melodies and countermelodies, that yielded to airs of such solemn mirth that Cyrus wondered whether they were perhaps hymns that the chimney sweep had overheard upon some Sabbath organ in Houndswick. Slowly these strains, like the tangled limbs of some gentle, shading vine, filled his brain and caused him to feel as though he were slipping beneath them again into the sleep that he had been forced to quit so abruptly.

Childermass, his gaze fixed upon Cyrus all the while that he played upon his pipe, noted the nodding head and drooping eyelids of the youth and, after a few minutes, slowly set aside his instrument. He rose and drew close to the sleeper, harkening to the slowed breathing and leaden motionlessness of the limbs. Satisfied, he then proceeded towards the coat that hung from one of the bedposts and, his fingers slithering into the breast pockets, searched for the book that he had felt in its folds when he had taken the coat from Cyrus that morning. Baffled disappointment suffused even the stern pallor of his face, but only for a moment – then the chimney sweep was casting his eye about the chamber, studying every shadowed corner of that chamber that might prove a hiding place for the missing volume. His steps, like the soft movements of some circling cormorant, brought him from one end of the room to the other – but so often as he passed the hearth of dying coals and inspected with care the contents of the tall wardrobe and the cluttered chest of drawers, so often he met with nothing even remotely resembling whatever it was that he had felt within the coat pocket.

He paused at last in the midst of his search and, while lost in thought, allowed his gaze to wander towards the sleeping youth. A look of thwarted malice deformed the chimney sweeper's countenance then, so that his lips grew grey, his living eye seemed to start from its socket with as fixed and ghostly a look as his marble one, and his face shone with a radiance that bespoke some awful passion kept at bay only by some implacable, inward strength of matching awfulness. His mind, ever possessed of a methodical craft, now raged as he demanded of himself why the stranger should have troubled to hide such a trifling item in the first place – and as the possibility that he might never have the chance of examining its contents now presented itself to him in all its most dejecting colors, his thin face grew as gaunt and haggard as a thirsting man who sounds a well only to find it as dry as his own tongue. Curiosity drove him, a curiosity as pure and untainted by personal enmity as an adder's instinct to strike at the hand that surprises it, but what compelled this Childermass to nourish so grim and implacable a curiosity and what it was that had first planted it so deeply within the black fastnesses of his heart and brain – these secrets could only be understood by the seeker himself. So intent was he in satisfying his peculiar thirsts, however, that the chimney sweeper rarely bothered to trouble himself with such metaphysical questions. At a much later date, long after the passing of this fateful night, would Cyrus perhaps glimpse something beyond the outward luminance that dazzles and blinds, something that would reveal a portion of the rotting, loathly core hidden beneath: the Leviathan heart that gnaws and recoils upon itself, submerged beneath infinite depths but capable at times of uplifting its monstrous head to reveal eyes like Hell's lanterns that penetrate with a gloating deviltry deep into some victim's soul before falling fast again beneath the waves. But let us, for the moment, leave such secrets untouched – let the black veil shrouding the chimney sweeper's heart remain drawn and impenetrable in its obscurity. No rude hand shall pluck from that secret garden a single withered rose this night nor shall the key to that gate be wrested until some wandering soul, perhaps, discovers an entrance that even the subtle Childermass himself has left unguarded.

But these thoughts did not enter Childermass's brain – only his blasting eye continued still to dart upon Cyrus a look of withering disappointment whilst he mused for the umpteenth time as to whether there was any hiding place left in that chamber that he had not already exhausted with his searching. A sudden thought struck him as he contemplated the sleeper, then: a thought that struck him with such hilarity that, where upon his countenance before had existed only gloom, now a smile lifted the corners of those thin lips and he thought, "What a fool I am! Of course – while trying all the secret spots in this chamber, I have neglected the simplest one all the while."

Without a single moment's worth of delay, he hastened towards the sleeper and, with a cunning softness, knelt by Cyrus's bedside, his fingers slowly feeling beneath the pillow. His heart leapt as they brushed against the firm edge of what was without a doubt a book. A gleam of gloating pleasure suffused his living eye as, with careful ease, he withdrew the little volume that Cyrus had hidden beneath the pillow and feasted his eyes upon it as though he were already sating his curiosity upon its contents.

"Now at last," said he softly. "If it does not displease you too greatly, Master Plainstaff, I shall perforce try the contents of this little book of yours and learn whether it may, perhaps, prove a more open and forthright fellow than you yourself have been. And, in good faith, I do only collect my due: have I not a right to know the name of the devil that I drove from your dreams?"

With a last mocking nod of deference, the chimney sweep withdrew then from the bed and, after one last glance back at the sleeping form of the hapless youth, departed from that chamber to feast in private.

The sky was cleared of clouds and the moonlight bright upon the Priory's high battlements where Childermass in joyance did alight. Settling himself at the sooty base of a smoking castle chimney, he withdrew the volume that he had clasped to his breast and began to turn the weathered leaves. Half of the book's pages were filled with hand-written scrawls, the other half being still blank and empty. Childermass paused for a moment to fortify himself against the midnight cold with a plentiful draught of wine and then commenced without further ado to read the following narrative.

Chapter Twelve: In which Childermass is acquainted with the narrative of the shepherd's son.

"Only a fool would set down a record of that which he least wishes others to discover – yet sometimes I believe that were it not for this little book, I would lapse into the mad forgetfulness of a Bedlamite and begin to think of all the events of the last month as but passing visions. Happier a man would I be with such a thought – but for my life's sake, I dare not. I will plainly set down as much as my heart has the strength and courage to recount and hope that these remembrances will be enough to keep my soul vigilant against that demon of destruction that has haunted my steps ever since my poor father's death in Essex and that, I fear, seeks after my own life even now.

"My father was Ephraim Colkins and, when he lived, he earned both his keeping and mine as a poor farmer upon a modest several acres that he possessed close by Chelmsford. My mother passed into the Lord's keeping when I was barely a week on this Earth and, being my father's only son, the two of us were often away to the marketplace to sell our fleeces and whatever surplus our fields had afforded us, leaving the farm alone until our return. My father, being as prudent as he was generous, often spent hours haggling with avaricious merchants who desired our produce but proved reluctant in giving fair return for its purchase, and so we often found the evening drawing on and the first stars brightening the nightly heavens by the time we began to wend our way back home from Chelmsford town.

"Even in tracing my father's name upon this cold page, I find my heart begin to quail before the task ahead and a thousand remembrances assail me from all sides, threatening to overturn my resolution to set these events down. Let me but recall my father in the colors that happier memories paint him in my mind's eye and may Heaven's power, which wards the fate of the innocent and helpless, drive away the awful speculations that now cloud my brain. He was a venerable man whose locks of silvery grey and whose lined countenance did nothing to lessen the look of intelligent humor that often shone forth from his eyes, though this brightness was often displaced with a heavy, melancholic shadow that would cross his visage unaccountably at times. His dress was always the tall, steeple-crowned hat and sober black cloth of the Puritan and regardless of the ill look that many a richly-cloaked Cavalier might cast upon him in Chelmsford, he preserved this plain style for as long as he lived. Men used to tell me that I shared his features to a startling degree and, if this is true, I suppose that I am glad. Would that I shared his wisdom as well – then perhaps I should stand a chance against the pit that now threatens to engulf the son as well as the father.

"One evening, my father and I returned to find a coach drawn up before the door of our cottage and a pageboy in royal livery approached us and declared that His Lordship the Earl of Linchester desired our acquaintance, wondering whether we would be so good as to invite him to dine with us tonight? My father was as surprised as me by this unexpected enquiry, for neither of us were particularly social and – save for the journey that we made every Sabbath morning to the church in Chelmsford – we rarely spoke to another living being but one another. Howbeit, my father – little knowing what else to do – bade the boy to tell his master in the coach that His Lordship was most welcome and that, if he would not be offended by the fare of a simple farmer, he might enter the cottage and be seated at our table.

"The Earl of Linchester, Lord Gomershall by name, cut a strange picture indeed within our rude dwelling as he stepped across the threshold and allowed his pageboy to catch his mantle as he unclasped it from his shoulders. His dress was rich but not ostentatiously so and his bearing was that of a man of power rather than of foppish fashion. As he turned his head to survey the rough, unpillowed chairs and single bookcase that ornamented what I blush to call a parlor, I could see his lip curl with a look that I – unacquainted with human emotions outside of those that I had seen in my father – could only wonder at.

"'A homely little dwelling thou hast, Master Colkins," he said at last, his voice steeped in the mannered accent of a courtier. 'Pray, tell me how long this home has sheltered your son and yourself.'

"'For my son, these last nineteen years, Your Lordship,' my father replied, wondering as much as I as to whither these questions tended. 'For myself, still longer. Will you not sit down?'

"Lord Gomershall seated himself at the head of our table, his piercing eyes turning from my father to myself. 'Will you not seat yourself, lad? I imagine that you must be wearied from a day's laboring at the market.'

"Embarrassed by my unkempt appearance, I replied, 'I shall, sir, once I have cooked a bit of lamb to serve both you and my father.'

"Lord Gomershall raised a brow in surprised consternation. 'What, have you no serving wench? None?' he shook his head, again with that peculiar expression that I could not quite define. 'Well, perhaps we shall see about that, my lad. Off with you, then, to the kitchens.'

"I retired from that room and set about my task, unable to hear anymore of what it was that the Earl of Linchester and my father discussed over the scraping of my ladle and the simmering of the hearth beneath the kettle. When at last I returned into that room with two steaming bowls, I was dismayed by the look of silent discomfort that had settled even upon my father's customarily melancholic countenance. To my further astonishment, Lord Gomershall turned his shrewd eyes upon me and said, 'Tell me, my lad, how would it please you to live with your father in the comforts of a mansion in Chelmsford rather than this hovel?'

"I turned my eyes helplessly from my father to His Lordship and, finding no clue in my father's grim visage as to how I ought to reply, said falteringly: 'I suppose I should like it very much, my Lord.'

"'Suppose!' he laughed, though I thought I detected a note of impatience now in his voice. 'What – are the two of you, father and son, both afraid of good fortune? Well, well – no matter. We shall think on it no more tonight, but return to the subject at a later time.'

"This last was directed towards my father who inclined his head in a silent nod of assent. The rest of that dinner was taken up in conversation revolving around London politics, a subject which I never had much of a head for and largely ignored in favor of my own silent thoughts. At last, Lord Gomershall arose and, dabbing at his lips with the edge of his kerchief, thanked my father most graciously for his hospitality. To me, he said before his departure, 'Your father, I have no doubt, shall inform you of the reason behind my visitation. Be certain, young man, that you argue most strenuously with him so that he chooses to make the decision that is most prudent for your own welfare as well as his own.'

"Once the Earl had departed, I pressed my father for some explanation behind all this mystery. To my disappointment, his only reply was a look of sorrow and a murmured promise that he would explain the whole business to me in the morning but at the moment that he was far too tired to do more than retire early to bed. Disappointed, I spent a somewhat restless night lying in my own cot, wondering what could have put my father in such a peculiar mood.

"It was early the next morning before my father had even arisen that I caught sight of Lord Gomershall's coach upon the horizon heading straight for our cottage. I abandoned the patient cow that I had been milking so sleepily before and hastened inside to awaken my father and warn him of the Earl's coming. No sooner had my father thrown on his somber raiment than a sharp knock sounded upon our door. I opened it and found myself face to face with His Lordship.

"'I should like to speak to your father at once,' said he.

"'Cyrus,' said my father. 'Go to the fields and see to the cows as you were doing.'

"'But – ' I protested.

"'And study this text,' he added tersely, thrusting a volume into my hand. 'Thou hast been lax of late in attending to spiritual matters and perhaps this will sharpen thy dull wits. Now get you gone.'

"The tone of my father's voice was not one to brook any arguing and so, with a heavy heart, I departed into the fields again and sat upon a knoll overlooking our sheepfold and waiting for the Earl to withdraw so that I might again tax my father with the questions that he had avoided the night before. As I sat there, I happened to glance down at the book that my father had given me. It was a copy of Reverend George Gifford's old discourse on supernatural prodigies, mostly of the diabolical sort, and was ill-calculated to put my mind at ease. I have always studiously avoided such texts, for my dreams are plagued with enough imaginative horrors as it is without my searching for true accounts of deviltry to populate them still further. But curiously enough, once I find myself with such an unpleasant volume in my hand, I cannot help myself: I must, albeit cautiously, turn the leaves in order to gather a notion of what the author's main argument is and before I know it, I have enlisted five and twenty new devils into my reluctant catalogue of terrors, all of which I am sure to be visited by in dreams soon enough. This perverse inclination, combined with my sleepiness, all resulted in my falling asleep after a quarter of an hour's passing and awakening only after having been assaulted by a series of visions that left me as shaken and anxious as a man who had experienced every single one of the prodigies so carefully illustrated in the good Reverend's text.

"The first thing that caught my eye was the departing figure of the Earl as he crossed the threshold of our cottage and strode in the direction of his coach. Disappointment was written large upon his features as was firm denial in my father's countenance. Catching sight of me, the Earl called out to me, 'Take this, lad – and if you would like richer profits besides this, then tell your father that he ought to forsake his tired old notions at the very least for the sake of his son.'

"He delivered something weighty wrapped up in a kerchief into my hand and then, without another word, entered his carriage and drove away. I unwrapped the cloth and found in my hand three golden guineas.

"After such a peculiar series of circumstances, my father was constrained to explain the meaning of the Earl's visitations. Apparently Lord Gomershall, having passed by our land on the road from Houndswick to London, took a great fancy to our pastures and was determined upon purchasing them from my father at whatever price my father might demand. Unfortunately, my father was equally determined that he should never accept so much as a farthing from Lord Gomershall for the land. Loyal son that I was and am, I could not help but wonder at my father's decision and reluctantly take the side of the Earl in the matter.

"My father seemed to read the conflicting emotions in my visage, for he said gently, 'I am not such an old fool that I cannot see the wisdom in accepting Lord Gomershall's proposal, Cyrus – and indeed I would, were circumstances of a different nature. But you must trust me when I say that it can never be and that I cannot at this time explain the reasons for my aversion. God willing, the Earl will forget this passing whim of his and devote his energies to the driving of less obstinate mules.'

"But my father, though a wise man, was wrong. From that day onwards, the Earl returned to press his suit with as much fervency as he had done that first day – and again and again, for a reason that must have baffled the Earl as much as it did me, my father rejected any offer that His Lordship made for our small estate. After his visits, the Earl would often leave me with some token present which only served to convince me of his generosity, but I left off demanding an explanation from my father, guessing that such inquiries would only be met with silence.

"So it went for several months. One day, however, as I returned from leading the sheep out to graze behind our cottage, I saw His Lordship depart from our cottage with an unprecedented haste, his face pale with an anger that I had not thought that noble countenance capable of. Before he entered his coach, however, his eyes happened to uplift and fasten upon my face. Coal-black they were, blacker than I ever thought a mortal man's eye could be, and as I gazed, he looked upon me with an expression of such intense malignance that I felt myself grow faint.

"As soon as Lord Gomershall had driven away, my father hastened from the doorstep and came to my side, inquiring anxiously after my health – for, in truth, after the awful look that I had discerned in that nobleman's eye, I had grown as pale as death and felt barely able to hold myself upright. Once we had entered the cottage and I had refreshed myself somewhat with a glass of water, I demanded of my father what the meaning of this new mystery was and told him as forcefully as my shaken nerves would permit that this time I would brook no mysterious silence.

"'No, I did not expect that you would,' my father said sorrowfully. 'And, in truth, you have had every right from the beginning to know why it is that I have denied a nobleman who could have made us both rich men by now. But I wished to keep silent, for I did not want to entangle you in a matter, the vicious nature of which might destroy you as well as it will me. However, methinks that the time is passed when I could preserve you from Lord Gomershall's ill favor and I fear that there is little harm now that the truth could do you.

"'You know that many years ago, I was a soldier in Oliver Cromwell's army – him whom the Cavaliers so scornfully term Old Noll – and that I fought in the early part of the war against the tyrant King Charles before my wounds discharged me from service and I retired here to Essex. Since that time, I have seen the rule and the death of Cromwell and now the restoration of the old king's son, King Charles II, who hath come to reclaim the throne of his father, the beheaded Pharaoh, and to throw the godly once more into confusion and distress. Yet am I content, for I know that I did as much as any man could to forestall this time of darkness and, in my old age, I possess still the memories of those days when liberty from this yoke of monarchy was a thing a man could fight for rather than dote on and wish for as so many men of this time merely do.

"'One memory in particular, however, abides in my old breast that does little to comfort but never fails to fill me with horror when I think on it. I recall once when I was marching under a regiment heading close by Chelmsford town that we were met by a herald from a small village called Wysterly Ford, begging for us to hasten along with him, for Prince Rupert and his band of merry Cavaliers were crossing the river there and had already laid siege to the cluster of farmhouses that made up the outskirts of the village proper.

"'Now the folk of Wysterly Ford had acted as a goodly and faithful garrison to Parliament's troops and so we, hearing of their distress, hastened on with speed – only pausing long enough to dispatch a messenger to ride ahead and inform our ally Lord Gomershall and his own regiment, all of whom were closer than we to Wysterly Ford, of our movements and requesting him to alter his own course in that direction so that his men might provide reinforcements.'

"At mention of Lord Gomershall's name, I started in surprise, but my father raised a hand for silence and continued with his tale:

"'After several hours' journeying we reached the outskirts of the Ford, but as Fate – nay, the Lord – for some indefinable purpose would have it, we arrived too late. Savage flames already lapped at the thatch rooftops of the farmhouses and, as we desperately searched the ruins of the village, we found that only pitiful corpses lying amongst the bloodied straw remained of those who had once been our allies and friends. Every one of them – man, woman, and child – had been put to the sword. Lord Gomershall – he who should have been their defender and savior – had, at the last moment, chosen to side with the King and had joined with Prince Rupert and his men as they celebrated their latest crippling victory against the Puritan rebels.'

"My father paused for a moment, and though his eyes remained as dry as before, a look of sorrow and hatred convulsed his features for a moment, causing his haggard features to resemble the grim lineaments of some awful death's head. Then, with a slight shudder, he cast off this gloomy pall and resumed his narrative:

"'I had hoped these last few months to pretend ignorance of my knowledge regarding Lord Gomershall's unmanly betrayal, not wishing to incur the wrath of so powerful a noble. But during this last visit, I could not keep the black bile that brimmed in my heart at bay – I poured out to him all the hatred that I had felt for him ever since that bloody day and now he has departed, bearing with him an enmity for you and me that, if the Lord does not choose to shield us, I fear shall be our ruin. What think you now, son? Is your father not a pitiful man to have rejected such a wealthy gentleman?'

"I denied this vehemently, my own heart filled with bafflement that a nobleman such as Lord Gomershall with a face that had before betokened such an affectionate concern for the wellbeing of my father and myself could truly be the author of such cruelty. I also voiced my hopes that perhaps after this last altercation, Lord Gomershall would darken our doorstep no longer. My father, however, was less optimistic in his expectations.

"'If he does not have a warrant out for my arrest already, then I shall think myself a fortunate man,' said he. 'I was the veriest of fools for having let my tongue gain an inch over my wisdom. If the Lord chooses to punish me for my foolishness, then it will be no great matter – but if you fall under the rod, too, my son, then I am a shamed as well as chastised fool.'

"But again, my father was wrong. No such warrant was issued, nor did we hear from Lord Gomershall for many months. Then, one October evening, a carriage drew up before our cottage door. It was empty save for a messenger who informed my father that, if he was available, His Lordship the Earl of Linchester would like very much to entertain him at his manor that very night. He added that the Earl wished to have it known that there were no hard feelings that he harbored against my father and that he wished, if it were possible, to make amends for any wrongs that he had committed in the past. For my part, I was highly doubtful of this invitation and sought to persuade my father against accepting it.

"'If this is a chance to appease His Lordship, then I must take it,' my father returned. 'Not for my sake, but for thy own.' Seeing the look of doubt on my face, he added with a smile, 'And, in good faith, though I have no love for the Cavaliers, I doubt that even they would wish to murder a poor old farmer in one of their rich manor houses – think of what a sight it would look on their costly Italian rugs!'

"I smiled at this jest in spite of the misgivings in my heart and watched as my father entered the carriage and drove away towards Lord Gomershall's manor. For hours, I sat up in the parlor, companioned only by a midnight lamp and Reverend Gifford's discourse on witchcraft, until at last the sound of footsteps brought me to my feet and I opened the door to see my father standing on the threshold. His face was bright with a merriment that I had rarely seen upon his melancholic countenance and, as he sat down at the table, I pressed him to tell me what had taken place between him and His Lordship.

"'More than I could have hoped for, my son,' he replied. 'All the ill will that I had feared would have poisoned the Earl against me is now a thing of the past – he told me himself that he was willing to forgive the enmity that ought to exist between a Cavalier and a former Roundhead and, indeed, that he had long ago repented wholeheartedly of the bloody fate that had befallen Wysterly Ford.'

"'But what could have provoked such a transformation?' I demanded, incredulous.

"My father hesitated and then said, 'Methinks it was our third companion – a Frenchman and a nobleman whom the Earl introduced as one of his closest associates: the Marquis Antoine St. Aubert.'

"My father went on to describe how throughout the entire dinner that he shared with Lord Gomershall, this St. Aubert shared the table as well and moreover, how when tempers threatened to flare, he would interpose in his measured way with a sparkling wit that would instantly lighten the spirits of both His Lordship and, my father confessed, himself. He was most impressed by the gentle gallantry of the Frenchman – used as he was to the coarser jests of the Cavaliers, it surprised him to find such sweetness of temper in a nobleman. And from France – the very heart of luxurious vice itself! The embroidered white lace at his throat and wrists, the powdered wig with its black ribbon at the back, as well as the jeweled, blood-red broach that burned upon his coat all bespoke a certain taste towards exquisite finery and fashion. But those eyes, blue as a robin's egg, were ever upturned in a look of such trusting amiability and friendship that, in conjunction with the short lamb-like curls of his white wig and the faint, cherubic spots of rouge upon his cheeks, created such an impression of innocence that my father could hardly believe such a thing were possible in one of Adam's fallen sons. He had a taste, St. Aubert did, for the English composers, particularly Mr. Thomas Tallis, and did Mr. Ephraim Colkins share his love for such music as well? My father, of course, assented and said that he enjoyed music that sought to uplift the soul as well as the senses. St. Aubert, delighted at this response, stated that he wholeheartedly agreed and that he would very much like to dine with Mr. Colkins one day himself, so well did their tastes seem to accord. He cared little for English politics – the whole fracas between the Cavalier and the Puritan left him as disinterested as the disagreement between the Papist and the Huguenot in his own country.

"'I have known a great many Puritan gentlemen and I have known a great many Cavaliers,' the Marquis St. Aubert had said. 'And I have enjoyed myself very much in both their companies. Why should Monsieur Ephraim Colkins fear for his life and that of his son while we, by virtue of our superior understanding of the Scriptures,' here he smiled most charmingly upon my father, 'grow fat on wine? Let us settle our differences tonight and satisfy ourselves with peace – then we shall have become a most amiable and efficient King and Parliament, shall we not, My Lord?'

"And, to my father's infinite surprise and relief, Lord Gomershall had smiled himself and nodded to this suggestion and the three of them had parted ways, the veriest of friends. My father still refused to sell his land to Lord Gomershall, but the latter insisted that it made no difference to him and that he was quite content with my father's friendship alone. As he bade my father farewell, the Marquis himself had added, 'I should like very much, Monsieur, to one day make the acquaintance of your son as well, if he is as delightful a companion as his father. Will you not accept this small present as a token of our friendship until then?'

"Here, my father disclosed to me a small pendant made of glass and fashioned in the shape of a dove – a piece of such lovely craftsmanship that I could hardly believe that the Frenchman had parted with it so easily.

"'He must be a most generous man, this Marquis,' I said.

"'We owe him our lives,' my father replied frankly. 'As far as I am concerned, that young Frenchman was no son of Adam but an angel of mercy – and you are safe now, my son, which was all the root and substance of my anxiety in the first place.'

"For my part, I still could not fully believe that Lord Gomershall had so easily relinquished his desire for my father's land, much less his hatred of my father – and, in spite of this St. Aubert's honeyed words, I wondered whether the Earl was not merely biding his time for some more opportune hour of vengeance. But in this suspicion, I soon felt myself proved wrong, for no such hour struck and, as October passed and November's first frosts whitened our fields, we heard no word from the Earl of Linchester. The business at last seemed finally settled and done with.

"Also, another trouble served to distract our attentions from this matter. Wolves, ever a peril to a flock of sheep, had begun to make scattered attacks upon our flocks, leaving only the bloody carcasses behind. Or, rather, we at first assumed these savage deeds to have been committed by wolves – as they continued, however, we were forced to admit that their perpetrator possessed a cunning and mystery about him that ranged beyond that of a mere wild beast. One proof of this was in the utter lack of interest that the attacker apparently possessed in eating the lamb's flesh: though there were manifold signs that the creature had been tortured with a variety of incisions before its death, there was no sign that any portion of it had been devoured. Another was in our utter inability to catch any sight of their murderer – whomsoever or whatsoever it might be that caught and slew the pitiful creatures, it successfully evaded all our attempts to witness it, signaling a certain amount of craft that a common wolf could never have possessed. Then, as suddenly, as these deaths had began, they ceased and we were plagued no more with mysterious corpses amongst our flock.

Chapter Thirteen: In which Childermass reads of Cyrus Plainstaff's encounter with the Marquis Antoine St. Aubert.

"November came and the snow covered the expanse of the pasture with a whiteness as pure as that of a lambkin's fleece. One winter's morn, only the week before the date upon which I write this narrative, I was standing watch over the sheep as they nosed past the snow for a few sprigs of grass hidden beneath, when I discerned a man standing atop a hillock on the outskirts of the field, watching me. I raised a hand to hail him and he replied by starting towards me, his steps tracing faint impressions of darkness upon the surface of the snow.

"'Cyrus Colkins, is it not?' he enquired as he drew nigh.

"I nodded, shading my eyes against the murky, livid glare of the winter's sun barely risen above the horizon. It was no easy thing to discern the stranger's form, for his hose and lace-fringed long coat were as white as the snow itself, as was the short, curled wig that crowned his head. But, as he approached me, I could make out the features of his face – the round, cherubic face, the merry twinkle of the eyes, and the smile that seemed in its good-naturedness to declare its full avowal of my own goodwill as well.

"'And you are the Marquis Antoine St. Aubert?' I asked, trusting in the description that my father had given of the man before.

"A smile of delight touched the dimples of the handsome Frenchman's lips. It was curious, the way in which there was such a child-like quality in his lively and attentive air, without the usual coddled, distasteful softness that usually accompanies such a personality.

"'You are as charming and clever a lad as I imagined, Monsieur,' said St. Aubert. He paused, his breath misting as he sighed heavily and turned his gaze towards the sheep that grazed quietly beside us. 'And what a lovely home you have. I always wished to live upon a farm.'

"'Is it my father that you wish to see?' I asked. 'If so, he has been most anxious for your visit.'

"'Presently, yes,' he said. 'But may I not watch the sheep for a little while with you? It seems a lonely watch that you keep.'

"'A shepherd's task is often a lonely one,' I replied with a smile.

"'Ah, but of course, Monsieur, shepherding is the noblest of vocations as well – was not Our Savior a shepherd himself…of men?'

"As he spoke, the Marquis knelt in the snow and, clicking his tongue, beckoned to one of the lambs that gamboled close by us. It had been born far past the usual time and had little hope of surviving the harsh frosts of winter, but still it crept upon unsteady legs towards St. Aubert's outstretched hand so that he caught it easily and drew it closer to him. The little creature began to sniff curiously at the starched lace at his cuffs and to suckle upon the velvet lining of his coat while he stroked its fleece with a practiced hand.

"'May I tell you a little tale, Cyrus?' St. Aubert asked, his eyes turning now upon my face.

"'Of course, my lord.'

"'There was once a nobleman who lived in the province of Auvergne. It would be most uncivilized and rude of me to expect you to be familiar with that part of France, when I myself am an alien in your charming realm. You must envisage to yourself, then, forests like the dense woodlands of some faery kingdom, full of murmuring brooks, ancient ruins, and occasionally a small village much like the Wysterly Ford that your father so lamented. Now this nobleman lived in a chateau close by one such village and one day he was out riding his finest horse across the meadows when he caught sight of a young maid drawing water from a little spring that ran from beneath a boulder. So taken was he by her beauty that, though she was but a peasant girl, he then and there determined in his heart that she would be his.

"'He soon discovered that she lived upon the outskirts of the village with only an elderly aunt as her guardian and, without further ado, began to court this maid for many months until, at length, she consented to be his bride. They were married within the Abbey of St. Clare and from thither the nobleman bore the maiden to his chateau and there made her his wife. A month of happiness passed for the both of them, a month in which even those blisses that one would think had been lost to man after the Fall seemed open to them. Yet even at the height of such pleasures, there was a certain dissatisfaction that often overwhelmed him at their closure. He would gaze upon the sleeping fair beside him long after the candle's flame had been extinguished and wonder what it was that caused him to feel such a churlish discontent in the presence of such an angel. Yes, he would gaze and gaze – and in his mind would rise a thousand visions, formless and vague, that sent shudders of delight running like coursers through his veins. But so vague were these visions that he could not fully understand himself in what direction his peculiar desires tended – and so his days were spent in longing and his nights in dreams that caused him alternately to recoil and to pant with an eagerness that he could scarcely contain even in the presence of his sleeping bride.

"'This state of affairs might have continued indefinitely had it not been for one fortunate occasion when the nobleman and his lady were seated together within one of the anterooms of the chateau. As I recall it, they were in the midst of conversing upon the state of England since the succession of the second Charles Stuart upon the throne when, quite by accident, the young woman pricked her finger upon the knitting needle that she had been employing and a few drops of crimson fell upon the skein of white fabric upon her lap. I tell you, Monsieur, that sight shot through her lord's heart like a transfixing arrow whilst, with every passing second his breathing increased, his face paled, and his heart seemed ready to burst from his breast with a transport that it had never known before – not even, I confess, upon his nuptial night. With a suddenness that caused the pretty little damsel to start, he hastened to her side upon the couch on which she sat and fastened his lips to her wounded finger, so that the drops fell therein. This was nothing compared to the sight itself of the crimson as it stained that white finger, but still the taste sent currents of life through him so that it was only the sound of his wife's voice that revived him from his joyous trance. Her expression was one of timid fearfulness and she shyly enquired as to the cause of his odd behavior. He made some lover's excuse of wishing to soothe the pain of her little finger and this must have satisfied her, for she smiled upon him and the conversation turned once more to their former topic of discourse, the incident dismissed altogether from her mind. But her husband did not forget – and a plan fomented within his mind that he thought might bring him closer to a fuller taste of this bliss.

"'Over the next several weeks, the nobleman began to comment upon the change that he claimed to perceive in his young wife. Though her cheeks were ever so rosy, he would remark on their pallor and though her eyes bright, he would discern in them the hectic glow indicative of a fever. Little by little, poisoned with these small falsehoods, the credulous girl began to believe that she was indeed the victim of some malingering illness and, as he continually insisted that she remain indoors and rest as much as was humanly possible in order to dispel this malady, in hardly any time at all she grew to be a bedridden invalid in body as well as mind. The melancholy that usually settles upon the human spirit when it is denied access to sunshine and open air began to encroach upon her formerly blithe spirit and, under her husband's eager, watchful eye, her cheeks became sunken and her eyes took on the hollow look of suffering. At last, as he had been hoping to do ever since the beginning of this charade, the nobleman summoned a physician from the village and requested that he provide some sort of remedy so that the health of his young bride might be restored.

"'The good man dutifully looked the lady over and pronounced her condition to be the result of melancholia. The only thing to be done, he told the nobleman sorrowfully, would be to draw out as much blood as could safely be lost and hope that such a treatment would, in time, restore her to health by bleeding of her the black bile at the root of her sickness. The nobleman gave his assent to this proposition, only barely containing the exultation that he felt at this news. This was, after all, what he had been anticipating ever since the commencement of his plot.

"'During this time, he began an extensive campaign to redecorate many of the chambers and anterooms of the chateau, replacing the medieval tapestries with draperies, all of the same rich, red dye. His lady would often enquire after this new obsession of his, to which he would respond smilingly, 'Why, somehow that color reminds me of you, my dear – and all that is of you, I love.''

"At this point in his tale, St. Aubert paused and a peculiar smile crossed his own face for a moment. For my own part, I was beginning to grow not a little unhappy with the direction towards which his narrative seemed to be tending, not to mention its length. We had, indeed, already strolled the entire circumference of the sheep's fold half a dozen times during the duration of the Frenchman's tale thus far.

"'This new all-encompassing absorption with the color red,' the Marquis continued, 'began to call to his mind a certain episode in his childhood when – '

"'I pray you, sir,' I interrupted. 'Do you not find it rather cold to be standing out here in a field telling such a lengthy tale to a shepherd?'

"I had hoped that this would cause him to cease altogether in the telling of his tale, but it merely drew from him a promise to pass over the childhood incident that he had meant to recount and abbreviate the remainder of his narrative as much as he could."

Here Childermass, his pale brow darkened with the intensity of his absorption, uttered a vehement curse against the incuriosity of Master Plainstaff (or was it now Master Colkins?) before turning his attention once again upon the text before him:

"'Night after night,' the Marquis went on, resuming his indefatigable narrative. 'This nobleman would sit by the bedside of his lovely damsel and watch as the physician made a delicate incision with his knife upon the inside of her left arm. He trembled as the warm blood began to pour in the basin, marked the few seconds when each drop would hang suspended upon her elbow before its descent, and grew pale with a breathless rapture when he beheld her own lips grow grey and wan from loss of strength. In his ecstasy, he well believed that he had never seen his lady in so fetching a state – nay, not even upon that blessed day when first he set his eyes upon her. He would often be forced to avert his gaze so as to conceal the full extent of his passion and, at such times, the suffering fair would take his hand in hers and clasp it, whispering words of reassurance – for indeed the sweet lamb thought that his odd looks were the result of a faintness that he felt at the sight of her blood – and perhaps they were, for he lost hold of himself at times when his excitement and fancy were provoked past all endurance by this delicious milking.

"'Unfortunately, however, this very passion of his proved to be its own downfall. His lady, influenced by the increased tenderness that she perceived in his regard towards her, began gradually to exhibit a certain renewal of that health that she had formerly lost through indolence and melancholy. Convinced that his ministrations were no longer required, the physician announced that one week longer would he stay – then he would depart, satisfied that his treatment of the lady had proved successful.

"'This sent the nobleman into a maelstrom of confusion and dread. Thus far, he had been amply content with the manner in which events had been proceeding. Now, met with the threat of all his plans being rendered null in a week's time, he found himself utterly bewildered as to how best to act. A kind of madness came over him for the space of several days and during that interim he sated himself somewhat with exercising his gruesome will upon several farm animals belonging to the serfs that lived in the fields by his chateau. When the servants noticed the bloodstained lace at his wrists, he merely explained that the thorny vines of the rose bushes were grown thick and had scratched him as he passed through the garden walks to pluck a few blossoms for his dear lady. And, after all, what did it matter if a few young lambs were found the next morning hanging from the boughs of a tree, their throats cut open and their blood still drying in a brown pool on the ground beneath them? He had harmed nothing that was not his to do with as he wished.

"'It was then that an idea occurred to him of such simple cunning that he marveled he had not hit upon it before.

"'That very night, when all others were asleep, he crept into the bedchamber of his lady and, unstopping the cork of a bottle that he had kept carefully concealed beneath his velvet mantle, and poured some of the liquid into the pitcher of water that stood by the sleeping beauty's bedside. This contained a potent, but not fatal, mixture of a drug that he knew would produce a relapse serious enough to cause any doctor to reconsider plans for departure. Just as he turned to leave, however, a rustling behind a nearby curtain caught his attention. The physician himself had remained hidden within that chamber, suspecting his employer's motives, and seeing this proof of the nobleman's true intentions, now stepped forward and began to denounce him as an unnatural monster, a cruel and treacherous husband, and threatened to have the entire village aflame with the news by morning.

"All the while, the nobleman gazed upon the outraged little man in utter disbelief – not because of the violence of his expressions, but because of the peculiar circumstances under which he had chosen to given vent to them. Now tell me truthfully, Monsieur: if you were indeed convinced that your employer was a madman consumed with bloodlust, would you confess your misgivings to him in the seclusion of a lady's chamber in the dead of night? *Par Dieu*, what an idiot innocence the man must have had, to think himself safe even then!'

"Here, the Marquis was forced to break off from his tale, overpowered as he was by a silent laughter that convulsed him for several moments. When at last he had regained his composure, his sparkling eyes fell upon me with a look that chilled me to the marrow.

"'Shall I finish the tale, then? Shall I say that the nobleman rushed upon the doctor in order to stifle his prattling while his wife, now awake, arose and screamed aloud at what she saw? You requested that I be brief: then let me only say that the doctor is dead and the lady followed him to the grave herself a year later. There now, Monsieur: what think of you my little comedy?'

"'And the nobleman?' I asked. 'What became of him?'

"St. Aubert smiled with that look of tranquil innocence so peculiar to him. 'I know that you have already guessed and so I shall give you an answer worthy of so patient an audience as yourself. He came to England upon a lovely ship named *The Christobel* and, as fate would have it, chanced to make the acquaintance of a most amicable gentleman titled the Earl of Linchester who, in turn, introduced him to a still more charming acquaintance of his – an Ephraim Colkins. Have you anticipated the ending to my tale yet, Monsieur?' I did not reply and he continued, 'The Earl, you see, was rather forgiving of my tastes – more forgiving, at least, than the unfortunate physician whom I described and he said that he thought he knew a gentleman who would prove an apt subject for such attentions. Furthermore, he claimed that this gentleman had a son and that – ah, but once more I digress.'

"My hand fell at once to the hilt of the hunting dagger that hung at my belt, but the Marquis put an end to this by drawing out of his own coat a silver musket. Pointing the firearm directly at my breast, he advised that I would be best served in complying quietly with whatever he requested. I demanded to know what request he intended to make.

"'Methinks that now I should like to be introduced to your father,' he replied.

"At first I was speechless with horror and thought to retort with a violent, impassioned refusal. Instead, I fell to my knees before the Marquis, heedless of my own dignity, and begged him to spare my father. I conjured him by the fair speech with which he had won both the respect of the Earl and my father – I conjured him by the nobility to which he had been titled from birth – I even conjured him by the name of the lady whom he had once perhaps loved, that he find some other victim's blood to feast his eyes upon. All of my words this St. Aubert attended to with the same expression of polite attention – when at last I lapsed into an exhausted silence, he then said, 'You are right, Monsieur. I am not at all interested in the strife that exists between your Puritans and Lord Gomershall's Cavaliers. I do not even believe your father to be more deserving of death than the Earl. But do you not see how much simpler it is to begin thusly? I would not wish to introduce myself into English society by first bleeding its most prominent members, would I? Absurd!'

"'Have you no pity at all?' I asked.

"'Pity? Of course I have – but that is altogether beside the point. You, I suppose, must pity the poor lamb that you intend to slaughter, but that does not prevent you from drawing the knife across his throat in order to satisfy your own hunger, does it? And why? Because this hunger was planted within you by some Divine Providence and must of necessity be satisfied, despite the sacrifice that may require.'

"'You are led astray by Satan, sir,' I said, my voice trembling with terror. 'A man is not a beast – nay, no matter how simple or wicked he may be.'

"But the Marquis shook his head and his eyes were bright and his cheeks were flushed and he seemed in every way to be a man suffering from a violent fever even as he turned his gaze from me to the cottage that stood a stone's throwaway from us. And, even as I began to consider shouting to my father in the feeble hope that he might hear my warning, I felt something crash into the back of my skull and I fell in a heavy heap upon the ground, my senses altogether forsaking me.

"I must have suffered quite a blow from the butt of St. Aubert's musket, for I awoke at last to behold the beginnings of twilight encroaching upon the land. I staggered to my feet and, in spite of my aching head, ran towards the cottage, still possessing the vague idea that I might find my father still safe after his visit with the Marquis. Instead, I found the place utterly deserted: only a pools of blood by the hearth seemed to indicate that some sort of horrible, fatal struggle must have taken place. Something lay upon the rough wood of the kitchen table. I picked it up – it was a glass dove.

"Of my father's death, I am somehow hideously certain, though the mystery that surrounds it still torments my dreams and even a good portion of my waking hours. After the token that the Marquis left in plain view for my benefit, I am also just as certain of my own imminent doom. All the grief that I feel at the fate of my unfortunate parent is irrevocably mingled with an added terror that the same doom will befall me as well. To remain at home would have been a paramount foolishness – thus, I packed what few provisions I absolutely required and fled from those mournful premises that very night.

"Ever since then, I have made my way as swiftly as possible to Scotland, hoping that my tenacious enemy will not trouble to pursue me over England's border. I know that he follows me even now and I dread whatever his intentions are. If only the justice which was denied my father might fall upon the head of my pursuer! Sometimes, however, a strange melancholy overcomes me and I cannot help but be convinced that whether I reach Scotland safely or not, that it shall make very little difference. I believe then that – "

The last sentence of the little book ended in a scrawl as though the author, grown weary of a narrative that could only recall past sorrows and bring to mind future horrors, had suddenly cast away his quill and put the volume forever aside as a silent reminder of the root of all his woes. Childermass closed the book himself and settled his gaze upon the distant horizon, lit only by the evening stars that hung over the moors lying beyond the Priory forest. His thoughts, of a bent ever dark and circular, revolved again and again upon the substance of Cyrus's history and the character of the man who had murdered his father and might even have pursued him upon the Scottish moors to serve him the same turn as well. At the remembrance of the young man's wistful yearning for his lost parent, the beginnings of a sympathetic tear rose unbidden to the chimney sweeper's pale eye – but only for a moment. Then a humorous laugh, no less unpleasant than the one that had disconcerted Feversham the night before, seized him as he remarked aloud:

"Poor Master Plainstaff! You could not have picked a more woeful sanctuary for yourself had Satan and all his angels directed your steps! Laughlin Priory…" Here his voice, so unexpectedly grave and musical for one with so set and stern a countenance, trailed away as he turned his gaze from the woodlands to the black spires and chimneys of the Priory itself.

"Yet perhaps," he at last continued, "what has befallen us this last year has some link to the horror that has plagued you as well. Perhaps with the Devil as with God there is no such creature as blind chance. But if, as I think, we are all tidily damned together, why then it will be the simplest thing in all the world for a neat snare to be made for the devils that encircle us. I like not this running about before the scourge of some tyrant whether he hail from Hell or France, though it seems to have served this Master Plainstaff well enough for now."

He produced the silver whistle with which he had entertained Cyrus earlier that evening and began to play upon it, his thoughts once again silent and private. There was something in the strange youth's narrative that struck a chord deep within the remote fastness of his heart and it was in vain that he sought to banish its effects from his soul. Again, pity rose in prominence, but also an imaginative sympathy that brought to his mind's eye all the landscapes of Cyrus's tale, many of which he had never beheld himself in all his life. Childermass's soul, crippled as it was by the narrow chimneys, silent cloisters, and cramped passageways of the Priory, now thrilled for the first time to the idea of green pastures in place of grey moorlands; simple cottages in lieu of smoke-filled kitchens and servants' quarters; and a clear, wooded horizon uncrowded by mountains or ruined towers. For the first time, the idea came to him that one day he might forsake the Priory, perhaps forever. As these thoughts, new and unfamiliar, assailed him, a gentle wind utterly foreign to the icy blasts of winter seemed to brush against the chimney sweeper's pale, thin cheek as though Nature herself sought to soften the harsh melancholy of his temper whilst the moon, emerging from behind a cloud, let fall her silver light over the proud battlements of the Priory, melting their steadfast blackness to an enchanting pallor.

Childermass put away his pipe then and gazed upon these effects with an attentive eye. No, he would never abandon the Priory – not when there was still so much left to discern, to marvel at, to master. When perusing Cyrus's manuscript, he had felt very like a blind man with his hand upon another man's face, able to determine the general pattern of the features but withheld from fully beholding them. Now, looking once more upon the vast, ancient pile that had been his home for so much of his existence, something in his very aspect changed, lending him a quality that seemed less human and more an element of some divine or infernal landscape. He rose and his flaxen hair lifted in the wind, casting a livid light all about his head like the luminance of some lost, angelic creature whilst his gaze fell like the pale eye of some sea thing that has discovered the sunken treasures of man and can alone glory in their beauty. A curious look then crossed his face – a mingled expression of longing and exultation that converged in his eye and brightened its intensity a hundredfold into the withering glance of the basilisk. Then, of a sudden, the moon fell again behind a cloud and all the light departed from him, leaving him in darkness: once again, nothing greater in appearance than a perhaps rather grim-faced, bright-eyed chimney sweep. Yet as he turned to depart from that rooftop, he allowed himself one last lingering look at the silent towers of the Priory before creeping through the narrow funnel of a chimney into the Great Hall below.

VOLUME II

Chapter Fourteen: In which a Worshipful Company of Grocers prepare to go a-wassailing and Master Shipwash makes a few adjustments to his itinerary.

Nat first noticed the dog when they were a day's walk out of Shrewsfield. The sky had been overcast with a milky tint earlier that morning and twilight had now deepened it to a dull, leathery color – but still amongst the shadows of the foliage that skirted the clearing, the small boy could distinguish the rustling leaves and bright red eyes of the creature as it paused in its scenting to raise its head and stare at him. He held out a stick with a scrap of dry, salted meat upon it, hoping to tempt the creature to his side. The dog, however, only opened his mouth and let his long, dripping tongue loll out a little in a curious pant before turning tail and disappearing into the thickets.

"A cup of broth for you, laddie?" enquired Master Shipwash, his chapped fingers curled around the handle of a cup steaming with some concoction fresh from the kettle.

The child shook his head.

"'Twill warm thee, lad, in this bitter December wind," Master Shipwash reminded him. "I trow we're but a day or so's walk from Houndswick and then shall have the hearth of some generous laird to warm our feet by, but 'till then 'tis best that you drink this down."

With a grudging acceptance, the boy took the cup and began to gingerly sip it down. Shipwash waited a moment and then, with the sad air of a man who already expects a rejection, added:

"Would you be willing to speak a few lines from Master Chapman's play? We are in sore need of a few more shepherds, you know."

Nat again shook his head, keeping his face turned towards the shadows at the edge of the meadow.

Shipwash sighed heavily and muttered to himself, "What's the use of anything if we've a score of angels and not enough shepherds even to countenance 'em. Well," he added to himself by way of consolation. "Perhaps some of the fellows playing the magi won't take it amiss to play the shepherds as well – as I see it, the beards ought to be enough to hide their faces."

Some explanation must be given for the drift of this conversation, else the reader become hopelessly lost in the obscure drift of Master Shipwash's musings.

On the same day upon which the events previously described in the last chapter befell, the Worshipful Company of Grocers – a host of venerable gentleman who identified themselves as members of that profession – had departed from their homes in Shrewsfield to go a-wassailing, as was their caroling custom every December. However, for the first time, Master Shipwash had been voted by his fellows as the head of the troupe for that year and, having been taken with – as he called it – a reforming spirit, it was his opinion that a few things ought to be improved and added to the company's usual wassailing program. Firstly, it was in Shipwash's mind that the usual practice of going about from household to household regaling the inhabitants with song ought to be supplemented with a religious play of some sort for variety's sake. Secondly, he intended that rather than simply pursuing the usual campaign of wassailing – travelling from the English border town of Shrewsfield to the nearby Scottish town of Houndswick and back again – that they pay a visit to several locales that had remained previously untouched by such overtures. And what better place to reside in during the duration of these ventures, he reasoned, than the ancient seat of the Gosselin family: Laughlin Priory?

Master Shipwash had expected his proposal to be met with unanimous agreement. After all, the Priory had a reputation in the past, did it not, for affording hospitality to wanderers whenever the opportunity arose? But his suggestion was doomed from the first moment it was uttered, thanks to the insinuations delivered by no less a personage than the former head of the troupe, Phillip Crawley. A large-shouldered, lantern-jawed man, so tall that he had developed something of a stoop from bowing his head to avoid collision with the low cottage ceilings of Shrewsfield, Crawley was perhaps the most influential member of the Company of Grocers, and well he knew it. His ability to exercise this influence had been most unfortunately curtailed, however, by the recent nomination of Master Shipwash to his former role of leadership – but the former monarch still had a few words to say to his upstart successor.

"Tell me, Shipwash," Crawley had enquired a fortnight ago, his large and faintly grey lips smacking and pursing as though they belonged to the mouth of some landed fish. "What do you know of the Priory?"

A hush had fallen over the Worshipful Company and all eyes turned towards Shipwash who blinked in bewilderment at the sudden pall that had fallen over that assembly in the wake of his innocent suggestion.

"Well," said he, clearing his throat. "I have heard superstitious tales – the sort that one usually hears bruited about a place as old as the Priory. Nothing, I assure you, that any but old wives would credit."

Crawley's moist, blue eyes narrowed. "And what were the nature of these tales, Master Shipwash?"

Shipwash's own gaze soared upwards towards the rafters of the barn in which they had all assembled as he collected what few vestiges of patience remained to him.

"Of course, there is the tale of Sir Etienne du Laughlin and his uncanny disappearance," he said airily. "And was there not some trifling legend of drafts rising beneath the stones in certain lower chambers, as though there were tunnels riddling some hidden, deeper portion of the place? Stories of witches and bloody murders shadow the place, but what Scottish castle has not been polluted by such a reputation at one time or another? I don't recall them all since I never put much store in their veracity anyway – and I am much surprised that you appear to, Master Crawley."

Crawley raised an eyebrow. "You read me wrong, sir – I am of your opinion in all these things."

Shipwash frowned. "Then I do not understand your objection."

The former ruling hand of the venerable company of grocers leaned back against the door of the horse stall before which he sat, a slow smile of satisfaction on his lips. "I take it, then," said he. "That you have not heard of the circumstances surrounding the death of Lord Luke Gosselin, the father of young Lord Withing and the son of the present lord, Sir Robert Gosselin."

"Certainly I heard of his death," Shipwash returned. "What man in these parts did not? But that misfortune befell the Priory a year ago – what has it to do with the matter at hand?"

"Tell me, how old would you say His Lordship was at the time of his death?"

Shipwash knew that somehow the screws were tightening, but he could not for the life of him fathom in what direction they were turning and so blurted out, "Why, forty-five or thereabouts."

Most of the men in the company nodded their heads in agreement at this, but a few of the men met Crawley's milky-eyed gaze with expressions of horror and remembrance that did little to set Shipwash's now thoroughly befuddled mind at ease.

"If this was so," murmured Crawley. "Then how came the corpse of an aged and withered man to be buried in his coffin?"

Shipwash turned pale. "What madness have you been spreading amongst this town, Crawley?"

"Nay, speak not so harshly, Master Shipwash," one fellow named Fenton protested, his own face turned a sickly shade as well. "He speaks the truth. As the body was borne in a coffin to be lain within the family crypt beneath the Priory, one of the bearers cut his hand rather badly upon a splinter and as his grasp slipped, the lid of the bier fell open, and the face of a withered ancient revealed itself to his astonished eyes. Apparently, he was the only one to behold this fatal transformation, before he recovered his senses and sealed the corpse up within its coffin again."

"Is it not also true," whispered his neighbor Bigley. "That the skin of the lich was so dry that when the blood from the bearer's hand fell upon its face, the withered flesh fairly drank it up?"

"Are you claiming," Shipwash demanded. "That Lord Luke Gosselin was not the man buried within the Gosselin crypt upon the Feast of the Holy Innocents a year ago?"

"Oh, no, Master Shipwash, it was His Lordship all right," Crawley replied. "The features could have belonged to no other."

"And it was soon after that," Fenton piped up. "That the other deaths began to happen."

"Deaths?" Shipwash returned. "I've heard of no such rumors from the townsmen of Houndswick."

"Aye, well, they were only a few young men of little standing," said Bigley. "No one took much account of them, except mayhap their family and those few who stood about to watch their pitiful burials. Yet their state was apparently very much like His Lordship's. Sometimes worse."

"Some had the marks of torture about them," Fenton muttered. "Others were withered up like His Lordship. What hideous plague could effect the transformation of a young man's body into that of a wasted, dried-up corpse? What common murderer could do what has been done to them?"

"And how came you all to grow so wise in these matters?" Shipwash snapped, feeling himself turn cold in spite of himself at these revelations. "Why is it that you are the only men who seem to be possessed of this awful knowledge of Lord Luke Gosselin's burial?"

"Because I was the only man whom Master Childermass happened to speak to during his last sojourn to Shrewsfield," Crawley replied.

At the name, Shipwash recalled what little he remembered of the chimney sweeper – the thin, parched lips, narrow shoulders, black garments, and most of all the peculiarity of that gaze made up of a pale marble eye and a single living eye. Come to think of it, he had not seen the lad himself since last December, soon after the burial of Lord Luke. "And what has made you so ready to believe his word?" he faltered.

"Nothing particular to himself," said Crawley. "Only that he happened to be the bearer who cut his hand on Lord Luke Gosselin's coffin."

Shipwash was turning all of these memories over in his mind once again as he watched the boy Nat slowly poke the end of a stick into the fire.

"Well, drat it all," he muttered. "I gave in to Crawley, didn't I? Agreed that we'd bypass Laughlin and take a route to Houndswick that avoided the moors and Priory forests. Then why have all my other plans fallen to shambles as well? Why are there not enough fellows in our company to perform all the parts in our play? Why does this road by which we now guide our steps insist upon taking the longest and most roundabout route to Houndswick through the most deserted and unsavory portions of this godforsaken forest? Why does Mr. Chapman insist upon composing every line in his play in rhymed verse instead of heroic meter? And why," he added, his voice now rising. "Does my finest young singer have to prove such a dour old Covenanter as to refuse any part at all in my play?"

The boy stared at Shipwash then with large, sober eyes until the good-natured fellow reached over and patted him on the head, saying in spite of himself, "There now, lad, don't mind my complaining. You stay good and true to your creeds and doctrines, though the Lord knows I'm glad they're not mine. I'm sure your mum and dad, God rest their souls, would be proud to see you so."

He turned his face towards the fire, then, warming his hands against its flames and so did not notice the slow tear that descended Nat's cheek before the orphan turned his gaze back in the direction of the forest, hoping for some sign yet of the mysterious dog.

Chapter Fifteen: In which Cyrus is plagued with nightmares.

There were red hangings everywhere; Cyrus could barely lift his head beneath the veils of crimson that fell about him, draping his shoulders and ruffling his hair. The carpet beneath him was a sea of rippling red as well, disappearing somewhere ahead into the folds of hanging cloth that hung suspended from some invisible ceiling. He thought he heard a whispering from somewhere close beside him – a muffled conference made up half of words and half of sobs. The voices somehow made him afraid, but every step that he took only prompted the sound of footsteps close behind him and, amongst the rustling curtains, the whispering continued. Not for all the world would Cyrus have turned to part the veil that separated him from his pursuers. He did not know them, but feared the sight of their faces more than knives.

Just as Cyrus stood there, however, debating what to do about the voices at his back that he could somehow not escape, the curtain directly in front of him parted and the Marquis Antoine St. Aubert appeared.

"Come, come," said he, his voice touched with the same gentleness that it had possessed when last they met. "Your father and I have been awaiting you for quite some time."

"My father?" Cyrus's heart leapt. At the same time, he wondered at his own emboldened spirit and the utter fearlessness that he felt in the murderer's presence. "But, my lord, this is only a dream."

"Dreaming is the noblest of vocations, Monsieur Colkins. Our own Saint John who wrote of the Beast and the Whore was a dreamer. Is it not so?"

As the Marquis spoke, his hand extended to part the curtain at his back. The white lace at his wrists was mottled with blood, but Cyrus did not even flinch as St. Aubert took him by the shoulder with the other hand and directed him into the chamber that lay hidden beyond the drapery.

"But the things that were whispering at my back," Cyrus protested, finding himself far more preoccupied with his first terror than with the immediate threat of the Marquis. "We must be certain that they don't follow us."

"But why?" the Marquis enquired. "Are you afraid that they will harm me? Foolish lad. Do you think they would dare?"

The chamber in which they found themselves was a simple affair: a window, a table, three chairs, and walls adorned only with guttering torches.

"You know already, Monsieur, that there are more levels of wickedness in this place than there are circles of Hell, I suppose," the Marquis said. As he spoke, he began to draw from beneath a linen towel that lay upon the table a sparkling fork and knife. The whispering continued outside the chamber, seeming to increase in volume, but St. Aubert remained either oblivious or disinterested, preferring to settle his attention upon the dish of steaming lamb that stood upon the table before him.

"Would you enjoy a portion yourself?" he enquired politely, knife poised above the skinless flesh.

"I would rather hear what you have to say about wickedness, my lord," the dreaming Cyrus returned.

"No, you would not," the Marquis smiled. "For then you would remain here all night, Monsieur, and no single dream has a right to last that long."

"Were you speaking of the wickedness of the Priory or of something else?"

"What is it that you think?"

"I came to the Priory to escape – from you."

"And no proper sanctuary could harbor wickedness, could it, Monsieur?"

The whispering outside the chamber had ceased and was instead replaced with a ringing ambience that filled the room like an invisible choir. Outside, a gale-blown tree branch tapped upon the glass pane of the window: the same staccato tattoo, like an insistent guest begging to be let in.

"Are you here – in the Priory?" Cyrus asked.

"Ah, do you expect to see me, standing at the end of a long corridor, waiting for you with a shining sliver of steel?" the Marquis enquired gently. "Or are you only wanting to hear the end of my story?"

"I thought your tale was finished."

"No tale is ever finished – utterly. Not even your father's."

In spite of the numbness that his dreaming self felt at all the strangeness that surrounded him, he felt his clouded eyes fill with tears at this. "I wish to see my father."

The Marquis shrugged and lifted one of the platters upon the table, revealing the head of the late Ephraim Colkins. Severed veins and muscles extended like tentacles of meat upon the bloodied porcelain of the plate and his father's grey hair was brightened as well with streaks of crimson.

"Cyrus," he whispered. "My son."

"You're alive, father," Cyrus said. "You're alive."

His train of thought was broken by a finger tapping at his shoulder. He turned to see Childermass standing there: a goblet in one hand, a dagger in the other.

"Meat and wine, my lord?" he enquired, bowing low.

Cyrus attempted to reply, but found his tongue as heavy as lead. As he sat there, speechless, the Marquis gestured for the chimney sweeper to occupy the empty chair that stood across from him.

"I thank you, my lord," Childermass replied. "But would prefer to stand."

He then took his place by the window, setting both chalice and knife upon the sill and watching the shadowplay of storm-tossed branches without.

"Put me to rest, Cyrus," Ephraim Colkins murmured. "I cannot – I cannot – work my tongue here."

"Your father spoke enough for the both of you when he was in my presence," the Marquis said, leaning the flat of his serrated blade against his cheek so that it added additional teeth to his smile.

"I will speak no more here," Ephraim Colkins said.

The Marquis lifted the cover of the platter and set it down gently over Ephraim's head, shielding him from view once more.

"Did you come to warn me?" Cyrus asked him, disbelieving the very words that issued from his mouth.

"It depends, Monsieur," the Marquis St. Aubert replied. "Upon which monstrous fate you wish to be rescued from. You cannot fly them all you know – there are far too many. Chimney sweeper, you are well acquainted with dust and secrets: have you heard of any pleasant tales from out this Priory?"

"Faith, not I," said Childermass, his living eye turning upon them with a look of sudden, leering merriment. "I know nothing of this Priory that I would willingly tell any soul."

"Then tell me," the Marquis said with a laugh. "For I have none."

"Then you already know of what I speak," Childermass said, his mask of grave composure restored once more.

The world of Cyrus's dream seemed to billow as though it were suddenly submerged beneath water; he found it hard to remain in his chair, for it seemed that all material things in that chamber were being drawn inexorably in a certain direction as though caught in the midst of an invisible maelstrom. Even the Marquis rose, unable to keep his seat, as the two of them looked to see from whence this new power had arisen.

The casement was unlatched and had flown wide open beneath Childermass's hungry fingers, now at last revealing the source of insistent rapping that he had heard so continuously from that howling, outer darkness. As Cyrus watched, a swarm of pale and fleshy serpentine limbs filled that chamber, scouring its walls like the scrabbling, jointed legs of an insect searching for a foothold. It was impossible in the darkness of that chamber to see what main body it was to which they were attached. Filled with loathing, Cyrus ducked and avoided their blind probing, trying to fight the sickness that welled up inside him as he saw that their tentacles appeared to be made up of the rotting remnants of human flesh and bone, all held together in a fantastic union by ropy guts and sinews. Cyrus managed to find a far corner of the chamber which even they could not reach, however, and saw that the Marquis as well had gained a safe ground as well, watching the Horror with a curious eye.

Cyrus looked about for some sign of Childermass, his gaze at last spying him at the opposite end of the chamber. It took no especial genius to deduce that the chimney sweeper's fate was to be less than fortunate. Childermass had been thrown against the chamber wall beneath the flickering light of one of the torches and looked to have already been savaged half to unconsciousness by the sinuous things that held him helpless. Yet as Cyrus started to him, Childermass suddenly raised his head. Breathless, he turned his glittering eye upon Cyrus and fixed upon him such a look of exultation that the pity that had once filled the dreamer's heart now turned to a bewildered, wondering horror. Childermass's lips parted – he seemed about to expire or laugh. The Marquis leaned forward, his fingers cupped about his ear, whilst Cyrus prayed himself deaf – and then awoke.

Chapter Sixteen: In which two gentlemen encountered previously come to call at the Priory and in which our hero is once again plunged into a state of alarm.

"Are you feeling well, Cyrus?" Withing had set his pitcher of milk down and was now gazing across the table at his new guest with real concern. "You look worse than I do after a night in one of Houndswick's alehouses. What do you think, Childermass?"

"Perhaps," Childermass speculated. "Master Plainstaff was afflicted with visions."

In the pallid morning light that flooded the great hall of the Priory, Cyrus could not discern whether the icy globe that was fixed upon him was the chimney sweeper's living or marble eye. In any case, he could not suppress the shudder that coursed through him as he recalled the circumstances – dream though it was – under which they had last met.

"I did suffer some nightmares, yes," he admitted. "Childermass saved me from one – but I suppose that as soon as he left the chamber, they returned."

"If this continues, we can always have Childermass sit up with you every night," Mariah suggested lightly, oblivious to the moue of contempt that Childermass made at this careless proposal and the look of unease that crossed Cyrus's own visage. "What was it that you dreamt?"

Cyrus cleared his throat. "Let's talk of something else, shall we, madam?" he said, forcing brightness into his voice. "Withing mentioned earlier that he had a little boat and I wondered whether this meant that you have a lake upon the grounds of this estate?"

Mariah hesitated, turning an anxious look upon him. "We have a boathouse," she murmured. "But then there are the stories I have heard told about the lake and the sights that some have seen there…the madwoman whose son drowned there and who every May Day will slay with a knife all those who go a-maying and forget their virtue…"

"Saints preserve us…" Cyrus groaned.

He started as the blonde-haired girl burst out laughing and even Childermass smiled as she said, between gasps, "Oh, Master Plainstaff, I know that our Scottish superstitions may be difficult for you English folk to understand, but I assure you that we do more than hide banshees and boggarts at every crossroad. It is my hope, sir, that we can prove this to you before you leave our company."

Clarice, who sat across from Mariah and beside Cyrus at that long table, silently finishing her own breakfast, could barely suppress a smile as she listened to this last remark. She had heard little the night before from Mariah that was not of the mysterious Master Plainstaff, his intriguing behavior, and what else could be made of him. That, of course, was after Mariah had managed to secret Clarice out of her locked bedroom where Childermass had left her, per Feversham's stern orders.

"My poor darling," Mariah had said, seeing the streaks of tears only half-dried that still stained Clarice's cheeks. "I shall tell Sir Robert of this tomorrow – I swear it. Feversham had no right to treat you with such indignity."

"I pray you, keep silent," Clarice begged. "If my uncle were to hear of this, he would be furious with me. It was partly his own idea that we keep the affairs of the last year a secret from Withing."

"Oh, very well," Mariah returned. "But come away now with me. We have much to discuss."

The two young women then went hand in hand back to Mariah's own chamber, whereupon Mariah began to expound at great length upon the many facets of Cyrus Plainstaff and his curious character.

"Did you note that he said nothing of his parentage, from whence he came, or even why he came here to Houndswick?" she demanded.

"That's easily answered," Clarice returned. "We hardly gave him a chance!"

"But he had no interest in speaking of it at all," Mariah insisted. "And yet he is clearly no commoner."

"How do you deduce that?"

"The sadness in his bearing, mostly," Mariah replied. "And the sensitivity in his eyes. Perhaps he is one of those poor unfortunates who lost all their wealth to the fanatic revolutionaries during the late uprising against King Charles. In fact, I am sure of it."

"You seem to be taking an uncommon interest in Withing's newfound friend," Clarice said with a smile.

Mariah blushed, but made no attempt to dissuade her friend from this opinion. "Well, what of it?" said she. "He has a comely appearance, does he not? And he is not so wicked as our friend Lord Andrew Montrose."

"No one is so wicked as our dear Andrew," Clarice said.

"Well, then," Mariah said, and the discussion was thus resolved firmly in Cyrus Plainstaff's favor.

Cyrus appeared to be utterly oblivious to the obvious admiration and curiosity that shone from Mariah's eyes, still far too discombobulated by his former nightmares and the present hilarity that his nervous response had generated. Fortunately, Withing suggested that perhaps that afternoon could be spent in an exploration of the Priory's lands – if Cyrus was curious to see the rest of the grounds.

As Cyrus replied, Childermass took this opportunity to approach Clarice and, laying a hand upon her shoulder, enquired lowly, "Is there anything I can fetch for you, sweet lady? Another platter of toast or another pitcher of milk? I hope," he added with a smile that could either have been sly or sincere. "That you have forgiven me for what I was forced by Feversham to do last night. It was never my will."

As he spoke, he took her hand and pressed it gently, gazing intently upon her face with that single eye of his.

"Of course I forgive you," she replied, always somewhat bewildered by the chimney sweeper's intensity. "Will you not sit down here?"

Childermass did not wait for a second invitation before seating himself beside her and helping himself to generous portions of toast and strawberry jam, washing these down with warm ale – the smell of which turned Clarice's stomach, but which he drank like water. He seemed to be listening intently to the conversation between Withing and Cyrus, though occasionally she found his eye settling upon her when she felt sure that he presumed her own attention to be elsewhere. Feeling a slight chill, in spite of herself, at his presence, she sought to break the silence that had settled between them.

"Are you afraid, Childermass?"

"Afraid? Of what, Miss Abelin?"

"Of what has been happening in this Priory for the last year? Of what happened to those young men in the village – to Lord Luke himself?"

"Are *you* afraid, madam?" he asked, his living eye gleaming with an avid attention upon her.

"Yes," she whispered.

"Then banish your fears," he said gravely. "One look at that face and all its pretty innocence and the devils and spirits will fly back of one accord to whatever Hell they emerged from, I warrant you."

There was always a dark depravity to his humor that did little to quiet her nerves, and she could not fully satisfy herself as to whether he spoke sincerely or leeringly. Either way, he retained a look of sobriety that rendered his true meaning impenetrable and she returned her attention to the conversation that was occurring betwixt Withing and Cyrus. Apparently, Withing was set upon the idea of Cyrus's joining him upon an expedition into the forests once springtime returned to Laughlin and was describing the beauty of the area with much enthusiasm.

"But surely," Cyrus interjected. "I cannot remain here for much longer. It has been kind of your family to allow me a roof for one night, but…"

"Nonsense." Withing's smile was still there, but dejection began to color his countenance. "Your foot still has a long way to go before it will be of any use for *real* walking and where shall you go once you have recovered? Have you any family in these parts, Master Plainstaff?"

All eyes were upon the young man, but only one of them – pale and watchful – glimmered like an uplifted sphere of silent, solitary inquisition. This single gaze – Childermass's, of course – went unnoticed amongst the rest of that party, all of whom were watching Cyrus with looks that under ordinary circumstances would have seemed bright with curiosity, but in comparison to the burning of that single globe, were as mere stars to a desert sun.

Cyrus's forthcoming reply never came, however, for at that moment the fall of horses' hooves were heard outside the Priory's walls, distracting the attention of all – even Childermass – from Cyrus. At the sound of an approaching visitor, Childermass slipped away from his place at the table, reappearing after some time at the opposite end of the great hall, with Feversham and Dagworth at his side, as the three of them ushered in both Squire Toby and His Grace the 34th Earl of Lauderness, Andrew Montrose. The two visiting lords were speaking to His Lordship Sir Robert Gosselin and the Reverend Hugo Abelin, for the moment oblivious of those seated who already dined within that chamber: the Squire as he pinched and elongated a fold of flesh at the center of his long throat whilst attending with a slight frown to whatever it was that the Lord of the Priory was remarking upon and Montrose as he listened with an inclined head to the conversation of the Priory's chaplain.

Most of that company eyed the newcomers with the usual amount of interest proper for the sudden intrusion of two guests upon an otherwise uneventful breakfast. Cyrus, however, felt the sickening pangs of dread fill his spirit and despoil the cautious contentment that had begun to grow within him in spite of his various misgivings and fears. He felt sure that at any moment, Montrose would catch sight of him and recall their less than pleasant last encounter. There was no chance of withdrawing unnoticed; all that Cyrus could hope was for His Grace to find himself in a better temper than that which he had possessed last night. Montrose's attention seemed to wander aimlessly about the room in all directions save that of Cyrus: rising up to the rafters in order to admire the embroidered hangings that depended from their lofty reaches, eying Feversham with an indifferent regard, touching upon Mariah with a drifting interest, and finally settling upon the pretty Clarice with a look that was difficult to translate.

"I understand what you say, good Reverend," Cyrus heard Montrose say, his voice slow and cynical, though still touched with that same lazy humor that had characterized his discourse the night before. "I also understand that Squire Toby has before owed me vast sums of money and that I have been more than forgiving to him on such occasions. Why should I not be treated with the same sort of circumspect sensitivity, pray? My purse strings and, indeed, my feelings are just as tender as His Squireship's, I assure you."

The Squire, in response, cleared his throat loudly and continued his own conversation with Sir Robert Gosselin at a greatly amplified volume, declaring with a nervous, sidelong glance in Montrose's direction: "This man – I mean, His Grace – was set to ruin me, My Lord, and last night's game was played only with the intention of reclaiming what I lost to him in a previous venture. Am I to be blamed for a sudden excess in good fortune? And how many others has this fellow – I mean, the Earl of Lauderness – driven to ruination, I ask? Is it so terrible a thing that he be educated in the suffering that he has inflicted upon countless other souls?"

"Spare us your sermonizing, dear Toby," Montrose interposed with a thin smile. "I am quite certain that those who have suffered at my hands, as you so romantically put it, would…would…"

His voice trailed off as, for the first time, his gaze at last chanced to fall upon Cyrus who had been watching the progress of the circumambulating foursome with a growingly apprehensive countenance. The Earl narrowed his eyes as though unable to completely convince himself that he was indeed looking upon the young man who had so stubbornly refused to play a hand with him the night before and whom, in the ensuing chaos of Alan's murder, he had abandoned to the tender mercies of the night. A prolonged inspection verified this first impression, improbable though it had at first appeared, as fact.

"Would what, Your Grace?" Squire Toby prodded. "Thank you for the privilege, I suppose?"

"Yes, Toby, however did you guess?" Montrose replied dryly, his attention completely disconnected from whatever it was that the Squire had said. His lips moved, mouthing that word of recognition – "you" – with a writhing motion as though it were a killing oath, his green eyes fixing upon Cyrus a look of bright hatred before turning once again to the Reverend Abelin who acknowledged this mimed digression with an arched brow. Cyrus stared down at his plate, his vision swimming in panic, wondering how it was that he had managed in so short a time to make himself the enemy of two highborn men of opposing nationalities but similarly ruthless dispositions. Surely no other man of his humble origins had accumulated such aristocratic enemies as the Marquis Antoine St. Aubert and Lord Andrew Ebenezer Montrose in the space of a mere several months. Cyrus managed to console himself, however ineffectually, with the remembrance that St. Aubert's murdering pursuit was probably to be taken more as a compliment than as a proof of hatred. He glanced up at Withing, expecting to read in the other's face a reflection of his own dismay. However, the youth was nonchalantly spearing a slice of buttered toast upon his fork and paying absolutely no heed to the jarring presence of Montrose, except to smile occasionally at the increasingly venomous insults that shot from both the Squire Toby and His Grace.

It appeared, however, as the four gentlemen neared the breakfast table, that Montrose was losing his side of the argument. Though the Reverend Abelin was uttering words of a conciliatory nature, the deep, dispassionate timbre of his voice also possessed a certain implacability that, in spite of His Grace's increasingly heated arguments, still remained undiminished. Likewise, Sir Robert Gosselin as he gave audience to Squire Toby's (by this time half-hysteric demands) continued to offer his own support to the plaintiff's case.

"I fear," Cyrus heard the Reverend murmur to Montrose. "That in this case, in despite of your higher peerage, My Lord, justice may have chosen the Squire's side."

Cyrus little knew how great a loss it was that the Earl of Lauderness had suffered the night before, but the look of malice and despair that crossed Montrose's face as he turned his gaze from the Reverend to the Squire left little doubt that it must have been crippling. Indeed, this look must have been caught by more eyes than those of our hero, for its passing seemed to implicitly signal an end to all deliberations and as those four figures stopped just short of the breakfast table at which Cyrus and his three companions sat, Sir Robert's nod held in it a finality that could not be gainsayed even by the violent temper of one such as Montrose. It was an extraordinary sight to see them then: the Reverend Abelin in his black robes, motionless as marble; Sir Robert's formerly generous and kindly countenance now transfigured in the morning light into a sallow parchment upon which was written an immutable judgment; Squire Toby pinching his already garishly painted cheeks and anxiously avoiding the Earl's gaze; and Montrose himself standing like a statue clothed in velvet, his green eyes now dark with the fullness of his bitter defeat. It was impossible to regard such a scene without experiencing the same thrill of awe and pity attendant upon the passing of a death sentence – and, in spite of himself, Cyrus felt a growing sympathy for the unfortunate Montrose that could not be abated even when he thought to consider the less than gentlemanly behavior that the Earl had exhibited upon their first meeting.

The awful moment was broken at last by Squire Toby hastily excusing himself, stating that his business at the Priory was done and apologizing that he could stay no longer. He seemed in a great haste to leave the place – and who could blame him with the green-eyed gaze of the Earl training upon him its glittering venom? In a moment he was gone; Feversham, Dagworth, and Childermass led him away with the usual shadowy silence that they employed in the presence of the Priory's lords and that differed so greatly from the boisterous mood of their private conferences.

Sir Robert and the Reverend Abelin at last acknowledged the bemused breakfasters before proceeding to sit across from one another at a far end of the table.

"Roasted eggs and a pitcher of milk, if you please, Master Feversham," Sir Robert requested. "Dear Montrose, I do hope that you will not allow this late unpleasantness to interfere with your friendship with our family and that you will dine with us before departing."

Cyrus had expected the Earl to reject this offer; however, with a faint moue of amused contempt, Montrose stepped forward and silently took his place at the right of Withing, directly opposite Cyrus's own seat. Paralyzed once more with apprehension and cursing his own cowardice, Cyrus turned his attention to the two other newcomers. This was the first time that he had ever laid eyes upon the Reverend Abelin and he found his gaze constantly settling upon the chaplain sitting at the far right of the table as, with elbows resting upon either side of his platter and fingers now steepled so that his chin rested upon their tips, Abelin gazed ahead with an unseeing eye past the dining table, past the cloistered landscape of the great hall before him, and into some invisible region of inner thought that fixed his eye.

"Uncle," Clarice murmured to him. "You look very tired."

That space of reverie into which only his eye could penetrate vanished in an instant and Abelin turned his attention to his niece with an affectionate, albeit humorless, smile. Indeed, of all the inmates of the Priory whom Cyrus had encountered thus far, the Reverend possessed the most unrelentingly stern appearance. There was a warmth to Feversham's melancholy, just as there was a merriness to Childermass's drawn pallor that startled at unexpected moments like the slipping of a veil and that somewhat softened the seeming sobriety of his spirit as well. But such marks could not be discerned in the dry lines of Abelin's visage, nor in those eyes like coals that set with a weary fire upon whatever person or object happened to attract their attention – but, more often, that lowered upon some obscure corner of the floor or ceiling of whatever chamber in which he was situated and seemed, by the very abstractness of their concentration, to reduce to an abstraction all of those other objects upon which they refused to acknowledge with a glance. Nonetheless, the Reverend was not an old man, being a good ten years younger than Cyrus's father and possessing a physique that was uncommonly powerful for a man of the church whom one would think had been confined all of his life to lecterns and Latin grammars.

Abelin's gaze then shifted from his niece to Cyrus and the young man felt for himself the peculiar heat of that indifferent scrutiny. "Your name, boy? I do not believe that we have been introduced." The voice that issued from the Reverend's high-collared throat could have belonged to the lungs of a tiger rather than a man, so deep and redolent was it. In spite of this extraordinary quality, or perhaps because of it, it was also the most clerical thing about the man: Cyrus could easily imagine how such a voice could ring out in a chapel or fill in a parishioner's ear the sublimity of the Scriptures and the terrors of Sheol all with the same rough, velveteen timbre.

"Cyrus Plainstaff, sir," the young man replied.

Montrose's languid eyes flickered upwards at the sound of this name, his gaze almost too bitter to be termed hatred any longer. There was a kind of familiarity in its contemplation that seemed at odds with his enmity. It was at this moment that Cyrus realized that there was more to Montrose's venom than mere hatred: it was an acknowledgement of the fact that Cyrus had been one of those few present at that fatal game, the night that had brought about the Earl of Lauderness's ruin. For better or worse, it was an exclusive confederacy of mischance that had brought them together; Cyrus had been witness to that terrible game and it was this that made the Earl's hostility ambiguous, his friendship uneasy. He could not fully hate the young man for having this special knowledge, but he could not love him for it either.

Abelin's own attention, abruptly disinterested in Cyrus's answer, had wandered once again into an obscure space of its own, alighting upon the warped wood of the dining table at which they all sat. Cyrus followed the direction of the chaplain's gaze and saw that, scattering upon the surface of the table like a swarm of sable insects, a series of shadows moved. They migrated in darkening undulations from the right to the left of the table, mottling porcelain and silver alike in one single, watery motion like a running river of darkness. And, as all the breakfasters turned their eyes heavenwards towards the eastern windows, they saw that the blue face of the sky was clouded over by a storm of pigeons and crows, wheeling past the Priory in a flight that was soundless save for the beating of feathers. Childermass alone, withdrawing the long pole that he had used to provoke the winged creatures as they rested upon the sills of the Priory windows, had his eyes upon those seated at the table, watching as they observed with wonder the heavenly riot that, unbeknownst to them, he had begun.

CHAPTER SEVENTEEN: IN WHICH MASTER SHIPWASH DEVELOPS A STITCH AND NAT FINDS A FRIEND.

Avoiding the road that ran through the moors was all very well and good, but it left Shipwash with the problem of deciding where precisely to camp his footweary and increasingly surly band of poets, minstrels, and players. Deciding that a benevolent despotism was the best policy in such situations, he forebore to confide to anyone the doubtful tendency of his introspections. This was difficult, however, considering the less than prepossessing landscape through which the Worshipful Company – now forced, thanks to Crawley's forebodings, to bypass the route that led past the Priory – were endeavoring to traverse. Only marshes and deep lakes surrounded by the encircling limbs of tall oaks, their waters dark as cavern tarns, populated that region and even the path that they traveled was narrow and choked with overhanging branches. As a result, at the very moment that Montrose took his seat opposite Cyrus Plainstaff at the table of the Gosselins, Shipwash and his band found themselves squelching through the black soil at the bank of one such slough – and, as if their situation was not made unpleasant enough, a light snowfall began to dust the landscape with its subtle notes of white, dampening their clothes and adding to Shipwash's already lengthy list of complaints against the day.

And it was still only morning yet. Shipwash turned his bleary eyes up to the equally bleary sun that managed somehow to shine a faint, blanched luminescence behind the wall of clouds overhead and cursed the threatening aches of a stitch that was beginning in his left ribs. In spite of the fact that they had only been walking several hours since sunup, he called for a halt and leaned against a tree, reminding himself that Houndswick would be within their reach by tomorrow morning. By coach, the trip from Shrewsfield to Houndswick only amounted to two hours. A young man by foot could have made the distance in double the time. But Shipwash was not only commandeering a group made up mostly of old men and children but also his own less than robust self through these hostile territories. Given these circumstances, it is little wonder that he was out of temper with the former monarch of the grocers: Crawley, whose complaint against Laughlin Priory he perceived, rather justifiably, as the parent of all these miseries. Indeed, had Crawley, who was somewhere at the rear of the train of wassailers, shown his face at that moment, it is quite likely that Shipwash would have performed some terrible violence upon it.

The boy Nat had been walking close behind Shipwash during the whole of their tedious sojourn and, just as the night before, his gaze continued to move silently along the line of trees that surrounded them on both sides, hoping again to catch sight of the dog that had accompanied them from a distance ever since their departure yesterday. Their trek through the forest for the last several hours, however, had revealed no further sign of their friendly, though bashful, companion and the boy had begun to give up any hope of seeing the creature again.

When Shipwash called for a halt, it was by one of those deep, still lakes so customary to that region and Nat, preferring solitude to the company of his fellow wassailers, set out for its bank, still silently hoping for another glimpse of the dog. He seated himself upon the moist moss and carefully unwrapped the dried meat that he kept bound in a little cloth in his pocket, dining upon this modest lunch with his eyes upon the far side of the opposite bank.

The sound of a snapping twig caused him to look up and see Shipwash carefully easing himself down upon the broken length of a log, still probing the area that had lately suffered the pangs of a stitch. After managing a little smile, the boy continued with his lunch, not uttering a reply even to Shipwash's friendly greeting.

The older man expelled a weary sigh and watched Nat with a careful regard, wishing to enquire after the child's thoughts but afraid of being met with the usual melancholy silence. His eye happened to fall upon a tiny, glittering object that the boy had begun to turn over in his fingers and he said, "Where did you find that pretty little toy, Master Nat? May I see it?"

The boy readily proffered it: it was a piece of glass, blown into the shape of a dove and cunningly shot through with a streak of red crystal, appearing like a crimson heart within the translucent bird's breast.

"This is a handsome piece indeed!" Shipwash said. "How did you come to find it?"

"It dropped out of one of your wassailer's coats, sir," the boy replied, sober as ever. "I picked it up in order to return it to him, but he told me I ought to keep it. He said that he was not in the habit of giving such gifts to children, but only to those on whom he intended to bestow a greater favor, but because I had been honest enough to return it to him, it was only right that I might keep it as an exception."

"That was most generous of him," Shipwash said, much surprised at this tale. He had not known that any among his group possessed the talent or the wealth to either create or purchase such a trinket, much less a whole flock of them, as this stranger's reply seemed to suggest. But then, considering the number of traveling merchants, journeymen, and grocers who had only recently begun to sell their wares in Shrewsfield, it was not surprising that there should be many who were strangers.

"Do you recall the gentleman's name?" he asked.

"No, sir," Nat replied. "But if I see him again, I shall point him out to you."

So interested was Shipwash in the circumstances of this case as he turned the crystal dove over in his calloused fingers, that it did not occur to him immediately that this was the longest sustained conversation that he had held with Nat since the boy had been orphaned. When this fact was recognized, however, it hit them both at the same moment like a thunderclap, causing Shipwash to smile and Nat himself to look ashamed as though somehow his unwonted outspokenness was an unforgivable crime against his dead mother and father that could only be repaired with a redoubling of silence.

"Now look here, lad," Shipwash said with good-natured impatience. "This melancholy of yours won't do anymore. Your parents would never wish it and God knows that I myself am weary enough of seeing you made miserable. What King Charles' men did to your family was a wicked thing, but you mustn't compound their sinfulness with this unreasonable grief. Your mum and dad are in Heaven now, are they not?"

The child nodded, too tearful to speak.

"Then what have you to grieve over, save their absence? And you will one day see them again, have no fear – though I hope it will not be too soon, as we would like to have your company a trifle longer here before you make your way to Heaven."

The smile that the child managed was heartbreaking in its trusting hope. Shipwash, feeling that he had done his virtuous deed of the day and amply made amends for his concession to fatigue, stood up and brushed off the dead leaves that still clung to his hose and trousers – but not before Nat had thrown his arms around the grocer's shoulders in a heartfelt embrace.

Shipwash returned it rather brusquely, angry at himself for the sudden emotion that welled within him at this display of affection, and was rather relieved when the boy suddenly broke away, his attention diverted by the sight of something across the lake.

"What is it, lad?" he asked, squinting in the direction that Nat was gazing so earnestly.

"I thought it was that dog, sir," Nat replied with a look of disappointment. "The one I saw the night before. It's been following us ever since we started out. Oh, if only I could lure it closer to camp, then mayhap I might tame and keep it!"

"Don't hunt after that stray," Shipwash returned. "When we arrive in Houndswick – if, God help us, we ever escape these damnable swamps – I'll buy you a fine little pup myself. But don't go after this one yourself, Master Nat. I don't like the look of these woods, nor the idea of staying any longer here than we must."

Nat nodded, though his gaze still searched for some sign of the creature – a flash of its gleaming black coat, a gleam of its crimson eyes. Shipwash himself was now noticing for the first time the ascending spiral of smoke that rose over the trees, many miles distant. "Then there are men who inhabit this region, after all," he said. "God willing, we'll reach the place by nightfall and have a warmer place to shelter ourselves than we enjoyed the night before."

Had Shipwash only heeded the advice that he had just delivered to Nat, how much more restful would he have found the coming night! But Fate decreed that he should not, and what harrowing perils this decision would ensure must remain hidden for the nonce as we return once more to the grim walls of Laughlin Priory and the company there that we so lately left.

Chapter Eighteen: In which a breakfast is finished, Cyrus displays the wisdom of a Solomon if not the courage of a Gideon, and Childermass begins his game.

"You perceive before you, Master Plainstaff and Miss Abelin, a ruined man."

Montrose was finishing the last of the cold partridge and had now paused in the midst of his repast to at last address Cyrus, whom he had been eying up until then with that mixture of enmity and curiosity noted previously. Now he was openly examining both the young man and Clarice as though he took a delight in his own sufferings, if only so that he might study their reactions. Cyrus, unable to ascertain what reaction was expected of him and not knowing whether open pity would more please or offend his already testy audience, simultaneously froze in his seat and began to stammer out several expressions of condolence in such swift succession that it was impossible for any of his auditors to make any sense of them. Montrose frowned at this dubious offering, but was fortunately distracted by Clarice who said, "But surely, my lord, you still possess enough holdings to pay back the Squire while still retaining your usual occupations and place of residence?"

"Your words, sweet girl, show how little you understand the thoroughness of my destruction," Montrose returned. "In a month's time I shall have to give up my residence in Houndswick and more than likely mortgage my estate in Shrewsfield as well. If my father was still alive, the old devil would probably have shot me through the head by now, but it looks as though I shall have to weather this myself, alive."

"But where shall you stay?" Clarice asked. "Surely you have relatives who would sustain you?"

"None that I would surrender myself to, were my very life to depend upon it," was the contemptuous answer. "I would sooner put myself under the mercy of Squire Toby himself than those who are my kin and who would gloat so at my misfortunes."

An uncomfortable silence ensued in which Cyrus overheard Sir Robert murmur something across the table to the Reverend Abelin.

"As for you," Montrose looked charmingly upon Cyrus. "You would be beneath the ground now by my hand, were it not for a certain…" he glanced at Withing, realizing that even he was unwilling to describe the appalling brutality of Alan's death in the presence of the young lord. "Tell me," he continued, clearing his throat. "Is it your usual habit to reject a man who has lost all that he owns by refusing him a game?"

Already unnerved by Montrose's casual reference to both his narrowly-averted murder and Alan's gruesome death, Cyrus could only remain speechlessly transfixed in his seat, wondering whether His Grace's question had been merely rhetorical or was yet another open challenge.

"Not everyone is so fond of cards as you, Your Grace," Clarice put in softly. "I have played a hand or two with you, but if it was against Master Plainstaff's conscience, then none of us have the right to demand such a thing of him."

Cyrus's cheeks burned with embarrassment at finding himself defended by a lady due to his own inability to summon any words of his own for the occasion. The merciless Montrose, noting his enemy's discomfort, returned, "And has Master Plainstaff forgotten the use of his tongue, which he employed so freely only the night before in defense of his precious conscience? Speak, boy – I asked you a question."

Cyrus found himself replying before he had quite grasped what it was that he meant to say. "My Lord, before I answer you, let me first put a different question to you – if I may?"

Montrose, too surprised by this sudden communicativeness to think of a properly sneering retort, gave the Puritan an automatic (though somewhat befuddled) nod of acquiescence.

"You told me that the reason that you enjoyed a game of cards so greatly was because of its ability to level the arbitrary differences of fortune that make one man a gentleman and the other a commoner – that you hoped that your virtues were such that whether you had been born an Earl or not, you would still possess the same ability to meet luck's smiles and frowns with the same sort of resourcefulness. Well, sir, it seems as though Fortune has dealt you a bad hand, but if you'll forgive my presumption, I don't see before me the ruined man that you make yourself out to be. I see a man who has lost his ability to live in leisure, but neither the intelligence that Heaven has given him nor the disposition to resist wallowing in self-pity. Perhaps I am wrong, but these, sir, are my impressions.

"As for my reluctance to play a hand with you myself," Cyrus continued, still maintaining his strained attempt at fearless dignity and all the while feeling his heart reverberating palpably all the way down to his stomach. "I meant no disrespect, but I do not wish to play cards with any man and you are not the first that I have refused. And if it is of any consolation, my Lord, I freely confess that I haven't more than several farthings on my person, and so had you won against me, it would have done neither you nor I any good – and had you lost, you would have hated me still more."

Having reached the end of this impromptu speech in his own defense and the personal improvement and character of a man several times his superior in rank, Cyrus cleared his throat rather noisily and deliberately transferred his gaze from Lord Montrose to a less intimidating portion of the breakfast table. Unfortunately, he happened to glance at Mariah instead who was fixing upon him a look of ravishing admiration and approval which succeeded in discomfiting him all the more.

"Well, well, well, Master Plainstaff," Montrose said at last. "Just when I believed that the events of this morning could astonish me no further, you surprise me more than anything else." There was a heavy pause and then he added, "And I suppose that all you say is true."

Everyone, even the customarily placid Withing, stared at the Earl in surprise, not least of all Cyrus himself. But Montrose, whose attention never remained fixed upon the same topic longer than was absolutely necessary, had already tired of the subject of card playing even though it had been he himself who had raised it, and remarked rather abruptly, "Well, I suppose that I must return home – I arrived here much later than I intended, thanks to that procession that I met on the King's road. They were ringing the bells in the old Houndswick church as well, so I can only imagine that it must have been on account of some lately departed soul." He glanced at Cyrus meaningfully – the two of them could easily guess whose soul this was.

"Some more ale, my Lord?" Childermass enquired. They had all forgotten that the chimney sweeper had been standing close by the table, silently listening to every word of their conversation whilst managing superbly to fulfill all the duties of an attendant servant so that he seemed as much a part of the backdrop of the great hall as the billowing tapestries and marble statues.

"Oh yes, thank you," Montrose said. "Now where was I?"

"The funeral procession," Childermass said obligingly.

"I am not certain whose funeral it could have been," Montrose paused. "But I think it was a young man's."

"Why say you so?" Sir Robert enquired.

"Why, sir, I heard talk in the town of a gruesome death," Montrose replied, after a moment's hesitation. "A young man, his own entrails disgorging from his mouth. A pitiable sight, so they say." He glanced at Childermass and seeing the chimney sweeper's watchful expression said, "Yes, I thought that lovely detail might catch your interest."

"Another death," Clarice murmured, disregarding the alarmed looks that arose in Feversham and Dagworth's countenances, the disapproval that flickered in Sir Robert's and the Reverend Abelin's, and the amusement that showed itself in Childermass's.

"Another?" Withing looked from her to his grandfather and from there to the Reverend, utterly bewildered. They remained silent, but Montrose who knew nothing of the stricture forbidding any to tell the boy of the recent events in Houndswick replied:

"Oh yes, something has been picking off the young men of Houndswick one by one this last year. Leaves their corpses either torturously mangled or without a drop of blood left in them. Dr. Erskine himself is at a loss as to what murderer could produce such…peculiar effects in a body."

"When did these deaths begin?" Withing asked. His cheeks had grown very pale and his eyes were bright, but no longer with their usual cheer.

"Why, I think not much longer after the last Feast of Childermass – that is the last Feast of the Holy Innocents in celebration of that day when Herod slaughtered all those Bethlehem children," he annotated, with a self-deprecating smile in the direction of the chimney sweeper as though to apologize for the fact that he shared a name with one of the more sinister days of the Holy Calendar. "An odd coincidence, is it not?"

"Then they began after my father died," Withing said.

The room had gone very quiet all of a sudden. Childermass's living eye, contemplating all of their countenances, was the only moving object in that immense hall: the apt pupil who had learnt by heart each varied cadence of the terror and pity felt by all of them.

"Yes," Montrose said.

Cyrus, who had only just begun to forget for the first time the tragedy and attendant perils that had haunted his own life for the last month, now felt a new fear seize upon him once again at this intimation of a mysterious horror. Withing himself had regained once again that look of paralyzed melancholy that had oppressed him the night before and neither the words of his grandfather nor those of the Reverend could awaken him from this dreamlike despair that had overtaken him.

Needless to say, breakfast was adjourned with as much haste as dinner the night before had been concluded.

***

Twilight found Cyrus wandering the secluded hallways of the Priory, gazing upon the lengthening shadows and faded old portraits of past generations whilst wondering what was to come next. He had thought that morning that after an hour or so, all those who had retired to their private chambers would reemerge again; that somehow, hopefully, he could find Withing and comfort him. But it was as though all the inhabitants of the Priory had vanished to another region of that manor altogether; a region that Cyrus, for all his endless explorations, could never penetrate.

He encountered the menial denizens of the Priory often enough. Feversham, carrying the smell of horses, would gaze gloomily at him before touching his forehead with a grave nod of deference; Dagworth would shuffle past occasionally, his thick fingers gripping the length of some leather leash, usually in the midst of his favorite peregrination betwixt the kitchen and the kennels. Childermass, too, must have been attending to his particular chore of cleaning the Priory's many chambers, for he would often pass by the solitary Cyrus, either with his sooty broom over his shoulder or with the immense collection of keys, all depending from a silver ring, that he would occasionally extract from his cloak in order to open the chambers that lay on his route.

As twilight descended upon the Priory, however, Cyrus found the chimney sweeper now bearing a long pole with a smoking flame at its end which he used to light the various torches and candles that lit up the hallways. Having been forced into solitude for nearly the whole day, Cyrus managed to overcome his natural bashfulness enough to ask Childermass, "Might I help you? A task such as yours could be completed in half the time were two men to do it."

Childermass's living eye lit upon Cyrus with a look that puzzled the young man; it seemed to hold in it far less of its ordinary reserve and instead a familiar, knowing look that struck Cyrus as somewhat unsettling. Half unconsciously, his hand went to the little book that he kept within his coat containing the full history of his misfortunes, as though to reassure himself that it was still safely there. Childermass, seeing this gesture, only smiled gloatingly to himself before replying with a look of irreproachable guilelessness and gratitude, "Why, of course, Master Plainstaff, if it would please you – but as you can see," he held up his ring of keys, "I have almost completed my rounds. Only these last," he pinched two of the keys between a pale thumb and forefinger, "only these last remain. But if you would still like to join me, it would be most kind of you, sir."

"Whose chambers do they belong to?" Cyrus enquired.

"They are no one's – or, rather, everyone's I suppose, sir," Childermass replied. "They are the scullery and the library."

Cyrus's heart leapt with the first start of hope that he had felt ever since the morning's gloomy end.

"Might I see the library?" he asked. "I promise that I shall take nothing – I should only like to look through a few of the volumes, if it would be all right."

Childermass gave a shrug of his cloaked shoulders before replying, "I see no harm in it myself, sir, and I doubt that young Withing, whose guest you are, would grieve overmuch either. But dinner will be set upon the table in half an hour's time and I doubt that you would wish to be roused from your reading so quickly, would you? Ask it of me again tomorrow, however, and I shall gladly take you there."

Cyrus thanked him and followed him to the last two chambers, helping him light their tapers as well and watching as the newly-lit flames expanded and revealed worlds of hanging herbs and dusty manuscripts. Childermass carefully instructed him how best to light the candles so that their wax did not spatter the silver sticks in which they stood and allowed him a few lingering moments in order to observe in the imperfect light of the single candle that burnt upon a library table, the glories that were in store for him tomorrow.

"I shan't leave it burning for long, of course," he said as they departed. "It would be worse than murder if such a room were to go up in flames. But the Reverend Abelin often studies here before retiring to bed for the evening and we keep it lit on his account."

Cyrus thanked him again as he followed him out of the hush of the library and once more into the open expanse of the great hall. In spite of the puzzling qualities that the chimney sweeper possessed, Cyrus found himself warming more and more to the young man. Blind though he was to the more enigmatic and baleful side of Childermass, he managed to detect enough of it to make him uneasy and yet somehow not enough to repel him. There was something in Childermass that made many feel as though they were in the presence of some great and awful secret that might be either the making or the end of them. Cyrus was not the first to feel this, nor the last to be intrigued and disquieted by it. It was what made the chimney sweeper seem at once greater than and indissolubly a part of the ancient, mazelike world that he inhabited.

"Do you possess a key to every chamber in the Priory?" Cyrus asked.

"Yes, sir – saving, of course, those that are never meant to be opened."

"What can you mean?" Cyrus asked, smiling in spite of his confusion at the theatricality of his companion's mysterious answer.

"Why, sir, this is a very large place as you have already seen, and I imagine that some chambers are meant for company, others for private habitation, and others to hide objects that mustn't be thrown away but mustn't be seen either. Surely you know that there are some memories that must be kept silent but must also never be forgotten?"

And Cyrus, whose heart was immediately touched by a remembrance of the secret that he kept lodged even at that moment within his breast pocket, replied in a hushed voice, "Yes, Childermass – I know too well what you mean."

Childermass arched a brow, a carefully constructed look of quizzical surprise crossing his face, though he could hardly keep back the smile that forced itself upon his countenance in spite of his mannered way. There was a touch of deformity in this smile, though Cyrus could not discern from whence this sudden impression had emerged. All that he could observe with certainty was that something darkened the dimples in those pale cheeks, as though an invisible, burning flame were held directly beneath the chimney sweeper's face to touch its crooked, quavering shadow and lurid gleam to his lips. In an instant it was gone and Cyrus was left wondering how he could have dreamt such a thing into a countenance that now gave only an appearance of grave interest.

Childermass, for his part, appeared suddenly restive; some instinct warned him that he had revealed almost too much of himself in the last several moments.

"The library," he said in a tone of leaden finality. "Tomorrow, sir, you shall see it."

And with these words, he disappeared into the shadows that skirted the many arches and pillars of the great hall, leaving Cyrus still smarting from the curious impression that the chimney sweeper's discourse upon secrets had left upon his heart.

Chapter Nineteen: In which Miss Clarice Abelin indulges a curiosity of her own.

Childermass himself kept to the scullery all through dinner, preferring even the dubious company of Dagworth to the chance of meeting the newest guest of the Priory once more. More and more this Cyrus 'Plainstaff' continued to intrigue the chimney sweeper – but at all costs, he must avoid the appearance of curiosity, lest it attract too much attention. Some stirring instinct within Childermass's cold brain whispered to him that the Priory's own history was now bound to whatever ghosts and monsters there were that at present haunted Cyrus – and, of course, anything that pertained to the Priory was of interest to Childermass, as its business was ever his business. So caught up was the imagination of Childermass by the tragedy that Cyrus's book had contained, that in his mind's eye he could already imagine the Marquis St. Aubert standing beneath the fluttering, crimson tapestries that hung within the Priory's chapel, genuflecting to whatever nameless spirit of Desire it was that haunted his heart and demanded those bloody sacrifices that he so delightedly proffered. He imagined as well Ephraim Colkins, his spectral hands and body adorned with chains and fetters of shining silver that to any mortal touch weighed no more than air, his eyes burning with an eternal sorrow and suffering as he wandered silent along the corridors of the Priory, bones, blood, and chains all one in a spectacle of gloomy glister. So absorbed was the chimney sweeper by these visions, that he did not think to question what such a specter or such a nobleman might have thought had they been confronted by such a voracious inquisitiveness; moreover it is likely that had the thought crossed his mind, he would have dismissed it as irrelevant. It is impossible to sway the heart of one for whom such horrors serve only to further arouse an already inflamed soul.

As soon as dinner was concluded, Childermass concealed himself within the shadows of the alcoves, observing each guest disperse and keeping his gaze particularly fixed upon Clarice as she made her way out of the Great Hall and down a hallway that traversed the western wing of the Priory's lower level. He recalled, of course, the Reverend Abelin and Sir Robert's injunction that he follow the girl and observe her actions in case she should say more that would disquiet Withing – but considering the indiscreet events of the morning, this command seemed somewhat pointless. However Childermass, never one to shirk a duty that happened to tickle his fancy no matter how little it might redound to the benefit of his masters, chose to pursue her at a distance and satisfy that elusive curiosity of his in another manner.

So cautiously did he follow her step down the narrow hallways and passages of the Priory, however, that once he at last emerged into an open parlor, he could catch no glimpse of his quarry, nor guess where she might have vanished. Disappointed, the chimney sweeper chose the door that led into one of the Priory's outer gardens, hoping with little expectation that perhaps his prey had chosen this route as well.

The clouds that hung low upon the horizon, grey and empurpled crimson, rose like frozen waves above the dense woodlands that surrounded the Priory or lent their stature to the haggard mountains that already raised their heads above the forests, so that it appeared as though the Priory and its gardens were close to falling beneath a siege of darkness. Occasionally, a flash of lightning followed by a gloomy report of thunder would sound from the west, and Childermass knew from the speed of the easterly wind as it raised the soot from his broom, that the storm would be upon them shortly.

Perhaps the mood of the evening reminded him of that earlier night – the night before the arrival of Withing and Cyrus – or perhaps an inclination of an obscurer nature possessed him at that moment. Either way, the chimney sweeper took it into his head at that moment to wend his way towards the abandoned watch tower that stood upon the outskirts of the Priory, the broken clock upon its face pronouncing an eternal noon or midnight upon the land. Using the ivy and weeds that clung to its walls as a perilous staircase, Childermass gained that locked tower and entered his silent and secret dominion. The rustling of the tempest-borne wind without the tower's windows sounded more faintly than before and the chimney sweeper knew well that he would not be missed by Feversham and the nightly shackles that awaited him for several hours more. Lying down upon a dusty hammock, he soon fell into a dreamless sleep.

***

Unbeknownst to Childermass, however, his steps had been watched with a curiosity equal to his own. Accordingly, as he climbed through the window of the lonely belltower, his spy followed at a short distance after him and resolved to do the same herself.

Ironically, Childermass had been correct in his guess that Clarice had chosen the door leading out to the Priory's outer gardens. If he had been more thorough in his search, he would soon have found her sitting beneath one of the arbors that adorned the perimeter of the garden, reading one of the volumes of history that she had borrowed from the Priory's library. As it happened, however, it was his intended quarry that observed him rather than the other way around and, as it had never occurred to the chimney sweeper that any activity of his could provoke anyone's curiosity, he had taken no care whatsoever in making certain that he was not followed.

The first order of business for Clarice was determining how best to ascend the steep wall of the watchtower. Her long muslin dress was hardly the most ideal clothing for such an endeavor; however, deciding that a few rips and tears were well worth the opportunity to discover what it was that the enigmatic chimney sweeper had hidden within that abandoned edifice, she set to climbing the ivies with less skill but ultimately the same success as he had obtained.

Once she had climbed over the sill of one of the tower's windows, she looked about for Childermass but found no sign of him. Crimson, gold, and violet draperies adorned the stone walls and floors of the spider-scuttled tower and, circling the chamber in which she stood, she found that a collection of rotted and rusted tables, candlesticks, and other contraptions that she could not even put a name to all had their place as well in that already crowded space. It seemed that she looked upon the accumulated castaways of centuries: the belongings of the Priory that her overlords had somehow forgotten to either acknowledge or dispossess. Now they had been claimed by the only soul who still remembered their existence or cared for it, existing now for his pleasure alone. Volumes and manuscripts lay beside heaps of rusted candlesticks and the crystal of broken chandeliers; bits of marble, the broken fragments of once whole and supple statues, lay upon the tattered velvet that carpeted the floor like the imperishable limbs of mutilated angels. One object stood hanging from the rafters: an iron cage wrought into the shape of a man that swung open as though one were supposed to enclose a living human inside it. Another chair of glittering silver was studded entirely with blades as thin as needles; though the make of the thing suggested that it must be ancient, she found as she ran a fingertip over them that its needles were still as bloodily potent as ever.

The sound of breathing from somewhere close by caused her to start violently and look about. Neither the lateness of the hour nor the objects that surrounded her were of a nature to quiet any mind – add to this her own guilt at having encroached upon what appeared to be the chimney sweeper's own private passion and she was now fearful of how he might respond to such a trespass. At first, her eye could not discern the source of the sound. Then, by chance, she happened to catch sight of a suspended ream of crimson curtain like a tongue of cloth, hanging from both ends by two rusted hooks. She saw that Childermass lay in this makeshift hammock and, as she drew nearer, she heard him draw another, still more labored breath before lapsing once more into his deathlike slumber.

This was the first time that Clarice had ever seen Childermass in such a state and the spectacle was not without an eerie sort of mesmerism. The winds that passed through the belltower lifted and spread aloft the torn curtains that floated above his hanging, crimson bed whilst the occasional gleam of lightning threw its own livid fire upon the peculiar devices and objects that surrounded the sleeper. She saw too that he had exchanged his usual plain garments for rich, though somewhat frayed and tattered, robes of black silk. Moreover, his eyes now being closed in sleep, it was impossible to catch any hint of the mysterious misfortune that had caused one eye to be replaced with a blind, milky surrogate; and with this one deformity shielded from view, the stillness of the chimney sweeper's pale features and the long gaunt fingers resting motionless upon his heart seemed as though they belonged more to the repose of a marble saint than that of a man. Hardly daring to draw a breath herself lest she awaken him and perhaps incur his anger, she gazed upon the sleeping Childermass with a curious sort of awe. Just as she managed to tear her enchanted eyes away from the sleeper and begin to depart, however, a crash of thunder far louder than those that had preceded it shook the tower, vibrating every chime and every bell within its eaves and rafters, and causing Childermass's eye to fly open and fall instantly upon the wretched young woman who stood beside him.

Clarice opened her mouth, a thousand protestations and explanations forming all at once within her mind, and yet found herself unable to speak, so thunderstruck was she by this unexpected occurrence. Instead, she bit her lip very hard, little heeding either the pain or the taste of blood that welled now upon her tongue.

Childermass for his part was so astonished at this unprecedented appearance that all he could do was gaze for a long while upon her wordlessly, a penetrating look gleaming within his living eye and a dull dispassion within his marble one. At last he spoke.

"You have injured your finger, Miss Abelin?" he enquired a bit sleepily.

Bewildered by this incongruous response, Clarice looked down at the finger that she had managed to prick upon the terrible chair of needles and replied, "Oh, yes – I am so sorry, I put my hand too carelessly upon your chair…" she did not know how to complete the sentence, for the peculiarity of such an item even existing within the chimney sweeper's secret tower now presented itself even more forcibly than before. Moreover, she hardly knew what to name such a device – nor, in her innocence, could she imagine what use such a chair could be put to, save that this use must doubtless be unpleasant.

"I believe that I know what you mean, madam," Childermass said, putting an end to the discomfiting silence that had ensued. "I wonder what should have prompted you to brave this lonely old tower only to prick your finger upon my chair."

The young woman thought that the subtle mockery of this speech was a sure proof that she had angered him. She little knew Childermass who, an ardent devotee at the altar of Curiosity himself, was in truth thoroughly amused by another's sacrifice to his favorite vice. That he had been the object rather than the pursuer of Curiosity in this instance intrigued rather than incensed him; and the fact that he had been the object of Miss Abelin's interest aroused some dark and obscure appetite in him as well that, had she known it existed, would possibly have unnerved the young woman all the more. As it was, she was thankfully spared this knowledge and managed to gather her wits enough to say:

"I am so sorry for intruding upon you. I shall depart and leave you in peace at once."

"Of course, madam," Childermass replied, rising and offering her a clumsy bow. Attired as he was in robes of black, doubtless absconded from some forgotten attic chest within the Priory, Clarice found it difficult to believe that she was speaking to the Master of Chimneys rather than to some nobly-born stranger. "Shall I show you the way out?"

As he spoke, he took her by the arm and led her to the window, pointing to the rain-swept ivies that clung to the wall beneath it. There was such a humorous incongruity to the chimney sweeper's gallantry amidst the wildness of his surroundings that even Clarice could not keep back a smile in spite of her apprehension.

"Truly, Childermass, you are not angry with me, are you?" she asked, gazing upon him with a searching earnestness. "I only meant to see your tower for curiosity's sake – I did not mean to surprise you in your sleep. But I am terribly sorry for my presumption."

She was embarrassed by the amusement that once again glittered within his eye as he took her hand and said, "I tell you plainly, lady, that your presence was no offense. Now will you believe me or not?"

The familiarity with which he spoke was so unlike his usual manner that she blushed at it and replied with some haste, "Thank you, Childermass. Now I ought to leave or my uncle shall be wondering where I am."

"Farewell, Miss Abelin," Childermass called after her as, without another word, she began to descend the ivies, managing them in half the time it had taken her to ascend. Once she reached the ground, she turned and, meeting his gaze, waved another goodbye before drawing her cloak over her head and running through the fog and rain back towards the Priory.

Childermass followed her retreating figure with his eye for some time before turning his gaze towards the roiling clouds and low clouds of mist that fled across the landscape. As late as the hour was, the sun had not lowered altogether beneath the horizon but still faintly colored the skies above with a dull crimson that vied with the black thunderheads for dominance. There was a violence to these colors, as though a murder had been committed within the heavens and the blood of some Titan had now covered the stars with proof of an unnamable crime. Childermass felt his heart grow cold within his breast; some strange instinct told him that this night called for something more than the mere raging of the elements. He longed to stay within his tower and watch until dawn, though he little knew what it was that he awaited. Only the remembrance of the chains that awaited him and that, if avoided, would bring a greater punishment upon his head, at last convinced him that he must forsake the woods and return to the Priory. As he did so, he thought of Clarice and her astonishment at discovering his secret treasures. What, he wondered, would the Reverend's lovely niece think if she only knew the whole of them? Perhaps one day he would see that she had this chance.

Chapter Twenty: In which Master Shipwash and the Wassailers take refuge from the storm, Nat is met once again by the creature in the woods, and a horror is discovered.

It happened that, at the same moment that Childermass was gazing upon the heavens and wondering at what impression could have prompted such a sense of imminent dread within his heart, Master Shipwash was attempting in vain to recall whether crimson skies in the evening signaled the approach of a terrible storm or whether they possessed an ominous significance only at dawn. One might have thought that the fact that the Worshipful Company of Grocers were, at that moment, suffering through one of the most frightful winter tempests to have raged through that district of Scotland in the last decade would have made the question somewhat irrelevant, but this did not abate his scientific curiosity in the least; indeed, it only made him wonder all the more nervously as to whether they could expect an even more violent outburst from the forces of Nature.

"Where shall we stay for the night?" Nat cried out above the din of thunder. "We've passed no cottages or farms ever since we left Shrewsfield!"

Master Shipwash was too cross to reply immediately, concentrating instead upon maneuvering his way past the muddy rivulets and upraised tree roots that crisscrossed their road. However, he heard someone behind him call out that they thought they saw the smoke of a chimney rising ahead of them. Blinking past the raindrops that fell from the brim of his hat into his bleary eyes, he saw that his unknown lookout had spoken the truth. Ahead of them, merely a stone's throw away, a cottage stood in a circular clearing and beside it he saw a flock of goats grazing in front of an immense barn, their curved horns glistening and dripping with rainwater.

"We'll stop here for now," Shipwash shouted over his shoulder to the rest of the company before pressing on ahead. As he did so, he felt a hand upon his shoulder. He saw that it was a man, his crimson cloak now drenched to a burgundy color under the relentless deluge, and his handsome, delicate face occasionally revealed in the intermittent flashes of lightning.

"Is it wise for us to trust ourselves to strangers in such an isolated place?" the gentleman enquired. "Bandits could infest these woods for all we know – or far worse, I imagine. And we have children in our midst."

Shipwash frowned; the man's English was perfect, but colored with an accent that he could not quite place. "We cannot linger in these woods on a night like this," he said. "And keep in mind the danger of wolves and other beasts. Our luck held out last night, but I cannot vouch for it a second time."

"I would sooner trust the mercy of wolves than that of my fellow man," the gentleman replied with a faint smile. It was a statement that ill-matched the guileless geniality of his countenance, but Shipwash was far too preoccupied with other troubles to deal with such an incongruity at the moment.

"Come, come," said he. "We shall lodge here and tomorrow we will have reached Houndswick and all will be well. You shall see."

"You are right in that, my friend," the stranger replied.

"Your fine clothes will thank me, I promise you," Shipwash said as he approached the door of the cottage.

By way of answer, the stranger wrung a portion of his cloak with a rueful look; beneath the crimson of the twilight sky, the moisture that he milked from it fell like drops of red upon the doorstep of the little dwelling. For his part, Shipwash removed his hat and began beating its soggy felt upon the door of the cottage with increasing impatience.

At last, this door opened to reveal the face of a young woman, her hair clinging to her cheeks and throat in long, damp ringlets of gold as though she had only just been exposed to the rage of the tempest herself.

"Alison Mackenzie at your service," said she. "And what brings you to these parts, masters?"

As she spoke, her quick, hazel eyes ran freely over the men who stood foremost in that company, seeming to study both their faces and the cut of their garments with an interest that puzzled Shipwash. They finally came to rest once again upon the befuddled grocer who, as it happened, had been absent-mindedly performing a similar inspection upon the lady herself. When she smiled at this realization, he cleared his throat in embarrassment and replied a little brusquely, "We are wassailers, madam, and would be most grateful for any shelter that you could provide for us this night."

"You won't be singing any of your carols out here, will you now?" she asked, her pretty face turning sour.

"Not if you wish us to refrain, Mistress Mackenzie," Shipwash said with as much gallantry as he could muster, a little irritated by this dismissive response.

"Then the barn is yours and supper as well, if you'll be wanting it," she said. "Gordon! Tavish!" she suddenly called over her shoulder. "We have some gentlemen as guests tonight."

In response to her summonses, two young men appeared behind her. She kissed both their hands in greeting, then nodded towards the bedraggled company of grocers before her. "Take them to the barn, will you, my sons?" she asked. "I shall tell you when dinner is ready and when they may all sup."

"Of course, mother," one of them replied. Then, to Shipwash and his company, "Follow us and you shall soon be out of the rain."

The barn to which they were led was a humble, but nevertheless warm and dry sanctuary for the company, filled with sweet-smelling straw and the less savory scent of goats. Shipwash was pleased with their accommodations and thanked the two young men heartily.

"We shall call on you and your men when supper is on the table," one of them replied.

Shipwash, feeling his clothes and – more importantly – his flesh already beginning to thaw and dry, settled back upon a mound of hay and exhaled a contented sigh.

"Good, wholesome country living," he murmured. "Could make a man live for a hundred years healthily, I do declare!"

The stranger in the crimson cloak lifted his eyes at this sentimental utterance and said softly, "Yes, friend, I do believe that you are right."

At that moment, the grocer happened to recall the sailor's maxim that he had forgotten earlier that evening and its reassurance that red skies in the evening were, in fact, as innocuous as an unborn babe. And Shipwash, never having felt so secure and untroubled since the beginning of their journey, smiled at the handsome gentleman and closed his eyes to settle in for a brief nap.

***

Dinner was brought out to them in the form of buckets of broth and with these generous portions, the two brothers Gordon and Tavish carried in blankets for the wassailers as well. There were about fifty men and boys in that company, all crowded together in that barn, and there were not enough blankets to accommodate them all in that damp and chilly place, and so it was agreed after the brothers departed that they should cast lots to decide who would be whose bedfellow. As they were all paired off, Shipwash began to dread that he would be forced to share a blanket with sour old Crawley whom he guessed would spend the rest of the night filling his ear with all the thousand and one reasons why their present circumstances were all due to Shipwash's inept planning. He was much relieved, as a result, when he found that his companion was to be none other than the handsome stranger with the distinctly Gallic accent. After all the lanterns had been extinguished, however, he found himself more talkative than drowsy.

"I have not yet decided," he confessed to his companion. "How I may tell Mr. Chapman that his play, though admirable, is not quite what I had in mind for our wassailing program."

"How do you mean, friend?" his companion enquired, looking quite drowsy himself but attempting for politeness' sake to maintain an expression of amiable interest. "What in it offends you?"

"Oh, I wouldn't say 'offend.' But must the fellow harp upon his end rhymes? Why cannot he employ heroic meter? That would be much more effective in a play of such breadth – and believe me when I say that the fellow would put a London printing press out of order with the amount of paper and ink it would take to put down this nativity play of his."

"I am told that end rhymes are much more highly favored in this country than their alternative," the stranger said.

"Yes, but which do *you* prefer?" Shipwash demanded, wishing to shake his companion out of the tactfully neutral position which he had hitherto maintained.

"One must never undertake two subjects in the same fashion," the stranger said. "For each one…there must be a special method."

Shipwash was profoundly impressed with this reply, delivered by his by now only half-conscious auditor. "Tell me, sir," said he. "Would you consider writing a moralizing play for our troupe?"

But the stranger by his side had already fallen fast asleep and Shipwash, finding himself deprived of an ear into which he could unburden his complaints, soon succumbed to sleep himself.

***

No matter how often Nat changed his position or turned his face to avoid the pallid glare of moonlight that shone through the cracks in the barn's roof, he could not fall asleep. He had lain beside the snoring Crawley, had heard the whispers that had passed between Shipwash and his companion on the other side of the barn subside and give way at last to the stillness of slumber, and still he found that sleep eluded him. It was not that he was hungry; he had felt so little need for food, in fact, that he had neglected to eat the bowl of soup given him by one of the two brothers. It was an indefinable restlessness that had possessed him, certainly not one connected with any bodily complaint. With every limb sore from the day's long march and a feeling of warmth suffusing him from the blanket of fleece beneath which he lay, the boy still felt an inability or an unwillingness to close his eyes and give himself up to the oblivion that his fellows had so readily succumbed to. For some unaccountable reason, he felt as though something more was needed of him this hour and that to sleep would be an unpardonable offence. What this offence could be, however, was beyond him and he was more than inclined to believe it a fiction that his exhausted brain had concocted for its own private amusement and his bewilderment.

To take his mind off of the disquieting sense of expectancy that pervaded his thoughts and sickened his stomach with its intensity, he began to watch the motes that floated in and out of view within the silver threads of moonlight, falling athwart the barn in livid crosshatches from ceiling to floor and across the walls, like the loose threads at the edge of some larger, unseen pattern. The motes of dust seemed too like the stars of some impossibly small universe invisible to any earthly dimension and as the boy held out his hand to catch one such constellation, it spun out of reach and into the darkness, hastened by the motion of air caused by his moving fingers.

He fell back again upon his makeshift pillow of straw, his thoughts turning abruptly to the scenes of the last several days: the chilly miles of marshland, the stranger who had given him the little crystal dove and who was now sleeping so soundly beside Shipwash, and lastly of all the dog who had followed them so faithfully ever since their departure from Shrewsfield and whom Nat hoped, in spite of Shipwash's warning, that he would have the chance to befriend. True, the creature had kept its distance since yesterday in spite of the boy's many attempts to lure it with scraps of meat or whistling calls, but it could not be altogether wild, for it had often looked at the boy and wagged its tail with a look in its eye that held none of the fear or suspicion that a feral beast possesses. Where did the creature come from, to whom did it belong, and why did it follow their company so closely? All these things Nat wondered before at last resolving to try again to court elusive slumber.

Just as he began to close his eyes, however, he noticed that the wooden paneling of the wall by which he lay had come slightly loose. It was the board by his head and it jutted out at such an angle that the child could feel the breath of winter upon his face in spite of the relative warmth inside the rest of the barn. He half-rose and attempted to wedge the board back into place, but this served to only loosen it still further. Impatient, he worried at it still more and as the plank of wood splintered and broke away he happened to look up and see what stood on the other side, barely a hair's breadth away from him.

It was the dog. Mouth open, tongue lolling, it stood there watching him with its great red eyes fixed and motionless and its black tail like a rearing serpent high above its body. It was so close that he could feel its breath upon his face and the wet drip of the saliva that fell in rivulets from between its parted jaws. Nat's heart beat wildly and his mouth had gone dry, though more from surprise than fear. There was nothing terrifying about the creature; it seemed as friendly as ever and even allowed the child to stroke its face before turning away and loping back in the direction of the forest. Nat propped his chin upon his elbows and whistled as softly as he could for the dog to return, but it only stopped at the edge of the woods and looked back at him, its eyes glowing and its breath drifting in a continual mist from its panting maw.

The boy managed to pry a few more boards loose and crawled beneath them into the winter night. The rain had ceased, but the thistles and weeds still glistened wetly and a sharp breeze stirred the thickets with its passing. Nat hunched his shoulders and hugged his arms, expecting to be overwhelmed by the bitterness of the weather. To his surprise, he found that the warmth that he had felt in the barn did not forsake him but seemed instead to increase as he approached the forest. The dog raised its ears at his approach and then trotted farther amongst the trees, turning its head occasionally to be certain of the child's pursuit.

Nat paused at the edge of the forest and looked back at the barn, remembering Shipwash's warning against venturing alone into these woods. But what harm could it do just to follow the creature a little way and lure it back? Shipwash had said that they would reach Houndswick by tomorrow; surely once they reached town, the creature would forsake their company and return to the forests. The lonely child could not bear to think of losing the dog who had companioned them so faithfully these many miles and as often as he recalled Shipwash's words, he glanced back at the creature that wagged its tail whenever he met its eyes and wished that somehow he could entice it back to the barn. He decided at last to follow it a little way and see if he could somehow catch the creature and that, if this strategem failed, he would return to his forsaken bed of straw.

So the boy followed the black creature into the woodlands and down the narrow, rain-sodden paths travelled only by wolves and thieves, trying his best to excel its loping gait and each time somehow finding himself one step behind his four-legged guide. Nat was so intent upon catching his errant friend that he lost all sense of time and forgot his own resolution to turn back if his attempts were not met immediately with success. The creature seemed tireless, but even the determination that the boy possessed was not enough to safeguard against weariness. He paused to catch his breath and the next moment found that he could see no sign of the dog any longer. It had continued onwards and vanished out of sight.

For a moment, Nat felt his heart clench with fear and tears sting his eyes as he realized at last not only that he had lost the dog but that he had no idea how far he had traveled into the forest, nor any notion of how to return to his companions. It was as though an enchantment had been cast over him all the while the creature had remained in his sight, clearing his head of any thought of his friends and rendering him immune to the biting cold of his surroundings. Now that it had been lifted, he found himself remembering the kindly Shipwash and longing for his familiar presence; and, fearing that he should never see him or any of that company again, the child began to cry bitterly.

A momentary flash of movement somewhere ahead of him caught his attention and caused his heart to thrill with hope. The dog's flitting shadow disappeared as he vanished behind the trunk of an ancient oak and Nat hastened in that direction.

The creature was nowhere to be seen, however. Instead, beneath the low-hanging, twisted branches of the tree, there stood a man. Nat could not see his face for his entire head was concealed beneath a black hood that only allowed the eyes to be seen past two narrow holes cut into the cloth. From head to foot, the stranger was muffled up behind veils and robes of black. As he approached, however, Nat noticed that his eyes were the only points of color upon that pillar of darkness, shining and crimson. They seemed the color of the dog's eyes.

Something was terribly wrong here. There was more to this night's horror than the terror of losing oneself to the woodlands and the marshes. Nat felt every nerve in his body, every primitive instinct in his soul, willing him to fly. But the man, as though sensing this desire, caught the boy by the wrist with fingers gauntleted in black silk. Nat knew then, by their strength and by the look within that awful gaze, that whatever hope of escape that might have existed before had ended now. In spite of this, however, he fought to wrest himself from the stranger's grasp.

The next moment, he felt a sharp pain in his ribs, just beneath his right chest that would have caused him to cry out, had the stranger not put a hand over his mouth to quiet him, at the same time drawing him closer so that he was wholly within his attacker's grasp. Nat saw the gleam of blood-stained silver in the moonlight and knew that he had been stabbed, though in his stricken state he could not ascertain how terribly he had been wounded. A dizziness swept over him and he fell back against the stranger, as he heard his persecutor speak for the first time, though in a whisper:

"Wonder not that you are still alive even now, child – for until dawn, alive is how I would have you."

But Nat had fallen into a faint and was deaf to this utterance as he was borne away deeper into the forest.

***

Shipwash started awake and found himself bathed in sweat and his heart racing as though he had run a mile in his sleep. He could not remember the nature of the dream he had been rescued from, but he felt as though he had been snatched only just in time from the very jaws of Hell itself. Expelling a pent-up breath, he glanced around at his sleeping comrades and found them as peaceful as they had been an hour earlier or however long he had been asleep himself. He half-hoped to find his companion awake at least so that he could find some comfort in conversation; the gentleman was wholly out of this world, however, though the heated flush in his cheeks and his labored breathing made Shipwash wonder at what violent vision was disturbing his rest. Truly this was not a night fashioned for gentle thoughts.

The grocer fumbled through his blankets for his purse, hoping to read a passage from the Scriptures in order to quiet his mind. As he lifted the tattered cloths, however, he accidentally caught his hand in a sewn-up pocket hidden on the underside of one of the blankets and, in an attempt to extract his hand, managed to rip the flap of cloth completely apart. He was about to throw the torn rag away, when he noticed that deeply-inked lines of crimson writing covered one side of it. Curious, he held it up to the moonlight, and read the following words:

I must write this with my own heart's blood, for I have no other ink with which to warn you of your imminent fate should you be unfortunate enough to be lying within the Mackenzie barn, enjoying the hospitality of that witch and her sons and little suspecting their intentions for you. If you were foolish enough to accept the broth they offered you, then like me you will have sunk into a stupor from which you will only awake once they have already plunged their daggers into your breast and robbed you of your wallet, leaving you to welter in your own blood as I am now. I also dread to think to what use the corpses of my companions and myself shall be put to, for I heard that wolfish woman speak to her whelps of the hideous progenies that are begat from the cold seed of murdered men. Truly, the bitch is insatiable.

As I have little hope of being found and avenged, this little scrap of cloth shall serve as my only epitaph. I pray that whomsoever reads it shall have better luck than we.

(Signed) *Sir Eustace Haverhill; barrister, MP, and sometime advisor to His Majesty King Charles II.*

Chapter Twenty-One: In which Shipwash discovers the benefits and the drawbacks of befriending a professional assassin.

By the time Shipwash had reached the end of this scrawled message, he was trembling so violently that he feared he would be too overcome with his own terror to prevent the very thing that had provoked it. So the worst had happened and they had fallen into the hands of bandits – or, as some of the lines in the late Squire Haverhill's message had hinted, far worse. The first thing he thought of was the broth: he had tasted a portion of it, but had fortunately not sated himself upon it. The same could not be said of his companions who were sleeping so soundly that he almost feared that they had been poisoned rather than drugged. Stricken by this new suspicion, he put his ear to the breast of his companion and was so grateful to hear the steady beat of his heart that he shed tears of joy. He set to shaking the man's shoulder; no matter how violently he did so, however, the sleeper continued to dream as deeply as before with not so much as the flicker of an eyelash to register that these motions were even felt.

You will only awake once they have already plunged their daggers into your breast, so Haverhill had claimed. In his desperation, Shipwash wondered whether pain alone could break the spell of the drug and began to fumble for his dagger. Taking his companion's hand, he pressed the point into one of the fingers. It was not until the warm blood began to flow that the crimson-cloaked gentleman at last awoke with a start. He spoke first in whispered French and Shipwash guessed that the man's consciousness was still half occupying the dreamworld that he had forsaken, though he could not imagine why a Shrewsfield grocer should know the tongue of a Popish enemy country. Under ordinary circumstances, he would have questioned the man but this was no time for arguments, not even with a possible subject of France.

Recalling himself, the Frenchman reverted instantly to English, saying, "What is it, friend? What means this blood and this dagger?"

In reply, Shipwash gave him the grisly rag upon which Haverhill's last testament was scrawled. A look of understanding dawned upon the man's face and he said, "Then this is how you woke me."

Shipwash looked at his bleeding hand and nodded. "We must do the same for the rest of our friends," he added, shivering.

"I hardly think that our wakefulness shall make any great difference to our chances of survival, my friend," the Frenchman replied. "How well armed are we, would you imagine?"

"In a company of children and tradesmen?" Shipwash returned despairingly. "They will be armed with no greater weapon than this dagger of mine and some of them not even with that! I greatly fear that we are lost."

"And shall have monstrous prodigies begat upon our corpses," the amiable Frenchman readily supplied the lurid thought that had been running silently through the grocer's mind already. As he spoke, he unlocked a chest that he had kept hidden beneath his blanket. The inside of the lid was decorated with the portrait of a beautiful, melancholic lady but Shipwash's eyes widened at the sight of the two silver muskets that lay gleaming in its depths.

The Frenchman handed one to him and kept its twin for himself, polishing its glittering muzzle upon the hem of his cloak. "They are unloaded but I have bullets enough to fill both. You know how to use such a weapon, Monsieur? I suppose by this time I should cease attempting to pass myself off as an Englishman."

"Who are you?" Shipwash whispered. For the first time, he began to feel a little afraid of his companion.

"We have grocers in France as well, my friend."

"But you are not one of them yourself, young man – you can't be. What grocer could afford such fine pieces?"

The guileless look in the Frenchman's eyes belied the outrageous nature of his ripostes.

"It is a lucrative service that I perform," he said.

The sound of footsteps outside the barn instantly recalled the two of them to their awful situation. Concealing the trunk and weapons beneath their blankets, they instantly lay still, pretending to be as unconscious as the rest of their company.

"There are too many of the lambs to slaughter them one by one," Shipwash heard their hostess say, and beneath his lowered lashes he could see her entering with her two sons Gordon and Tavish following closely in her wake. Her hair was unbound and flowed past her shoulders to her waist; the light from the torch that she held occasionally set a particular curl alight so that it gleamed like spun gold before falling into shadow and turning to honeyed auburn. Her eyes were hazel jewels that radiated cruelty and beauty in equal portions as they wandered over the sleepers that lay at her feet. Shipwash felt his stomach tighten as she neared the place where he and the Frenchman lay.

"It would be so much simpler," she murmured. "To simply padlock the door and burn the place down this time. Then we could pick the gold and silver from their ashes without bothering to bloody our knives."

"But, Mother," one of the young men interposed with a smile. "Methought that you enjoyed more from some of them than merely their wealth."

"From these withered old peasants? What do you take me for? Not even as dead men could they please me." Her glance happened to fall upon Shipwash and the Frenchman, both still feigning sleep. "Indeed, these two appear the only likely ones in this company."

As she spoke, Shipwash noticed that at least a dozen other men stood in a semicircle by the shadowed entrance to the barn. A few held naked swords pointing earthwards and watched the proceedings with the same lifeless gaze. Others had only stumps for fingers and had been obliged to sharpen the broken knobs of bone at the ends of these severed joints into makeshift talons. Dried blood stained and spattered all their garments and the horrified grocer thought that in the unsteady flickering of the torch, he could discern the mortal wounds that marred their temples, breasts, and throats. Their lips were shrunken, dried and frayed as though they had been wandering for an eternity in a raging furnace. In the empty eye socket of one, Shipwash imagined that he saw the black head of a serpent emerge for a moment and peer down upon the sleeping wassailers, lending its own two emerald eyes to the single dull orb remaining in the skull of the creature that it inhabited.

His attention was distracted from these grisly details by the witch herself as she knelt by his side. He instantly closed his eyes entirely, praying with all his heart that she should not know that he was awake nor find the musket concealed beneath his pillow. He felt her fingers wantonly cover him with caresses and though his memory was still fresh with the sight of the dead men who stood watchful at the door, he could not prevent his senses from responding to the effects of these ministrations, in spite of his best efforts. Still worse, the horror of his situation – rather than lessening his receptiveness – seemed instead to intensify it, so that he soon approached the point when he felt certain that he could no longer contain the response that his own treacherous senses now called for. To his relief, she abandoned her work before its completion, murmuring, "Let us wait until these sweet springs have grown colder, love – then we shall see what nectars we may draw from them."

She pressed her lips against his mouth and he felt himself grow warm beneath her kiss, at the same time wishing foolishly that he could open his eyes and see the face of the beautiful witch under whose power he lay. Too quickly, she left him for his companion and he watched with mingled relief and envy as she began to serve him the same turn.

"Why you would almost think that this fair one was awake," the young witch said with a little laugh to her sons as they watched. "See how he blushes if you but touch his lips?"

"Methinks that we shall see those roses bled to lilies before the night is out," one of the sons speculated.

"And that shall make them all the fairer," the witch said, rising and moving towards the door. "Let me see to my cantrips and then we shall return to our little flock in an hour's time. I'll suck their sweet bones, my dears, like honeycombs."

Once that ghastly assemblage had departed, Shipwash instantly sat up and whispered shakily to the Frenchman, "What shall we do now?"

His companion was already methodically filling his musket with cartridges and offered Shipwash several shining pellets with which to feed his own firearm. Once the Frenchman had finished with this operation, he began to fit a curious series of silver rings over the fingers of his left hand, all melded together in a row and yet perfectly fitting his hand.

"Are those made to break a man's jaw?" Shipwash asked curiously.

The Frenchman smiled at this. "Oh no, Monsieur, I haven't the strength for that. But if you touch a little spring here," his thumb pressed an upraised trigger at the bottom of one of the rings, "then you shall see their magic."

As he spoke, Shipwash saw five separate knives of silver fly out from the rings, extending like talons several inches past the Frenchman's fingers.

"If our pretty mistress comes too close again, her cheeks will bear the memory of me," he said, caressing his artificial pincers against the skin of his own smooth cheek.

There was something in the man's voice that made Shipwash's skin crawl. Certainly, he was glad to have the assistance of someone with such composure, particularly in circumstances that were contributing greatly to the deterioration of his own equilibrium; but he didn't like the way in which his companion spoke so familiarly of the rending of flesh. He shook his head, trying to force these unpleasant speculations from his mind: he still could not resist being somewhat unsettled, however, by the sight of this gentleman with his mechanical claws of silver and was somewhat grateful when these talons were sheathed and his companion was once again wholly human.

"I saw no muskets on them – did you, Monsieur?" the Frenchman asked Shipwash, as though unaware of the eerie effect that he was producing.

"No, sir, I did not."

"Tell me, then: have you any flint?"

"Yes..."

"Then we have fire and two muskets against their many numbers and sorcery."

"You forget that we have to awaken all our comrades and somehow leave this place without pursuit as well," Shipwash reminded him despairingly.

"No, I have not."

"Then what do you propose?"

"That we leave them to their fates."

Shipwash could not believe what he had just heard, nor could convince himself that these monstrous words had just issued from the mouth of the delicate-faced young man before him.

"You cannot be seriously suggesting that we leave our friends to the cruelties and lusts of this woman and her sons," he said.

"I can see no other way for us to escape. You see, my thinking is this: we can use the fire and the muskets to surround their cottage and create an illusion of numbers that we do not possess. But how we are to awaken all our company and have them make their escape while putting on this shadow play for our captors – that is beyond me."

"But we must try," Shipwash said helplessly.

"We must?" his companion asked. There was no passion in his retort, only a curiosity regarding how Shipwash would convince him of the logic of this conclusion.

But they were losing time; moreover, the events of the night had worn a hole through Shipwash's rather thin reserve of patience.

"Why do you think that I woke you?" he snapped. "I was afraid, yes – but it was also for pity's sake. Will you let them lie there and die as I could have done? Have you no pity yourself?"

The grocer's impatient grief gave way to a bewildered astonishment as he saw the haunted look that suddenly tainted the Frenchman's eyes; he could not have known it, but his companion was recalling those same words as they had been voiced by a young man in a snowy Essex field, pleading upon his knees for the life of his father.

"There is a reason why I came to this land," the Frenchman murmured at last. "And it was not to be slain by this woman and her brood. Yet perhaps I can provide a means for the escape of this company and have a question of my own answered by this Mistress Mackenzie."

"Then we shall help them all escape?"

"If you insist, Monsieur – then yes."

Shipwash grasped the Frenchman's hand, his eyes shining with gratitude. He did not know what had provoked this change of heart, nor did he care. At another time and place, he could have been the victim of the man he embraced so earnestly, but Fate had decreed that they should be comrades on that awful night and only the Frenchman realized the irony of their situation. Shipwash saw the tears shining in his companion's eyes and thought them provoked by tender pity and remorse. In truth, they were the tears of barely-contained hilarity.

"If we live past this night," Shipwash said. "I shall always consider you my friend."

"And if we do not," the Frenchman replied brightly. "Then we shall spend an eternity as soulless corpses jointly servicing this lustful young woman. Either way, Monsieur, you shall always have my regard."

Needless to say, this was not the heroic note that Shipwash would have preferred their perilous deliberations to end upon.

***

Midnight found the grocer nearly finished with the tedious task of awakening all his comrades. He could not tell how swiftly time passed nor how close the hour drew nigh when the witch and her sons meant to return and carry out their cruel sentence. From time to time, he would steal a glance between a crack in the boarding of the barn wall to see if he could glimpse the Frenchman and spy whatever it was that he was planning for their captors. When he could see no sign of him, his heart began to sink and he wondered whether they had been abandoned. But as soon as this thought entered his mind, he thought of the peculiar look that had entered the Frenchman's eyes for a moment and his enigmatic remark that he must put a question to their hostess. More than anything else, Shipwash trusted the resolution that he had seen in that glance, though he was heartily glad that he was not the one whom his companion intended to question.

"Where is Nat?" he asked Crawley in a low voice once he had finished rousing the rest of the company.

"How am I to know?" the surly grocer returned sourly. "I fell asleep long before he did. When I awoke just now, he was gone as you see."

Shipwash anxiously inspected the place where the boy had lain, but could find nothing save footprints in the damp earth that led from the barn into the forests.

"Foolish lad," he murmured. "Did I not tell you to leave the woods to themselves?"

To distract himself from the fear that welled in his heart at the child's disappearance, he began again to watch the cottage for any sign either of the Frenchman or of their intended murderers. At that moment, he heard a distinctly Gallic voice outside cry:

"Mistress Mackenzie – come and face thy judge. Hell itself has come for thee!"

Shipwash barely suppressed a groan. The Frenchman's sweet-tempered voice, even when raised in a shout, sounded more like a friendly call to arms than a deadly threat. However, this was their signal, God help them. Gesturing to Crawley to lead the way, Shipwash watched as the company of grocers began to slowly depart from the barn through the splintered hole that he and Crawley had smashed through the wall, all the while keeping his musket trained upon the door.

A series of blood-curdling screams erupted in the stillness immediately following the Frenchman's ultimatum; these piercing shrieks had no human quality to them, however. Shipwash hastened to the barn door to see if he could glimpse their source, but could see nothing save the two sons of the witch standing upon the doorstep, their faces registering the same confusion and terror that he himself felt at those fearful cries.

But the cruel little drama had only just begun. From the forests, dozens of creatures came loping towards the cottage, white figures on all fours out of the mist, their sides and faces darkly streaked and their horns mounted with flaming brands. One passed by very close to where Shipwash stood and he saw that it was one of the Mackenzie's goats that he had seen grazing earlier. The creature was running in a maddened, erratic fashion and occasionally it and its kindred would let out that same cry that had harrowed Shipwash's ears earlier. He thought its eyes looked particularly bright and wondered at this for a moment; then he saw the streaks of blood upon its face and saw that where its eyes had been, there now stood instead a pair of glittering rubies. Shipwash realized in one horrific instant that it had been blinded by jeweled broaches driven like pins into its skull and as this realization came upon him, he felt a wave of sickness rush over him such that he fell upon his knees in the doorway of the barn, hardly able to prevent himself from retching.

"Shipwash!" Crawley hissed behind him. "The whole company has made their escape and are already on their way down the road. You must come along now yourself."

Shipwash could not believe that time had passed so quickly; yet he could not wrench his eyes from what was unfolding before him. He knew that he would forever curse himself for witnessing this night – that future nights would come when he would awake with a sweat-drenched brow and long with all his heart to tear the visions that he was about to see from out of his memory forever. He knew all this and yet as though his own heart had been transfixed by one of the Frenchman's jeweled skewers, he continued to kneel in the doorway of the barn with cheeks newly wetted by tears of horror and pity, while Crawley snorted and turned away himself to follow the rest of the company.

And indeed, this was only the first act. While the tortured beasts blindly raced forward, their burning horns setting the fields and thatched walls of the cottage ablaze, the shadowed figure of the Frenchman followed them with a long branch in his right hand that he employed like a switch in order to drive them on whenever they slackened or veered in the opposite direction. The dead men who served Mistress Mackenzie stepped forward to seize the creatures and prevent them from causing any further damage, but it was a fool's game, for while they busied themselves in attempting to catch the pain-maddened creatures, the fires that had already spread to the main house continued to rage all the more, some even catching upon the living corpses themselves. It was like witnessing a scene from Hell: the groping fingers of the dead, animated men and the screams of the driven beasts. One of the sons ran at the Frenchman with a dagger; the silver fingers of his intended victim's left hand caused one of his cheeks to weep blood as, swift as a shadow, his opponent touched his face and then moved away into the darkness.

He's playing with them, Shipwash thought as he watched with a kind of sickened fascination. The Frenchman still had hold of his musket, but he had not used or even threatened with it once. It was as though he preferred the gradual build of terror that his present technique created to the more efficient method of simply dispatching his enemies. In spite of their cruelty, Shipwash pitied the witch and her sons at that moment: they had thought that they had only to contend with children and defenseless merchants that night. Instead, they were facing an enemy who was their equal, if not their superior, in hellish ingenuity. It was a contest between demons and Shipwash knew with a mingled pride and horror that his own infernal champion, though outnumbered, would be the victor.

But in spite of this belief, he could not simply abandon the Frenchman to the mercies of the witch and her sons while the rest of the company made their escape. The dead men were already rallying and had almost beaten the blazing fires down to smoking ash, though the flames still leapt high enough to prevent any of them to leave off battling them and give chase to the escaping wassailers. In the meantime, the two brothers were circling their antagonist, hoping to overpower him by the sheer force of numbers.

Shipwash could bear the suspense no longer.

"Friend!" he shouted. "Come away – our work here is done!"

For the first time since he had commenced his bloody performance, the Frenchman paused and looked in Shipwash's direction. An expression of delighted surprise crossed his face and he held up a knived finger as though gesturing for the grocer to give him a moment. Then, he at last drew forth his two muskets and shot first the one son and then the other in the knee, effectively disabling them from any further mischief.

Shipwash watched mutely as the Frenchman approached him, while the witch's curses and the crackling flames touched his consciousness only dimly as though he heard them all from a great distance. He saw his companion come closer, eyes alight like blue fires and the distended, claw-like knives upon his left hand glistening with blood but his face remaining otherwise as tranquil and guileless as always. The grocer felt a simultaneous wave of revulsion and gratitude as he looked upon the man whose cruelties had saved them all from becoming the victims of the witch's abattoir.

"You should leave, Monsieur," the Frenchman said softly. "You will be left behind by your companions if you do not."

"And what of you?"

"I still have something to ask of our Madame."

"Then you are not coming with us?"

The Frenchman shook his head with a regretful smile. "From here, I shall continue alone."

"These woods are dangerous to travel oneself."

"And so again I repeat that you should leave now, Monsieur," the Frenchman said with another smile. As he spoke, he began to polish his finger-knives upon a silken kerchief before holding them up to the moonlight in order to study their brilliance.

As Shipwash prepared to leave, he turned one last time and said, "I suppose that I shall never know who you truly are."

"Oh, I would not assume that, Monsieur," the Frenchman said. "Perhaps one day we shall meet again under different, more amenable circumstances. Now, my friend, how would you enjoy that?"

As he spoke, Shipwash thought that he heard the bleating of one of the blinded goats from somewhere close by and felt a chill of dread come over him as he looked at the man who stood before him.

"Farewell," the grocer said at last, falteringly.

The handsome stranger waved him away with a playfully insincere show of impatience before continuing to pick at the clotted spots of crimson that marred the shine of his deadly gauntlet.

***

Alison Mackenzie looked up as the shadow of the stranger fell athwart the body of her groaning sons by whom she knelt. Her full lips curled with contempt as she saw that it was the Frenchman, though the terror that she felt was evident in the trembling of her fingers as they tightened on the hilt of her dagger. Her hold instantly relaxed, however, when she felt the cold metal of a musket pressed against the side of her head. He then put his own fingers, now clothed in leather gloves, beneath her chin so that she was constrained to lift her face towards him and meet his eyes.

"What more do you wish?" she demanded. "Get you hence or I shall have my dead slaves tear you asunder."

"I think not, Madame," the Frenchman replied evenly. "For if they so much as approach me, I shall put the light of your pretty eyes out forever with these." Here he traced a caress down her throat and across her lips with his knife-gauntleted fingers.

"What do you want?" she asked at last.

"I wish you to answer a question and to keep this exchange a secret between us, sweet lady. Will you do this for me?"

He then knelt beside her and, after drawing her close with his hand still firmly about her throat, he whispered his question in her ear.

"I know of whom you speak," she whispered. "My two sons saw a young traveller answering to your description several days ago. He was upon the road passing through the moors and leading to Houndswick – a day's journey will bring you there. But," her eyes gleamed. "He is there no longer. He has taken refuge in a place of walled darkness."

She pointed in the direction of the Priory.

In an instant, he released her and with a gallant bow said, "Thank you, Madame, for your assistance. If you and your charming sons," he nodded in the direction of the two fallen young men, "had murdered my quarry, I should have had the delightful duty of dispatching the three of you myself. As it is, if I learn that you have lied to me, I shall return here, I promise you."

He threw a purse at the witch's feet before turning upon his heel and pursuing his way in the direction that she had indicated.

"What is this for?" she hissed.

"It is my experience that cripples make rather ineffectual bandits – and, as I have been negligent in my alms-giving, I only thought that I would leave your two young beggar-sons with their first offering of charity to encourage them at the start of their new and illustrious career. A very good night to you, Madame."

To his surprise, the young witch laughed at this and said, "A good night to you, pretty lad, and a good hunting as well. If you ever fall under my power again, I shan't make the same mistake that I did this night."

The Frenchman turned as if to reply, but the woman, her wounded sons, and even the smoldering ruins of the cottage and the bleating goats had all vanished entirely, leaving behind only a desolate, shrubless meadow. It was as though, having performed their service to darkness, the forest and the night had swallowed them utterly until the advent of tomorrow's twilight.

Chapter Twenty-Two: In which Cyrus discovers the Priory's library, Childermass continues to pursue the object of his elusive game, and death visits the Priory.

The morning following these fateful events was as sublimely tranquil as the evening before it had been violent and tempestuous. When Cyrus awoke, the sun had only just risen above the horizon, transforming the pale sky into a mixed palette of gold and roseate color. Its rich light filled the chamber in which he slept and crept into the edges of his dreams as well so that they were filled with a light, joyous anticipation rather than the darkness that had filled his visions of yesternight. He threw the coverlets aside and after dressing and combing his hair into some semblance of tidiness with the aid of the looking glass on the mantelpiece, he departed from his chamber.

He met Feversham in the great hall; the ostler bowed and enquired whether he would like to have his breakfast served early.

"No thank you, sir," Cyrus replied. "I was in fact wondering whether you could tell me where I could find Master Childermass?"

"Oh, I can take you to him, young man," Feversham replied. "I was on my way to see him myself."

"I know this is a very early hour yet."

"Fear not, Master Plainstaff – he will be awake, I assure you."

Cyrus followed the aged servant out of the spacious quietude of the great hall and down into the servant's passages, the steep and choked stairways that led into the lower levels of the Priory that the young man had never beheld since his arrival. Even in comparison to the stately decrepitude of the Priory's upper floors, these corridors and cobbled inclines seemed to be made up as much of cobwebs as they were of cold stone. There were far fewer windows on these floors as well and even with the arrival of dawn, Feversham was still obliged to hold a candle above his head in order to keep from stumbling over the uneven stairs and scuttling creatures that darted into the shadows at their approach. There were no hearths to warm these hallways and Cyrus found himself shivering slightly as they continued on their way. It was easy to imagine that time had reversed and night had resumed its reign in this dank and silent world beneath the Priory.

Finally, Feversham paused before a certain door and after turning a key in its lock, opened it to reveal a cramped closet of a room furnished only with a cot and lit by the flame of a single cresset attached to the wall. Cyrus recognized the broad, hulking Master of the Kennels, Dagworth, standing by the bed and speaking to Childermass who lay with his wrists and feet shackled to the bedposts.

"Why – " Cyrus began, but was interrupted by an explosive laugh from Dagworth. He had apparently been thoroughly amused by some remark that Childermass had made, for he took no notice of the Puritan lad as he replied:

"Oh yes, you would know all about that wouldn't you, you devil?"

Feversham was fumbling in his pockets for the keys to the chimney sweeper's shackles as Dagworth continued:

"There's an ugly little whelp in the kennels who reminds me of you. His only talent is in bedeviling me. Even a good thrashing can't seem to cure him of his nasty little habits." Several heated drops of wax from the candle that Dagworth held fell upon Childermass's hand and Cyrus heard the chimney sweeper give a barely suppressed gasp of pain.

"Oh, did that sting a mite?" Dagworth enquired. "Well, as I was saying, I don't know what should be done with the little cur but I was thinking that perhaps on this coming Feast of the Holy Innocents, I shall take my knife to one of his eyes and see if I can't make the resemblance between the two of you all the more complete. What do you say to that, Master Chimney?"

Childermass kept his own single eye agonizingly fixed upon the candle held above him as he replied, "An excellent conceit and while you're at it, why don't you take off his ears as well? Then he will look just as lovely as you would were the hangman to have his way with you."

Dagworth's lips twisted with hatred at this and he inclined his candle again, allowing the white drops of tallow to fall again upon the chimney sweeper's flesh. Childermass bit his lower lip so deeply that blood spotted the corner of his mouth, but remained unmoved.

Cyrus, however, did not remain so stoic.

"In God's name," he cried, his voice low with horror as he snatched the candle out of Dagworth's hand. "Leave him alone! What mean these chains? What has he done to deserve this torment? Well?"

Both Childermass and Dagworth stared at the young man with nearly comedic expressions of astonishment: Childermass with a look of both relief and confusion (for indeed, no one had ever before interrupted the cruel interludes that so frequently occurred between him and the Master of the Kennels) and Dagworth with a face crimsoning with rage and a rare feeling of shame at having his viciousness so bluntly recognized and named.

"Now see what you've done, Master Dagworth?" Feversham said wearily, at last finding the key that he had been seeking all this while. "You've shocked Master Plainstaff with your brutal games. Why don't you return to the great hall and make yourself useful by preparing the table for breakfast?"

Dagworth withdrew from the chamber, but not before casting a look at Cyrus that made the young man inwardly quail, though he did his best to maintain his former look of indignation. Childermass in the meantime was sitting upon the edge of his bed, chafing life back into his wrists.

"Breakfast will be ready in a half an hour, Master Plainstaff," Feversham said with a bow before departing.

Once the Master of Horses had left, Childermass cast an inquisitive eye upwards at the young man who stood before him.

"I was not expecting to see you up so early, sir," he said. "What can have brought you to this out of the way place, I wonder? I did not forget to light your hearth last night or some other such foolishness, did I?"

"Oh no, not at all!" Cyrus replied hastily. "I only wanted you to show me the Priory's library."

Childermass gave a humorless laugh. "Ah, yes."

"But first I want to know why you were chained to your bed and why Dagworth was treating you like that."

"It is Sir Robert's express wish that I be shackled to my bed every night and has been for the last year," the chimney sweeper replied. "And as for Dagworth, 'tis a riddle simply solved for he hates me and I him."

"He seems a brute," Cyrus said.

Childermass did not reply, busying himself now with buttoning up his loose white shirt and attiring himself in the sooty black coat and tall, dirtied boots that he always wore.

"I should have done the same to him were I in his position," he said at last. "Our hatred is mutual."

"I cannot believe it of you," Cyrus said.

"You do not even know me," the chimney sweeper said with a perplexed look that held in it a great deal of amusement as well. "Or are you a reader of hearts as well as of books, Master Plainstaff?"

Cyrus recalled the terrible nightmare that he had suffered – his vision of the Marquis St. Aubert and Childermass, with the latter's hideous fate still lingering freshly in his memory. Though Cyrus knew of the illogical nature of such visions, he could not fully dispel the disquiet that now haunted him at the thought of it. He averted his gaze from that of the chimney sweeper, embarrassed now into silence.

"I am sorry," Childermass said, and his voice contained a genuine note of apology in it. "I jested poorly. I should have said that it is very kind of you to think so well of me."

Cyrus met the chimney sweeper's pale eye and now found a look of surprise and even concern in its customarily cold depths.

"I take my breakfast much earlier than the family," Childermass continued. "As you're up so early, would you perhaps like to join me, sir?"

Cyrus was not acquainted with the chimney sweeper's usual custom of dining alone; else he would have been struck speechless by this unwonted invitation. As it was, he stammered, "Certainly – I would like that very much."

Childermass smiled at the lad's embarrassment and, catching up his long, dusty broom, led the way out of the darkness of the servants' quarters and into the sunshine of the scullery beyond.

***

The poached eggs and slices of white bread that piled Cyrus's plate smelled inviting, but he found his eye constantly straying to the window that looked out upon the moors and forests that surrounded the Priory. He wondered if perhaps he would have the chance to explore the grounds as he had hoped to do yesterday and turned to Childermass in order to ask him what he thought of such a plan.

The chimney sweeper was in the midst of carefully pouring heaping spoonfuls of sugar over four slices of toast, already glazed with a thick layering of strawberry preserves, before topping these with generous helpings of cream. These daubs of cream he likewise christened with sugar before finally committing one of these carefully constructed offerings to his mouth. Following the slow and methodical mastication of one of these slices, he cleared his throat with a full glass of strong ale, the smell of which caused

Cyrus's eyes to water uncontrollably. Bizarre as it was, the whole process had about it a ritualistic quality that was absolutely mesmerizing.

"You were about to say something, sir?" Childermass enquired before beginning to devour a second portion.

Cyrus blinked and reclaimed his former thoughts. "Oh, yes – I was just going to say that it seems perfect weather for a walk in the forest."

The chimney sweeper's pale eye turned towards the scullery window and flickered, as though cowed by the naked brilliance of the sunlight.

"A walk in the forest," he said. "Do you like to do that often? The forests in this land have their peculiar perils, or did you not know?"

The question was childishly simple, but Cyrus realized that he had no real answer for it. After all, he had only just set foot in Scotland for the first time in his life several days ago; how was he to know whether he enjoyed strolling its forests and moors for the pleasure of it or not? Withing, in his careless fashion, had neglected to enquire after his guest's history; now for the first time since Montrose's own interrogation in Houndswick, Cyrus found himself confronted with the need to give some sort of explanation for his presence. Finding himself unprepared, he hesitated before Childermass's expression of innocent curiosity as though confronted with a riddle.

"Are your eggs too well done, sir?" Childermass asked abruptly after swallowing his second slice of toast and taking up a third. "You've hardly touched them."

Cyrus began to poke at his food, trying a bit too obviously to show an interest in it. Finally he said, "To tell you the truth, Childermass, I hail from Essex and have never seen these forests before my coming here."

Childermass was more startled by this frank admission than he would have been by a bald-faced lie. He continued with his breakfast but listened intently as the young man continued:

"My father died a month ago and so I decided to come here to find some employment."

"But why to Scotland, sir? What work could you possibly hope to find here?"

"I have some relatives in the north," Cyrus said, averting his eyes. It was a poor lie, but what else could he say? He could not confess himself a poor farmer's son on the run from a vengeful English lord and a bloodthirsty French aristocrat-turned-assassin. He was among the peers of his persecutors – and though he found himself warming more and more to the society of those in the Priory, very much against his better judgment, he could not be certain that were his true identity to be made known, he would not be cast out. He had seen the broken statues in the great hall and knew of Scotland's allegiance to Charles Stuart, the defeated former King of England and father of the current king, whom Oliver Cromwell and the rebellious Parliament had executed. How could he, Cyrus Colkins, the Puritan son of a former soldier in Cromwell's army, expect to find a permanent refuge in a place that must have been partially ruined by the invading forces of Parliament and was now inhabited by those very aristocrats who had most abhorred the enemies of Charles? The best outcome would result in his being turned out of the Priory; the worst would be his arrest which, he was certain, would lead him into the waiting hands of the implacable Marquis St. Aubert. Better, then, to remain as Cyrus Plainstaff and forget his past as much as possible than to reveal his true identity and make himself homeless and vulnerable once again to the unknown but awful fate that had befallen his father.

"St. Aubert," Childermass almost whispered.

Cyrus started and felt a sudden eerie sensation creep over him at the sound of this name. "What did you say?" he asked falteringly.

The chimney sweeper glanced at him with a carefully fashioned look of perplexity, as though he had been shaken out of some inward reverie. "Forgive me, sir," he said. "I was thinking aloud. There is an encyclopedia of saints in the library, but the volumes are all out of order and I believe the second book of H's with St. Hubert's name on the spine is missing."

There was no such volume in the Gosselin library, but Cyrus's start of terror at the sound of that very name had been enough to entertain the cruel and subtle sport that most amused Childermass. In spite of his delight, however, the chimney sweeper's features remained as pale and unmoving as marble; the only sign of his soul's response came from the unconscious wetting of his lips with the tip of his tongue and the peculiar tremor that began to course its way through his long, white fingers.

Cyrus gave a convulsive shudder himself, attempting to expel the vague shadow of unease that seemed to fall over him whenever he was in the company of the chimney sweeper, though he had not quite discerned why this was always so. There was something strangely familiar about Childermass, something that made him feel as though he had met a presence like this before; but he couldn't for the life of him remember when or where. It was like a childhood fear, a nightmare experienced in the cradle, blotted and obscured by the passage of time and the memory of fresher visions, but always remaining beneath the lake of one's consciousness, waiting to surface again. He felt as if only one more element was needed to show itself and then the mystery would be solved.

He shook his head; it was impossible. He had never met anyone like the gaunt young chimney sweeper before in his life and this impression was only the result of badly jangled nerves. But he had lost his appetite and was ready to leave the scullery before these morbid imaginings returned to take up residence in his mind once again.

Childermass sensed the young man's change in mood and rose as well.

"The library now, Master Plainstaff?"

"Yes," Cyrus said heavily and the two of them departed, leaving the scullery to the nosing of rats.

***

The library had appeared imposing by candlelight the evening before; as Cyrus stepped into it for the second time, with the half-concealed glow of sunlight spilling in through the crimson glass of the window, it seemed nearly as spacious as the great hall itself. A long oaken table, its length clothed with a cloth of velvet dyed a rich columbine blue, stood in the center of the chamber. High shelves of oak stood against the walls and each shelf was filled with books, the loose leaves of manuscripts, and drifts of dust: an embarrassment of the forgotten songs, ravings, and visions of poets and theologians. Cyrus's mouth watered as he took them all in with his eyes.

"What would suit your taste?" asked Childermass.

Cyrus disregarded the question, instead pointing to several iron trapdoors that were situated at intervals betwixt the shelves and tables of the library.

"What are those?" he asked.

Childermass traced the outline of one such door with the pointed tip of his narrow, soot-smeared shoe.

"Doors," he murmured. "Passages that lead to other, deeper chambers of the Priory."

"What sorts of chambers could be hidden beneath the library?" Cyrus asked. He could not help but feel a thrill of amazement at the sheer breadth of the place: he recalled his first glimpse of the Priory (it seemed as though it had been ages ago) and knew that it had seemed a vast edifice from the outside, but he had never imagined that its walls held so much. It was as though, in spite of the time he had spent as a guest of the Gosselins, he had only scratched the surface of what their residence contained.

"Faith, sir, I know not," Childermass said, his quick, pale eye moving towards his questioner. The next moment, however, he rushed to the young man's side as Cyrus, suddenly overcome by a feeling of faintness, fell to his knees, clutching at the edge of a nearby table for support.

"What is wrong?" he asked, bewildered by the sudden pallor in Cyrus's cheeks and lips. "Shall I fetch you some water?"

Cyrus did not hear a word that the chimney sweeper uttered. Before his eyes, a recurrence of the vision that he had suffered the night before last swept over him, and again he heard the words that Childermass in his dream had spoken in that chamber, past the red hangings, the whispering voices, and the cries. Indeed, as his eyes flickered open and he found himself supported in the chimney sweeper's grasp, he thought that Childermass's moving lips mouthed once more those words:

"Faith, not I – I know nothing of this Priory that I would willingly tell any soul."

Gasping for breath, Cyrus recoiled from Childermass, trembling from head to toe with a terror that even he could not put a name to, whilst the chimney sweeper – now grown paler even than he – stared at him with a look of commingled contempt and horror. He started towards Cyrus, but the young man backed away from him as though his outstretched hand were the head of an adder.

"Have I offended you somehow?" asked Childermass. His voice – by custom, soft – was now harsh and unsteady.

"I must be alone," Cyrus managed. Without even a glance in the direction of the chimney sweeper, he reached the door of the library and had soon departed, leaving Childermass to himself.

For a long while, Childermass stood motionless in that shadowed place, gazing with an unseeing eye upon the rumpled cloths that decorated the tables and chairs of that chamber and watching the dancing motes that floated before the crimson glass of the windows like a thousand glowing embers. At last, he sat down in a chair that stood before the hearth, digging in his coat for a velvet-bound book of chivalric legends that he carried with him always. For a long while, he gazed upon it without opening it, his living eye as glassy and remote as his marble one. Then, at last, he opened it, the worn leaves of the book spreading open beneath his gaze like a fan, revealing at turns a printed page or the gilded scene of a roseate bower and an enchanter's tower.

He could not lose himself even in the world of his book, however; the repulsion that he had seen upon Cyrus's visage was still too fresh in his memory, and his wounded soul still smarted from the unspoken terror that the young man's eyes had held. What vision, Childermass wondered with a quiet welling of hatred within his heart, what thing in him could so have frightened this Master Plainstaff that he had shown such a response? Was it, the chimney sweeper speculated, something to do with his visage – some grotesquerie therein that Cyrus had only spied at that very moment? The chimney sweeper lifted a hand to his face as though he thought to feel for the offending disfigurement that could awaken such horror. That pale, statuesque visage held nothing to revolt the senses, however; even the marble eye in his right socket seemed too much a natural, though arresting, part of his peculiar appearance to startle. At last, he let his hand fall to his breast while a single tear stole its way down the lean flesh of his cheek.

As though some part of his being remained cold and untouched by his own grief, however, he began to work his fingers methodically in his pocket until they caught around the loop of the key ring that he always carried on his person. Catching hold of one small, slender key, he knelt before one of the library trapdoors. Without a moment's hesitation, he fitted it within the notch at its center, gave the key a sharp turn, and pulled it open. For a moment he paused, recalling Cyrus's last question.

"Oh, no, Master Plainstaff," he murmured to himself with a curiously contemptuous twist of his pale lips. "I haven't an inkling what lies beneath this library or whither these doors could lead. How could I?"

And with these words, he crept into the world beneath the trapdoor, pulling its iron bulk softly shut above his head.

***

Cyrus made his way back into the cool quiet of his chamber, his head still throbbing as though he had suffered some blow. Once he had collapsed upon his bed, he closed his eyes and attempted to clear his mind of the memory of what had just happened, but the words and the scenes spoken and seen in his nightmare continued to pass through his mind, matching in violence his own desperate attempts to quell them.

A young man as anxious as our hero, however, could not have endured the vicissitudes of life without having developed some sort of method for dealing with his travails. In Cyrus's case, talking aloud to himself was a close cousin to the main cure, which required that he dissect every attribute of whatever it was that had caused him to feel terror in the first place until, by the very banality caused by his familiarity with it, it had ceased to cause him any sort of disquiet.

"I'm only having another of my usual nightmares," he thus murmured aloud to the empty chamber. "True, I appear to be having them now when awake as well as when asleep, but this can easily be accounted for by all that has happened this last month, can't it? Anyone under my circumstances would suffer from nerves, I expect." He took a deep breath, already feeling his racing heart beginning to slow. "It's quite obvious why I should be having dreams about the Marquis St. Aubert." His skin crawled, even though he had dropped his voice to a whisper as he uttered the name. "But Childermass?"

He again felt a chill, but the sensation was markedly different from that provoked by the thought of the Marquis, if only in one respect alone: for while St. Aubert was forever to be associated not only with a sense of horror but also with the grief of a parent's loss, the horror that he attached to Childermass's person was less easily definable. Indeed, Cyrus could not be certain that what he felt existed outside of his own imagination. It was true nonetheless that while St. Aubert, had he not freely admitted himself to be a man of cruel and peculiar tastes, might have remained a charming acquaintance, the same could not be said of Childermass who was, in Cyrus's eyes, tainted with an atmosphere of dread that followed him regardless of whatever deeds he may or may not have committed. It was an atmosphere as natural to him as the movement of the wind amongst the chamber curtains or the night call of an unseen bird. The nightmare that he had experienced must, Cyrus reasoned, have only been a natural manifestation of the state of mind that this dread induced.

Reassured by this rational explanation for the vision that he had seen in the library, Cyrus arose from bed and knelt by its side, intending to pray before heading downstairs to find Withing. His Puritan father had patiently taught him a number of the psalms in metrical form, renouncing the hymns of the Church of England as any hot-headed Dissenter should; but as these psalms had no fixed melody to accompany them, the elder Colkins had resorted to singing them to the tune of whatever street song happened to have lingered in his memory from his day spent in the market. Cyrus, having acquired this rather haphazard habit himself, began to sing one of the rough stanzas from his Psalter to the first melody that arose in his head:

"O Lord, how many are my foes?
How many now against me stand?
Some say, O Soul, there is no help,
From God for thee at any hand."

The stanza had been arranged by translators more concerned with its spiritual, rather than poetic, value and Cyrus's voice was hardly the gift of an angel – but the beauty of the melody coupled with the strength of feeling in the young man's voice, gave it an arresting quality that, unbeknownst to Cyrus, caught the attention of someone in the outer corridor who paused to listen as he continued, oblivious of his audience:

"But thou, Lord, art my shield, my glory,
And the uplifter of my head;
With voice to God I call'd, who from
His holy hill me answered."

He hesitated for a moment, wondering himself from whence the song that came so readily from his lips emerged. Had he learnt it from his father and somehow forgotten? His eyes stung with tears at the thought of having neglected to remember even such a trifling thing as the day that his father had taught him such a melody. And yet…and yet the tune that teased and floated within his brain and flowed so easily from his untrained tongue did not hold the customary cadence of an English ballad. It would fly aloft into the highest reaches that the human voice could reach only to fall with a soft flourish as though to turn the triumph of its ascent into a bittersweet tragedy. In the morning light that fell past the curtains, it seemed to Cyrus the most joyous thing that he had ever heard; but he could easily imagine that in the space betwixt midnight and morning, it could have seemed as melancholic as it now seemed merry. And as he realized this, he suddenly recalled where he had heard the melody first: it had been upon that night in which he had suffered from visions and Childermass had come to lull him back to sleep with music. It had been from the chimney sweeper and from him alone that Cyrus had learnt what it was that he now sang.

While Cyrus was contemplating his newfound hymn and its unlikely source, his unknown audience – who had been standing quietly by the door – wondered at what had caused the young man to stop so abruptly in the midst of his singing. Several times a slender hand hovered above the brass doorknob and the muscles in the fingers tensed, the heart behind them willing them to open the door. Just as they seemed at last to gather the courage to do so, however, they dropped abruptly and Mariah Gosselin, with a sinking and bashful heart, quietly withdrew from the door that she had approached before the singer had the chance to discover her presence and learn its meaning.

***

But let us take our leave for a moment of the Priory's principle inhabitants: the Puritan praying within his chamber, the golden-haired daughter of the Gosselins who lies within her own room wishing that she had not lost her courage outside the stranger's door, the dark-haired niece of the chaplain who sits in the morning sun of the garden lost within the world of her own reveries, and the chimney sweeper who has betaken himself to a lower place whither we shall not follow until another time. To their solitary hopes and fears we shall return soon enough, but more builds within the walls of the Priory than these private, simmering apprehensions.

For a celebration is anticipated. Christmas and the Feast of the Innocents approach and the few servants of the household are busying themselves with preparations for these two holy days. The kitchens are hot and swarming with a thousand activities performed by those menials who are rarely glimpsed in the other portions of the Priory, but whose handiwork – whether it be a roasted hog dressed in spices or a quivering dish of pudding – appears as though wrought by invisible hands upon the table of the Great Hall. It is the duty of those three servants who are allowed a freer access to the Priory's other wings, floors, and corridors – the Master of Horses, the Master of Hounds, and the Master of the Chimneys – to see to the adorning of the Priory's outer appearance. But Childermass cannot be found and so for the nonce it lies in the hands of Feversham and Dagworth alone to make of those cobwebbed walls and dusty hangings a place fit for festive celebration.

Feversham gazes long and critically at the time-stained statues and the ancient tapestries in the Great Hall, his long face redolent of more than his customary sobriety and his brow wrinkled as he attempts to view them with the eyes of a guest. It is a vain exercise. He can only see them as he himself has always perceived their presence, as an inseparable part of the Priory. He knows that he must do his best to polish and obliterate the dust and antiquity, but he cannot bring himself to rid the Priory of any of her unspeaking denizens, for they seem to him as much a part of the fabric of the place as its living occupants. Instead, he spends the morning in polishing the limbs of the decapitated saints and dusting the frayed edges of the tapestries, as the morning sunlight marks the hours in its golden progress across the far western side of the Great Hall.

Dagworth holds a dirtied rag in one hand, a vial of bergamot oil in the other, going from chamber to chamber and liberally polishing the ornaments therein before returning to the corridor from which he departed, leaving behind him the overpowering atmosphere of his favorite scent. In many of these windowless hallways and closets, it is easy to forget the brightness of the day, but the cool darkness of these enclosed worlds does not affect the Master of the Hounds. He wishes rather sourly for someone's company, but more for the sake of conversation than for any fear of his grim surroundings. If his loathed nemesis Childermass were here, the two could have shared a delightfully vicious interlude by filling each others' ears and the echoing chambers with their own poison. As it is, Dagworth curses Childermass for his unprecedented absence and occupies his time instead by rehearsing what he will do to punish the chimney sweeper for his unlawful absence.

It is close to high noon now and the shadows are at their sparsest in the Priory's few sunlit halls and chambers. A young boy wanders between the sunbeams and the dark spaces that lie between them, but casts no shadow himself between the face of the sun and the stone floors upon which his feet fall. It is as though he is not even there, passing by Feversham and Dagworth, even seeking to catch their attention with a plaintive word or a gesture, but remaining invisible to their eyes. At last he wearies of his fruitless attempts and settles himself upon the straw floor of the Great Hall, curled into a huddled mass of invisible rags and floating mist. He is a stranger here, but even if his friends who know him as Nat could see him in his present state, they would perceive too closely the change that has come over him and perhaps blanch to behold him. The child's breast is dark with blood, his face deathly pale, his lips bloodless: he is a sight that would rivet any who could see, but none here are able.

He has wandered far through the woods to reach this place of strangers – but though he has at last found a refuge, he cannot make himself heard or seen by those from whom he wishes help. His hand reaches out to touch the passing Feversham as the Master of Horses shuffles back and forth, observing his own finishing touches to a statue that he has been polishing with especially meticulous detail; but the man merely shrugs his shoulder as though the light touch of a moth has brushed him by, before continuing to pace as before. The child, now tearful, calls out to him, pleading for him to hear, to see. His intended listener does not even pause in his stride and Nat falls back upon the straw again, wondering what it is that has happened to him and not daring to consider the awful thought that rises in his heart all the same.

The Priory remains aloof, humming with the distant sound of kitchen-work and the occasional, hoarse cough of a hawk huddled somewhere in the sanctuary of the rafters. Hours pass, marked only by the movement of a spider as it journeys along its gossamer thread from one perilous corner of the Great Hall's ceiling to another. Outside the low, glass-paned windows, two dark figures occasionally pass. Withing and Cyrus are exploring the grounds of the Priory, the circle of withered flowers that make up the gardens of that place and stand in such stark contrast to the grey, tall grasses of the moors. For Cyrus, the sunlight of the outer world has dispelled whatever vision of baleful warning it was that he perceived within the Priory and even the sinister aura of the chimney sweeper seems garishly ludicrous amidst the frost and soft sunlight of the gardens. He feels only wonder and awe as he gazes upon the ancient walls of the Priory and the tangled grounds, finding a new revelation of color and darkness in every flower and shadowed brier unveiled with each passing step.

Feversham has polished the last statue to perfection and pauses at last in his labors, gazing out the window at Cyrus and Withing and wondering whether it will rain that evening, for there is a hint of shadow upon the horizon, only barely touching the farflung summits of the outlying mountains. He is distracted by the sound of Dagworth who now enters the Great Hall, rubbing his greasy hands upon his now thoroughly loathsome-looking rag and announcing that he has finished his own duty to the house. He slumps at the table just as Childermass enters, broom over shoulder, from the opposite end of that vast chamber.

"Where have you been, Master Chimney?" he asks with a sneer. "You know how particular Sir Robert is of the Priory's appearance before feast days and if those hearths still stink of old soot, it will be you alone who is to blame for it."

"Ah, but I have already finished scrubbing each and every one of them, Master Cur," Childermass replies with a more than usually theatrical bow. His pale hands, streaked with coal, are proof of the truth of this statement. He sits upon the edge of the table directly before Dagworth, feet resting upon the seat of a chair, the cold tranquility of his smile as much an unspoken insult as Dagworth's contemptuous leer.

But Feversham approaches with a look of weary reproof, setting a tankard of ale on the table and seating himself in a chair betwixt the two, placing a cup in front of all three and pouring himself a modest draught. His two companions follow suit, all three sharing the heady mixture without a single word passing between them, enjoying that silence that can only occur between the most comfortable of companions, while the afternoon's sun begins to turn towards twilight.

***

Just as Cyrus and Withing reached the front door of the Priory and were about to reenter the warmth of its interior, the sound of approaching horses drew their attention back to the pathway upon which they had been wandering. They saw then the coach of Squire Toby Wadham, pursued closely by Lord Andrew Ebenezer Montrose, mounted himself upon the back of a coal-black steed. As Cyrus and Withing neared, Squire Toby emerged from the left door of his carriage exactly in conjunction with His Lordship's dismounting, the two approaching each other with a synchronicity that even a pair of professional performers might have had trouble duplicating. The expressions that showed upon their countenances, however, belied this more than passing resemblance to a stage act.

"Well, as you have seen, my dear Squire," Montrose said in his usual smooth and mannered way, only superficially concealing the fury that simmered behind his words. "As you have seen, my horse neatly outpaced your carriage. If, indeed, your fine Arabian horses cost as much as you boasted several nights ago, then I am afraid that you sorely wasted the pittance that you won from me!"

"Were it not for the respect that I held for your father, long may he rest in peace, then I would call you a liar, Your Lordship," Squire Toby returned, his temper flaming his rouge-tinted cheeks to an unnatural shade of scarlet that neither Nature nor man's art alone could ever have hoped to produce. "However, I shall merely presume that your sight is somewhat impaired and earnestly beseech you to procure for yourself a pair of spectacles from Dr. Erskine as soon as may be in order to spare yourself future embarrassments."

However, Montrose's eye was already darting towards the Priory, in the hope of spying some impartial witness to their arrival whom he could conscript immediately to his side. Instantly, fatefully, his gaze fell upon the miserable Cyrus. Without a moment's hesitation, the Earl's long-legged stride brought him to the young man's side and he instantly seized Cyrus by the arm in a grasp that, for all its seeming friendliness, pinched like a vice, as he pulled his unfortunate recruit before the Squire.

"Now, Master Plainstaff," he said with a smile. "Tell this gentleman what it is that you saw and which of us arrived first at the doorstep of this Priory."

"I cannot say for sure, sir," Cyrus replied, doing his best to assume a diplomatic air. "But it seemed as though you and the Squire arrived almost in unison."

"Nonsense!" both Squire Toby and Lord Montrose declared in perfect chorus. Then the euphony of their voices divided into two separate streams of reproach: the Squire on the one hand saying, "Why in God's name are you taking up for him?" and Lord Montrose on the other whispering viciously, "Are you attempting to undermine me again, you whelp?" Fortunately for Cyrus's peace of mind, their overlapping voices made it impossible for him to distinguish even one word of their complaints. And, at that moment, Feversham, Childermass, and Dagworth appeared as three welcome distractions to a situation that Cyrus did not know how to handle and Withing did not seem to care to.

"I feel as though something is still terribly amiss in the Priory," Feversham was muttering to his two comrades, the customarily weary baritone of his voice now tinted with an uncharacteristic note of apprehension. "Once the holy days arrive, I am certain that there will be some hanging that Sir Robert shall object to, some choice of floral arrangement that will offend him. We have done quite a lot already to the place this day, but I fear me that it is still not enough. And what with Christmas approaching and after it the Feast of the Innocents…"

"We've done all that a body can, Master Feversham," Dagworth said, his gruff voice little used to providing comfort to any save the curs that housed the Gosselin kennels. "If His Lordship is still displeased, why, certain it is that Master Chimney here is to blame and will take the punishment that is justly his. Isn't that so, my obliging young devil?"

Childermass was not even listening to the man's ruthless prattle. His eye was fixed upon Cyrus with an expression that was void of reproach, void of hatred, void of grief – void even of that cold fire of curiosity that so often charged his glance. Instead, it possessed the look that a telescope or a spyglass might have had, were its metal made sentient: a thing purposed for a single thing, the act of mere looking, without sentiment or even revulsion. Cyrus felt his soul grow cold beneath that desolate eye, yet he could not wrench his own gaze away from its motionless pallor. A bullet might have passed through his heart – he still would have remained standing, his own eye held to that awful, gleaming emptiness by a magnetic horror that could only be revoked by the withdrawal of that other eye. Indeed, only when Childermass himself at last glanced away did Cyrus realize by the force of his own expelled, caged breath that he had ceased to breathe the whole time.

The import of that moment, however, still remained horribly fresh within his memory. He had somehow made an enemy of the chimney sweeper with the incident in the library. If he did not somehow regain his good will, Cyrus knew that he could count on this Childermass's hatred – however deeply it ran – to remain unwavering for the entirety of his stay at the Priory. Inwardly, he chided himself for his inexplicable terror in the library that morning and resolved to somehow make amends to Childermass. This thought comforted him somewhat and exorcised much of the fear that had welled in him the moment before. After all, he was certain that Childermass would understand him once he had described the visions that he had so lately suffered – and if, even then, Childermass continued to hold a grudge against him, what had Cyrus to fear? It was not as though the chimney sweeper could deal him any real harm – why, Childermass hardly knew Cyrus as a guest, let alone as a man seeking refuge from a fearful fate. Where then was the harm?

Childermass followed Cyrus with his eye as the young man left the outer gardens with Withing, Squire Toby, and Montrose into the great hall of the Priory. The traces of a smile played like an afterthought about the corners of his lips. The silent dispatch had been sent and received; he knew it by the pall that had fallen over Cyrus when their gazes had met. Now it was time to let events run as they would.

While Childermass stood there, deep in thought, Dagworth set a hand upon the young man's shoulder, about to make another of his cruel sallies. This was no evening for humour, however – not even Dagworth's brand of levity. Quick as a deadly trap startled by some blundering beast, the chimney sweeper had his knife out and had drawn its edge swiftly across the back of the man's hand, leaving a lurid streak of crimson in its wake. A low sound, like the growl of a whipped dog, erupted from deep within Dagworth's throat, but he made no move to restrain his attacker who was breathing heavily and gazing with a ghastly fixity upon him, the dripping knife still clenched in his hand as though waiting to gut at the first sign of a retaliation.

"You mad little wretch," Dagworth said at last, withdrawing a few steps. "You disgusting, contemptible whoreson. The Devil take you – if he'll have you – but I'll be revenged on you for that little insult myself before this week is out."

Childermass laughed in reply and Feversham stepped away from the gardens and in the direction of the Priory's door, as though to avoid the sound of it. Dagworth stood his ground, but his lip twitched almost imperceptibly and his hand convulsed about the hilt of his dagger. Then, abruptly, the chimney sweeper's mirth died away and his lips resumed their usual bloodless repose.

"You're rather tall and burly for a milkmaid, aren't you?" Childermass enquired.

"What are you saying, devil?" Dagworth said, his voice trembling.

"In faith, I wouldn't know you for one," the chimney sweeper replied, keeping his cruelty slow and deliberate whilst his mode of speech became oppressively close and familiar. "Were it not for your manner of speech and action. I forget that it is your way to tease a man and provoke him with trifling torments in the manner of a girl but that at the first sight of blood, that delicate heart of yours revolts. Forgive me for mistaking you for something manlier than what you are. God's blood, I think that not even a maid would shake as you do now."

This time, not even the knife could prevent Dagworth's reaction. Before Childermass could recoil, the Master of Hounds had brought his fist into the chimney sweeper's face with all the force that his pent-up fury and muscled arm could afford.

Childermass staggered back, his countenance frozen from the shock of pain that the blow had delivered. Then, his nose and lip were welling with blood, appearing all the more ghastly in contrast to the pallor of his flesh. Dizzied and panting, he gazed steadily upon Dagworth with his one good eye, blood instead of words trickling now from between his lips. Though now the sufferer rather than the inflictor of pain, the sight of his blind marble eye mingled with the blood that now ran down his face, lent him a ghastly quality that even his boorish oppressor did not possess.

Still not satisfied, Dagworth moved closer, prepared to deal another, still worse blow to his enemy. So absorbed was he in his desire to humiliate the chimney sweeper that he did not notice Childermass stiffen with surprise, nor see Feversham suddenly draw himself up to attention and gaze in the direction of the forested valley below the Priory. Only when he heard the faint sound of music at his back did he loosen his grip on the chimney sweeper's collar and turn to see what had caught the attention of his two companions.

At first, it looked to his bewildered eyes as though the stars were forsaking the heavens for the moors, for from a nearby hilltop (the summit of which only barely touched the evening sky) to the valley below, he perceived an unbroken train of golden lights. Then the spell was broken as, by their flickering light, he distinguished the faces of men as well as the several shapeless white bundles that they bore. They were travelling slowly but inexorably upwards in the direction of the Priory itself and, in spite of their sluggish progress, it was clear that it would only be a matter of minutes before they approached the gates. As they neared, the singing of the men grew more audible, though it never seemed to rise above a subdued murmur, no louder than the faint breeze that stirred the utmost branches of the silent oaks.

"Wassailers?" Dagworth murmured.

"It would seem so," Feversham said softly, his eyes following the approaching train of men. "But it is no carol that they sing."

“Nay,” said Childermass, wiping some of the blood from his face with the back of his hand. “But it is a familiar tune nonetheless. See their burdens?”

Feversham saw the bloodied rags carried upon the shoulders and in the arms of several men, as well as the faint stains of blood that marred their hands and he murmured a faint prayer under his breath. His two companions, one with a bloody hand, the other with a bloodied face, either out of fear or respect, remained silent.

Chapter Twenty-Three: In which Shipwash recounts the history of his trials to the inmates of the Priory and Childermass continues to weave the thread of his devious and unknown plot.

They were in the midst of dinner when Feversham, Dagworth, and Childermass broke in upon them. The grey figures of the scullery servants, customarily never seen outside of their quarters, were shuffling to and fro with silver platters in their hands and Sir Robert, seated at the head of the table with his grey-haired head framed by the coat of arms painted upon the wooden back of his chair, demanded where in Heaven's name the three had been all this time. Feversham explained then in a curiously unsteady voice that a group of men who referred to themselves as the Worshipful Company of Grocers from Shrewsfield sought audience with the Lord of the Priory – and that they appeared to have a dead child in their midst as well. After a moment's hushed silence, Sir Robert nodded and Childermass withdrew whilst Feversham and Dagworth stood by the entrance to the Great Hall, their eyes turned down towards the flagstones, neither of them speaking a word. Even Montrose and Squire Toby, both of whom had been absorbed in their usual, venomous disputations, allowed an uncomfortable truce to intervene for the nonce between themselves.

Shipwash was waiting outside in the courtyard to deliver whatever answer he received to his comrades. The last several days – the escape from the witch Alison Mackenzie and her sons, the disappearance of Nat (and the finding) – had weathered him beneath their buffeting; not with fresh streaks of grey in his hair or a stoop in his walk, but rather with a great weariness of mind that he had not possessed when he had left Shrewsfield. Yet in spite of this new spirit, numbed and bruised with shock, he could not look upon the dark Priory that rose above him without a sense of awe mingled with sorrow, an emotion that somehow softened the sharpness of his heartache like chilled dew upon a parched thorn. He took an almost perverse pleasure in feeling his thoughts lift free for a moment from the cage that his mind and memories had become and pursue altogether new avenues of speculation. The high windows, stained crimson and cobalt blue; the solitary towers that rose above the battlements like the broken pikes of a disused iron fence, their shutters hanging slack and open to reveal the nests of owls and crows that now alone enjoyed their forgotten eminence; Shipwash's eyes took it all in with a kind of desperate fascination, naturally drawn to the look of fallen grandeur that the Priory exuded and, at the same time, happy at the relief that this change of scenery afforded him. It was a more than welcome refuge from the little bundles of blood-soaked rags that he had left behind with the rest of his company, for the moment.

He recalled with a start the gossip-laden whispers of Crawley and his comrades – their tale of Sir Luke Gosselin and what had been seen beneath the overturned coffin lid. Who was it whom Crawley had cited as a witness? That young man with the marble eye, the broom, and the soot-stained clothes who had been the coffin-bearer. What was his name? Childermass. Named after the Feast of the Innocents, Shipwash presumed; the feast day set aside on the twenty-eighth of December for those Bethlehem children whom King Herod had murdered when he sought the life of the Christ child. Crawley mused after why any mother, looking down upon her child, would christen the infant with the name of the calendar's blackest day – perhaps blacker even than the horrors of Good Friday, for it was followed by no visible resurrection. The heaven that the children attained was implied, but never described. All that was left for a dispassionate onlooker to observe were the gutted infants and the empty cradles. There was nothing hopeful or holy to be found in such a spectacle – certainly not in such a name.

Feeling the rot of disgust and despair build again within his heart, he turned his mind back, almost fiercely, to the idea of Luke Gosselin and that riveting image that Crawley had so cunningly conjured of the withered corpse and the coffin-bearer with the cut hand who had seen the horror of his face. He did not know why, but there was something peculiarly comforting in the evocation of that tale: the motionless portrait of the wonder-stricken servant, the shocking look of the coffin's contents. Perhaps it was because the whole thing, in spite of its mystery, seemed to suggest a purpose, a hint of meaning behind its awfulness. That purpose did not rob his imaginative tableau of its terror; rather it gave Terror a mind and a face, something that a man could either fight or, were his nature inclined to it, pursue.

"Master Shipwash?"

Startled, Shipwash turned to find – as though summoned through the alchemy of his reminiscences – a half of that very portrait that he had been contemplating. The marble eye of the young man standing before him winked and glimmered with the light of the moon whilst his living eye ran over Shipwash's countenance with a methodical curiosity as though it were gathering, like crumbs, the traces of the grocer's former, pensive mood. The lower lip was swollen, the nose still slightly stained with a trace of dried, black blood, the countenance unmistakable.

"Childermass, is it?" Shipwash asked.

"How right you are, sir. His Lordship, Sir Robert Gosselin would like for me to inform your company that they are most welcome within the walls of our Priory." Childermass clasped his pale fingers together over the handle of the broom upon which he leaned and added, "He would also like to know what it is that you intend to do with your dead."

"I would like to speak to His Lordship regarding that matter myself," Shipwash replied. Grief had leant him a firmness of purpose that he had not formerly possessed. He would very much like to see Master Crawley come at him with another of his dolorous prophecies now. But Crawley, perhaps sensing the change in him, had kept his distance all that day.

The chimney sweeper gave a courtly bow.

"As you wish, sir," he said gravely. Then, raising his right hand, he gestured for the rest of the company to pass into the courtyard and follow in his wake. Unconsciously, Shipwash inspected Childermass's hand to find some sign – perhaps a scar – that would serve as proof of Crawley's tale. Then, catching himself, he looked away. He had enough griefs to glut his mind for the moment. The addition of a ghost story would be a surfeit – and Shipwash had his own tale to tell.

***

For Shipwash, the next hour was less a relation of events and more a revisiting of them. As he recounted the journey from Shrewsfield to Houndswick, the circumstances of their coming to the home of the Mackenzies, the mysterious Frenchman who had rescued them from the witch and her sons, and finally the discovery of Nat after a long day's search, his worn face alternately flickered with amusement, relief, and at the very last, weary horror. So preoccupied were his eyes with looking inward that he did not see the start that Cyrus gave (nor Childermass's flickering glance) at mention of his French savior. The only spectacle in that room that he seemed to take note of was the sight of those seven fellow grocers who entered the Great Hall of the Priory, bearing in their hands the misshapen, blood-soaked bundles of cloth.

"Methought that you said it was but one child in your company that died," the Reverend Abelin said.

"Good Reverend," Shipwash replied, his face stony in spite of his tears. "These all belong to him."

***

They had searched the road and countryside between the Mackenzie cottage and the forests from morning until mid-afternoon, following their escape. A sleepless night does not make a thorough scout of any man, but Shipwash's fear overcame his exhaustion and he spurred the company on, mile after weary mile.

At this point in his tale, Shipwash found that his voice had begun to tremble. Mercifully, Crawley took up where his comrade left off, the deep tones that his own sepulchral throat gave forth causing an audible break from Shipwash's plain, gruff way of speaking.

"And then we found what was left of the child. He was all up in the branches – " Crawley, for all his gravity, was an expressive sort of man and so he gestured towards the rafters as he spoke, " – like – like the piecemeal remains of a little creature left scattered by a hawk."

Shipwash gazed at the man beside him, feeling a sense of wonder at Crawley's unexpected little simile. Was that really what the man had seen? He had never looked upon the broken scraps of the child as the remnants of a murderous, ravaging flight. They had seemed somehow fundamentally stationary, fixed in his memory forever as seven shadows dappling the gold of the moss in that meadow: seven shadows that had caused him to look up as he had stopped in that clearing for breath – looked up to see at last the dried, brown rivulets of blood tracing their way down the trunks of seven separate trees – shadows that would remain in his thoughts and beneath his closed eyelids, he felt, forever and ever and ever and ever, memory without end.

A faint, crumpling sound beneath his feet startled Shipwash out of his morbid reverie. He looked down and found that he was standing upon what appeared to be a vast, unraveled scroll of paper that covered the floor of the

Great Hall from the hearth to the feet of the marble statues standing at the opposite end of the former chapel and marked by two winding paths of black ink, the which were bordered by an array of formulae and ratios, half-Greek, half-numerical. By shifting his foot ever so slightly, Shipwash had managed to cause the paper that he stood upon to rustle, thus bringing this unorthodox carpet to the distracted grocer's attention for the first time.

"Pray, do be careful, sir," Squire Toby called out. "Those are all my formulations, tracing the trajectory of my coach and the horse of His Lordship Montrose here. We were in the midst of measuring the ratio of speeds when you arrived. But all that is much beside the point. Pray, continue."

"But that is the whole history, my masters," Shipwash replied.

The great hall was silent but the faces that surrounded the grocer were eloquence enough. Squire Toby and Lord Montrose were brothers in discomfort. The former had his painted face of rouge and white averted as though the sorrow on Shipwash's face was too stark for his taste and the latter had his bright eyes turned upon the grocer with a look that was half sympathy and half incredulity. The Reverend Abelin, whose own eyes were so often transfixed by some remote pattern on a hanging tapestry or a particular section of masonry in a nearby wall, was now devoting his entire attention upon Shipwash with the discomfiting look of a man who was looking into rather than upon a subject. Sir Robert Gosselin, dreary with wine and old age, seemed as though he expected the grocer to continue his tale. Childermass, standing off to one side of the long table, was watching him with that same forthright look of curiosity in his one good eye that he had possessed when they had first met; there may have been pity in that gaze as well, but it was difficult to discern, outshone by the gleam of reflected candlelight that glittered from its marble neighbor.

Only the young man clothed in the worn garments of a shepherd, his countenance rigid with the configurations of sympathetic terror, seemed to fully comprehend Shipwash's feelings and the retribution that he desired. But it was not for Cyrus the stranger to speak for the Priory. Shipwash's heart, formerly sorrowing, now fell beneath the weight of resignation. It appeared that neither his tale nor his loss had made any impression on those who were in a position to offer him or his company aid. He began to turn away.

The creak of an ancient chair and the sudden scrape of a chair leg, however, caused him to turn around in surprise and look to its source.

Withing appeared flustered with embarrassment as he perceived all of the surprised looks that were now turned upon him, but somehow he retained his composure as he stood and said to Shipwash, "What is it, sir, that you wish of us? I am sure that my grandfather would agree that the Priory and all that we can offer are at your disposal."

Withing looked first to Sir Robert Gosselin, then to Reverend Abelin. Their visages were curiously apprehensive, though they made no remark. Then he looked back at Shipwash – and both the grocer and Cyrus were amazed at the look of nervous resolution on the boy's face. For a youth of only fourteen years, Cyrus was struck by the sudden resemblance that Withing now possessed to the noble portrait of his late father Luke Gosselin that he had beheld in the Looking Glass Cloister.

Shipwash was stunned for only a moment by this sudden change from cold indifference to ready alliance. Then he swiftly said, "First, we would like to have Nat given services and buried as soon as possible, my lord. Secondly, and most humbly, we beg for the hospitality of your walls for the duration of our stay here in Houndswick. Then, we would seek your aid in helping us hunt down the bloody person or thing that destroyed one of our children."

At this point, Reverend Abelin finally arose and put a heavy hand upon Withing's shoulder, indicating that the boy should sit once more. Then, turning to the grocer, he replied: "I myself shall see to the funeral arrangements, Master Shipwash. And it will be counted as an ornament to our household to have you and your company dwell with us during this Christmas season. But as for your last request, how can we grant it? This land has been plagued with these strange deaths for nearly a year's time now. What can we do to prevent or solve the mystery of them?"

"You are the lords and the regents of this land," Shipwash replied. "The death of this child did not occur in Houndswick or on its borders. We discovered his body within the forests of your Priory." Several persons visibly stiffened at this revelation. "Whether it was a beast or a man who committed this offence, it is your duty to bring him or it to justice – else the blood of Nat will be on your heads." He hesitated and then added, "Or can it be that I found in one Frenchman more kindness than in a host of my own countrymen?"

No one noticed Cyrus's pallor nor Childermass's sardonic smile at this mention, once again, of the mysterious French noble who had rescued the

Company of Grocers from the knives of Mistress Mackenzie and her sons. Instead, everyone looked once again to Withing as he said, rising before Abelin could forestall him or utter a word of reprimand: "Then we shall do all in our power, Master Shipwash, to find the one who committed this crime."

At these words, the company of grocers gave a shout of rejoicing and the host of them, formerly so grim and cheerless, now began to embrace each other as though this sign of promised justice was all that had been needed to lift the weight from their spirits. Even Shipwash, though still far from animated, managed a smile as Crawley shook his hand with a gruff nod. Lord Montrose and Squire Toby, unable to resist the contagion of relief that now permeated the great hall, exchanged amused glances whilst Clarice and Mariah embraced Withing.

"Methinks that we've a riddle of horror on our hands to unravel, Master Colkins," a voice behind Cyrus murmured, cold and soft. He felt his blood freeze at this utterance of his true name, but turned nonetheless and saw Childermass standing beside him. The chimney sweeper's marble eye was dead and white; his living eye was lapping fire.

"You stole my diary," Cyrus said, lips bloodless with terror and shock. Then, cheeks flushing for the first time with anger as well as fear, he whispered: "I trusted you."

"As your father trusted the Marquis St. Aubert?" He hesitated as he saw Cyrus's eyes gleam with tears, then continued with a look half mocking, half surprised: "But why? You do not know me. You have no reason to believe that I wish you well. And what great wrong is it that I've done you in reading your heart? Was it not a just payment for my ridding your sleep of nightmares?"

"You won't tell them will you?" Cyrus whispered. Though the great hall was filled with the sounds of conversation and merriment, it seemed to Cyrus as though all voices had died, all candles had dimmed, save the voice that was Childermass's and the light that was his devouring eye. "You know that if Sir Robert knew that my father fought for Parliament against the King's father – "

"Have no fear of it," Childermass said. "It is true that Sir Robert and the Reverend would be grateful for the knowledge so that they might send you out upon the road again. There is little love for strangers here at the Priory. But if they knew that I had stolen into your chamber and read your volume without your permission, they would have me whipped at Dagworth's hand. There is little love for curiosity here, either."

"If I were cast out of the Priory, I am certain that I would either be murdered by St. Aubert himself, or by the King's men."

"Did I not say you had nothing to fear?" Childermass returned.

"First you tell me that I should not have trusted you and now you ask me to rely upon your silence." Cyrus wished to regard the chimney sweeper with contempt, but the forthright look in Childermass's pale eye made such an emotion impossible. Instead, he felt only a quiet, heated fury for him. "What is it that you hoped to gain from your prying?"

"I little knew at first myself," Childermass said, his smile now grave in its ruthlessness. "You see, there are times when a madness of curiosity overshadows me that I am altogether powerless to resist. Then I must follow my desire whithersoever it may lead. It led to you, Master Colkins. From the morning that you arrived, I desired to know your history. We have so few visitors here and you were so very closemouthed. It was impossible for me to restrain myself. And God save you, sir – your stolen diary did not disappoint my appetite."

Cyrus felt himself growing lightheaded. He sank into his chair, still deaf to the sounds all around him. "I feel unwell," he murmured. "Please tell me quickly, Childermass, what it is that you want of me?"

The chimney sweeper knelt in a motion as seemingly innocuous as that of a servant pausing to sweep up a crumb from the floor by his lord's table. Then he whispered to Cyrus in that voice of his, musical as the passing of wind through the organ pipes of a razed, unpeopled abbey: "Soon, Master Plainstaff. Soon."

Then he rose and left Cyrus's side to take his place once again by Feversham and Dagworth. Cyrus averted his eyes from those of the chimney sweeper, but when he did occasionally glance at him, he saw that the look on Childermass's face was hardly one of deference any longer. It was one of exultation.

Chapter Twenty-Four: In which Clarice ventures into the Priory's lower levels and discerns two separate terrors.

Clarice suspected that her uncle wished to avoid her company when he sent her after the wassailers, asking her to make certain that they were comfortably settled for the night. She did not know what the object of the Reverend's grim introspection was, but she imagined that it would be best to leave him to himself as he wished rather than ply him with unwanted questions. For all the years that she had known her uncle – and it had been many, for she had lost her mother and father to smallpox when she was only six years old – she had learnt when he wished her presence and when he wished her gone.

Moreover, this errand gave her an opportunity to explore a portion of the Priory that she had never beheld before. Ever since her arrival from London, the Reverend Abelin had forbidden her from a free exploration of the Priory and so she had remained confined to the ground floor and second level of the place. All other doors remained locked, including that one door of black oak that led from the Great Hall to those interminable passages connecting the Priory's first floor to its subterranean levels. Of course, she only knew this because of what Feversham had told her when she pressed him to tell her what lay beyond this forbidden entrance: and even the ostler confessed that he had only passed through that door once or twice, both times as the member of a funeral procession. The Priory's crypts as well as its former dungeons lay there and Feversham mused that he would not be surprised if there were chambers in those depths that had not seen the light of a candle or felt the footstep of a human in over a century. Childermass alone – save, of course, the Reverend Abelin and Sir Robert Gosselin, who rarely bothered to venture into the Priory's lower levels – held the key to that door. It appeared that the wassailers would be expected to make berth in the darkness behind it. It seemed a cold arrangement for guests, but Clarice supposed that she had no right to question a decision made by the Priory's lords. Certainly, such questioning would little profit either Shipwash's company or herself.

Furthermore, the hush that lay behind the door of black oak forbade any thoughts that did not center upon the immediate, visceral quality of the atmosphere that now enclosed her. Her uncle had told her the directions – left, right, left, another left before the marble statue of Venus, and another right – and she had dutifully marked these down with a bit of ink on the back of her palm. But it was difficult to adhere to instructions when confronted by the dusty labyrinth of corridors that made up the Priory's lower world. They snaked before her on either side, twin passages of darkness: the one to the left with walls of moldy stone and the one to the right with walls and floor made of white, stained marble. It was as though they had been constructed at different periods in the Priory's history – and, for all Clarice knew, they had. She wished that she knew more of the immense, enigmatic place that she had inhabited for so much of her life; more, at any rate, than the small portion that her uncle had allowed to her. Clarice knew very well that her uncle had little interest in the orphaned niece that Fate had thrown into his power, but would it have been too great a sacrifice for him to give her freedom in lieu of love?

So it was that although Clarice had the Reverend Abelin's strict charge to follow his directions to the letter, she could not resist the temptation to explore the corridor to the right – the passage made of marble – before reluctantly carrying out his wishes and turning to the left.

Her footsteps echoed differently in that place from the sound they gave above ground. There was a watery, faraway sound to them, like the ricocheting of a stone flying down a cistern, and Clarice began to wonder how far the darkened hall continued. Her candle, though its flame burned bright, had only an inch of wax left and she promised herself that she would go no further if the passage took her too far.

She was relieved to find, however, that it was quite short and stopped at yet another intersection diverging into two separate branches: one a staircase leading down to yet another level beneath the Priory's foundation and the other a corridor similar to the one that she had just explored. She glanced back at the passage that duty prompted her to be exploring instead and then returned her curious gaze to the passage that promised to bring her even further beneath the Priory than she had already travelled. Was it fancy that prompted her to imagine the sound of whispering ahead of her or was it only the footsteps of vermin that she heard? Clarice at last expelled the breath that anticipation had held within her lungs and chose to venture down the forbidden staircase.

Her heart beat loudly within her breast as she raised her candle above her head and let its light dapple the stone floor beneath her feet. She gazed with wonder and awe at the silver cressets carved into taloned hands and untenanted by torches, though still stained with the black remnants of ancient pitch. At the same time, she noticed that a draft seemed to emanate from betwixt the stones upon which she stood. Kneeling, she held her candle above the crack in the floor. This action most unfortunately confirmed her suspicion – for in one breath, the candle died instantly, snuffed by the wind that whistled between the stones.

Clarice's first reaction was stunned surprise rather than terror. True, it was the same night that Shipwash had told his tale of the orphan boy Nat's bloody and mysterious death; and it was true as well that she was in a strange and unfamiliar place, alone and unable to call for help with any hope of being heard in such a remote portion of the Priory. And yet, imagination had had no time yet to insinuate its dark fancies within her mind's eye. She began feeling her way back up the stairs, but she went too hastily, slipping to her knees upon their sharp edges and feeling the wetness of blood on her scratched legs. Drawing in her first anxious breath, she proceeded more cautiously, keeping to the left wall and steadying herself against it to avoid another misstep.

Once she had reached the top of the stairs, she began to feel to her right, searching for the passage by which she had come. Ahead, she thought that she heard that whispering sound, like a scuttling of echoes ahead. She stopped, tried to listen, to distinguish the syllables as they ricocheted like scattered stones before her: *See me, see me, see me.*

"Who is there?" she whispered, feeling at last the slow rise of dread. "Who is it?"

It continued, however, without pause for breath or reply – *oh see me, see me, please, please, see me, oh see me, see me, see me* – as though it were deaf, ending at last in a short gasp as though its lungs had been stopped by some violent interruption, allowing only a low, strangled cry. Then silence. She stood motionless, suddenly afraid to move in that darkness as though her footstep would muffle some further sound made by the unknown voice ahead.

A hand fell on her shoulder, cold as a rain-soaked, withered leaf. The low sobbing of a soul *in extremis* then filled her ear and as she began to tremble herself with tears of paralyzed fear, the entire corridor began to vibrate with the throes of a shriek, mounting, mounting, and unbearable in its agony. Covering her mouth to bite back the cry that threatened to escape her own lips, she stumbled back down the passage that led towards the stairs and groped her way to the right, regardless of what turns she took or how unfamiliar the floor beneath her feet felt, so long as she could be sure that she was far from that awful passage and that the sound at her back had faded to nothingness. Only when silence at last reigned once more did she allow herself the luxury of tears.

Presently she rose and began to feel her away along the passage in which she stood. She was now drawing in ragged breaths and, for all she knew, every step she took brought her further rather than nearer to the oak door through which she sought to escape the Priory's underworld.

She froze once again as a sound again echoed from somewhere ahead. This time it was more readily identifiable than those that had assaulted her before: the familiar rhythm of footsteps, advancing nearer and nearer by the second. A panicked courage inspired her heart at that moment. Rather than fleeing, she called out in a voice that trembled only slightly, "Who goes there? Please, I pray you, tell me!"

"Miss Abelin?" The familiar voice of Childermass fell on her ears like the notes of an old and well-loved tune – perhaps the first time that it had ever had that effect on a listener. "How is that you are here – and without light?"

She ran towards the sound of his voice and, so relieved was she at the company of something human, that her tears began to fall once more as he caught her in his arms. Childermass let her lay her head against his breast and took the liberty of offering a silent prayer of thanks that fate had placed her into his hands upon that night when he was still celebrating his awful and enigmatic triumph over Cyrus. As he felt her slender arms go about his neck, he longed to put his pale lips to the crown of her head, but cold instinct told him that this would be too much too soon. He could not suppress a martyred sigh, however, at his own self-denial.

"I am very well now, thank you, Childermass," Clarice said at last.

She was about to gently withdraw, but he continued to hold her close as though he had not heard her. Not wishing to appear rude to one who had saved her from loneliness and terror, she continued to remain quietly in his arms and listen to the faint sounds of the Priory settling all about them.

"How is it that you are without a light yourself?" she ventured to ask.

"Well, Miss Abelin, candles are scarce as you know and I have every turn and passage of this portion of the Priory memorized. I had no need of fire."

In any other man, such an announcement would have astonished. In Childermass, however, such a knowledge of the Priory's routes was only a matter-of-course. Surprise was thus supplanted by admiration.

"I verily believe that you know the Priory better than its lords," she declared.

"How kind of you," he said. Then, hesitating and for the first time employing her Christian name, he added, "Clarice."

"Yes, Childermass?"

"Oh, I merely wished to say your name. It is a beautiful name – *Clarissa* – like the name of a tragic lady in Mr. Webster's plays. It caps a phrase like the little flourishes of an Italian libretto."

"What a strange thing, speaking of librettos and tragedies in the darkness of a dungeon," Clarice managed. She wished her voice to sound light, but she knew that she was breathing as heavily as she had been earlier when overcome by terror.

"Do you think so, Clarice? Would you have me do it in a garden or under a snowy elm? Is it that you are too much afraid of this place?"

"Afraid? Of course I am not afraid." She knew how foolish this reply must sound, but rankled at the presumption in his voice. "It was because I wished to explore it myself that I accidentally had my candle extinguished." After a pause, the duration of which she somehow knew was filled with his silent, mocking smile, she added, "And now, if you don't mind, I should like to be taken out of this horrible place."

"Of course, Miss Abelin," he said with sardonic formality.

He took her by the hand and conducted her down several corridors, pausing at last and reaching into his pocket for a key before unlocking a certain chamber. Clarice blinked in the sudden light and the two of them stepped through, Childermass shutting the door behind them.

"This isn't the Great Hall," she said. Her eyes were filled with a quiet dismay as she turned to look upon the chimney sweeper.

"No," he assented. "But there is no longer only darkness here either." He gestured to the low hearth that burned in the bare, dusty little room. "You may light your candle there, if you wish."

With a silent sigh, she did so and then set it upon the low, three-legged stool that stood by the hearth. "What a lonely little room," she mused. "What is it used for?"

"Oh, I make use of it myself when I have need to light a candle and show guests through these passages," Childermass replied. "'Tis the only reason I keep this hearth burning, for other than that it is little more than a broom closet."

"If you had not found me, I would surely have been lost in that labyrinth out there," she said. "Thank you."

Childermass stood utterly still and silent with surprise, and at last Clarice ventured to look upon his countenance. At first she thought his look was one of cold, unsympathetic appraisal but then saw that she had mistaken the milky pallor of his glass eye for his living eye, the latter of which glittered in the hearthlight with a mixture of emotions too powerful and contradictory for her to fully understand. Pity it seemed was there, but also a curious look that observed the gratitude of the young woman before him with a brightly avid eye, as though hesitant to speak lest speech should destroy the fragile moment that had brought them together. The shadows of the moving flames danced madly across his face, obscuring the kindly sympathy that struggled for dominance in his eye against the hungry exultation that sought preferment there instead.

"What was it that frightened you?" he enquired at last.

"A whispering," she replied, her voice soft with fearful remembrance. "It wouldn't stop but kept on like the scuttling of rats in a passage, and it seemed to keep saying – "

"'*See me, see me, see me*,'" Childermass said with an eerie look of recognition. "I know – I have heard it too, all of this day."

"What is it?"

He gave a slight shrug. "The wind has a curious effect on the Priory, even in so deep and windowless a place as this. It finds its way into passages that not even the rats can channel through and insinuates itself into the household draughts that already waft through these halls. I would not be surprised if what we have heard was something so simple as that."

"Perhaps you are right," she said doubtfully. "After the tale told by the grocers, however, I couldn't help but be afraid."

"My poor Clarice," he said. "How like the heroine of a tragedy you seem, sometimes." He began to draw nearer, so close that the smell of soot and coal again filled her senses. She pretended to prefer the light of her candle to the center of the room and drew back to the other side of the chamber, but his advance continued in spite of her retreat until she found herself pressed against the far wall, Childermass only a breath away from her.

"But I am not afraid any longer," she continued a little too hurriedly. "And my uncle will be wondering where I am and it is getting quite late. "

She wished to evade him, to tell him that she was not afraid of ghosts but of *him* now. The hearth's flames lit his hair in such a way that it seemed to have blanched to ghastly white and his pale and living eye was upon her with that fixedness that she had noted in him before but had preferred then to disregard. There was no averting one's gaze from it now, however. More than any other before – more than even Cyrus who now feared him and Dagworth who hated him – Clarice saw into Childermass's soul and beheld the swallowing fastness, the devouring purpose. Too frightened even to tremble now, she stared – fascinated – into that eye as though it were a necromancer's glass, filled with a fearful vision that she could not wrench her gaze from no matter how greatly she wished to. The coldness that so often characterized his visage was now giving way before something more heated and compelling, though he still attempted to preserve the passionless façade that he so carefully cultivated.

"You mustn't be afraid," he said at last, a little hoarsely. "I came for you, did I not?"

She nodded slowly.

"And so?" He smiled. "Come, come. I've something to show you, but you mustn't breathe a word of it to anyone. Do you wish to see it?"

She nodded again, warming in spite of herself to the chimney sweeper's air of theatrical intrigue. With a mysterious look, he withdrew from his coat pocket a small, silver device, rounded and silver, bejeweled with various precious stones, with a small key attached to a screw at its end. It had been one of the curious trinkets that Clarice had marveled at in Childermass's watch tower and now she gazed with a new fascination at it as the chimney sweeper held it before her.

"What is it?" she asked curiously. "And wherever did you find it, Childermass?"

"I discovered it in one of these chambers," he replied. "And was as bewildered as you by it. Then I read of its use in a volume that I found in the Priory's library."

"And what was it?"

He put the tip of it between his lips and then twisted the key at its end. Then, extracting it, he said, "Do you see how well it fit? And look what happened all the while I turned its key."

She saw that the rounded end of the device had now parted into two separate petals and that with each twist they had continued to separate.

"The Pear of Anguish," he said. "It appears a pretty and delicate toy at first, but it could break a man's jaw when employed by its inventors. Or," he added decorously. "Any other place into which it could be thrust. You see, our ancestors did not possess the elegant manners and tasteful decency of our modern age."

Clarice shuddered, her eyes fixed to the terrible instrument. "And to think that you found such a thing within these very walls!"

"Forgive me," Childermass said, a sardonic look in his pale eye as he returned the glittering device to his pocket. "It slipped my mind for a moment, Miss Abelin, that one is expected to speak to a lady of librettos and tragedies rather than medieval tortures when one is in a dungeon. Would you have me do so again instead?"

"I think," Clarice replied with a long-suffering sigh that ill-concealed her amusement. "That I should like to finally see the Worshipful Company of Grocers as my uncle wished me to. If, of course, it would not inconvenience you, Master Childermass."

"The hour is late," Childermass replied as they stepped out of the chamber, she with her newly-lit candle. "And I must return to my quarters or I shall be punished. But come to me tomorrow and I shall see what I can do."

"My uncle shall be angry with me," she said sorrowfully.

"But how is the Reverend Abelin to know that you preferred my company to that of the wassailers?" he returned with a pale-lipped smile, holding an icy finger to her mouth. "It shall be our secret."

Chapter Twenty-Five: In which the Priory readies itself for the coming of Christmas, the annual hunt, and the presentation of a mystery play by Mr. Chapman followed by a tragedy of anonymous origin.

If the snows came late to that area of Scotland in the winter of 1665, then when they at last fell upon that frosty December midnight, they fell with all the force of a thwarted power that will no longer be kept at bay. They fell as the wassailers slept beneath the roof of the Priory, as Cyrus lay awake contemplating with a mixture of fear and bewilderment the last words spoken to him by the chimney sweeper, and as Childermass himself placed the tip of a torturing device between his lips. They set their dominion over the moors, the forests, the gambrel roofs of Houndswick, and the battlements of Laughlin Priory, heaping the skeleton branches with banks of frost and muffling the silent graves of the newly-dead beneath their immutable white. Travelers fancied that they saw, rising above the trees at some distance from the Priory, the thin wisp of smoke and thought of the legends that they had heard of the witch Alison Mackenzie and her murderous sons, but such tales are a comfort only to those who have a hearthside to warm them against the inevitable chill of dread that follows such storytelling. The traders and wayfarers who by custom followed the road from Shrewsfield to Houndswick recalled too the stories of murdered young men and thus kept their distance from both Houndswick and the immense, grey-stoned Priory that seemed to preside over these happenings.

Though few guests were expected at the Priory, the next several days were still spent in a flurry of preparation not only for the religious festivities of the Advent season and the Feast of the Holy Innocents, but also for the annual hunt. Dagworth's fingers grew numb from the bitter, northerly wind as he spent hours upon the moors with his curs, keeping them in practice for the scouting of quail, pheasant, rabbit, and fox. Feversham garlanded the doorposts and walls with branches of pine and fir, crosses of beaten gold and silver, and candles of colored wax while Childermass divided his time between stirring the coals of every hearth in the Priory and keeping a ministering eye upon the Worshipful Company of Grocers, whose charge he had been given. For Reverend Abelin, understanding the chimney sweeper's temperament, had judged that this occupation would keep him sufficiently distracted from his odious custom of spying upon his superiors, satisfying that obscure love of mastery that Abelin had sensed in Childermass's soul.

The chaplain was correct in a very limited fashion, as it did give Childermass no small amount of pleasure to lord it over the wassailers in his cold and passionless way; but unbeknownst to Abelin, he also slaked his other, more heated compulsion, in the shadows of the library, wherein he had begun to read the chronicles of Lord Stephen Gosselin, who had reigned as the master of the Priory during the early reign of Charles. Curiosity had driven him into the lower vaults of the Priory's library just as it had compelled him to steal into the diary of Cyrus and make himself master of a history that was not his own. Ignorant of his own past up until the point when he had begun as a young child to work as a chimney sweeper in Houndswick, he was a veritable reader of every narrative other than his own. Their faults and their virtues were the weapons which could restore or wound according to Childermass's pleasure, whilst those whose hearts he could read could do nothing to touch him, for his history – like that of a beast or an angel – was all a blank. His was all the advantage, while the world and its denizens, titled or otherwise, remained defenseless against his single, penetrating eye. So it had been for years; yet it was Childermass's hope that the time was approaching when he would do more than merely watch.

Gaily whistling "In Dulci Jubilo" beneath his breath in time to the piping of one of the grocers, Childermass compassed in several long strides the immense, arena-like chamber in which the wassailers had been placed. His movements were swift and sinuous and what he lacked in regality, he made up for with a peculiarly boneless, fluid grace. He had exchanged his stained and ragged garments for the fresh coat and doublet, both of the same black hue, that the chaplain had grudgingly offered him and instead of his usual sooty broom, the chimney sweeper now held a straight cane of ebony oak in which was sheathed a thin blade that could be drawn out with the twist of its end. This deadly ornament he pivoted and swung with a pendulum-like precision in time to his measured walk and song, until he paused at last before Shipwash who was witnessing a rehearsal of Mr. Chapman's "On the Nativity of the Christ-Child" with an expression that was less than commendatory.

"They can certainly keep a tune, though, can't they, Master Shipwash?" Childermass remarked.

The grocer started violently and exclaimed, "Good God, lad, can't you stomp about a bit before approaching a man from behind? This creeping habit of yours has subtracted several years from my life already." Shipwash had not been so easily startled before, but the death of Nat had altered much of his former nature. That, and the fact that, for all his generosity, there was something in the pale-eyed chimney sweeper's presence that unaccountably repulsed him.

"Forgive me, sir," Childermass returned with that humorless smile of his that seemed, somehow, to lower the corners of his thin, bloodless lips rather than raise them. He would have disliked Shipwash intensely for his hostile attitude, had they been equals; on account of the chimney sweeper's authority over the wassailers, however, Childermass merely regarded him with indifference. "I was only remarking on the progress of your company."

"Progress?" Shipwash snorted. In spite of his aversion for Childermass, he did not mind gossiping freely with him. The young man, for all his peculiar ways, at least had good ears. "If you term this progress, Master Childermass, then you are either generous or a fool. Were little Nat still with us, we would at least possess a tolerable enough choir. As it is, his death has left us nothing."

The grocer's eyes grew bright with tears and Childermass averted his gaze. When his mysterious hints happened to inflict pain or terror, then the chimney sweeper's living eye would be trained with a curious gloating upon his victim. Grief, however, seemed to baffle and subdue him. Shipwash, for his part, took this aversion as a further sign of the calloused soul that lay behind that pale eye.

"As it happens," Childermass at last said. "I came to inform you, sir, that the child's funeral is to be held tomorrow morning. Tonight, as you know, is the third and last night of his wake."

"Who will watch him?" Shipwash asked. He knew that Feversham and Dagworth had remained by the side of the coffin upon the first and the second nights.

"I shall," Childermass replied.

Shipwash looked at the chimney sweeper with an expression of surprise and scorn. "You?" he shook his head, sorrow paling his face once again. "You shall not play cards over his poor little body, will you?"

"I shall do as I have been instructed, sir," Childermass replied. "I shall watch over him."

"You Priory folk here are all very good at watching dead children," said Shipwash. "I wish that you lot were more clever at catching their killers."

Childermass looked at him and said nothing.

In truth, the chimney sweeper was closer than most to comprehending the mystery behind the horror, but even he possessed only the vaguest of hints and visions – enough to whet his curiosity but not enough for him to prevent further horror. These secrets he had kept to himself, turning them over and over in his mind whilst Withing had been away to Oxford. Now the young lord had returned to the Priory and with him a friend who brought at his heels a new peril.

A killer who left the limbs of his victims scattered in treetops and a French nobleman with a taste for blood: both now converged at once upon the Priory. But Childermass had them in his heart. None else knew the Priory as the chimney sweeper did and it was impossible for any force to encroach upon it without his own soul feeling the violation as well. He had already exceeded his authority by informing all servants that there was a villain abroad in the land and that they should admit no stranger within the Priory's walls without his personal consent, warning that those who kept their doors and windows carelessly unlocked were inviting a murderer into their midst. Torturing and subtle though he could be, the ties that bound Childermass to the Priory were made of cords that could bind and compel him to the performance of heroics and villainies alike; to him, they were all of a similar cast, so long as they served his turn.

"What are you smiling at?" Shipwash enquired abruptly.

Childermass gave a brief shudder as though divorcing himself (for the moment) from a thought both pleasurable and somewhat terrifying. He then extracted a sheaf of papers and put them into Shipwash's hand.

"When you tire of watching your men rehearse Master Chapman's heroic couplets," the chimney sweeper replied. "Then read this and tell me what you think of it. I should like you and your children perform this upon Christmas Eve."

"That allows us little time for preparation, Master Childermass," Shipwash said, his brow furrowing.

"Enough time, I assure you."

"What sort of piece is it and who is its maker?"

"'Tis a tragedy with comic elements – or a comedy with scenes of tragedy in its midst. A tragicomedy, if you will, sir. It is called 'The Orchard and the Lamb.'"

"And its author?" Shipwash persisted.

"Myself. But you will announce it as written by the Chevalier Christophe des Saints-Innocents. I pray that you do this thing for me. It shall be worth your while, I assure you."

As he spoke, he produced the jeweled torturer's instrument that he had showed Clarice the night before. Its precious stones twinkled luminously in the candlelight.

For a moment, Shipwash was tempted. He took the device in his hand and turned it over, unable to determine what its use was but certain of the high price that it would fetch. Then, abruptly, he returned it to Childermass with a gruff shake of his head.

"Keep your little trinket, Master Childermass," he returned. "I'll not be bought with baubles."

"Then you will not perform my play."

"I will. But I must warn you straight off, young man, that I don't like the look of you and that the only reason that I am willing to do this without recompense is simply because I'm reluctant to accept any payment from you. How can I be certain that it is not stolen?"

Childermass laughed, then. It was not that hellish laughter that made Feversham wish to stop his ears, but an unexpected mirth that caused his pale eyes to twinkle and his thin cheeks to take on a rare intimation of color.

"Thank you, sir. I wish that I could pay you properly, but you see that they give me nothing more than my lodging and keep in return for my services."

"Then I only have one request," Shipwash replied. "I notice that you have this one fellow in your dramatis personae called the Visconte Cavalcanti, the one you call your villain-hero. But I have only old men and children in my company. I therefore request that you play your protagonist in our performance."

Childermass hesitated and his eye grew subtle as though he were considering the wisdom of such an action. At last he gave a slight nod. "If you wish it, then I shall, sir. Though I must warn you that I have no experience in the art of mimicry at all."

"Sir," Shipwash said with a heavy sigh. "If you but say half your lines and look at your fellow player instead of the audience during the performance, then you shall already be the Richard Burbage of our troupe."

Of course, Shipwash little suspected that the drama he held in his hand was more a torturer's love-thing than the device that Childermass kept in his pocket. Nor did the circumspect Childermass realize that his decision to act the part of thespian in his own tragedy would put him in greater danger than he had ever known. Alas, for the lot of man! Even his subtlest machinations are at the mercy of forces that he cannot see and the invisible worlds of spirit and of mortal craft may affect the plots of both the lowly and the great alike, be he an exiled Marquis, a Puritan lad, a sweeper of chimneys, or a Shrewsfield grocer.

Chapter Twenty-Six: In which an extract of Lord Stephen Gosselin's journal from December 28, 1633 is here reproduced and in which Childermass's light is stolen.

"And I came to the forest, I and my men, and we waited there beneath the trees for a long space, until the coming of midnight. It was a cold, clear night, still and dark as a well of ice water, and it came into my mind many a time that she would not come to us and that I would return empty-handed to the Priory. The dogs grew impatient at first, and restless. As midnight approached, they fell to crying and shivering, and that was when the Mistress at last appeared.

"She took one of the dogs, a swarthy black cur, and put its throat to the knife, letting the blood fall into a pail. Then she removed its pelt and gave the skin into my hand, telling me that I would have need of it in the future.

"'Give to my sons the gold that you brought us, Master Gosselin,' said she, her smile a mockery of goodwill in the moonlight. 'Then we shall tell you what next you must do.'

"And I commanded my men to give to the two young men by her side – "

Childermass broke off from his reading of Stephen Gosselin's journal, distracted by a sound that seemed to come from somewhere at his back. He strained his ears for some repetition of the soft utterance or cry that he had fancied, but when none came, he set his attention upon his true charge rather than the stolen volume that he had been perusing.

It was the third and final night of Nat's wake and the chimney sweeper had begun his own watch over the child's body. The little fragments had been assembled beneath a layer of rags, but Childermass could still discern their shapes: the hill and indentation of a nose and lip, the arch of a knee, the round curve of a head separated from its throat. Little wonder, then, that he would rather attend to the pages of Lord Gosselin's diary than fix his eye upon the eerie stillness of those human fragments alone. But it was difficult to concentrate in the empty darkness of the Priory chapel; even for Childermass, accustomed as he was to the Priory's atmosphere, the unaccountable sounds that continually caught his attention only to echo once more into silence were enough to set him uneasy.

He had spoken to no one since the hour that Feversham and Dagworth had set him at his post and then left, assuring him that they would be back in several hours with a fresh candle. They had chosen a great, oak-backed medieval chair that stood beside the altar and Feversham had carefully wound the chains all about him, tightening a coil about his chest, about his waist, about his legs, and fitting manacles about his wrist, allowing his hands a certain freedom of movement, but restricting his ability to rise from his seat. It was, after all, nightfall and the old rules of his punishment still applied in spite of the special circumstances of the wake.

The two other servants must not have relished their own shifts in the chapel, for Childermass had thought that he detected in them an uncharacteristic distaste for their task. Even Dagworth watched Feversham go about his business with a look of reluctance, his gaze frequently moving from the chains to the coffin while he shook his head. Feversham, ever more sympathetic than the Master of Hounds, went so far as to ask the chimney sweeper if he should like an extra candle for light and warmth.

"The one that you have left me sheds enough light for me to see my charge," Childermass had replied with a faint, humorless twist of his pale lips. "And my chains are too tight, sir, for me to shiver. I believe that I have light and warmth enough as I am."

Once Feversham and Dagworth had departed, however, and Childermass had found himself alone, the passionless mask slipped slightly and the chimney sweeper gnawed at his lower lip, a look that seemed almost pitiful now distorting his face. And yet what, he argued with himself, could he be afraid of? The mangled remnants of a child's murdered body. Surely it was a thing to be sorrowed at rather than feared. As he reminded himself of this, he felt the terror within him begin to dull somewhat. His heart still throbbed against his chest, his anxious breathing still ached against the chains that constricted him, but his mind now remained coldly unimpressed by his surroundings. Save for the peculiar sounds that occasionally set his pulse quickening once again, there was nothing unusual in his circumstances.

Furthermore, the tale that Withing's great-uncle Lord Stephen Gosselin told within his sparely-written journal proved a sufficient distraction from Childermass's unenviable task. The chimney sweeper had found the volume tucked away in the library's hidden vaults and had begun to devour it as swiftly and thoroughly as he had assimilated Cyrus's own tragic narrative – but the tale that he found within was less redolent of tragedy than of horror mixed with farce. It was clear that the conventional account of Lord Stephen as a pious Catholic was not an entirely candid portrayal of the Cavalier gentleman. Nearly every page that Childermass had read thus far dealt in some way with His Lordship's occult researches and his obsession with gleaning from a woman whom he referred to as 'the Mistress' the secret to earthly immortality. For Lord Stephen believed in the immortality of the soul; yet, he wished to avoid death altogether and prolong his existence amongst the living, keeping not only his soul but his flesh intact as well. To this end, he required the help of the mysterious lady and her two sons, but Childermass could discover no further description of them or any explanation for how Lord Stephen had first come to hear of their existence.

Again, Childermass started at the sound of something rustling close by, straining as well as he might against his chains in order to catch a glimpse of what stood behind his chair. This time, he saw his mysterious visitant for who he was: a long, thin cat with white whiskers and streaks of grey fur along his cheeks. The creature flashed its two spheres of emerald fire upon him before vanishing into the darkness, startled in its turn by the laugh that he gave at the sight of it. His fear was completely gone now, replaced by his usual wintry dispassion. After all, Childermass could only respect and love what awed and daunted him. It was as though terror somehow disarmed his heart, allowing the entry of an emotion that it was otherwise entirely void of. When comforted by the banality of his situation, he was also cheated out of whatever might have stimulated him in it as well. With a sigh half of relief, half of regret, he trained his gaze upwards.

Across the airy space between the eastern wall of the chapel and the western, a single thread of spider gauze stretched, its silver length occasionally catching the light of the guttering candle or revealing itself in the moonlight that streamed past the indigo stained glass, like a hidden path discovered for a moment only to mingle once more with the darkness above. Childermass followed its glistening course from one end of the chapel to the other, finding no sign of its poisonous architect, but marveling all the same at its unbroken expanse. The thought of climbing an invisible staircase into those vaulted heights pleased him immensely. He could have dreamt upon those cobwebbed rafters for an eternity and forgotten the shackles that held him to his chair. There had been a time, he knew, long ago in the Priory's past when the chapel had been ornamented with hanging cressets depending from chains of silver and iron and surrounded by streaming banners of crimson. The cressets had been stolen away by Henry VIII's knights and the tapestries used as blankets by Cromwell's men. All that remained were the unburdened chains hanging pendulously from the rafters and the tattered rags of red that fluttered and billowed beside them in the uneasy, draft-driven chapel air. The cracks that ran between the ancient rafters allowed melted snow-water to drip down the lengths of the chains so that they appeared to sweat with an icy perspiration in the moonlight.

Childermass's successive breaths were rhythmic plumes of mist as he mused upon the vaulted atmosphere above him. The cold of the chapel and the constricting embrace of the shackles were beginning to effect in him a growing drowsiness. Unable to move or shake the chill that was spreading over him, he presently closed his eyes and gave himself over entirely to the approach of sleep, his thin cheek resting against the arm of the chair, his flaxen hair nestled in the crook of his own chained arm. With the closing of his marble eye and the quenching of his living one, he seemed as innocent as a drowsing child and, in spite of his cramped and ungainly position, he soon fell asleep.

He awoke several hours later to what sounded like the baying of a dog. Only half-aroused from slumber, Childermass tried to sit upright, then winced at the pain of his stiffened muscles. For a moment, he was startled by his surroundings, forgetting briefly that he was in the chapel and wondering why he was out of bed. Then he caught sight of the coffin on the altar and remembered.

The dog's baying had grown louder and Childermass turned as well as he might in the direction of the chapel's twin doors. He heard the creature's heavy, racing steps as it semi-circled the church. As the chapel was only joined to the main Priory by a long, open-air corridor, the beast was constrained to run from the southerly wall to the northerly one. Occasionally, the chimney sweeper would hear it scratch at the door of the chapel with a tentative paw and then give a low, peremptory growl, before again pursuing its skirting path around the building. Childermass had the distinct feeling that the creature would have liked nothing better than to get at something inside, but was hindered by the practical barrier of the closed door. He wondered what it could possibly be that motivated the dog to pursue this odd course of action again and again with so fixed a purpose.

Ordinarily, Childermass would hardly have taken an interest in such a matter. His recent reading of Lord Stephen's diary, however, with its grisly mention of the slaughtered dog and the bloody pelt came to his mind at that moment and made him uneasy as he listened with bated breath to the beast's claws against the wood of the church along with the thin, high baying that it gave throat to from time to time. If the creature was attempting to frighten its quarry into quitting the Priory, it might have been successful. Childermass would have had half a mind to leave the church if only to shoo the creature away – his chains prevented him from carrying out this intention, however. Captive, he continued to listen for close to an hour until at last he heard its steps retreat and fade away. Without even being conscious of it, the chimney sweeper let a breath of relief pass his lips.

With the departure of the beast, the ensuing silence that filled the Priory seemed more profound than before. Childermass would have liked to resume his dreamless sleep, but his rest was now light and unsatisfying, filled with visions of a heated and wanton nature, and all accompanied by the elusive face of a young woman, her face colored by torchlight and moonlight, and her eyes filled with a fearful fascination. He awoke with a start and, in spite of the numbing coldness that filled the chapel, he found himself drenched in a burning sweat.

Spent, Childermass gazed upon the now-extinguished candle that stood upon the altar by the child's corpse, and waited for his heart to slow to a steadier rate. It was obvious that Feversham and Dagworth had forgotten their earlier promise to bring a fresh candle to the chapel. Left in a darkness too profound for reading, Childermass turned his attention once more to sleep. Another man might have dwelt longer upon his former vision, but Childermass had already put it out of his memory with an uncanny ease. If there was any desire that existed in his narrow heart for any fellow creature, he himself was too unaware of its secret development to consciously give it any nourishment. Moreover, as he had remarked quite truthfully to Cyrus earlier, he hardly ever remembered his dreams past a few moments after awakening. Only the fever of their former presence continued to glow beneath the pallor of his face. As soon as he closed his eyes, however, a sound from somewhere above again caused them to wearily open.

There was a movement in the hanging chains of the rafters – not the rustling of a draft, but the swaying caused by some great disturbance in the upper reaches of the chapel's vaulted ceiling. In chains himself, Childermass could only watch as the gossamer threads of the cobwebs came undone, their white lines drifting in fallen tangles like the loosed moorings of an invisible vessel. Again and again, the chains rang and jostled against each other, and beneath their jarring sound, Childermass heard the sound of sharply drawn breath, as though something sobbed close beside him. Like a cruel, teasing finger tracing its way along the back of his neck and causing his hair to rise with dreadful anticipation, the chimney sweeper felt the first touch of horror in his heart. This was no mere painful apprehension, such as he had felt when first left alone in the chapel: this was true and solid, the knowledge of a presence that smote him and made ragged his breathing, as though his body hoped that by starving him of breath, it could enforce a swoon and thus save itself the agony of sighting whatever was to come. Yet Childermass continued to breathe and his living eye, though it wavered, did not close.

There were two presences in the chapel: the thing that moved amongst the chains in the rafters and the other that cried somewhere invisibly at his side. The latter's sob was unmistakably the same as the curious, half-heard voice that Clarice had heard in the lower labyrinth of the Priory and that Childermass had noticed himself and mocked as only the wind. The former, however, was unknown to him even as a shadow and as it approached like a billowing darkness from the rafters to the altar before him, it seemed at first no more than a hanging cloak, its sleeves revealing only a vague outline of arms that terminated in interlinking chains, falling at its sides like serpentine fingers. Further and further down it lowered itself, like a man hanging by a noose that is lowered inch by inch to the ground and at last a glimpse of its face caught the moonlight. Childermass shrank before it like a child afraid of a blow. It was the face of Cyrus Colkins.

Or at least it seemed so at first. The lineaments were the same, the expression of faint sorrow uncannily similar. But the face was stained with blood and the body was gutted by the chains that hung from the rafters, as though it were a puppet only animated by their motion. Riveted himself, though only with fascination, Childermass watched the being advance and felt his blood curdle as both curiosity and guilt stirred within him. For if this were some vision connected with Cyrus, how could it wish him anything but harm? What he had done last to the young stranger had been nothing short of blackmail and, furthermore, he felt no remorse for it. If this spirit could read his heart, it would surely have little love for him.

"Who are you?" Childermass asked softly.

The tortured man stood above him, his eyes fixed and unremitting in their anguish. His lips parted, but no words came forth – only blood, that fell in crimson droplets upon Childermass's knee. Biting his own lip to prevent himself from recoiling, the chimney sweeper repeated his question, this time in a voice that shook ever so slightly.

"He cannot answer you, my lord," a child's voice replied. Childermass looked down and saw that by the side of his chair, the figure of a young boy now knelt and gazed upon him with a look of hope that nearly outshone the glistening wounds that circled his neck, his shoulders, and other portions of his body. "Or at least not with words. But I can understand his thoughts. He is Ephraim Colkins."

"And you are Nat." Childermass delivered this as a statement rather than an enquiry, for he recognized the face of the apparition as belonging to the child in the coffin.

"You can see us!" the child breathed. Childermass could smell rot and blood upon his breath. "You can see us! No other could – and we have tried to gain their attention many a night."

With the dead child's flayed hand pressing his own hand in gratitude, Childermass could almost forget the slitted cheeks, the bloodied stumps where ears once had grown, and the fingers each cut short by a joint – the few tokens that the moonlight revealed of the complete havoc that had been done to the child's body. It was strange to be embraced by this ghost, to feel its coldness as though it were the coldness of a living presence and knowing all the while that its true flesh lay in a coffin only a few feet away. Childermass felt himself grow cold and his heart slow as though he were growing close to death; only when the child withdrew did he feel warmth and life return to him again.

"How is it that I can see the both of you now and was not able to before?" he asked.

In reply, the uplifted sleeve of Ephraim gestured to Childermass's face and Nat supplied the dead Puritan's answer: "You did not look away, my lord. All the others looked away. You did not."

Childermass's bewilderment turned to understanding. It was no special power that he possessed but merely a stroke of luck that had gifted or cursed him with this sight. Had the apparitions not tried their utmost to make themselves seen within the Priory as well as to Feversham and Dagworth on the first two nights of the child Nat's wake? The whispering, the shadows, and the sounds must have been apparent to others as they had been to Childermass. Only one difference existed: the chimney sweeper's chains. Others had averted their eyes, paced to the opposite end of a chamber, disregarded or been repulsed by the sign of a separate presence when first they had sensed it. Childermass's shackles had prevented him from following this instinct and so he had kept his gaze perversely fixed upon the flowering rift between the visible and the invisible worlds when others would have fled, thus allowing the first light of their coming to penetrate his own eye and enable him to perceive what he had formerly been blind to. And with this coming had followed also a tangible quality to the visions; he could see them and they could touch him, whereas before their fingers would have passed through him like air. His very looking gave them flesh.

He closed his eyes and felt their presences begin to fade, though he could hear the child begin to cry.

"Please." Nat begged. "Please look upon us, my lord."

They regained their substance as soon as his living eye opened, coming alive like two pale flowers that can blossom only under moonlight. The child was gazing at him with a tear-stained face and Ephraim's own transfixed eyes regarded him with sorrow.

"What do you wish of me?" said Childermass. "I am neither your friend nor your murderer. Do you wish love or revenge? I can only offer pity."

"Protect me," the child whispered, pressing his hand again. "Protect me from *him*. If he catches my soul, then he shall torture me again – and I shall never get to Heaven. Please help me to Heaven, sir – please."

Childermass smiled at the dead child, all the while feeling himself begin to lose hold of his wits. There is a reason why the human eye instinctively flinches and averts its gaze from the rift between the worlds; like gazing upon the sun too long or awakening to full moonlight in one's eyes, it is neither good nor healthy to look too long upon the dead. Childermass looked and the health of his mind suffered greatly for it.

"And who is it who will catch your soul, child?" he asked.

"You have heard him howling, sir. Surely you have heard his howls. But he will not find me with you. You will show me how to get to Heaven, won't you, sir?"

Childermass felt something wet chill his hand and saw that Ephraim had opened his mouth as though to speak, but again only cold blood had issued forth.

"He says that he wishes you to warn his son of something, my lord. Someone is coming for him and he has a sign that you must give his son on his behalf. But he has no hands with which to offer it to you."

Childermass glimpsed the stumps that terminated the ends of Ephraim's wrists and knew half of what the inventive St. Aubert had performed upon his victim's person. The other half, he surmised, lay within the now tongueless mouth of Ephraim.

"Then how will he deliver it to me?" the chimney sweeper enquired.

"There will be two signs," the child replied. "The first will come to you soon – the second will come at a later time." Childermass turned cold at the next words that Nat uttered: "But before that, he says you must be punished. You have done his son a great wrong and frightened him terribly. Ephraim has seen it and there is no use denying it. For this, he says you must suffer too." The child's eyes were large with pity. "I tried to change his mind, sir, but he would not listen."

Childermass had never loathed his chains so greatly as he did at that moment. Ephraim's eyes were fixed upon him like cold spheres of ice, but he made no movement towards the chimney sweeper. Childermass closed his own living eye and prayed that the ghosts would be gone, rendered insubstantial, and that whatever vengeance Ephraim wished to wreak upon him would be averted by this action. He remained so for a long space until he was certain that the sounds all about him had died away and that the two had left him – that the only presences that remained were the hanging chains and the wintry drafts of the chapel. Then, at last, he opened his eye – and, with this action, knew in an instant the manner of suffering that he was condemned to endure. And with this realization, in the comfortless cold of the darkened chapel, Childermass began to cry.

VOLUME III

Chapter Twenty-Seven: In which plans are made, a warning delivered, and a visitor arrives.

Cyrus awoke earlier than usual, long before the rising of the sun, and found himself unable to resume his sleep. Again and again he was tormented by the memory of Childermass's words, last spoken to him in the Great Hall. He could not discern what it was that had provoked the chimney sweeper to interest himself in a stranger's history – Childermass had said something about a "madness of curiosity" that had possessed him – but Cyrus felt certain that there was more to his malice than mere whim. Or was it even malice? The chimney sweeper had insisted that he did not intend to expose Cyrus to scorn by revealing the young man's true identity. And yet Cyrus could not shake that empty look that Childermass had given him in the twilight – that look that promised him no forgiveness, only an eternal remembrance of the terrified repulsion that Cyrus had exhibited towards him in the library. Cyrus had never found the opportunity to ask the chimney sweeper's pardon for his involuntary reaction; would he now suffer Childermass's own private, bitter vengeance for it? At length, Cyrus ceased in his attempts to comprehend the marble-eyed servant of the Priory. Whatever it was that compelled Childermass was too tangled a mixture of malignity and method to be discerned by a stranger, like a cobweb so marred by its withered burdens that its underlying pattern is altogether obscured.

Cyrus heaved a rather fatalistic sigh. First the Marquis St. Aubert, next Lord Andrew Ebenezer Montrose, and now this Childermass. He was beginning to think himself a lodestone for villainy. The only consolation left to him was that he possessed only one life for them to devour.

Pushing aside the heavy blankets that covered him, he rose out of bed and crossed the floor to stand by the shuttered window, unfastening it and breathing in the rush of winter air that surrounded him. It was a relief to feel the freshness of the wind in that close and chilly chamber and for a time Cyrus stood by the open casement, looking out upon the forests, the far moors, and the mountains with a pensive eye. The sun had not yet risen, but a faint light touched the summits of those prominences beneath the deep, indigo darkness of the sky and illumined the highest towers of the Priory with its piercing radiance. The whole world beneath this light seemed a study in cerulean, a cosmos made of mist, dew, and low-hanging cloud. This mingling of gold and shadow, darkness and light, struck Cyrus with an impression of beauty that affected him more than any other dawn that he had ever beheld. He had seen many a sunrise before in Essex whilst watching his father's sheep, but never one such as this – one in which Nature presented herself in such stark contrasts, at once painting the lower gardens of the Priory and the outflung forests and moors with a brush of darkness whilst blanching the mountains with her coming light. Gazing upon the melancholic beauty of the land that lay beyond his window as well as the cold, grey stones of the Priory that loomed above, Cyrus realized at last why it was that he dreaded so deeply the injury that Childermass could deal him. In his own hesitant, faltering way, he had come to grow fond of his sanctuary. The thought of not only departing from it, but of finding himself hated by his friends therein unaccountably hurt him to a degree that he had not expected.

Impatient at these feelings that rose unbidden within his heart, Cyrus abruptly closed and fastened the shutters, deciding that he would prefer to take a turn in the Priory's shadowed corridors rather than nurse these fancies that could lead only to his own unhappiness. Perhaps when all was said and done, it would be in his best interest to simply leave the Priory of his own accord. He could see no use in adding to the tragedy that had already befallen him.

The world that lay beyond his bedroom door seemed a tunnel of darkness leading in both directions: to his right hand a lightless hallway and to the left the staircase that led to the ground floor, only barely illumined by the spectral blue of the dawn sky. Against the carved arch of the staircase railing, a figure leaned motionless, only the profile and a gleam of golden hair visible in the uncertain light of that passage. What could have brought Childermass to such a place at so early an hour? Was he not still confined in chains? There was something eerie about the youth's stillness and silence and Cyrus, in spite of his desire for solitude, approached him and whispered tentatively, "Childermass?"

Instantly, the figure turned and, with a drowsy, drunken slur in his voice, replied, "Cyrus, is that you?"

It was not Childermass at all, but Lord Withing Gosselin. The instant that Cyrus saw the dreamy, half-closed eyes, he wondered how he could have ever mistaken the young lord for the chimney sweeper.

There was something eerie, though, in Withing's countenance as revealed in the half-light of the corridor. Cyrus could not discern the nature of the disquiet that he felt; he only knew that it made him conscious for the first time of a mysterious fragility that hovered like the smell of a disease in his newly-acquired friend. It had been no mere superficial resemblance that had led him to mistake Withing for Childermass. They both seemed to be haunted by an aura of peril; but if, in the chimney sweeper, this aura took the form of an excess of depraved energy that hung about him like a predatory musk, then Withing's own aura was that of one laboring under an invisible curse. With this realization, Cyrus also comprehended the reason why he felt so disturbed by this insight: in the last few days, he had come to think of Withing as though the lad were his younger brother rather than an eccentric, coddled lord. It troubled Cyrus profoundly that he could not discern the source of his new friend's unhappiness.

"Yes, it is me," Cyrus said, adding anxiously, "But are you well?" For Withing had suddenly sunk down to a sitting position upon the cold stone of the floor, his back supported by the tall bannisters. Cyrus saw that the boy was wearing only his white, rumpled nightclothes and that his hair was still mussed from sleep. He looked, in fact, as though he had inexplicably wandered directly from bed to this corridor without so much as a look in the mirror or a change of clothes.

Withing looked up as though genuinely surprised by the question. "Why, of course," he replied. "Why shouldn't I be?"

Cyrus shrugged, concealing his bewilderment. "You have risen very early, my lord."

Withing recoiled as though struck.

"Why do you call me that?" he demanded, almost angrily.

"You are *Lord* Withing Gosselin, aren't you?" Cyrus returned.

"Yes," the boy replied. "I suppose so." His voice trailed off and he said no more. But the look upon his face was infinitely sad.

Cyrus shifted his weight from one foot to the other, feeling decidedly awkward. He had seen something of this peculiar mood of melancholy before, first when Withing had drunkenly introduced him to the Looking Glass Cloister and the second time after Cyrus mentioned at breakfast that he ought to depart from the Priory soon. It had never seemed so potent as now, however. There was something inconsolable in the slump of the lad's shoulders, his bowed head, and the dreamy despair that haunted those bright, visionary eyes. Cyrus, like his father, had never possessed much tact and, in a circumstance as much fraught with mystery as with sorrow, he felt himself utterly useless. Again that comforting cowardice, that urge to abandon the Priory, stirred within his breast. But it was eclipsed by an alternate determination that welled in Cyrus's heart: a decision that yes, he would assuredly leave the Priory soon, but not before he had set whatever was troubling Withing right again. The young nobleman had saved his life – the Puritan felt that the least he could do was save his rescuer's peace of mind.

"If you must know," Withing at last said, not meeting Cyrus's eyes. "I was troubled with dreams and moreover my room was stifling, so I thought I'd like a breath of air. I feel like myself again now, however," he added after a pause.

"I am glad," Cyrus said.

There was another moment of silence. Then Withing said, "Do you know, it's a funny thing: I spend such a great deal of time hating the Priory that I forget how much I love it at hours like this, when no one else is about. I don't know why – perhaps because it seems so lonely and forlorn. You can't hate something that's lonely, can you?"

"No, I suppose not. But how can you hate the Priory at all?"

Withing gave a faint movement of his shoulders, a motion of helpless weariness. "I don't entirely know myself. And, after all, what does it matter?"

"Methinks it matters a great deal," Cyrus replied. "If by it, you are made unhappy."

He was about to say more, but at that moment he heard the crash of a door from somewhere a floor beneath them as it was rudely forced open. Both Cyrus and Withing looked down and discerned the tall, lank shape of Feversham enter the Great Hall. In his arms, the ostler held something limp and lifeless.

"Feversham!" Withing cried. "What has happened?"

The Master of the Horses turned and shook his haggard head. "Childermass."

"Dead?" Cyrus felt his throat tighten with an odd grief that surprised even him. And yet perhaps his hatred for the chimney sweeper had become something like Withing's for the Priory – and hadn't the young lord said that it was difficult to hate something so lonely? The chimney sweeper, motionless upon the table that Feversham had laid him down upon, seemed forsaken by life itself.

But Feversham replied, "No, not dead" and Cyrus felt relief return – and with it, the old reserve and reticence –as he looked upon the still form of Childermass. "I found him as you see him," the ostler continued. "Still chained to the chair in the Priory, but in a swoon. He would not awaken when I shook him, nor even when I took water to him."

Cyrus and Withing had descended the staircase and were now standing by Feversham. It seemed somehow unreal and out of joint to see the chimney sweeper lying there upon the very table that he had every day waited upon – lying there with his flaxen hair drenched from the ice water that Feversham had splashed to no avail upon his face, his lips bloodless and still, his hands incongruously composed at his sides. The ostler had said that he was not dead; had it not been for the occasional rise and fall of Childermass's breast, Cyrus would have doubted this affirmation.

"My lord, where are you going?" Feversham suddenly cried.

Cyrus followed the ostler's gaze and saw that Withing had already crossed the Great Hall and was standing at the entrance of the foyer. Against the solid black oak of the immense door, the boy in his white nightclothes appeared pitifully small.

"I'm going to fetch Dr. Erskine," Withing replied. "There's no time to wake everyone else and explain the situation to them. Don't trouble yourself about getting a horse ready, Feversham, I can do it myself. And no, Cyrus, you shall not go in my stead." He gave a faint smile. "I want you to watch Childermass and be with him when he awakes. I doubt that he should be left alone. Now – I must be off."

Feversham glanced at Cyrus. "You heard Lord Withing's request. I shall take Master Childermass to the sick tower in the west wing and you shall look after him until His Lordship's return."

***

As they proceeded to the place where Childermass was to be laid, Cyrus came to appreciate the silent strength of the ostler. They ascended no less than six flights of steep and winding staircases and all the while, still bearing the chimney sweeper in his arms, Feversham proceeded without the slightest indication of fatigue.

"I pray you," Cyrus at last managed to say, between gasps for breath as they paused between the third and fourth floor. "Why must we go so far to find a chamber?"

Feversham looked at him in surprise.

"Perhaps such matters are dealt with differently in other places, Master Plainstaff, but it has always been so at the Priory. Those who are suffering from a malady should be kept separate from the rest, but as there is only one chamber that is in decent condition in this portion of the wing, I shall lay him in Lord Luke Gosselin's sick chamber."

"Withing's dead father?" Cyrus asked as they continued on their way up a further flight of stairs.

"Aye. His Lordship died in that room, I fear, close to a year ago. But Lord Withing must have told you all about it already."

"He told me of his father's death, but not of its cause."

Feversham expelled a ragged breath, more from the weariness of remembering than from than any physical exertion.

"That is because Lord Withing does not know what the cause is," he said at last. "Nor, in truth, do we." The ostler shook his head. "I have said too much already. But what is there to keep back? His Lordship died upon the last Feast of the Holy Innocents, after several days of wasting away until he seemed a haggard old man – nay, the dried husk of such a man. After Lord Luke Gosselin's funeral, Withing was sent directly to Oxford and Sir Robert told us not to breathe a word to his grandson of the deaths in Houndswick. I know not why." Feversham adjusted his arms into a more comfortable position, so that Childermass's head rested in the crook of his elbow, and smiled with a weary irony at his burden, remarking, "One would almost mistake him for something human when he is like this. It was after the funeral that he was condemned to wear those chains, you know."

"Why?" Cyrus asked.

"We caught him one night in the crypt by Lord Luke Gosselin's coffin – he would not tell us what he was about, but it was evident from the signs of disturbance around the place and the tools that he carried, that he had intended to pry open His Lordship's casket and look upon the corpse."

"But for what purpose?" Cyrus demanded, aghast.

They had, by this time, ascended to the sixth floor of the Priory. After passing several feet down a long hallway, lit only by the great, glassless window at its far end, Feversham stopped before one of the doors and gestured for Cyrus to open it. As they continued inside, he replied, "As I said, Master Plainstaff, we were never able to learn what purpose drove him to such a ghastly deed – and believe me, Dagworth did his best to beat it out of him. But methinks that the motive ought to be as obvious as his marble eye. Won't you draw the curtains while I lay him down here on this bed?"

Cyrus crossed the room and did so, saying, "But what motive is this, sir?"

Feversham glanced up at him, a look of frank exhaustion in his eyes. Then he gave a shrug of his shoulders. "Some men take delight in the hunt, some in wealth, some in a mistress. Childermass delights in frailty and corruption. Pray that he never chooses to turn that eye of his upon your heart, or you shall regret it, I assure you. There is only one amusement that delights him more than this cruel sport and that is whatever power the knowledge of such frailties can offer him."

Cyrus, who had learned too late the truth of this statement, made no reply as he gazed upon the still form of the young man. He knew the damage that could be done to him by this creature were he to awaken. As he looked upon Childermass, Cyrus could not prevent the dark little prayer that welled within his heart, that the chimney sweeper's eye should never open again. He was instantly struck with horror at the hatefulness of his wish and before he could compose himself, tears half guilty, half pitying, wetted his cheeks.

Feversham saw the young man's woeful looks and allowed himself a grim smile. "Come now," he said. "It's not so bad as all that, Master Plainstaff. You'll awaken again, won't you, lad?" He ran a rough hand through the chimney sweeper's pale hair, then shook his head at the stillness that met his caress. "I will admit that I do not like this swoon that he has fallen into. There is something unnatural in it. I shall be off now, Master Plainstaff. If you have need of anything, there is a bell-rope to your right hand that will summon either Dagworth or myself."

***

Only a half an hour had passed since Feversham's departure, but to Cyrus it felt as though time had ceased to move. The morning sunshine that streamed in through the narrow eastern window illuminated the curtains that surrounded the bed, their folds depicting scenes of the virgin-goddess Diana and her silver-antlered stags. Soon the sunlight moved its golden fingers towards the crimson coverlet upon which Childermass's head lay. In shadow, the chimney sweeper's hair was like gold; when set afire by the morning light, it seemed as pale and resplendent as the goddess's bow. Cyrus watched the shadowplay of light and darkness upon the moving, painted curtains for some time, before at last rising from his seat and taking a turn about the room.

The paintings that covered the four walls contained a similar theme as the canopied bed, presenting a mixture of subjects both pagan and Christian: Venus moving with her Adonis through a brook-haunted glen; the Redcrosse Knight and Una from the first book of Sir Spenser's "Faerie Queene," wandering through Error's forest; Pygmalion and his creation in the midst of her transformation, supple stone beneath moonlight; the dark sorcerer Busirane, his countenance burning with lust as he traced in dripping blood with the end of his wand a wanton's incantation while kneeling at the feet of his captive mistress, a slave to the very beauty that he sought to enslave. For the man who suffered illness or the approach of death, there would at least be much for his eyes to linger upon, even as he remained confined to bed for days or weeks on end – and Cyrus found himself absorbed by the excruciating detail with which the unknown artist had rendered every wall alive. It was with a great effort that he at last wrenched his gaze from the walls and happened, instead, to glance at the mirror that hung in the midst of the Venus and Adonis scene, its gilt frame wonderfully mimicking the painter's foliage.

After all the shocks that Cyrus had sustained in these last few days, the youth had rather naively begun to hope that he had developed nerves capable of remaining steady no matter what new horror might present itself to him. But no human torture, no violent murder, no grief could ever have suitably prepared him for what he saw within that mirror.

For Childermass in the reflection was sitting up. His eyes had flown open, pale and vacant, but otherwise he remained motionless. The peculiar expression upon his face had never belonged to the chimney sweeper.

Cyrus started horribly and instantly turned his gaze from the mirror towards the bed by which he stood. He received yet another shock, however, when he saw that Childermass still lay prone and unmoving where he had formerly lain. It was as though there was Childermass and Childermass-in-the-mirror and the two were somehow divided when they should have been one.

Cyrus was trembling violently, but still he ventured a glance once more upon the mirror. Childermass-in-the-mirror returned his gaze and raised a hand, pointing to his breast and saying in a voice that belonged to his lungs but not his soul, "Cyrus. My dear son." The voice shook with both effort and emotion; tears fell athwart the cheeks. "Do not be afraid. I am come to warn you and – "

But Cyrus had recognized the voice and gave an anguished cry as he tore his eyes from the mirror and buried his face in the merciful darkness of his hands. Whether it was madness that had descended upon him, some tormenting demon, or a true visitation from his father, he could no longer support the shock of what he saw. When he at last ventured to raise his eyes again, the mirror's reflection showed nothing more remarkable than Childermass as he had been for the last several hours: a young man laid low by the power of some mysterious swoon.

Cyrus approached the head of the sleeper, almost afraid that the chimney sweeper would start awake and begin to speak again in the voice of his father, as Childermass's reflection had done. But Childermass remained as still as though he were dead. With an outstretched, trembling hand, Cyrus touched his shoulder, wishing to reassure himself of the chimney sweeper's solidity – and, also, half-remembering the vision's command. Not even the barest of movements indicated that Childermass's nerves had felt the touch.

Cyrus had just turned away when a sound in the bed brought his attention back to the bed. He watched in mounting dread as he saw Childermass begin to convulse beneath the sheets, his movements resembling those of a man struggling violently against some invisible source. In a desperate attempt to calm the sufferer, Cyrus took hold of Childermass's shoulders, hoping to keep him from injuring himself in the midst of his convulsions.

"Feversham!" he cried. "Someone! Help!"

He would have pulled the summoning rope, were it not that he was afraid to leave Childermass's side while the young man was still in such a violent state. Unfortunately, his attempts to restrain the chimney sweeper proved entirely ineffectual as he lost his balance and found himself overcome by the greater strength of the sufferer whom he had hoped to help. Helpless in Childermass's preternaturally strong grasp, Cyrus saw a rivulet of blood begin to flow from a corner of the chimney sweeper's lips and, as he watched with stricken eyes, he saw Childermass put his pale fingers into his blood-stained mouth and draw out a thing that Cyrus had not seen since the night that he had fled his father's house, a thing that he had never hoped to see again – a little piece of glass, pressed now into his hand and shaped into the likeness of a dove. St. Aubert's dove. And, as Cyrus's gaze fell upon it, he felt a chill overspread his soul, and he whispered in a voice hushed with horror, "Where did you find this?"

But Childermass, who was himself again, cast his pale, living eye somewhere over Cyrus's shoulder as though he were not sure of where the youth's face was, and replied, his voice still choked with blood, "Find what?"

Cyrus was not used to this new look of pale, listless sorrow in Childermass, nor was he accustomed to the peculiar shadow that seemed now to darken the fire of his only eye. The chimney sweeper did not meet Cyrus's gaze but continued to gaze steadily in his direction and though Cyrus passed a hand before his face, Childermass did not so much as flicker an eyelash. Cyrus knew, then, what the difference was.

"God have mercy," Cyrus whispered, his voice hoarse. "Poor Childermass. What has been done to you?"

Childermass made no reply at first, a look of unutterable sorrow passing silently over his countenance. Then, at last, the blind chimney sweeper said: "A thing no worse than what befell your father, Master Plainstaff. Oh, I know it all now, sir – I know it all. More than your account could ever have told me, more perhaps than even your St. Aubert himself could have guessed. I have been plunged into darkness, yes – but you wander in a denser darkness than even I. You and, I fear, Lord Withing as well."

"Why do you wish to be my enemy, Childermass?" Cyrus said, appalled at the exultation in the chimney sweeper's voice. "What harm have I ever done to you?"

"Your enemy, sir?" the blinded Childermass returned mockingly. "I have never thought of you as such, you may be assured. Indeed, methinks that I shall be your savior, after all is said and done."

"How do you imagine that will happen?"

But Childermass's lips had gone white again and he fell back again upon the pillow, lost again to the world. He did not feel the stricken Cyrus anxiously chafe his wrists and brow, nor hear the sickroom bell as it rang for assistance, nor hear the door open as strangers entered to minister to him. Just as the world of wakefulness held only darkness for him now, his sleep was filled with visions of the two specters who had visited him within the chapel. He watched as repeatedly, with silent, pointing fingers, they indicated to him the gaping wounds, the long places where their flesh had come undone, and waited for his nod before resuming their lesson. "I will remember," he promised these strangers. "You do not have to teach me again. I will remember." His promises began as tears and then inevitably melted into laughter as he looked upon their solemn, dead faces and felt his sanity drift away like sand beneath a black tide, while his dreams bore him deeper still into darkness, a darkness of tongueless specters, tortured victims, and the offspring of his own malformed, panting Desire.

***

And at the edge of the Priory's forest, making his way through the snow and the white-petaled hellebores that bloom at his feet, there stands the saint-faced stealer of tongues himself, the remaker of bodies, cheeks flushed from the winter air as he gazes up towards the towers and battlements of Laughlin. 'Tis here, 'tis here, that the witch whispered to him that the son of Ephraim Colkins has fled – it is within this grim fastness that, Fate willing, St. Aubert shall take his sweetest pleasure.

For here, the flying and the running shall all end at last – and the sporting begin.

Chapter Twenty-Eight: In which a History is Told and an Expedition to the Crypt Resolved Upon.

Several days passed since Cyrus beheld the vision of Childermass's possession in the mirror; several days spent in hushed whispers as Dr. Erskine locked himself, often hours at a time, alone in the sick-chamber with Childermass before reappearing, as mystified as before by the chimney sweeper's inexplicable blindness. From Childermass himself, Erskine could learn nothing: the young man spoke at first of an awful visitation in the night, but he soon sensed the doctor's skepticism, for he soon grew reserved and silent, returning Erskine's questions either with feigned weariness or with a vacant look in his staring eye. Erskine at last departed the Priory, advising rest for the chimney sweeper, but saying that he could do nothing to dispel Childermass's blindness. If ever it departed, it must do so of its own accord – no human agency could banish so miraculous a darkness.

Cyrus would have spent these days in the seclusion of his own chamber, turning over the blood-encrusted dove that Childermass retrieved from his mouth, were it not for Withing who insisted upon showing him about the Priory. They wandered beneath the floating tapestries, through the Looking Glass Cloister with its waxen effigy of the dead Lord Stephen Gosselin, and even far down into the servants' quarters. But there was something strange and empty in the long shadows, something not-quite-right in the angle of certain chamber corners. It was as though the shadows were missing the added darkness of the broom-shadowed servant, the corners of the room lacking a certain added angularity of sharp cheeks and high, narrow shoulders. As much as Cyrus had begun to loathe and fear Childermass, the peculiar young man's absence felt like that of a missing tooth – the ache was gone, but so was a space once filled within the Priory's mouth. For all Childermass's distressing qualities, the Priory was left gap-toothed without him.

Mariah often accompanied Cyrus and Withing upon these indoor expeditions, her eyes wandering as often upon the melancholy face of Cyrus as upon the paintings or the marble ornaments pointed out by her cousin. The sadness that she had traced in his countenance before had deepened in these last few days, leaving imprints of grief along the tender pallor of his flesh. A look of faint, unceasing shock had entered those eyes as well, as though the knowledge of something both hideous and inevitable had made itself known within his very soul – not with the soft subtlety of a spoken betrayal, but with the rudeness of a dagger plunged into a breast. She saw the sorrow with which he looked upon the broken saints and imagined that it was the sorrow of a displaced noble. Ah, daughter of the Gosselins – there is nobility in that countenance, but it is not the sort of nobility that you dream after. But Cyrus was too occupied with his own reveries to notice the Earldom of Air that she had constructed for him and the history of fond falsehoods that her heart had painted.

As for Clarice, these days were spent in a dread made all the more terrible by the cloud of mystery under which she was kept. Strict orders were given by the Reverend Abelin that Childermass should not be disturbed and so, unable to see him and unable to account for why this wish of hers had grown so desperate, she often knelt upon the floor of the hallway across from the invalid's chamber, a lantern at her feet, horribly tired but too afraid to sleep or even to cry. Instead, she waited and watched as though she expected that such vigilance would bring an end to the tortuous prolonging of terror and mystery.

Feversham and Dagworth, in the meantime, had their own difficulties to sort out.

"The day of the hunt approaches," Feversham observed mournfully. "And yet ever since we buried that poor child, I fear that no one has bothered to recall it."

"I've spent the better part of this month in training up those whelps for just that occasion," Dagworth commiserated. "What sort of hunt will it be, where the curs, the horses, and the servants are more prepared for it than their masters, I should like to know? – I should indeed. If that hateful little devil Childermass was only well again, what a laugh he would have at their expense! Aye, and I'd share it with the young fiend, though only in this instance."

*   *   *

At the end of the third night, Mariah, Cyrus, and Withing were departing from the Looking Glass Cloister when it suddenly entered Withing's head that they should venture to the sixth floor. Mariah, naturally, pointed out to him the strict injunction that both Reverend Abelin and his grandfather Sir Robert Gosselin had made against approaching Childermass.

"But I don't mean to disturb him," Withing returned brightly. "I only want to see that portion of the western wing before we go our separate ways. There's no harm in that, is there? And Grandfather and the Reverend are not about anyhow."

It was true: Sir Robert had taken to retiring directly after dinner and the Reverend Abelin now spent all his nights cloistered within the Priory library. There was little chance of the three finding themselves reprimanded for their forbidden explorations and so, without further argument, they followed Withing upstairs. For Cyrus, it was the first time that he had ventured to this floor since his last, terrifying meeting with Childermass and he felt his heart begin to beat painfully as they approached the sixth floor of the Priory. It was entirely deserted, Cyrus guessed, save for that single chamber that Childermass now inhabited – and the sight of the dark corridor, relieved only by the faint glow of firelight that spilled beneath the invalid's door, only emphasized the utter desolation of this portion of the Priory.

"Clarice!" Withing cried. "What are you doing here?" For by the light of his candle, he saw the pale young woman sitting on the floor by Childermass's chamber, her eyes dark from lack of sleep.

With a trembling finger, she beckoned for them to lower their voices, herself whispering, "My uncle wishes Childermass to remain alone."

"Has he left that room at all since his blindness?" Withing asked, his voice soft.

Clarice shook her head.

"No, though I can hear him moving about as though he were walking from one end of it to another. I – "

They all went quiet at the sound of footsteps behind the door. Then, after a painful moment of silence, the door to the sick chamber slowly opened.

The thing that shocked them most at first was the apparent lack of change in him. They had expected after these days of confinement and darkness to behold an altered creature, not the same Childermass who had stood by the long table in the Great Hall, helping himself to his masters' ale and conversation; the same bloodless, sharp-boned insinuator who had whispered such frightful intimations to Cyrus only several nights past.

Then his living eye moved and they saw the difference. The pale light that had formerly burned behind that eye had now changed direction; its cruel searching had turned inwards rather than outwards, so that there was something distant in his stare, something of a grey sea's horizon and poignancy in that single eye's depths. It was the closest that Cyrus had ever seen Childermass's eye come to sorrow unmixed with malice.

"Lord Withing, Lady Mariah, Master Plainstaff. Clarissa." He murmured this last name most softly. "I am glad that you have come to me, for I have something to show to you."

They watched as he withdrew from his pocket a battered volume of dried leaves and rotted leather.

"The diary of Lord Stephen Gosselin," Withing whispered. "But, Childermass, this is from a portion of the library that Reverend Abelin has kept locked away."

"So it is, my lord," Childermass said with a bow. "I trust that you will forgive my presumption in making use of the effects of your late great-uncle."

Withing gave an innocent shrug, but Cyrus heard the mocking color of Childermass's tone and shuddered when he thought of the brutal treatment that his own history had been afforded by the inquisitive Master of Chimneys.

"But what about it interested you?" Withing enquired, still with that same deference.

Childermass withdrew into his sick room and beckoned for them all to follow. In spite of himself, Cyrus felt a renewed shudder, this time redolent of awe, pass through him as they entered. Something in Childermass's manner seemed to promise an answer to some, at least, of the mysteries that had dogged him ever since his arrival in Laughlin Priory.

Childermass found his way back to his bed and resumed his former place there, whilst Mariah, Clarice, and Withing took a seat at its far end and Cyrus stood by the hearth, his heart full of foreboding. Had a stranger come into the room at that moment, he might have fancied that he had stumbled upon a group of young people gathered in anticipation of a winter's ghost tale and he would not have been far wrong. Of course, it was no mere tale that the cold brain of Childermass intended to devise for his audience that night: but if it was the truth, it was the truth twisted cunningly to its tellers' advantage, to impress some secret lesson upon its hearers' hearts. Like the political philosophers and moral fabulists who teemed within London's printing houses and royal courts, Childermass possessed a preternatural guile: he would teach his rapt students not *how* to think, but *what* to think.

***

I fear, masters and ladies, that you know already (said Childermass) that every night for this last year, I have been forced to sleep in chains as though I were a common thief instead of one who has served this House for nigh ten years. This came about because of a mishap that befell me upon the last Feast of the Holy Innocents, my own birthday so they say – and also the day that Sir Luke Gosselin was laid in the Priory crypt.

Some have heard that when I was bearing the coffin of His Lordship, that I happened to lose my footing and allow the lid of the casket to fall open; that by so doing, I beheld the face of a withered man instead of the youthful features of Sir Luke. I fear it is true. The wasting effects that have been seen upon many of the murdered victims this past year are identical to those that I saw in His Lordship. But Master Feversham shut the coffin up before I could be certain of what I had seen, and so I was left in a state of doubt and apprehension.

That night, I chose to return to the crypt to look upon Lord Luke a second time, so that I might be sure once and for all that I had not dreamt. I managed to gain my way to the entrance, before I was caught by a man so muffled in his cloak that I could not discern who he was. He struck me across the face with the back of his hand and then, after supposing me unconscious, lifted me to his shoulders and carried me out of that place. I was brought before Sir Robert and after I had revived somewhat, I was told that I had attempted to commit a terrible desecration and that, for my pains, I must needs wear my chains every night for as long as I should live within the walls of Laughlin Priory.

Naturally, I protested my innocence and – for evidence – made mention of the transfiguration that I had seen within the features of Lord Luke Gosselin. They would not believe me and thought that I meant some awful disrespect by talking so. I was flogged by Dagworth and then left chained and half-unconscious to the gate of the crypt for three days, with only water to sustain me.

As you may imagine, these precautions only served to inflame my curiosity still further. But there was nothing that I could do to sate it and thus every night I spent in chains, with only my questions to companion me. But luck chose to favor me yet, for one day whilst I was lighting the candles in the library, I happened to discover the private journal of Lord Stephen Gosselin and in it, I found many of the answers after which my heart had so long thirsted. You will forgive me for my (perhaps) presumptuous curiosity, Lord Withing, when you yourself hear what I found within those leaves.

Your great uncle Stephen was not merely a secret Catholic. He was a soul on fire with a desperate fear of death itself and he soon convinced himself that his only escape could be found in a study of the occult. He employed the aid of a Scottish lady whom he only refers to in his writings as 'The Mistress,' and with her two sons they performed many acts, the like of which even Lord Stephen seems to have been reluctant to commit again upon paper.

(At this point in the narrative, there were several gasps from Childermass's listeners and Mariah murmured, "Shipwash told us of a Mistress Mackenzie and her two sons and of how the witch made an attempt upon their lives. But surely she was far too young to have been the same."

Childermass only gave a slight shrug of his shoulders and continued his tale.)

One of the few rituals that Lord Stephen chose to describe involved the killing of a hunting dog and the removal of its pelt. This pelt was 'consecrated' and the Mistress informed him that he must never destroy it or lose it, for if this should happen, he would surely die. The whole time I read of this, I thought it all sounded like nothing more than the most childish of fairy tales. And yet, and yet…the voice of the diary seemed full of a true terror and belief in the deeds described therein. I could not but wonder at it all.

Several times Lord Stephen made mention of your father Lord Luke Gosselin, but said nothing more save that it was all a pity – though he never said what he meant by this. There does seem to have been some sort of connection between Luke and Stephen's eventual renunciation of the Mistress, however, for his diary ends with an affirmation that he shall never set his hand upon a book of wicked wisdom ever again and that he must keep himself pure and holy for the sake of his nephew.

Years later, of course, he at last succumbed to the malady that would eventually prove fatal to him. He told the physicians, if I recall the gossips correctly, that there was a change in the quality of his blood – that something in the terrible sciences that he had explored in his youth had altered his constitution so that, without the consumption of some certain saving liquor, he would surely die.

Well, my masters, whether his account of black magic was made of truth or not, he certainly now occupies a narrower resting place than the living.

***

There was a long hush after the closure of Childermass's tale. It was curious, how swiftly a new and subtle hierarchy had been established within that bedroom since the chimney sweeper had first begun to speak. Though all of those present stood higher than him in rank by virtue of either their titles, their birth, or their guesthood, they all looked to him as though to their master. Mariah and Withing gazed at him with eyes dark with terror and apprehension; Clarice, with a look of wonder and awe; and Cyrus, hands clasped and yet still restless against his breast, watched him and speculated how such a fantastic tale could possibly serve Childermass's obscure purpose, and yet remained too mastered by his fear of the chimney sweeper to voice his suspicions aloud. Childermass himself, though blind in sight to these effects, sensed the change. While those about him felt their hearts grow cold, his own head and heart felt as though they were encircled by a coronet of flames. He felt at once half-dead with exultation and curiously, almost demonically calm.

"What does it all mean?" Withing asked. His voice was soft and guilty, a child speaking out of turn in the sanctified silence of a church.

Childermass spoke with his usual quiet precision. "Blood is the common link that I noticed between Lord Stephen's tale and the deaths in Houndswick. Blood and the death of Lord Luke Gosselin. Stephen described in detail the ritual bloodletting of a dog; all the deceased victims have been found shriveled and bloodless. Likewise, Lord Stephen's diary ends with his concern for his nephew just as the deaths in the village began with the death of this nephew. We must know what horrified Lord Stephen so greatly that he abandoned his quest for earthly immortality. And we must know the reason behind the ghastly state of Lord Luke Gosselin's body within his casket."

"Please tell me," Withing said. "What you want us to do. I will do anything – anything if it will stop the deaths."

It was the same resolution that Cyrus had seen in Withing when the boy had promised Shipwash that he would seek justice against Nat's murderer. But there was a different quality to it now, a kind of relief. Cyrus could see in Withing's eyes that the boy was throwing himself desperately and wholly under Childermass's authority, as though glad to follow any voice that promised an escape from the Priory's labyrinth.

Childermass hesitated before replying. Perhaps he, too, was surprised at the young lord's wholehearted trust. "What I require is not pleasant."

"If you require it to solve this mystery, it is yours."

"Then it is mine. The signet ring of your father."

Withing paled and stole a quick glance at Mariah who returned his look with one of equal horror. "Then you mean for me to open my father's casket?"

"I wish to know what it was that I saw in his face a year ago. The signet ring I require, to find if it corresponds with a ring that Lord Stephen describes within his journal."

"And if it does?" Withing asked, after a dreadful pause. "Then what shall that mean?"

"Lord Stephen wrote that he offered the ring to his nephew so that Luke, at least, might be protected from the wicked forces that he had conjured, should they seek revenge against his family. If that ring were proven to exist, it would show that at least the whole of Lord Stephen's narrative was no mere dream."

Another long silence followed. Then Withing at last said, after a trembling sigh departed his lips, "Then it must be done."

They left the sick chamber, their hearts too full to recall that throughout the latter half of the evening, Childermass had wholly neglected to address his superiors by their usual titles of nobility. But the chimney sweeper remembered and derived no small amount of amusement from the recollection.

CHAPTER TWENTY-NINE: IN WHICH THE ANNUAL HUNT IS HELD, WITHING AND CYRUS EMBARK UPON AN EXPEDITION TO THE CRYPT, AND CHILDERMASS CONTEMPLATES A COMING COMPLICATION.

Lord Andrew Ebenezer Montrose, 34th Earl of Lauderness, was having a difficult day of it. Indeed, as he found himself trapped in the freezing interior of his coach, his head pounding like some hapless, sentient anvil at the mercy of a rabid blacksmith's flying hammer, and surrounded on all sides by the morning traffic of Houndswick's citizenry, he began to wonder whether it would not have been more prudent for him to remain in bed after all rather than choose to wend his way to Laughlin Priory.

There were several reasons for his current predicament. The first and most oppressive was a consequence of the former night's excesses. Montrose was quite certain that he had been solicited by not one but at least five separate ladies as he had left his dear friend Lord Loosefair's house in the company of the ubiquitous Mr. Pursegood and Mr. Finegrange. He was equally certain that he would have happily added these five charming companions to his troupe had he been capable of replying with something other than a few, maudlin stanzas of "When I Was on Horseback." Once he had arrived within the safety of his apartment and been safely maneuvered up the twisting staircase to his own bedchamber, Montrose had reclaimed something of his soul from the bottle of Loosefair's port that he had downed with such gusto earlier that evening and even begun to speak again in prose rather than verse.

Mr. Pursegood and Mr. Finegrange then suggested that perhaps a taste of brandy would revive the Earl's senses. Midnight found Montrose as insensible as a corpse, whereupon, after exchanging shrugs and looks, Pursegood and Finegrange departed from the tenement to sleep in anticipation of the next night's jollities.

The Earl of Lauderness awoke to find the world of his bedroom moving all about him as though it were a separate sphere revolving around his prostrate, sickened body. Every pore of his body exuded the vapor of alcohol and his very breath was a noxious gas that recoiled to poison him. It hit him, then, like a two-pronged thunderbolt that this was the day of the annual hunt at the Priory and that he had drunk not one but six bottles of strong liquor upon the previous evening. He struggled to a sitting position – then collapsed once again upon the pillows as he felt his brain and stomach move as though in two separate directions.

"Dear God," he murmured. "I shall die today."

Mrs. Leaske entered at that moment, bearing in her withered hands a tray of burnt toast and a glass of milk. The housekeeper's piercing black eyes took in the sight of her employer with a single glance as though to verify that he had satisfactorily awakened from his stupor. She had been obliged to change his garments herself the night before as he had been too far gone to do so himself, but if she felt any embarrassment at this, her demeanor certainly did not register this emotion.

"Come, sit and eat this, my lord," she said, setting the plate beside the bed. Montrose waited until she had momentarily turned her back before pouring a generous dose of brandy into the glass of milk. Then, as she glanced back at him, he leaned back again upon his pillow, altering his expression into a picture of heart-rending pathos. It was not difficult; he already looked fairly awful.

"Will you be well enough to go to the hunt, my lord?" Mrs. Leaske enquired. "I would advise against it."

Montrose had been hoping that she would ask this very question, just so that he could insist all the more vehemently on the necessity of his going. He required an opportunity to voice this argument aloud, for he was beginning to question the wisdom of such an action himself.

"And have Squire Toby sneer at my absence?" he cried. "Besides, I am certain that I shall feel myself again once I have lain here for a bit."

He was about to turn upon his side and pray for sleep, but Mrs. Leaske seated herself at the side of his bed and commanded him to eat.

"If you wish me to remain in your employ, my lord," she said with emotionless candor. "Then you shall have to abide by my law. And I will not have you lie there like a common drunk when I have gone to the trouble of preparing your breakfast. I doubt that, considering your current financial predicament, many servants would be willing to take my place at a reduced rate."

Montrose allowed himself to be helped into a sitting position against his pillow and dutifully consumed the portions of toast that Mrs. Leaske systematically spooned into his mouth, washed down with brandied milk. At intervals, she dabbed at the corners of his mouth with a handkerchief as though he were a little boy. It was all thoroughly humiliating.

"My dear Mrs. Leaske," Lord Montrose protested wanly with a look of ill-concealed enjoyment. "Have you forgotten your place?"

The housekeeper only returned the Earl's question with the faintest of smiles.

***

"Scroggs," Montrose called to his coachman once he had finally emerged from indoors. "Are the dogs and horses ready?"

Scroggs touched his cap and winked at the Earl. "Dogs in the back and horses hitched to the coach already, my lord."

Montrose stared hard at him for a few moments and was reassured to find that the figure of his coachman was not undulating from side to side. He was beginning to hope that perhaps the worst effects of his overindulgence had been dispelled somewhat by brandy and breakfast.

"Excellent work, Scroggs," he said at last.

"Had a devil of a time getting the creatures out of the kennels, let me tell you, my lord. Something had them riled last night. Expect they'll be glad for a change of scenery."

"Then let us be off, Scroggs. The sooner we are gone, the better a chance we have of avoiding the morning traffic."

It was only a matter of minutes before Lord Montrose found himself in his coach, surrounded on all sides by what seemed to be every citizen of Houndswick who owned a horse, cart, or coach. He sighed and glanced at his dogs who sat in the opposite seat of his carriage and returned his sullen glances with wagging tails and panting tongues. Montrose, being in a villainous mood, would have cheerfully given one of them a hearty kick, but finding no room for the commission of this deed, decided instead to indulge in a much-needed nap. The dogs, seeing their master's action, happily followed suit themselves.

***

The elevated, hilltop prospect that Laughlin Priory commanded was not conducive to the ritual of preparation that Feversham and Dagworth were obliged to perform. Yet every annual hunt for close to two decades they had been faced with the same challenge and surmounted it with the usual mixture of ingenuity and improvisation that marked the commission of most of their duties. Childermass was not with them, of course, but when he had first come to serve at the Priory, the chimney sweeper had provided them with a rather clever solution to their annual dilemma.

The difficulty had always been in erecting tents for the hunt. As there was no clear and flat expanse save the moors beyond the forest, it had always been the custom to raise the tents there. Yet this was an inconvenience, for it set the tents at such a distance from the Priory that it was a wearisome task both for the servants to erect them and for the spent hunters to return from the tents to the Priory.

So Childermass had devised an alternate solution. In the boughs of the trees, the chimney sweeper had spread with hooks and ropes a curtain of opaque tent cloths, turning an entire patch of forest into a space set apart and sheltered from wind and rain. Torches were tied to the trunks of trees to set off the artificial dusk that these cloth coverings created, curtains of silver draped to set that portion of the forest apart. For the last decade since Childermass's employment this had been the custom, and even in Childermass's absence it remained so.

Lord Montrose, being an old friend of the Gosselins, was well accustomed to all these procedures. He had Scroggs pull up before the Priory's gatehouse and, after one of Feversham's stable boys took the horses and dogs away, Dagworth led him to the canopied forest. This was Montrose's first intimation that something was wrong.

"Where is Childermass?" Montrose enquired, for it was the chimney sweeper who had always formerly acted as his guide from the Priory's gatehouse to the forest.

"Taken ill, my lord," the Master of Hounds replied, not for a moment slackening his shambling gait.

"Ill? How?" Montrose blurted. The idea of a bedridden Childermass seemed as peculiar to the Earl as the thought of one of the marble statues in the Great Hall catching cold. It was not as though he held any sort of sublime reverence for the chimney sweeper – indeed, he would have laughed if anyone had suggested such a thing to him. But he had come to expect the pale youth in the same manner that one expects a familiar fork in a road or a handrail at one's side and it was a disconcerting thing to be brought up short by so unprecedented an absence.

"We aren't entirely certain what it is that ails him, my lord. But certain it is that he has gone blind."

Something in Dagworth's evasive manner made Montrose nervous, in the same way that the news of the child Nat's death had affected him. A violent, reflexive motion like the snapping of a wolf's jaws quivered through his soul, then dissipated; the relaxing of a drawn tendon. The Earl took a shuddering breath. Below them lay the forest, but before they descended the hill, Montrose cast a backwards glance at the Priory. His eyes happened to fix, then, upon Nat's fresh grave just outside the Priory walls and something in him, like a dry bone, snapped.

"My lord?" Dagworth broke in upon his musings with a dubious edge to his voice.

Montrose turned on him, bloodless with anger. Then, enchantingly, he recalled himself and recovered his usual grace with a smile.

"Forgive me, dear fellow," he said. "My mind was elsewhere."

Dagworth nodded; though a head taller and several shoulders wider than the Earl, his mouth had gone completely dry. The Earl's temper, like his blandishments, was not a thing easily forgotten – nor the rapier that hung at Montrose's side, the hilt of which his hand had flown to at the very peak of his fury.

Dagworth judged that it would be prudent to keep a generous distance between himself and the Earl of Lauderness for the remainder of the morning.

Sir Robert Gosselin and the Reverend Hugo Abelin were both already seated upon tall thrones of oak. Several foxhounds prowled at their feet and at a short distance Lady Mariah Gosselin stood by, loading her musket. At sight of Montrose, Sir Robert raised his hand in a cheerful, though weary, greeting whilst the chaplain observed him with the same unsmiling disinterest with which he tended to contemplate every scene and soul that fell beneath his eyes.

An oak reared behind them, its trunk as wide as a tower and its branches rising higher than its fellows. In the past, when Childermass stood in his own belltower and looked clear across the forest, it was often the topmost boughs of that tree upon which his pale eye would settle. He had sometimes even climbed those evenly-spaced limbs as though they were a staircase made of circling, knotted arms and sat astride the highest branch that he could safely mount, watching the sun burn and lower behind the western mountains. Montrose's own eyes traveled along the bleached wood of the tree and recalled how those branches had streamed with black ribbons upon the day of Sir Luke Gosselin's death. It was the Laughlin Oak, fabled to have been planted by Etienne du Laughlin himself: a bare, white monarch in a forest of leaning, leafless courtiers.

Montrose caught sight of Withing Gosselin and Cyrus Plainstaff, both standing at the foot of the Oak behind Sir Robert and Reverend Abelin. They were conversing, their voices too low for the Earl to comprehend. Withing's expression was one of disquiet; Cyrus's, uneasy caution. Intrigued, Montrose took a step towards them, only to find his arm almost immediately arrested.

"My lord," Mariah said, smiling up at the Earl. "You look exceptionally pale this morning."

Montrose bent to kiss her hand; he did not notice Mariah's distracted glance over his shoulder and she hastily recovered herself and returned his gaze with a forced smile.

"You have arrived early, my lord. Squire Toby is not even here yet."

This was the best thing that Montrose had heard all that dismal morning.

"Delightful!" said he. "Now where is your cousin and that peculiar Master Plainstaff? I thought I saw them only a moment ago."

As the Earl spoke, he looked up; then blinked. For no one stood any longer beside the Laughlin Oak. The two had vanished entirely.

***

They were out of breath by the time they had reached the top of the hill. Beneath the shadow of the Priory's western wall, they were invisible to Montrose or anyone else in the forest.

"We've perhaps half an hour before anyone notices our absence." In spite of his run, Withing's complexion was still as pale as it had been in the forest. For a moment, Cyrus's own, private anxiety was replaced with a real concern for the boy.

"Truly, my lord – I mean, Withing – are you sure that you wish to carry through with this? It was only Childermass's suggestion and if we are caught – "

"We shan't be caught." Withing bit his lower lip and turned his eye again in the direction of the Priory's main gate. "But we cannot go in through there. Let's try for the scullery instead, shall we?"

Cyrus followed the young lord to the doorstep that led into the servants quarters. The entrance was locked but, after Withing knocked and was glimpsed by the flour-dusted face of a kitchen maid, they were soon admitted.

"The door is always kept well-locked?"

"Of course," said Withing, an unexpected but familiar smile brightening his countenance. "One never knows what sorts of villains wander these moors, does one?"

Cyrus felt his own heart lighten, though misgivings yet lingered within his breast. "You trust Master Childermass so very much," he remarked as they proceeded from the kitchens to the Great Hall.

"Oh, you would too, if you only knew him better."

They were passing through a windowless corridor. Cressets were affixed to the wall of the passage at regular intervals, lighting Withing momentarily with their radiance before his forward steps brought him once again into shadow. Cyrus's own steps faltered; the hypnotic effect of the candles momentarily obscured his vision to a dizzying blur.

"How well must I know him before I can trust him?" He knew that he could not keep the sharpness out of his voice if he spoke, so instead he whispered. At any rate, Withing was too occupied with his own terror and thoughtless resolve to notice such subtleties of emotion.

"Why, he knows such a lot about the Priory – far more than me. I cannot tell you the number of times when I was a little child that I would have lost myself if he had not happened to find me. There was one time in particular when I felt as though I had wandered for hours, unable to find my way back to the Great Hall, and Childermass saved me from the darkness – and he only a few years older than me!"

"But what has he ever actually told you of the Priory? What tales, what histories? Has he ever bothered to draw you a map of the more difficult passages so that you might find your way without him?"

Withing paused and turned, facing Cyrus with a puzzled look. "What odd questions," he said at last, softly. "He is a chimney sweeper, not a mapmaker, Cyrus. Why do you distrust him? Has he injured you?" He paled and added, "Do tell me, my friend, if anything at all has happened."

Cyrus shook his head and turned away, shielding his eyes from the glare of the candles as well as the look in Withing's gaze. The source of the boy's incomprehensible faith was at last beginning to grow clear to him. There was a raw power that Childermass embodied for the young lord; a power made not of blood or wealth but of the mind; and Withing, for good or ill, had been drawn to this intimation of authority from childhood so that he now met it with the familiarity of a pupil in the presence of a master. With a word, Cyrus might have brought to dust the airy castle that Withing had constructed for the pale, marble-eyed chimney sweep, but his heart faltered at the thought of explaining his own past to this nobleman's son. Childermass's power was no empty boast, no mere parlor trick played for the benefit of a credulous boy. The chimney sweeper, he now realized, had sensed in Cyrus a possible threat, a future friend to the brotherless Withing, and had acted accordingly. What Withing admired and trusted from a distance, Cyrus felt – and keenly. But what was the purpose of it all? Was it only the heady joy of dominance that inspired Childermass? Not long ago, Cyrus would never have believed that so slender a motive existed, but the last month had taught him a great deal about the heart.

"I meant nothing," Cyrus at last said. "Let us continue."

***

And so they continued on through the honeycomb of kitchens, pantries, and closets, running and faltering to their own separate rhythms, while all about them the Priory lay prone and empty, a hollow drum. The merest touch would have set its drawn skin trembling.

Childermass stood by the window of the sick chamber, his sightless eye and his false one both fixed upon the glass, his ear bent upon every sound that violated the darkness outside his room. For once, it was no idle curiosity that prompted this blind watch. He could recognize the soft, hesitant tread of Cyrus; Withing's faltering yet certain steps; the heavy approach of Feversham. But the footfall that he heard without his door did not belong to any of these. It was soft, yes, but wonderfully steady; not measured and winding like Childermass's own worming course, but gentle and constant like a heartbeat felt beneath a muffling pillow, or the fall of dirt upon a casket. It played upon the floorboards outside his door like the theme of a tongueless song, then paused as though considering the chamber that lay beyond. Childermass waited, pale and braced, breath pent up within his breast. Then, after an age, he heard the steps again as they traced their way down the corridor. He continued to listen until he could hear them grow faint no longer.

Clarice's voice brought him out of his horrible reverie. He had entirely forgotten that she still slept in a chair by his bed, exhausted after a night spent reading aloud from the diary of Sir Stephen Gosselin.

"Childermass." She spoke softly, her voice still slurred with sleep. "Are you well?"

"Methought I heard someone pause outside our door."

"I heard no one. And hasn't everyone, saving Cyrus and Withing, left the Priory to watch the hunt?"

"Not everyone, Miss Abelin. There are always servants at the gatehouse and a few attendant in the scullery." His reply was swift and curt, for he had thought of all this before and had swiftly dismissed the mysterious footsteps as belonging to any of these servants. "I think, though," he added, "that one of them was a fool."

He said this with a smile, but his face was drawn. Slowly he tightened his fingers together until they cracked musically, like splintering bone. The chimney sweeper could not see it, but Clarice was watching him with a look of dread.

"You are afraid of something," she murmured. "Not the Houndswick murderer, but another thing altogether. What is it, Childermass? You must tell me!"

He turned upon her, then. His blind eye was pale and mad, his marble orb a dull weight that lowered and sobered his countenance. The look upon his face was nothing like what she had ever seen in him before.

"There is only one soul whom those footsteps are after," he whispered, half to himself. "And, thankfully, that soul does not stand in this room."

"What are we to do?"

"Call Feversham and Dagworth here. Tell them that they must search the servants' quarters without a moment's delay. I suspect that we shall all too soon find the fool who gave our new guest entry. Then return to me. I have something in mind for you."

Clarice gazed for a moment at the averted face of the chimney sweeper, a look of bewilderment and doubt upon her face. Then at last she said, "Very well."

Childermass waited until the young woman's retreating steps had receded before returning to his former train of thought. The thought of St. Aubert's coming both troubled and intrigued him, for it introduced a gnarl into the fabric of his own invisible scheme that he had not foreseen. Yet, it also amused him in a fashion that even he could not readily define. He was no thirster after murder; but his brain, like a sphere of ice divorced from the heating rush of his burning heart, could contemplate these things with a detachment almost inhuman. And so, while his heart could gloat with desire or melt with pity, depending on whatever stimulus fell into its flames, his mind remained an eternal winter of rapt and methodical deliberation.

Childermass's heart pitied those who would surely suffer for having disobeyed the measures that he had set forth in order to prevent the Torturer's intrusion; hated the distraction and peril attendant upon it and how these two elements would tax his own careful stratagems.

But his mind turned to the mysterious murderer of Houndswick and how he, too, would be baffled by the coming of this new wickedness in a land made foul already by his own excesses – and the thought of this imagined bafflement brought a ghastly smile to his lips.

Chapter Thirty: In which an intrusion is discovered, a murder found without a trace of the murderer, and Childermass prepares to play the part of a villain.

In spite of the mulled cider and lanterns, the wood beneath the canopy had grown colder since the hunt's commencement. A wind from the south had intruded, negotiating the barriers of coats and scarves with an almost sentient alacrity.

The hunters were abroad, in the forest and amongst the close thickets and grey grasses of the moorlands. The report of their muskets came again and again: raucous barks, the breath of which sent forth plumes of fragrant smoke, obscuring the woodlands with a new and denser fog.

Sir Robert Gosselin and the Reverend Abelin felt the cold more keenly than did the hunters on horseback, sitting motionless in their oak thrones and listening to the approach of hooves as the hunters wheeled back and returned to the Priory. Montrose and Mariah were in the lead, their horses halting several yards before the place where the two men sat.

"Did Withing and his new friend Cyrus accompany you?" Sir Robert called out.

"No, my lord," Montrose replied. "Come to think of it, I have not seen them since the hunt began."

Sir Robert's mouth began to tremble violently and he stood with a suddenness that caused even the statuesque Reverend Abelin to glance sharply up.

"Not Withing," he murmured. "Christ in Heaven, let him be safe." To those about, he called out in a voice that shook: "Find him – find my grandson. Do you hear me?" He suddenly shouted: "Why do you all still only look? Go forth – now!"

The trees rang with their own soulless echo, but still all about stood motionless. Sir Robert at last, stricken though he was, turned and saw what it was that they all looked upon so silently.

Feversham was descending the hill. His hands were dripping, blazing a spotted trail of crimson at his back; his face remained grim and impenetrable. Dagworth was at his heels, bulky in the long coat that he always wore.

Sir Robert staggered towards the two before the Reverend caught his arm, urging him to quiet himself.

"Withing..." Sir Robert managed. "It is not Withing you have found, is it, Feversham?"

The ostler slowly shook his head and color flooded back into Mariah's cheeks. "Oh no, sir," said he.

"Then..." Sir Robert stepped back. "What has happened?"

***

When in 1085 (following the untimely death of Sir Etienne du Laughlin) the Priory was appropriated by an order of Dominican monks, her new masters installed a series of cells in the castle for their novices, some on the ground floor and others beneath it. These cells were only large enough to allow for a narrow cot, a desk for the purpose of study and contemplation, and a low bench at which to kneel. A crucifix of wood was nailed to the wall above this bench and when the Priory's present owners converted these cells to servants' quarters, they had not bothered to pluck down these ancient relics of the old religion. The particular cell that Feversham led them to was above ground, lit by the glassless slit of a single window.

The bench was meant for the support of a worshipper as he knelt and clasped his hands before it in inward prayer: not for the young woman who lay stretched across its length, her hair a stream of gold trailing to the floor and her white arms composed upon her breast. The eyes, sea grey, were open and tranquil, the lips parted. Only the wound below her abdomen and the pool of blood that darkened the floor beneath her white dress showed that any violence had been performed upon her at all. When death had come, it had come so swiftly and suddenly that the girl had not had the chance to recognize it; and so, as her blood had chilled and her limbs had stiffened, that look of languor, too, had remained. She was as those transfixed saints who, though riven by a thousand arrows, still hold the same look of eerie, unremitting pleasure.

The death instrument lay upon the nearby bed, its end blotting the sheets with a single, small speck of blood. It was a hunting knife with a handle of silver, mottled with embossed roses; as much an ornament as a weapon.

The rest of them continued to stand outside the cell, hardly drawing breath. Sir Robert's tongue was passing over his dry lips; Montrose's eyes were remote; the Reverend Abelin alone appeared unaltered. Mariah averted her gaze, tears darkening her vision.

"Who did this?" Sir Robert said at last.

Feversham shook his head. After a silence, he said, "Jennie Sandys, one of the young women who worked in the scullery, my lord. She has no kin that any in this Priory know of. Dagworth and I shall see to her burial. Then we shall have the castle searched for any sign of the murderer."

"Searched?" Montrose's gaze flew from the dead girl's form to Feversham's face. "But what if the murderer is already an inhabitant of the Priory?"

The ostler's face did not even twitch as he repeated the lie that Childermass had taught him. After all, it was easier to tell than the truth – that Childermass had stolen a diary and read of a French assassin with a taste for torture who wished for the life of the Priory's newest guest. "My lord, we have it by credible authority that an inmate of the Shrewsfield madhouse escaped less than a month ago. Last week, he was sighted close to this area and this is why we have kept such a strict guard against the entry of strangers. Miss Sandys acted against our precautions and you see the result of her disobedience."

Robert Gosselin appeared too overcome to question the ostler further. Reverend Abelin, however, said softly, "A madman, you say. Then I suppose this murderer will make his presence rather conspicuous."

"Well, Reverend, I am not so sure of that. They say that this madman is also a man of noble birth and that his bearing still accords with his blood, whatever disease has corrupted his mind and causes him to relish the suffering of innocent girls."

Sir Robert flinched at these last words. "And this monster is now within the Priory's walls."

"I fear so, my lord."

"You seem to know a great deal about this murderer, Master Feversham," the Reverend remarked, a faint smile rising to his lips. "Perhaps you might astonish us further with an account of his general physiognomy, so that we may recognize him?"

Feversham disregarded the Reverend's sardonic tone and doggedly replied, "Yellow hair, blue eyes, and a fair complexion."

As they at last turned to depart from that cell, Sir Robert murmured, "How came Feversham to grow so learned in these things when we never heard a single rumor of such an escaped murderer ourselves?"

"That," replied Reverend Abelin. "Is simply answered, my lord. The chimney worm. It is only for us to have him teach us as well as he has taught Feversham."

At these words, Sir Robert again passed a nervous tongue along his withered lips.

"But do you think it would be wise to use him so? My grandson will not approve – and this Childermass is still stricken with blindness, as you know."

"With the greatest respect, my lord, I have never heard that eyesight made a man's nerves less keen. But if, out of some misguided sense of mercy, you wish to delay our lesson, we shall wait until the Eve of Christmas. That shall give him enough time to recover – if recover he ever shall."

***

And so they all went their separate ways; Montrose, to steal a sip of brandy from the Priory kitchens and attempt in vain to clear his head of what he had witnessed in the servant's quarters; the Reverend Abelin and Sir Robert to pursue their own dark, disquieted thoughts; and Mariah to the Great Hall, her own mind so unsettled that she nearly cried out when she happened by accident to run into Clarice.

"Oh, my dear friend," she said. "Cyrus and Withing must still be within the crypt. We must find them and tell them of what has happened."

Clarice returned her friend's terror-stricken look with a dark, melancholic glance. Mariah had not noticed before how very pale and drawn the Reverend's niece had become in the last week. She wondered whether the young woman was not spending too much of her time, perhaps, in the sick chamber of Childermass.

"Clarissa," she said more gently, though she could not keep the tremor out of her voice. "Did you not hear me, dear one? I said that we must go down to the crypt and find Cyrus and Withing."

Clarice pressed Mariah's hand. Her sudden smile mingled with the peculiar sadness of her countenance. "Yes – but you must go without me. Childermass wished me to go to him."

"He is the one who knew that something was amiss from the first, wasn't he?" Mariah murmured.

Clarice nodded. For a moment, her face became radiant with a shining pallor and her dark eyes flashed with both pride and fear. Then, she flushed and turned away.

"Do be careful at least," Mariah said at last. "Remember, the murderer is still within these walls."

"Oh, but I am not afraid of him at all," Clarice smiled. "Not with Childermass as our guide. Do you not think, Mariah, that he, more than any of us – more than even my uncle or Sir Robert – has the power to prevent the horrors that have come upon us?"

Mariah was astonished by the pure faith of the girl's ardor. She had known that Clarice was fond of the chimney sweeper, but she had not realized how great this partiality had grown. Moreover, with her loosened hair floating about her shoulders and her eyes shining like altar candles, Clarice had a witching look about her that Mariah had never beheld before. It made her friend wonder all the more as to what state of mind she had succumbed to.

Mariah, too, recalled at that moment the peculiar look that she had seen in Childermass's eye the night before – the look of him whilst he told the eerie tale of Luke Gosselin's burial. She had been too terrified to notice it; the way in which, every now and then, he would pause and, still watching them, wet his lips. It had seemed such a natural thing, but now as she thought back on it, there seemed something hateful and gloating in that innocent gesture. But beyond its initially repellent appearance, she could not tell what it was that made her shudder at this particular memory.

"The preventer of horrors," she murmured to herself before turning again in the direction of the crypt. "Or the nurturer to them."

She stopped before the bolted barrier of solid black oak that stood between the Great Hall and the lower floors of the Priory. Just as always, it was locked and when she held her ear to the cold wood, she could hear nothing beyond it. Mariah recalled, then, that only three persons held the key to this door and that Cyrus and Withing already possessed Childermass's own. That left only the Reverend Abelin and her uncle Sir Robert Gosselin.

To gain another key would be to confess not only their secret mission but her own complicity in it. Furthermore, she reasoned, there was little chance that the murderer of Jennie Sandys would reach them behind such a barricade. She chose, then, to leave the matter alone for the moment and trust that Cyrus and Withing would return of their own accord.

Yet noon and afternoon passed; the sun fell and evening came; but they never did.

***

The long shadows of dusk fell athwart Childermass as he lay awake upon his bed and listened to the dead child whisper in his ear. He had learned how to listen to the ghosts now, just as he had learned how to look for them when he had possessed sight. At first, it sounded like the scratching of something sharp and smooth against rough wood. Then, as he listened, it grew more distinct; the noise became words and the ringing in his ears, a lost little boy's plaintive voice. Shipwash would have been amazed had he seen Nat in this state; the child had never spoken so much since the death of his parents as he did now to the chimney sweeper.

"When will you take me to Heaven, sir?" Nat was asking. He had the pleading tone of a child who is certain that he is being denied something that would easily be performed, if only he were to ask for it in the right fashion. "Will it be soon?"

There had been nothing else for Childermass to do all that afternoon and evening but lie and listen to Nat's voice and think of what had happened to the dead scullery girl. As he had requested, Clarice had returned to him and told him all that she had seen in that chamber. He had then asked her to depart and return to him later that evening after dinner, again refusing to specify what it was that he required. She would learn of it soon enough.

And so, while he waited, he thought of all that Clarice had told him of the murdered girl lying across the bench like a slain saint, of the silver knife upon the bed and of how it had stained the coverlets so sparingly, and wondered why these details dissatisfied him. There was something wrong in them, some flaw in that simple portrait of death that he could not at first define but, as he continued steadily to think upon it, became starkly apparent.

For St. Aubert had murdered the girl. Childermass was darkly certain that he alone had done it. But, save for a few touches, the death did not bear his signature at all. The silver knife, yes, as well as the eye for aesthetic detail that the languorous look of the corpse had indicated: but one thing –

the most necessary of things – was lacking from the tableau. The room was starved of blood.

True, there had been the stains beneath the dress and the faint smear upon the bed. But these had been nothing to what Childermass knew the Frenchman's heart would have preferred. Something, then, had caused him to exercise a curious restraint in his crime. The girl's death, free of agony, had not merely been a necessary act; it had been, for the Marquis, a mercy killing. But what had she done to deserve in his eyes such an easy death?

In all this mystery, there was only one thing that the chimney sweeper was certain of. The Marquis had been forced to quit the cell more hastily than he had intended. Only this could explain why he would carelessly leave behind so fine a weapon. Perhaps he had heard the approach of footsteps. Childermass imagined that it must have happened just after he had wiped the knife clean with a handkerchief – how else had it stained the bed with only a dribble? – and when St. Aubert had turned away again towards his handiwork. He had departed without a sound, for no one had seen either his coming or his going, and had taken the bloodied handkerchief whilst leaving the murdering knife behind.

Of course, St. Aubert would have looked upon such a trade as infinitely more preferable to its reverse. There were many knives in the world – even fine silver pieces such as the one he had abandoned – but only one cloth with which he had blotted with his own hand the blood of his prey. It was a horribly poignant gesture, the wiping of the blood: one so homely and mechanical as to seem almost innocent, and even Childermass could not prevent the coldness that came over him as he thought of it. Though his heart was often resistant to the warming influences of sympathy, it was more than susceptible to a chill, and it galled as much as it amused him that St. Aubert, whom he had so far only read of with an illicit curiosity, had forced his way into the Priory in spite of the chimney sweeper's measures. There were any number of places in which a murderer could hide himself away but it was impossible in his blindness for him to guess what place St. Aubert had chosen. More than anything, Childermass despised the darkness that had enslaved him and forced him to become even more a prisoner than he had been when he had submitted to his nightly shackles.

So Childermass's thoughts continued to run their dark and chilling course, like a brook that flows beneath a black and moonless sky, until slowly the voice of Nat began once again to grow large in his consciousness.

"I will get you to Heaven," the chimney sweeper replied at last, his voice soft and poisonous. "When you have given me back my light."

"Then it will be never," the child said, his voice full of despair. "For I did not take it and so I cannot give it back."

"Then let it be never," Childermass said and turned away, hoping that the ghost could not see the single tear of pure sorrow that left his living eye to mark his cheek with its glistening path. To be left in darkness, with no hope of sating his curiosity either upon ancient books or the mere sight of the Priory – there could be no greater curse. It allowed him only the cruel satisfaction of feeling the child's suffering as keenly as his own and even this was tainted by the reluctant pity that welled within even Childermass's torturing heart.

"Perhaps I do not know how to help you to Heaven," he said. "Perhaps you are a little fool to trust in me."

"Who else can I go to? All else save you are blind to our existence."

Childermass smiled. "All else are blind save me. And yet I still am ignorant of your murderer."

"He did not want me to go to Heaven, but he did not want me to become as I am now either. He hurt me because he wished me to say the words written in his book. It was big as a Bible, his book. But I did not know how to say them because they were written in a language I could not understand." The child was crying again. "And I was afraid to say them because I didn't know what they meant. And so he cut into me with his knife. Oh, don't let him come near me again! He would torture me even as a spirit, sir, if he found me."

"But for what purpose?" Childermass's mind was racing, driven like a mad beast beneath the flogging of his own relentless curiosity. "Surely he was not torturing you for the mere enjoyment of it?"

"No, sir, he was full of only anger. There was no joy in him at all."

You have heard him howling, sir. Surely you have heard his howls. A man who howled like a beast, who dismembered a child limb by limb because he would not read aloud from a book, and who had for the last year turned healthy bodies – including perhaps Lord Luke Gosselin's – into bloodless corpses. Who was it? Or perhaps more to the point, Childermass mused, what was his purpose?

"Childermass?" In the Great Hall, dinner had ended and Clarice had now entered the room silently to stand by the side of his bed. "You wished me to see you?"

He turned, his blind eye as immobile and impenetrable as his marble one. There was something in his appearance that fascinated her. It was impossible to discern what thoughts were passing through his mind, but she felt as though they must have been powerful, for his lips were white and his eye shone with a luster that was almost too harsh to gaze upon.

His only reply was to point to the side of his bed, indicating that she sit at his right hand. Clarice did so, feeling again that odd thrill of expectancy that always went through her when in the chimney sweeper's presence.

"Withing and Cyrus," he said. "Have they returned?"

"No," Clarice replied. She did not want to sound afraid in his presence, for she feared that such frailty would cause him to despise her, but the strain in her voice betrayed her heart. "No, they are still gone. Mariah at last told Sir Robert and my uncle what happened and they opened the black door and searched the crypt, but could find no trace of them."

"Could find no trace of them," Childermass repeated flatly. For the first time, he felt frankly flabbergasted, a rare state for the chimney sweeper and one which he took little pleasure in. "Could they have lost themselves in the maze of corridors beneath the Priory, as you did?"

"How could they have? You know that the crypt is the simplest thing in the world to find. One only has to take the first set of stairs to the left of the black door, pass through the iron gate, and one is there."

Childermass nodded. Clarice was right; there was no way that even a fool could have lost himself on his way to the Priory crypt. And yet they were gone – whither, though, he could not guess.

"What are we to do?" she asked. "Sir Robert is beside himself with grief and fear – too afraid even to be furious with Mariah and myself."

"Lady Mariah did not, I suppose, hesitate to mention my name as well."

"There was no need for her to. I told them that I stole the key from you while you were asleep."

"Clever girl." Childermass took her hand in his own and ran her fingers along his cheek. "What would I do without you, locked away as I am in this wretched darkness?"

She made no reply. Her brow and cheeks burned headily, however, as though her head and heart would burst. She little realized that this curious consternation that she felt was far exceeded by Childermass's own carefully suppressed inclinations. The most confirmed prude would have been amazed to see how thoroughly the chimney sweeper had managed to leech all evidence of his desire and, by a tangled mixture of cold logic and deliberate disavowal, had denied any affection that existed in his heart and accounted the labor of his breath and the trembling sickness of the heart that took possession of him as a more hateful symptom of the Curiosity that so often came over him when confronted by certain objects or persons. He had starved his heart so well, in fact, that this affection had grown in him like a dead, twisted tree within his heart and – lacking the nourishment that would have caused it to flourish – needed only the searing lightning of some prodigious event to send it ablaze. Woe to the object of such a love when such a fire is kindled! But these are the makings of a future nightmare and have no concern with our present horror.

"What is it that you wished my presence for, Childermass?" she asked.

"A play that Master Shipwash and his grocers will perform upon Christmas Eve. None know of it saving myself and now, Miss Abelin, you as well. I have already promised to play the part of the villain. You shall be my heroine."

Her cheeks caught fire again. "But I know nothing of the theatre."

"Nor do I. We shall suit each other admirably well, will we not?"

"But what am I to do?" she protested, trying with little success to keep the anticipation out of her voice.

"Speak a few lines, scream affectingly; nothing too exerting, I give you my word."

"And you?"

"Why, I shall torture you, Clarice. What else is a poor villain to do?"

Chapter Thirty-One: In which we learn at last the reason behind the long and unwarranted disappearance of Lord Withing and Cyrus Plainstaff.

We have lingered so long upon the hidden movements of the Marquis St. Aubert and the dark observations of Childermass that we must return once again to the start of the day recounted in our last chapter in order to understand what act of hidden treachery prevented Withing and Cyrus from returning. In the shadows of the Great Hall, they hid themselves as Feversham and Dagworth passed by and, alone once again, put Childermass's key into the cavity of the black oak door. The bolt flew back the instant that Withing turned it as though it slid upon oil, and soon they were through the entrance and safely in the darkness. As Childermass had warned them, once the door was closed, there was no light whatsoever, and so Withing had come forearmed with a candle to light once they reached the corridor leading to the crypt. This corridor, Childermass had told them, was always kept in light and it would be the simplest thing in the world to find it if they kept their wits about them and veered left of the main passage.

Cyrus kept a firm grip upon Withing's arm and paused for a moment, disoriented by the abrupt passage from morning light to the close confinement of this underground world.

"You are a little ahead of me," he said at last. "If you feel your way leftwards, you can lead us both to the crypt."

He could feel Withing's arm tense at this instruction and knew that Withing would have preferred that Cyrus take the lead. But it seemed worse somehow to fumble in the darkness and exchange places, for there was always the fear that they might disorient themselves. After a nervous pause, Withing began to grope his way in the direction that they had been instructed. It was a mercifully short space of time in which they crept along before at last spying the first wavering hint of torchlight ahead.

"Does this place look at all familiar to you?" Cyrus asked.

"I believe so," Withing whispered. "Yes! That iron gate was where we all stood while Childermass, Dagworth, and Feversham took my father inside to be sealed up." His face threatened to contort again with fresh grief, but something kept the tears at bay. In the morning air above, perhaps, the tears would have enjoyed their usual triumph. But the air beneath the Priory stifled such sorrow. Perhaps it was the suffocating closeness of the atmosphere; perhaps it was the drafty heat that seemed to rise and fill the passages at intervals, as though they stood in the throat of some stone monster. Certainly there was something more than mere anxiety that caused both their hearts to race, caused them to draw breath more deeply as though it was difficult to fill their lungs with adequate air.

They approached the gate of iron that stood at the entrance of the crypt and Cyrus took the second key that Childermass had given them, unlocking this final barrier. The space they entered seemed, to Cyrus, the grimmest of all the Priory's spaces that he had seen thus far. It was a world where the walls were made of dark, rectangular cavities filled with dust and dead remains; where the ceiling was low and thick, forcing the two to stoop in order to make their way forward; where silence, save for the achingly distant sound of some heavy footstep from somewhere up above, had been banished. Cyrus imagined that what he felt at hearing these sounds could not be dissimilar to the feeling of a diver who has passed down to the uttermost depths of some lake and then looks up to see what chance gleams of sunlight he can spy from on high. There was still a world of life and sunlight, but it existed far above them; were it not for these nearly imperceptible manifestations of its presence, it would seem to have vanished entirely behind the door of black oak.

"Do you know where your father was laid?" Cyrus whispered.

Withing pointed to an alcove ahead of them, separated from the rest of the crypt by a passage lit at intervals with crimson votive candles.

"There," the boy said. His voice, like Cyrus's, was amplified in this narrow sanctum to a startling degree; here, a whisper seemed a raised voice and even the soft, barely perceptible sound of the candle wicks as they smoked, shriveled, and burned seemed as audible as a roaring furnace. Only a moment or so longer, thought Cyrus, and they would be above ground again with this narrow world beneath their feet, as it should be. There was no reason to shudder at the long, solemn caskets of stone and the carven skeletons, the relics of some Norman sculptor's macabre imagination or Dominican's apocalyptic inspiration. Was it not for the living to pity those who died with an evil conscience, to envy those who died well and holily?

They were already walking down the length of that votive-litten hallway. Cyrus glimpsed a shape ahead; the dark, oblong shape of a sarcophagus. Withing saw it too and his legs buckled so that he fell like a kneeling devotee before the sealed bed of stone that bore the name of Lord Luke Gosselin. Cyrus knelt before him, desperately wondering what to say, whilst the boy buried his face in his hands, his sobs shaking him so cruelly that it seemed as though his body was seeking to forcibly expel a sorrow too great for it to healthily harbor.

"Oh, Father!" Withing whispered, raising his face at last, his cheeks streaming, his eyes those of an anguished and uncertain child. "Oh, Father! In the name of Jesus Christ! Pray, forgive me for what I must..." His voice faltered and the tears flowed afresh, though there was a resigned rather than violent quality to his emotions now.

Cyrus caught the young lord by the shoulders. "You are not obliged to do this!" he cried, his voice thrown back at him like a discordant mockery in that narrow, echoing vault. "Come to your senses – it is Childermass who wishes this, not yourself or your father! Let us go back and forget this ridiculous errand."

"But I am obliged to do this." Withing returned Cyrus's pleading stare with one of calm sorrow. "Don't you see, Cyrus? It is a horrible thing to kneel here in this cramped place, surrounded by all these bones and coffins – but it is a far worse thing to return above ground and still be cursed with not knowing. I have been kept in this state of unknowing for a year now and I've hated the Priory for it. But I am weary now of hating and fearing. I only wish to know once and for all what it is that we must face – and what it has in connection with my father."

"But must you do it in this fashion? Must you follow Childermass's advice? Half of what he says seems a riddle and the other half too wild to even be countenanced."

"You mean that you are skeptical of the witch tale he told of my great-uncle Stephen?" Withing asked, puzzled.

"I mean," Cyrus said. "That I do not think Childermass sent us upon this mission for our own good, but rather his pleasure. I think that there is some dark purpose in his wishing to have your father's signet ring and I think that following his advice will lead us farther rather than closer to the truth that you are seeking."

Withing shook his head and rose, moving past Cyrus until he stood beside the sarcophagus. He looked up at the Puritan youth, then, his expression startlingly direct.

"Tell me, Cyrus," he said, and it was his own voice that had a plaintive, pleading quality to it. "If we do not follow Childermass in this matter, then whom shall we follow? My grandfather and Reverend Abelin? We must trust him in this, for we have no other. He is our guardian angel."

"And if it is revealed that you are following a destroying angel instead?"

The boy appeared bewildered, as though such a thought were too absurd even to have crossed his mind. "The only fear I have is that we shall do nothing while still more suffer and die." He hesitated. "You will help me, won't you?"

If anything had been revealed in this conversation, it was the fact that Withing's faith in the chimney sweeper was truly unshakable. Cyrus's own heart burned to tell Withing of Childermass's treacherous behavior towards himself; but, as before, he feared too greatly the effect that this revelation might have upon his own fate. He only prayed that either Withing's faith was not unfounded or that something might soften Childermass's relentless heart.

And so taking opposite ends of the sarcophagus' stone lid, they lifted and set it aside against the wall.

"Let me look alone," said Cyrus. "There is no need for you to see your father."

"Thank you," Withing replied softly.

The boy turned his gaze back towards the corridor through whence they had come and so he did not see the look of shock that crossed Cyrus's face as he looked into the sarcophagus. Instead, his own eyes happened to fall upon a different source of peril.

"Cyrus…" Withing whispered. "I think that someone else has entered the crypt after us."

"What did you see?"

"That shadow."

They looked down the shadowed length of the corridor. At the far end, Cyrus could make out the distant movement of a shadow, but he could not satisfy himself as to whether this belonged to a man or whether it was merely thrown by the erratic flickering of a candle flame.

"Wait here," Cyrus said at last. "I will see if someone is there."

He left Withing to stand beside the stone bier and moved softly down the hallway that led from Luke Gosselin's tomb to the crypt proper. At first, he saw nothing. The altars, the candles, the arches made of carven stone and ornamented with the angel wings shorn of bodies and grinning heads shorn of flesh – all looked as they had before. Cyrus turned his eyes about the silent chamber for a minute longer and then at last returned to Sir Luke's tomb, satisfied that Withing had imagined an intruder.

In the shadow of the crypt's iron gate, the man watched as Cyrus disappeared down that crimson hallway. His eyes remained fixed for a long space upon the place where the young man had stood; time in that world of dust was measured by the fall of wax, a cobweb in movement to the rhythm of some stray, wandering draft. So, for the durance of several rolling drops' worth of wax, four or five moth-like flutterings of a web against a stone wall, the man stood and waited. Then, silently, he drew closer to the entrance of the corridor down which Cyrus had returned.

Cyrus had left the entrance of the corridor in time to find Withing. The boy was motionless, rigid, gazing into the sarcophagus with eyes dry of tears, drained of everything – even horror.

"Cyrus, it's empty." He looked up, his gaze stark, hungry for an answer – any answer. "My father isn't here. Where could he be, if not here?"

Cyrus opened his mouth to reply, for the very shock that Withing was experiencing was identical to his own of only a minute ago – though, of course, the boy's deep love for his father served to deepen his suffering and bewilderment. Before he could, however, the unmistakable sound of a footstep outside the alcove forced their thoughts from the sarcophagus to a more immediate complication.

This time, the shadow that fell athwart the corridor was unmistakable. Cyrus, with an instinctual presence of mind, shoved Withing into a corner of the circular chamber so that he blocked the boy from view as much as was possible. He could hear Withing's labored breathing at his back, echoing his own terror. It was only moments before whoever traversed the corridor would enter and see them. Cyrus thought of St. Aubert – for some desperate, unthinking part of his soul was sure that it was none other than him – and felt his legs lose their strength. As before beauty, so too before horror, the body must kneel.

Cyrus's mind oscillated between a loathing for his inadvertent frailty and a hopeless searching for some way out of the trap that had caught them so effectively. The alcove was perfectly circular save for the gap that gave way into the corridor leading to the crypt. Only the cornices of fluted stone at the opposite ends of its far wall served to interrupt this pattern of smooth stone and Cyrus pressed himself and Withing as far into the shadow of the nearest cornice, sucking in his breath and praying even at that last moment that the coming steps might turn away from their inexorable approach.

He was startled by a movement at his elbow. In spite of his fear, Cyrus could not help but look back and was startled to see that the wall beside the cornice had swung open ever so slightly. A gap, thin as a door that stands only a quarter of the way ajar, was revealed behind the wall of the seemingly solid of the crypt.

"Inside!" Cyrus whispered. Withing needed no further prompting. The secret passage was too narrow to enter head-on, but a fear of the unknown spurred him to flatten against the wall and side-step his way deeper and deeper into the cramped and swallowing darkness. Cyrus followed him, edging along by his side until the rectangle of candlelight at the opening of the passage had been reduced to the merest thread. There they stood, waiting; their faces and backs both pressed by the damp, stifling stones that rose on either side of them.

A shadow blocked the thread of light. A moment passed and then another in which Cyrus knew with a dreadful certainty that someone looked in upon them, trying to catch a glimpse of who they might be. In that space, Cyrus thought he caught a fleeting glimpse of the stranger's profile: an arched nose, a high brow, the dent of lips. For a moment, Cyrus had a fleeting impression that there was some familiar quality in this half-seen shadow of a face; but he could not for the life of him recall what brought about this notion. Certainly it bore no resemblance to the Marquis St. Aubert. Cyrus felt relief flood his heart at this.

At last the stranger withdrew his head from the gap. The thread of candlelight returned to illumine the far end of the passage. Cyrus strained to hear the sound of receding footsteps.

It never came. Instead, the echoing groan of stone against stone filled his ears. The thread of light winked out. The entrance to their passage had been closed.

Even then, a part of Cyrus's mind persisted in believing that this new development was a trap and so he remained motionless for an interminable amount of time before at last edging his way back, along the way that they had come. He found the place where they had emerged, but could find no latch to open the way – nothing save a circular indentation in the stone. He pushed against the wall with all his might; the stones were as solid and motionless as though he strained against the side of a mountain. At last, in spite of his former fears, he called out for someone, anyone, to open the wall so that they might emerge. No reply came.

Buried beneath the labyrinthine floors of the Priory, trapped under solid masses of stone, and held on either side by the suffocating pressure of the choking passage, Cyrus rested his cheek against the wall and listened as Withing began to breathe heavily, strangled by the close air. He could feel his own lungs begin to labor for air. The silence was only broken by the sound of their breaths.

The darkness itself was utter.

Chapter Thirty-Two: In which the Priory is graced with the nobility of England and Scotland; Mariah, Montrose and Childermass expound upon their individual notions of a rescue operation; and Clarice learns the secret of the Priory's walls.

Night had fallen and yet the great hall of the Priory was still alive, transformed into a vision of candles and wreaths, a moving panoply of richly-clothed figures, all the noble guests of Sir Robert, who would remain under the Priory's hospitality until the feast of Epiphany. Their jewels and buckles shone like distant stars against the firmament of tapestries and torches that made up that festive scene whilst far above it rose the piping melody of a lament, set to a tempo of indescribable gaiety, and effecting upon the hearts of those who listened to it a nearly unbearable vicissitude of successive emotions. The effect was akin to the delicious torture of ringing glass set to music.

"I could never bear the sound of bagpipes," Montrose began – then caught himself when he saw the distant look of enchantment that had riveted Childermass' visage.

They were all standing together upon the landing of a staircase, looking down upon the Great Hall – Lady Mariah, Clarice, the Earl of Lauderness, and, of course, Childermass: voyeurs rather than participants of the evening's merriment. Sir Robert was absent from the feast and his guests, having been too distressed by his grandson's disappearance to emerge from his chamber. A search had, of course, been organized for the errant young lord as well as for Cyrus Plainstaff, but it had revealed nothing, not even a hint of where the two had disappeared. Mariah had confessed their plan to search the crypt, but even an investigation of the lower floors of the Priory had revealed nothing. They had well and truly vanished.

Montrose stood, his elbows resting on the bannister, his face drawn and morose. Anxiety made him petulant, for it foisted upon him a sobriety that was unnatural to his constitution. Yet even the hot-headed Earl could not simply dismiss the vision of the murdered young woman from his memory; and though he would have liked to participate in the evening's revelries, he simply had not the heart to do so. He could still see Feversham and Dagworth hauling out the body through one of the back doors of the kitchen, preparing to have it carted into town for a Christian burial. The memory made him feel ill and long for another taste of the brandy which had so far fortified him against the more unpleasant extremes of his present mood.

Mariah stood beside him, her own pale face set like stone and impenetrable. She was thinking not only of her cousin Withing but of the mysterious stranger who had vanished along with him, wondering whether she would see them alive again or whether they too would surface either as corpses gutted with a silver knife or sapped of blood. The horrors that had mounted since Sir Luke Gosselin's death had at first served to paralyze her with terror. But this December was not as that past one had been. The chill of paralysis had melted into a desire for activity. Fear was now a spur to action.

"We must do the searching ourselves," she said. "Feversham and Dagworth could easily have missed a corridor beneath the Priory."

"That is undoubtedly true, my lady," Childermass replied. "For I am convinced that both Lord Withing and Master Plainstaff are within these walls."

"Where shall we begin?" Clarice asked. For the last hour, her hand had remained within the chimney sweeper's vice-like grasp and held against his heart as though he wished to be sure at all times of her presence. There was nothing consciously sensual in this possession, for he held her fingers with the passionless desire to simply know that she stood by him. When she uttered this question, however, she felt the beat of his heart quicken beneath her fingers and her own pulse began to race, though she hadn't the slightest idea as to what had prompted the sudden coursing of Childermass's blood.

"We must search still deeper," he said.

"But we haven't a key to the crypt. Withing and Cyrus still have yours."

"Ah..." Childermass said as though he had already thought of this, but was not inclined to remark any further.

Mariah turned her eyes to the pale, sharp-featured chimney sweeper. "And what convinces you, Master Childermass, that we shall follow your instruction? It was heeding your advice that led my cousin and Master Plainstaff into their present predicament."

Childermass's lips twisted into the semblance of a conciliatory smile as he replied, "My lady, you are, of course, at liberty to disregard my advice. My words, as always, have ever been merely suggestions, not orders."

"I am gratified," she replied, her eyes flashing, "that you are aware that you are in no position to deliver orders."

Childermass's lips turned as white as a corpse's, but he made no retort. Mariah, however, felt a sense of unease chill her heart as she looked upon the chimney sweeper's inexpressive countenance. Clarice started to turn away from the two of them, but Childermass tightened his fingers about her wrist.

"And what think you, Clarice?" said he. "Shall we two look for the lost ones ourselves?"

Caught between Mariah's look of disapproval and Childermass's blind look of enquiry, Clarice felt herself trapped.

"Well, we must do something, mustn't we, Lord Montrose?" she said at last, helpless.

Montrose, who had been listening to this conversation with a feeling of detachment bordering on ennui, replied, "Well, of course, the great thing is to do something. But what, what, what? It would appear that the Lady Mariah and Master Childermass have diametrically opposed notions of what must be done. What is required is, of course, an objective opinion. Mine, I believe."

A frown shadowed Childermass's brow and Mariah appeared even more ill at ease than when the chimney sweeper had put forth his own suggestion. Clarice attempted in vain to hide a smile.

"Feversham and Dagworth did a fine job of exploring the interior of the Priory, but perhaps the grounds are in need of a search. What think you, Lady Mariah? It is a novel approach, you must admit."

Mariah disliked the flippant tone of the Earl, but there was no denying that he had a point. Furthermore, she had absolutely no desire to either accompany the chimney sweeper or follow his suggestions.

"Very well," she said at last. "Clarice, won't you come along with us? I know the hour is late, but it is best if we do it tonight, whilst the rest of the guests are preoccupied. I doubt that Sir Robert would take too kindly to our exploring without his permission."

Clarice thought for a moment. Though she was often mistaken as impressionable, she never for a moment lost possession of herself and her own desires. Her heart was her own and neither the disapproval of Mariah nor the bitter, provoking look of Childermass could force her to one side or another. There was something in Childermass's way of speaking, his intimations, and his conduct, however, that caused her to inexorably find herself drawn to elevate his opinion above even the advice of her dear friend. And so, of her own free will, she said at last with all the candor of an enraptured heart, "I would go with you, Mariah, yet I cannot but think that Childermass is right."

"As he was right in sending Withing and Cyrus to the crypt?" Mariah returned bitterly.

Clarice returned her friend's look without defiance, but with steady resolution. "It was not Childermass's fault that something happened to them there. But it is our duty now to save them."

Mariah lifted an eyebrow and smiled with a grim sort of resignation. "Very well. My lord Montrose," she said, turning to the Earl. "Let us go to the stables and be about our business at once."

Montrose pointed to the staircase with a gallant bow. "After you, Mistress Mariah," he declared and the two of them departed to form one half of the Priory's covert search party.

Childermass remained silent for a long while, his sightless eye and his marble one both settled upon the feast and the guests that lay below him. His thoughts were uncharacteristically disordered, violent and confused, his heart baffled before Clarice's devotion. He would have understood, would have delighted, had he been constrained to use some force in order to draw her to his side. Then he could have been sure of what cause provoked her to remain in his thrall. As it was, this free allegiance bewildered and troubled him. It was a mystery to him, what this young woman could love in such a one as he; and before such a mystery, Childermass found himself unwillingly captivated. He did not believe that he loved Clarice; no, not for a moment would he have entertained such a contemptible thought. Yet he was very close to enjoying the mystery of her, as he enjoyed the mystery of the Priory itself. His tongue had gone very dry and yet he murmured softly, "I thank you for remaining with me."

"Of course," she said, surprised by the look in the chimney sweeper's eye. "I would follow you wherever you wished to go."

"Well, and if you will follow me," said Childermass. "Then I swear by my life that I shall show you secrets that these others have never even dreamt of. How would you enjoy that, my pretty friend?"

And Clarice, who could not imagine what Childermass meant but felt herself inflamed by the mystery of his words, said breathlessly, "Very much."

***

Childermass, with Clarice at his side, descended the staircase that led into the Great Hall, until they both stood in the mist of the Priory's host of guests. The chimney sweeper had devised a plan, and this he whispered into Clarice's ear, telling her the part that she must play in the comedy that he had so craftily composed.

"You will find the most richly-dressed noble in this gathering," he said. "One whom you are certain cannot be denied anything without causing a serious embarrassment. Tell him of an exquisite Portuguese port kept in the cellar. Tantalize him with it until he demands a taste. Then come to me, for I've the key to the cellar. There must be no suspicion that we go down for any cause but to bring up the wine."

"But the cellar gives no access to the crypt."

"'Tis true, and yet you shall soon know how cunningly we two shall flit there in spite of Sir Robert and your uncle's wishes. Now, away!" he added with a smile. Then, as though ashamed of the unwonted gentleness in his own manner, the chimney sweeper's countenance grew cold and he turned away, conducting his way by memory back to the staircase to await the girl's return.

Clarice gazed after him, bewildered by this sudden change in mood, but hardly troubled by it, as she was by this time accustomed to the curious vicissitudes of the chimney sweeper's temper. With a wry smile, she turned her attention to the guests who surrounded her – some standing by and talking amongst themselves, others seated at the long table that stood in the middle of the hall. It would not be difficult to find the lord whom Childermass's plan required – and oh, what new plan had the chimney sweeper in mind once they found their way into the cellar?

"I must not take such delight in all this," she told herself. "But if I do, then it is Childermass's fault. Somehow, he makes it all seem so light-hearted, like a game. But that's not what it is at all."

And yet she could not shake off the feeling. It reminded her of the first time that Dagworth had offered her a sip of his liquor – the burning sensation that lingered for hours in her brain. This was very much like it; the only difference was that it was now her heart that was on fire.

***

The night was cold and the sky as clear as glass, revealing the black heavens and the stars that shone above like distant windows in the wall of some celestial fastness. Even the bitter northern wind that customarily haunted the Priory's forests at this time of year was absent, leaving in its place a frosty stillness. Save for Montrose at her side and her own breath misting before her mouth, Mariah saw no movement in this world: only the stars, like brilliant motes of ice, and the dark growths of oak that rose about them as they walked the path that led from the Priory to the watchtower.

Lord Andrew Ebenezer Montrose, feeling his face go cold and dry in that wintry vacuum, was beginning to seriously regret having suggested that they brave the Priory's grounds at this hour. True, there was still the possibility that they might find Cyrus and Withing in this way – though Heaven knew what could have possibly detained the two youths this long in such disagreeable weather – but Montrose would have preferred an expedition indoors to the one that he had so cavalierly insisted upon within the warmth of the Priory.

"The devil take me for a fool," he swore ripely under his breath. "For not siding from the very beginning with the chimney sweeper! A wiser fellow he, conducting his charitable deeds indoors."

"You do not mean to tell me, dear Montrose, that you are already having second thoughts about your own scheme."

The Earl met Mariah's ironic smile with a strained smile of his own.

"God forbid, sweet lady," said he. "But I do wonder at your reluctance to follow Master Childermass's advice. It seemed sound to my own ears."

"Master Childermass has a talent for seeming sound," Mariah replied. "He has already enchanted Withing, appears to have enchanted Clarice, and I will not be a whit surprised if he enchants you as well."

Montrose laughed. "'Enchant?' That pale miscreation? Aye, he has a fair enough face if one were able to ignore the marble eye, that knife of a nose, and the prudish mouth, but I should hardly revere him even without these defects."

"I do not mean that you revere him – though I believe that Withing and Clarice do. What I mean is that he has a talent for always finding someone willing to follow whatever it is that he asks of them."

"Even that is hardly a crime, my lady, if his desires are perfectly reasonable."

"You think me only an anxious woman," Mariah said, her manner still unruffled though terse. "I only hope that you are right in thinking so."

"Well, what proof have you that there is anything to fear from Childermass? He has lived within your walls for as long as I can remember. Surely if there were anything underhanded in him, it would have been revealed by now."

They had reached the belltower by this time and as they stood beneath its shadow, they could see the face of the broken timepiece with both its hands exalted in a ceaseless worship of midnight.

"It is only in a few odd looks that I have seen cross his face from time to time," Mariah admitted at last. "I do not know how to put it but – do you sometimes feel that he loves the Priory a little too well?" When Montrose's only reply was a bewildered frown, she continued, "More than its masters, I mean? That he would be happier to wander it without the cumbrance of its other inhabitants or that he would prefer to somehow rule it rather than serve it?"

Montrose laughed. "It is probably the dream of every poor chimney sweeper. I see nothing in it to fear."

"Perhaps you are right," Mariah said. "Only – "

She stopped short and Montrose halted beside her.

"What is it?" he asked.

"I thought I heard something – almost like a – there it is again!"

This time Montrose heard it too: a desperate, melodious keening, like the sound of a bird trapped in a chimney. It rose and fell in volume like the approach and retreat of an invisible minstrel, yet Mariah was certain that its source was somewhere to the left of their path.

"It could be the wind."

"There is no wind, Your Grace," Mariah replied. Before Montrose could answer her, she had already taken off in the direction of the faint call. With a sigh, he followed after her.

They both broke into a run, however, at the next sound that cleaved the silence of that chilling night. It still echoed for several seconds afterward in their memories: that unmistakably human scream.

The woodland flew past her as she ran, a flock of twisted growths rising to shadow the heavens. Up ahead, the stars were further obscured by a sloping hillside, dark and overgrown with a tangle of thorny underbrush. As she continued on, she saw the trees fall away to reveal the arched entrance of a cave that entered into the hollow side of the hillock. Without a doubt, this was where the sound had emanated.

A flood of light covered the forest and hill with its brilliance, quick as the blink of an eye, before leaving the moonlight alone again. The sky was clear of clouds and so Mariah knew that it had been no lightning burst that had momentarily blinded her. And after all, what light from the heavens ever erupted first from beneath a hillside?

Some part of Mariah's heart perceived these signs and knew that the closer that she drew to the source of that cry, the closer she came to some knowledge that was beyond whatever horror she could have imagined in the quiet of her own chamber. Her own imaginings could not have produced what it was that drove now into her breast with such urgency and caused her to feel her traitorous limbs threaten to lose all resolution. It was not panic, for it turned her to stone rather than water. It was something that turned her into a single eye, without brain, hands, or feet: able to see and feel but incapable somehow of action or even judgment. Something, she knew, stood beyond the veil of darkness that shrouded that grotto – she willed herself to move forward, but her feet remained as stupid as stones.

"God in Heaven," she whispered, her teeth ground tightly together. "I've not even seen what is in there and already I am faltering."

She remembered the scream and know that even as she stood there, enchanted, another's nerves were still riveted in a different and much more visceral fashion. With an effort, she forced herself forward and almost instantly felt the dream-like weight lift from her shoulders and carry itself beneath her feet so that now, conversely, she felt as though she walked towards the mouth of the grotto with the ease of air. She heard Montrose behind her – judging by the intemperate rhythm of his steps, he too had been afflicted by a similar epiphany of the senses, but her own movement had shaken him free as well. Together, they approached the grotto, their ears filled with the sound of a chanting plainsong and the tortured voice that sobbed beneath it as a faithful accompaniment.

There was a child standing against the far wall of the shallow cave. It was from his mouth that the weeping came, but now in a muffled fashion as though something other than tears now filled it. His arms were raised and gathered together at the wrists with ropes so tightly knotted that threads of blood ran down the taut flesh. Of a sudden, the awful sobbing ceased and gave way to a sound that seemed halfway between a cough and a gulp. It was difficult to see the boy's face; the eyes were tightly shut, the cheeks drained of blood, and the throat was lost to shadow as though something leaned over it, obscuring it from view. At the opposite end of the grotto, a dark figure in a hooded mantle stood, open book in hand, chanting a song in stately Latin.

The victim's struggles were growing feebler by the moment. When she saw the little spill of crimson that had begun to fall down the child's shirtfront, Mariah could bear it no longer. Forgetting her terror, she stepped forward and delivered her most ear-splitting and blood-curdling shriek.

What happened next, Mariah could not be certain of. The singing ceased as though someone had stopped the throat of the singer by force. The figure that leaned over the victim raised his head and looked in her direction. The eyes were young, clear and grey; the curve of the cheekbones, or that part of them that the moonlight touched, possessed of an angle oddly familiar. It was difficult to make out the mouth in those uncertain shadows, but it almost looked as though something long and ribbon-like fell from the lower lip, spilling down nearly to the figure's chest. This illusion – more than likely caused by the peculiar slant of some shadow – had the grotesque effect of causing the figure's lips to appear oddly slackjawed, as though a solid stream of dripping blood ran straight from his mouth to his feet. The next moment, swift and leaping, the figure ran out of the cave and away into the woodlands, his own darkness becoming a part of the forest's. As for the robed singer, he had taken advantage of this momentary distraction to vanish even before his companion.

Chapter Thirty-Three: In which Childermass proposes to Clarice an ingenious theory and St. Aubert discovers for himself a new object worthy of attention.

Clarice had waited upon the landing for nearly half an hour before she caught sight of Childermass's approach. She hastened to him then, whispering, "Is it safe for you to wander alone? Jennie's murderer – "

"Will have no desire to harm me," Childermass replied. "Have I not already told you this? That is not to say that I recommend your wandering about the Priory alone."

She gazed in astonishment at the chimney sweeper's utterly humorless face. "What a hypocrite you are, Childermass!" she said at last. "One moment you pretend that we are safe and the next you tell me that I should not go about by myself. Are you often in the habit of revising your opinion to suit your own interests?"

"I should hardly revise it to suit another's," replied the chimney sweeper. "Now, shall we wile away the hours debating my character or shall we go now to the cellar?"

"I feel that there is more to Jennie's murder than you are telling me," Clarice murmured.

"And how came you to imagine that?"

"Only the look upon your face when I happen to mention it and the way you seem both less and more afraid than the rest of us – as though you knew more about it."

"Should I put a guard over my face henceforth?"

"It would be a kindness to me at least! I confess that I am nearly frantic with curiosity to know what it is that you yourself know."

The cellar was less a chamber than a cavern made of vaulted ceilings and walls of dusty, narrow cells. The sheer multiplicity of these cells attested to the wealth that must have belonged to the Priory during its time as a seat of the Dominican order. Under its new masters, the Priory's stores seemed stunted by comparison, though in a wine cellar of more moderate proportions it would have appeared magnificent.

Childermass led the way into that shadowed world, himself blind but still able to navigate his way between the ancient caskets of wood as easily as though he not only possessed sight but made his way through a bright, unfurnished hall.

Clarice held her torch high, taking in the splendor of cobwebs and the dull glitter of dust-covered glass.

"We haven't much time," she said. "My uncle will notice that I am gone before long."

Childermass had reached the western wall of the cellar and was climbing it by way of the empty cells in the wall, which his nimble fingers and narrow feet made excellent use of. He scuttled up, hand over hand, until he had gained the uttermost shelf, which terminated a few inches from the ceiling. From there, he beckoned for Clarice to follow.

She eyed the makeshift staircase dubiously.

"I'm not certain that I can ascend as easily as you," she called up.

"Certainly you can. And I require your eyes in this matter, Miss Abelin, as I have not even one left for myself any longer."

Gritting her teeth and not daring to look down, the Reverend's niece began to slowly climb the stone shelves, the torch held precariously in her right hand as she maneuvered upwards with her left. At last, breathless and dizzied, she reached Childermass's side.

"Now tell me," said he. "Do you see anything strange about this wall at our backs?"

She felt the sightless gaze of his pale eye trained upon her as she transferred her own attention to the stones that completed the space betwixt the shelf and the vaulted ceiling.

"Save for a few cracks in the stone, I can see nothing remarkable," she confessed.

"And those cracks? How deep are they?"

She put her fingers into one of the wider cracks, expecting to soon feel the surface of stone. To her surprise, though the crack was hardly deep, she was able to put her whole finger into the crevice without encountering a single impediment. With a little extra effort, she managed to pry the stone loose and shone the torch's light into that narrow opening. Now there was no doubt at all: a narrow crawlspace had been built behind the cellar wall.

"I am convinced that a great many of the Priory's walls are hollow," said Childermass upon hearing her discovery. "Do you remember the breath of air that you felt that night that you lost yourself in the Priory's lower floors? I chose this particular wall as it adjoins the place where Sir Luke is interred. I would not be surprised if our two friends somehow trapped themselves in the maze of these walls."

"Why?"

"Their sudden disappearance. Our complete inability to find any trace of them. Had they fallen prey to Jennie's murderer, I assure you, they would not have remained hidden for long. Our new guest is not modest in respect to the largess of his talents. What other way could they so effectively have vanished, save by losing themselves in the very walls?"

It was impossible to imagine what it must be like to crawl, cramped and constricted, between those two tight walls for hours on end – searching for an escape and finding only the endless progression of slithering corridors and blind, hollowed-out alleys.

"But how?" Clarice asked. "How did they trap themselves so?"

"They could not," Childermass replied, "unless a trap had been laid for them."

The chimney sweeper and the Reverend's niece descended again to the floor of the cellar. This time, Childermass led the way to the northern wall, to a space bare of shelves.

"What do you see here?" he asked.

The rough stones were all equal in appearance, save one which bore upon its face a circular bas-relief image of a leafless tree. Clarice instantly recognised it.

"The tree of the Gosselins," she whispered.

"And the symbol engraved upon their signet ring. A perfect fit for this engraved ornament, do you not think?"

Clarice traced a finger over the curious keyhole and said, "Then you think that Sir Robert's signet ring would open this wall?"

"Perhaps. But there are other ways to coax it open, I am certain."

His pale eye, sightless though it was, had settled upon some distant corner of the cellar, and his already spare lips had drawn themselves into a still thinner line of taut flesh. It was only when his tongue happened to moisten that dry mouth that Clarice caught a glimpse of something like anticipation in the chimney sweeper's mien. In an instant it was gone, subsumed by a bitter gravity. Yet there was something in that casual motion that reminded Clarice of an earlier occurrence – something that she could not, at that moment, recall but that nagged, invisible, in the recesses of her memory.

"We must tell Sir Robert and my uncle about this at once," she said. "There will be no need for us to force the wall open if Sir Robert employs his signet ring."

"Ah, but he will not."

There was something chilling in the surety of Childermass's dour retort.

"Why will he not?" she demanded.

"Do you not know by now that there is something both terrible and wonderful hidden at the very heart of the Priory's power? Something that they wish to keep hidden, for if it were revealed, it would be the death of the Gosselins? Do you not imagine that these hollow walls could reveal secrets that others might wish to leave to the dust and curiosity of rats?"

"They will do all they can to save Withing and Cyrus," Clarice returned.

"We can only pray, my lady," said Childermass, but his tone was dry.

And it was then, all in a moment, that Clarice recalled what it was that the chimney sweeper's tongue had brought to mind – for it had been with that same hungry gesture that Childermass had followed the last request that he had made of Withing: that he bring to Childermass the signet ring of Lord Luke Gosselin.

"You desired Lord Luke's ring," she said, unsure even of what suspicion it was that prompted her to speak. "But was it truly to prove the truth of Sir Stephen Gosselin's account?"

Never before had she seen so sudden and so complete a transformation in a visage as she beheld after the close of her simple question. Instantly, the face of Childermass grew as white as though it had been bled of all blood: white as his marble eye, white as the center of a flame, whiter even than the bare bone beneath a deep and brutal cut. This unholy pallor had an odd appearance: it seemed to set Childermass's flesh burning with an inward fire, much like that of an ember that flares brightly before collapsing inwards upon itself. Clarice felt afraid to stand any longer in the company of this transfiguration; she felt herself in the presence of a spirit rather than a mortal and the sensation was fraught with a paralyzing awe and fright.

Before either Childermass or Clarice could dispel the enchantment of horror that had fallen over them both, the sound of raised voices from above shook their attentions free. There was a quality to their pattern and cadence that suggested that some new happening had once again taken the Priory by storm.

"We must go," Clarice said.

"Yes," Childermass said, with a pale and tight-lipped smile. "I think we must."

With a sightless instinct, he stepped forward, feeling for her hand. As his fingers closed about her wrist, she felt her spirit sink, though she could not for the life of her have told why. It was as though his hand had passed through her flesh and taken hold of her heart instead and that there was nothing she could do to shake that implacable grip. Their eyes met – or at least her eye fell upon the translucent flesh that made up his own unseeing orb.

What a riddle it would have made, the look that passed between them: the bewildered look in her able eye and the bitter gaze of understanding in his blind one. It was a corruption of the ordinary and only the two of them, by virtue of their union in the paradox of that look, were unable to recognize it for the sublime subversion that it was. Had an outsider seen it, his own gaze would have been riveted by the impossibility of their wordless communion.

And then Childermass spoke and his speaking was the most exquisite perversion of all, for it was the truth, the pure, unadulterated truth, that fell from that artful tongue as he told her: "And no, it was not for Sir Stephen Gosselin's account that I sought the signet ring. It was for myself."

***

Save for Cyrus, Withing, the chaplain, and Sir Robert, they were all there to see it – all the nobles, all the inhabitants of the Priory: the child laid out on the long table of the Great Hall, breast heaving, blood streaming from his mouth.

Everything had been leading to this moment. The year of secrecy and desperation, Withing's return and Cyrus's coming, the party of wassailers – even the advent of St. Aubert, though he came as a separate shadow to, unwittingly, join the darkness that already held the Priory by the throat: they had all formed into the limbs of a single inexorable Event, all moving as one towards an equally inexorable ending. Childermass's eye had been put out, his one light snuffed by the Essex farmer who had now arrived as a hanging spirit made up of chains and the weightless, glowing memory of lost flesh. Yet out of all of them, it was the blinded Childermass who saw the ragged pieces and the matter of chance meetings and hidden plottings that sewed them together – saw them as a single, sinewed Horror, powerful enough to separate and sift the Priory's stones like seashells.

Whatever the Horror was, it had become something beyond the Houndswick murderer and the bloodthirsty Marquis, for it had escaped its original confinements. It was meant to have been a thing of forgotten woodland walks and lonely moors, or the sealed privacy of a torture chamber in one of Gomershall's manors; Cyrus had brought it into the Priory by fleeing from it and now Lady Mariah had carried its other half, bleeding and grey-lipped, into the Great Hall itself. Childermass was certain that the original engineers of these nightmares had not reckoned on the sewing together of these two unwieldy and separate creatures and it was their fusion and resistance to each other that created the present chaos. They infected one another like a pair of ill-grafted limbs – worked and destroyed with an animation beyond the skill of their creators to contain them. The two-headed Horror had grown into a thing that surely bewildered and dismayed the murderers as much as their victims. The dour line of the chimney sweeper's lips twitched with pleasure. He wore a look of gratitude, the look of a saint who after years of watching has been granted a particularly gratifying vision.

In the darkness of a stairwell, another shadow stood, watching Childermass as he blindly listened to the spectacle and the whispered description of the child's condition as Clarice recounted it in his ear. It was this unseen stranger alone, standing with his fingers clothed in knives and his throat and wrists muffled with reams of crisp, patterned lace, who saw it all: the convulsion of the lips and the accompanying look of pale, nearly religious intensity that flowered in Childermass's visage as he listened and murmured to the young woman, "I shall set it right – believe me, I know what it is that ails this Priory."

Bloodstained as those soft hands had been so often before, the intruder watched the chimney sweeper's countenance and the dying child and felt the first intimation of fear that he had experienced for as long as he could remember. Why he should fear, he could not tell; he was more than able to protect himself against the Houndswick murderer, or so he believed – and as for Childermass, the young man was hardly a threat to him. Childermass's expression at the moment, though curious, was hardly cruel; it had in it the cold tranquility of an angel, not the gloating of a fiend. Yet St. Aubert watched that pale eye and felt his blood turn to ice, his heart clench as though it were a fist. With a last lingering look, he withdrew from that place, trembling as though he had been shown his own headstone. His momentary fear was soon displaced, however, by an emotion more recognizable to him than terror. It was that old, familiar hunger – and if he did not remove himself immediately, he knew that he would approach this Childermass in front of all that company and take him then and there with his knife. He doubted that the nobles there would care very much about the loss of one chimney sweeper, but St. Aubert hardly wished to expose himself so crassly. It was not that he feared justice; it was simply not his way.

The child on the table had suddenly grown still, a trail of blood still streaming from his parted lips. Montrose closed his eyes at this sight, his own face very pale; Mariah leaned forward, taking the child by the shoulders and whispering, "Come awake, please – please, come awake."

There was utter silence. Then, with a start, the boy came awake and shouted, "I will say it! Oh, I promise I'll say it, sir! Caelum te nego, caelum te nego, caelum te nego, ave terra – now let it stop, I beg you. Let it stop."

And as naturally as though he had finished his bedside prayers, the boy fell quietly into a deep and utter swoon.

The door at that moment opened and Feversham entered, the apothecary at his side, moving so swiftly that his cloak rose behind him as though it rode on water. After several minutes of silent inspection, the apothecary raised his eyes and said briefly, "The child will live. But he must be kept under careful watch and be made to drink as much water as he can. He has suffered a terrible loss of blood and it is a miracle that he has survived the shock of it. A little more and I tell you frankly, he would have ended like all the others."

As Feversham and Dagworth carried the sleeping child up to Childermass's former sick chamber, Clarice murmured, "I did not understand what the Latin the boy spoke meant."

"Not at all what one would expect from a cobbler's apprentice," said Childermass, for he had recognized the child's voice immediately. "'I renounce you, heaven. I renounce you, hell. Hail, earth!"

"But what did he wish to stop?" Clarice asked. "What was it that he hoped these words would end?"

"The torture," Childermass replied. "The same torture that tore Nat limb from limb and forced all the other victims to say those words. But there was a difference – Nat did not say them all. That was why he was taken apart, whilst the others were not. There were more words than only those to say."

"And what were those?"

"Words that would keep a victim's tongue silent – forever."

"They were dead," Clarice said. "How could they ever hope to speak again?"

The chimney sweeper thought of his recent acquaintance with the dead child and the tongueless Puritan and said nothing.

Chapter Thirty-Four: In which Childermass reviews the last generation of the noble Gosselins and arrives at several conclusions, none of them particularly savory.

Childermass had first come to the Priory in the year of 1656, nine winters previous to the events recounted here, when Withing was but a child of five and his father Lord Luke and uncle Sir Robert both lived out their rather comfortable exile in France. This was the time of the Protectorate, when Oliver Cromwell ruled and the Puritan poet John Milton, though blind, continued to dictate his tracts on behalf of the new Commonwealth with the faithful Marvell by his side. Yet in Scotland, there were still many Scotsmen who despised this new English yoke as much as they had the former and felt no substantial change between Cromwell's reign and that of the monarch Charles Stuart.

It was hardly an era of peace. But for Childermass, who had spent all his life in Houndswick laboring by day for the local chimney sweeper and spending his nights in the pews of the local kirk, it was indistinguishable from what it would have been had King Charles still sat on the throne. He did not know of the hard old Presbyterians who had resisted Archbishop Laud's tyrannies, nor did he know of Scotland's support and then renunciation of Parliament's cause and her subsequent defeat at the hands of Cromwell and his generals. There was nothing of Scotland's history in him: he knew little of the moors and heathlands that surrounded him save what he learned from travelers and in tavern songs and could only appreciate the beauty of the land during those few hours when he was not climbing the grimy walls of a chimney or sleeping off a draught of ale. He had never known his parents, for he had been left as a foundling at the church and given away to the master sweep as soon as he was of age to work. Whether they had been loyalists to the crown, firebrand Presbyterians, or rebellious Roundheads, he little knew nor much cared.

They had first named him Childermass because he had been found upon the Feast of the Holy Innocents. They continued to call him it, in honor of his face, which was cold and humorless even when it smiled, and for his fortune, which was naturally desperate, as he was a chimney sweeper. He had seen many of the other children die, most only several years his elder, and did not expect to live much longer himself. Sometimes, he would drench the wood of a church pew with tears, but those nights of sorrow did not arise out of any fear of death but rather of how he would die. He remembered the terrible burns that he had seen on one body before they had covered it with churchyard loam and imagined those welts rising upon his own flesh, burning him with an unutterable agony. The reverend spoke of Heaven and Childermass believed in it; but he wept to think of how he must suffer before he would be let in.

***

Childermass had heard rumors all his life of the House of Gosselin and its history, mostly in the form of songs and tales told by tavern guests who hoped to win a drink by recounting a particularly gruesome ballad. He learned in this way of Lord Stephen Gosselin and his quest after earthly immortality and he heard in some of the bawdier songs of his consorting with the witch Alison Mackenzie and her two sons, all three of whom were said to be as deathless as the spirits they served.

In most of the townships of southern Scotland, the Feast of the Innocents was remembered only in song and prayer; but in Houndswick and Shrewsfield, it was still celebrated as a time of carnival, just as it had been in the days of King Alfred. Cobblers would dress as kings while magistrates would, for one day, masquerade as beggars; children would rule the house in honor of those slaughtered by Herod and would dress in the finery of princes while their parents wore the sackcloth of mourners. For the orphaned chimney sweepers who could not afford rich clothing, Childermass among them, the long white robes of holy martyrs were enough.

At the start of his ninth winter, upon the midnight of that very feast day, Childermass first heard the tale of Lord Stephen Gosselin and the tongue of Satan. The bartender's daughter, Bridgette McEwan, said that it was upon the Feast of the Holy Innocents that he had been offered this chance at immortality and had, at the last moment, chosen to reject it. When she paused to take a long draught from her glass of ale, Childermass leaned forward and said, "But why did he reject it, mother?" All the chimney sweepers called Bridgette McEwan their mother, even though she was no older than twenty, for the sweets that she would coddle them with and the ale that she gave generously to help them sleep.

"And wouldn't you have, too, lad, if it had been the Devil himself and his mistress offering it to you?"

"I wouldn't crave eternal life at all myself, for then I'd have to sweep chimneys forever, wouldn't I? I would rather be done with it all, hand my broom in, and go to Heaven. But His Lordship was already so close to gaining what he desired. I hardly know why, after sacrificing all those dogs of his and singing psalms backwards, he should change his mind. It seems a poor waste."

"Ah..." Bridgette smiled mysteriously. "But no man kens what the last ritual that he was meant to perform was to be, nor why he spoke so often of 'the tongue of Satan.' They say only that he left the glen that night a changed man and that it was then that he began his penance of gazing upon a waxen image of his corrupted body, in order to prepare and mortify his flesh for death." She shrugged then and, gathering up their empty cups said, "Aye, well, 'tis the way of them fine and noble folk. Can't even keep a deal with the Devil, can they?"

Childermass could learn nothing more of what 'the tongue of Satan' meant, though the phrase persisted in every telling of the tale that he heard. There was a peculiar variation on it, though, in some versions of the tale in which Mistress Mackenzie gave to Lord Stephen a ring of silver and told him to place it beneath his tongue at midnight. In these versions Lord Stephen, fearing some unspecified horror, had refused to do so and had kept the ring locked away instead, never daring to use it.

***

The coming of Childermass to Laughlin Priory was a premeditated thing, but one so cunningly contrived that it was never known to be such by any but the chimney sweeper himself. It was one thing to gaze upon the battlements a mile away and another to plan the trespass of those grounds – a thing that could easily cost him his life. He knew of the foresters whose duty it was to guard a lord's lands from poachers and thieves and he knew of the punishment that he could very well incur upon himself were he to be found by one of these. Worse, his plan could not succeed without such a discovery.

It was the sort of strategy that could only seem reasonable to a fanatic or a man whose only other option was death. Childermass, in terms of temperament and station, suited both criteria admirably. Whatever the groundskeeper did to him, he reasoned, could be no worse than the inevitable death that awaited him were he to remain safely as he was.

Characteristically, after having devised a scheme both complicated and perilous, Childermass devoted himself to every detail of its planning with a compulsive energy that left little to chance. He would come with a dead hare over his shoulder and several in his satchel, all the guilty marks of a thieving hunter upon him; he would conduct himself with enough insolence to earn him an audience with the lord of the Priory, but not so much that the groundskeeper would choose to take matters into his own hands. Once inside the Priory, for whatever duration, he would be satisfied. It was only to see the place that he schemed at all. They could do anything they wanted to him after that.

The evening was warm when he first left for the Priory, but chilled as the night drew on. He felt his heart burn as he drew closer, and though he could not see its towers in that dense forest, he knew that every step brought him further beneath their shadow.

In general, his plan unfolded to perfection. He only wandered an hour before he felt the end of a musket touch his back and a voice order him to stand still and account for himself. The forester's usual custom was to give the offender a beating and then send him on his way. Childermass's insulting manner, however, made it impossible for him to feel as though it was right to send the boy on his way so quickly. He spent the better part of an hour attempting to correct the chimney sweeper's lack of respect, then gave the case up as hopeless and took him to the Priory for a more effective solution.

If he had been obscure in his purpose with the forester, Childermass was perfectly frank with Thomas Micah Stoddard, the man of Parliament's choosing who now held the Priory. He told the steward, wiping the blood off his mouth and gazing up at the stained glass and arched rafters, that he had come to see the place that all the gossips had spoken of: the Priory where witches had sacrificed and lords had consorted with them. The explanation was so mad that Stoddard could not fully believe it, but admitting that Childermass hardly looked a Royalist spy – and what was there to spy upon in these wilds anyway? – he promised to show him about as long as the boy, for his part, gave some account of what these rumors contained.

The truth was that Stoddard had been troubled by these tales already to some degree. A London man himself, he was not used to the customs of the North and was eager to hear at last some explanation for the odd whispers that he overheard from time to time in Houndswick and Shrewsfield: whispers pertaining to the Priory's exiled, former tenants. Feversham and Dagworth, though obedient enough, were taciturn and gave no indication of what they knew. This chimney sweeper, however, though young, was a veritable repository of oral legend and, if all the boy wished in return was to remain in the Priory, Stoddard thought this an easy exchange.

Every evening for a week, Childermass gave him a variation of the tale and Stoddard, though he scoffed aloud at the superstitions, listened and felt the old, familiar mixture of fear and intrigue that keeps such tales in constant circulation. He confessed with some embarrassment that when he had lived in England he had been most fond of the pamphlets pertaining to apparitions and the perils of the occult, but that he had never fancied that one day he would find himself the inhabitant of a place with such a haunted history. Afterwards, they would light candles and explore the Priory's corridors, hoping to find Lord Stephen's secret chamber where it was said that he conducted most of his occult experiments. It was, of course, in the way of a game: Stoddard hardly expecting that they would find anything more than the usual dust-strewn cellar or room full of cabinets and chairs, and Childermass desiring any opportunity to see more of the Priory.

He was given the room that Cyrus would nine years later occupy as a guest and spent the days in wandering freely about Laughlin and its grounds whilst Stoddard remained in his study, reading letters from London and writing out long and labored replies. When Childermass would bring him volumes of verse and history from the forsaken library of the Gosselins, Stoddard – glad of any distraction – would read aloud from them. Slowly, through both a keen attention to the relationship between the sounds uttered and the words upon the page as well as Stoddard's own occasional instruction, Childermass learned how to read himself.

The chimney sweeper should have left after a week's stay. How he came to live four additional years within those walls was a circumstance borne both out of Stoddard's lonely, fatherly affection and their mutual interest in the hidden chamber of Lord Stephen. Stoddard would often say that the boy had a kind of sharp, dispassionate eloquence that made him most persuasive, no matter how foolish-seeming his enterprise might be and it was true that the Englishman's dormant curiosity caught fire from the force of Childermass's arguments. But Stoddard was not the only one changed by their acquaintance. The dour Presbyterianism that the chimney sweeper had been born into and fed upon all his short life was not supplanted but instead grafted to a new sensibility that he came to adopt from his study of the pamphlets that the Puritan gentleman had brought from London. For a nature like Childermass's, as conscious of the supernatural world as a saint and yet as coldly practical as a fishmonger, it was almost too easy a thing to take into himself the stern mysticism and political radicalism of the Dissenters that had flourished so well amongst certain circles and had eventually grown powerful enough to kill a king. It mingled with his innate, visionary pragmatism, adding ice and fire to the set stone of his character.

Childermass's memories rarely lingered on these (what he considered) trivialities. The poignant melancholy that they caused was something to be loathed and avoided in favor of the more exquisite terrors that were also discovered in those years. Thus, with icy efficiency, he passed over the happiness of those first years and the doubt and foreboding of Thomas Stoddard after news of Cromwell's death and Parliament's subsequent confusion came – and settled instead upon that January night in 1660 when they had at last discovered the secret room.

It was a mere few months before Charles II would return from France to England as her restored monarch. Stoddard knew, as did many of the other supporters of the rebellious Parliament, that his doom was near. He did not flee to the American colonies, however, for he preferred to have his trial in a familiar land and hope for an acquittal rather than live out the rest of his years as a refugee. He urged Childermass to go to Massachusetts Bay, but the young man preferred the Priory to America. Moreover, the chimney sweeper had always been sure of a near death and was more accustomed to it than the unfortunate Stoddard, who often lapsed into unquiet reverie as the months drew on, a melancholy that no amount of conversation or music could draw out of him.

One January evening, Childermass suggested that they search out Lord Stephen's hidden chamber. Stoddard was surprised, for it was a pastime that they had not indulged in since the first intimation of Parliament's slow dissolution had come to them. Childermass did not press him, but Stoddard of his own accord arose, took up his candle, and nodded. They searched all the dark, familiar places of the Priory, they ascended staircases and descended into cellars and crypts, and at last came to rest in the library.

That was when Childermass suggested that they descend further, into the deep cavities that existed beneath the library. They had explored these only once or twice, but it was difficult to keep a candle burning in those passages. Moreover, the walls were crowded from floor to ceiling with books and manuscripts, it was a perilous to hold a light there, for fear that the whole would go up in flames. Yet they descended through one of the trapdoors and down its spiraling iron staircase, past the moldering books and loose papers, until they found themselves facing the wall at the end of the passage. On this wall was blazoned in brass lettering the words FIAT LUX: *let there be light.*

***

Childermass awoke with a start. It was past midnight and he was asleep in his chamber. He felt just as he had upon awakening in the chapel to the sound of a baying hound and wondered if it had not been the selfsame sound that had forced him awake now. In his blindness, he could not hope to see if anyone approached, but even if his sight had been restored, his chains rendered any chance of escaping an intruder impossible. He would have returned to the flow of memories that his dreaming had begun in his head, letting them run their course to its natural conclusion, were it not for his awful certainty that someone stood outside his door – that someone had heard the start of his breath as he had awakened – and that someone was waiting for his breathing to resume its sleeping rhythm before entering.

He forced his breathing to slow and closed his eyes, willing himself to concentrate upon the approach of the footsteps by his bedside, denying himself the ability to recall the look of all the dead young men whom he was certain had fallen victim to this very approach. If he must die now, let him die unafraid and curious, knowing at least the thing's identity at the very last. Its breathing sounded strangely gentle and as it approached, he felt it touch his hand.

"Childermass," Clarice whispered. "Are you awake?"

"God save you, Miss Abelin, speak more quickly next time!" said Childermass. Only now that relief permeated his being did he feel the chill of sweat that had drenched his brow. "I thought you to be something else."

"You appear somewhat disappointed," she whispered.

"Truly? Then I suppose that is my look when I feel myself saved from a bloody death," he returned a bit sarcastically. "Or perhaps when I realize that I must wait a little longer to know the mystery of the Priory."

Clarice, now sitting at the edge of his bed, gazed at the chains that held him fast and said, "I have begged my uncle to ask Sir Robert to take away your punishment, considering the dangers that have violated this Priory, but he refused."

"I did not expect him to," said Childermass. "Besides, the man who haunts this Priory has no desire for my life. He knows that were he to take it, I would oblige him to introduce himself first and he has no intention of ever satisfying my curiosity. He is a torturer, after all."

"Do shut up, Childermass," she said brightly. "I made an impression of Feversham's key a few days ago, took it to a locksmith in Houndswick, and had him make me a copy." As she spoke, she unlocked the shackles at his wrists and began at the ones at his feet.

For once, Childermass was too surprised to do more than stammer out his thanks.

"But if they find me free in the morning – " he began.

"I will come back to chain you again before then," she promised him.

"Thank you." His awe and astonishment at what she had done rendered him stupidly dumb for the whole of a minute. Then it came to him in a rush – this would be the first night since the last Feast of the Holy Innocents that he would be free during the night. Free, when the scourge of the Priory was free. Christ, what he would not have given for this! And the girl had bestowed it on him herself, so freely. He started up, so abruptly that she felt a little frightened – both at his haste and the look upon his face.

"We must go to the library at once," he said.

"Why?" she seized his hand. "Childermass, please don't act as rashly as you did last year, I beg you. If my uncle and Sir Robert discover what I have done – "

He laughed, dry and bitter. "They will not."

"How can you know?"

"Because if they do," said he. "Then it will prove that they were complicit in the Houndswick deaths – and they could not very well have that, could they?"

"In the name of Christ, Childermass, what are you saying?"

"Let me tell you as we pass along our way, for time is short and I would that you were as schooled in these things as I. I fear that it is the only reward I can repay your kindness with."

***

He began by telling her of the old legends of Lord Stephen Gosselin and his occult experiments, then of Thomas Micah Stoddard and how he had searched with Childermass for the secret chamber in which Lord Stephen was said to have kept his blackest secrets, and finally of that one night when they had gone together to search for it and had found their way into that deep, underground room beneath the library.

They had always taken the FIAT LUX to be a monkish maxim from the Priory's early days – a reference to the illuminating nature of the Scriptures and the writings of the ancients. But that night, Childermass had taken it to be something different. He had taken it to be a call to ritual and he had used as the crux of his theory the verse from which it was taken.

"Darkness and water," he said. "That is how the world was before the coming of light. Perhaps that is the only way for there to first be light."

They had blown the candle out and they had brought water and poured it on the floor of the passage before the bronze-lettered legend, stone by stone. They had not really expected anything to come of it, but it gave Stoddard's mind something new to dwell upon and it amused Childermass's fancy. When they heard the echo of water beneath their feet, beneath a certain stone, they were too astonished at first to believe that they heard aright. Childermass brought a lit candle and together they lifted the loose stone and found beneath it a trapdoor. Upon it, too, were carved the words "Fiat Lux." They lifted the trapdoor and opened a door to the darkness directly beneath them.

What was the use of describing it when they would see it in only a few minutes' time? Suffice it to say that the old legends spoke truly. Lord Stephen had most assuredly dabbled in dark magic and had been very close indeed to finding the ritual necessary to ensure his own earthly immortality. They had spent that night in reading his journal, taking it in shifts with the one reading aloud whilst the other listened, and knew that they had unearthed either the imaginative visions of a madman or the most profound study of diabolism that had ever been recorded. They had found the pelts of the creatures whom Stephen had sacrificed at Mackenzie's command, as well as the sacrificial knives that had been wrapped in their furs after use. They knew too what had stopped Lord Stephen from carrying out the final stage of his experiment – what the tongue of Satan truly had been. Not only because he had made shuddering mention of it in his account, but because they had found it in a silver, velvet-lined case. It was not a ring, but instead a small strip of dried leather, with a forked end – the tongue of a viper. This was the thing that Mistress Mackenzie had told him to place beneath his own tongue every night for a year. This was the object that she had promised would bestow upon him immortality, if he only followed its 'direction,' as she put it. He had balked and so had died as any other man.

After the Restoration of Charles II, when Thomas Micah Stoddard had been executed for treason against the Crown and the Gosselins had returned to their seat of power in Priory, Childermass had remained as the Priory's chimney sweeper, occasionally visiting that secret room and rereading that mysterious account. But the night before Lord Luke Gosselin's death, he had discovered the dried coil of tongue missing; and after Luke's funeral he had been condemned to chains every night and thus was ignorant of who it was that visited that chamber nightly. He knew one thing, however: whoever the thief was, he was carrying out what Lord Stephen had blanched at doing. He had stolen the tongue and now he was carrying out its desires.

"Then you believe that what happened to all those murdered men in Houndswick was not the act of some madman but rather the work of sorcery?"

"With all my heart," Childermass replied.

Clarice helped him down the stairs leading down to the passage where the trapdoor leading to the secret chamber lay. Childermass, though blind, felt along the floor and paused before one stone.

"This?" she whispered.

He nodded. Together, the two of them lifted it and she saw beneath it a square door made of oak leading downwards. Taking up the handle, she struggled to lift it. It would not open. Childermass, hearing her struggles, came to her aid. Their combined efforts could not move it.

"Horrible," he murmured, an odd smile on his face. He then raised his sightless eye. "There is no keyhole on our side, so the door may only be fastened from the other side. This can, of course, mean only one thing. He is below us even now."

Chapter Thirty-Five: In which Cyrus and Withing make an end at last of their explorations in the darkness.

It was incredible that they were still sane.

A day of suffocating darkness, brought up against countless dead ends, forced to retrace their steps and search for a new turn in the sheer maze in which they were entrapped, weak with hunger, but driven on by that terror – still unspoken between them – of actually dying in the narrow space between those endless walls—

At first, the whole situation had seemed too unreal, too dreamlike, to admit of the fear of death. But as hour after hour progressed and as they felt along the walls and floors, finding no end to the rough stone that held them in above, below, and at every side, they knew it to be too probable a possibility. Either the walls were too thick or they were in too remote an area of the Priory to be heard, for they had shouted themselves hoarse to no avail. The only hope for escape, then, lay in finding another passage that would open to them like the one they had found to their misfortune in the crypt.

Upon the very hour that Childermass in chains dreamt of his childhood, Withing and Cyrus paused to rest. It was too cramped and narrow to kneel, let alone sit, and so they leaned their faces against the wall and drew in long and weary breaths.

"Where are we, do you think, Cyrus?" Withing whispered.

"I can't say," the Puritan youth replied. "We have gone down several steep drops that, I suppose, lead to lower floors – but what can lie lower than the crypt, I cannot imagine."

"Childermass would know," said Withing. There was something hopeful and plaintive in the way he said it. Cyrus could not decide himself whether this declaration gave him relief or merely made him suspicious that it had been Childermass who was the cause of their predicament.

"But Childermass is not here," Cyrus said. "We have only God and ourselves to save us."

Withing did not reply and Cyrus instantly regretted his hasty retort. If it gave the boy hope to believe that Childermass was an angel rather than a schemer, then why not let him harbor the illusion? It could do no more harm in their present position.

"I'm sorry—" he began, but Withing instantly made a hissing sound, signaling for silence. Cyrus listened, wondering what was about. Then he heard it too.

They were not quite footsteps, but they had the same pattern, the same pauses and hurryings, of a sound belonging to something sentient. For a moment, Cyrus was overcome with the sheer wonder of hearing something that was not the sound of their own steps or the dripping of groundwater. Then, in a raised voice, he called, "Help! We are here, in the walls! Help us find a way out!"

The sounds gave way to silence. Cyrus had the distinct impression that something had stopped and was now attempting to ascertain the direction from which his voice had come. He thought he heard a sound like the quick breathing of an animal from somewhere above them, but it sounded as though it came from a distance, as though separated by some partition.

"We're here!" he called once again. A tentative movement from above, then silence again. Whatever it was, it was thinking out the problem of their separation, but had no intention of replying to their calls. Cyrus began to wonder whether it was not an animal rather than a man, after all. But what animal could have trapped itself within these walls and survived for so long? The relief that he had felt at first now gave way to discomfort at the thought of having to share these blind alleys with some unknown creature whose movements certainly suggested a size larger than that of mere vermin.

"What do we do, Cyrus?" Withing whispered.

"We go on," Cyrus said at last. "There is nothing else to be done. It was a false hope."

An hour later, however, and they still heard the thing above them. It was following them along its own route, tracing their steps on a path that was intercepted by a ceiling of stone but somehow lay along the same line as their own. There was something unsettling about this thing that had the footsteps of a man but breathed like an animal. It was close enough for them to hear, but not enough for them to ascertain how to either reach or avoid. Cyrus began to dread its presence as much as if St. Aubert himself were its source and bent all his energies to feeling for some passage that took them in a different direction from its course.

After an interminable time, he paused at last, breathless. Withing was crying softly behind him. Cyrus thought of the boy's fear and hatred of the Priory; of his kneeling upon its cold stones and saying how he only loved it in the early morning, and then only because it looked so lonely; and now of how they were pressed between its walls, trapped in this darkness that was as close as a coffin. For Cyrus, it was a terrible enough fate – but he was a stranger and had already suffered the horror of having a father tortured and finding himself pursued by the self-same torturer and this seemed only a logical continuation of the same, endless trial. But Withing in the same day had undergone the awful shock of finding an empty coffin in lieu of his own father's corpse and was now trapped within the very walls that he had feared all these years. Cyrus listened to him cry and thought that it was a wonder that the boy did no more. Perhaps his soul was so crushed that it could do no more than protest in amazement at the swift succession of horrors that it was forced to endure, rather than rail against them. Sorrow always staggers as much as it dismays with its power.

Cyrus at last managed to speak.

"We won't die here, Withing – I promise you. Childermass will find us, or we will find our own way out, but one way or another we shall make our escape."

As he spoke, trying to put some amount of feeling and conviction in his words, he happened to bump his elbow against the wall and felt one of the large stones shift slightly. For a moment, he felt as though his heart had leapt out of its seat. He began to cautiously feel at it, while Withing's sobs now subsided into sniffs.

"But how do you know we'll escape?" he asked plaintively.

"Because…" Cyrus said, swallowing the lump in his throat. "I think I've found a passage already."

The two began to work at the loose stone until it came out on the other side. Cyrus stretched his hand through the hole that this made and felt open air. Moreover, a faint light poured out of that aperture, promising something more than further darkness beyond the wall. Immediately, they began to kick and push at the stones that had surrounded the dislodged one. The ancient mortar could not withstand these efforts and at last they managed to break an opening large enough for them to force their way out. They tumbled headlong upon the cold stones of a large and circular chamber.

The place was windowless, but a muted light shone from candles sheltered in lanterns of crimson glass, allowing a red, wavering luminance to touch the furthest corners of that room. The floor dipped occasionally into pools of water upon which the reflection of these flames moved dancingly.

Save for the shelves filled with books that lined the walls and the pelts of fur that hung in bloodstained folds from the rafters, it was like moving through a cave rather than a chamber made for habitation.

"What have we stumbled into now?" Cyrus wondered aloud.

"I don't know." Withing's face was white. He looked at Cyrus, the relief in his face now replaced by a new fear.

Cyrus could not understand Withing's emotion. He found himself suddenly unable to connect with the terror that the boy felt. It was as though Withing stood apart from him on a separate stage, one that the character Withing found terrifying but that Cyrus the observer found strangely compelling and curious. He shook his head, seeking to clear his head, for he felt the hysterical impulse to laugh come over him. It suddenly came to him as a clear conviction that this was what Childermass felt when he saw what merely horrified others.

He did not know what caused him to feel so himself. Perhaps there had simply been too great a surfeit of darkness in the last few days. Perhaps, like wine, one could grow drunk on horror and find in it something exhilarating as well as terrible. Whichever it was, Cyrus would leave it for the philosophers to conjecture. It felt like walking on air, moving from the table of sacrificial knives, the shelf of black-bound books, and finding that the sight of them had no effect upon him whatsoever. It was like walking through fire and yet not feeling even a brush of heat. He thought that he had either reached so far above himself that, like a saint, he could tread on dragons without any peril to himself, or that he had sunk so low that the dragons were unable to distinguish him from themselves. Was this what Childermass meant when he spoke of curiosity?

"There's a ladder leading up." Withing was pointing to stairs made of wood leading up to a trapdoor in the ceiling. "Please, let's leave."

"Does your grandfather know of this place, do you think?"

"I don't know." Withing's gaze was wondering, in spite of its misery. It was clear that Cyrus's newfound immunity to terror perplexed him as much as it did Cyrus himself. "What are you looking for?"

"Aren't you curious as to how these candles came to be lit? Someone visits here – and often."

The stones beneath them trembled ever so slightly; the sound of the Priory settling. Cyrus, pausing to listen to it, felt himself slightly awed, in spite of his numbness, by the thought of the weight of floors that existed above them and (for all he knew) beneath them as well. Some explorer in these reaches had found this hidden cave of a chamber, just as they had, and made it his own. But who could it be?

Something gleamed silver upon one of the shelves carved into the stone walls. Cyrus took hold of it; it was a box of silver, lined with velvet and empty. Next to it lay a heavy signet ring, also made of silver, with a leafless tree embossed upon its face. Cyrus lifted it and watched as the branches caught the crimson light, making out of it a miniature twilight in the world of the ring's crest. This was, without a doubt, the signet ring of the Gosselins – the thing that Childermass had desired from Lord Luke's coffin in the first place.

It was while Cyrus was putting the ring in his pocket, that he heard that animal breathing somewhere above him. He turned around, but saw nothing within the circular confines of the chamber. In fact, the place looked so still and the world had gone so suddenly silent that he was almost sure for a moment that he had imagined it. Then he saw the movement of the trapdoor above them as it swung open – a movement followed by the entrance of a man as he silently climbed through the shadow of that breach, twisting his wrist as though to lock the door behind him, before descending to stand beside the broken wall.

Cyrus could barely make out the features of the intruder; he only knew from the shadowed contours of the face that there was something blank in the expression. The eyes were dilated in the darkness; they turned from Cyrus to Withing with an eager stillness. Still, in spite of the alien look of the stranger, there was something familiar in his countenance, particularly in the quality of those eyes, that Cyrus could not, for all his efforts, entirely place. He did not recognize the man, but he was certain that somehow he had seen him once before.

As the stranger stepped forward, Cyrus fell back for there was something sweet in the air that surrounded him, like rotted apples, and it turned his stomach. He kept his eyes fixed too closely upon the man and as a result, stumbled and fell back upon the stones; the stranger, however, passed him by, all attention fixed upon Withing.

The boy was half-crouched, half-standing by the far wall of the chamber, his own eyes riveted upon the stranger with a look of terrified recognition. The look reminded Cyrus of an old tale that his father had told him once. In the tale, there had been a woman who had lost her son – he had been hung as a murderer – and she had gone to an enchantress and begged the witch to restore her son to life. A year passed. One wintry night, the woman heard a knock at her door and rose to answer it. "I am come home, mother," said her son – and it was her son, but him after his neck had been throttled by the hangman's rope, after his body had been thrown into a wooden coffin, and buried for twelve months beneath the dirt of a pauper's graveyard. Cyrus's father had never detailed how the young man had appeared, but in Cyrus's dreams there had always risen ascendant in his imagination the look on the mother's face as she had seen and recognized the rotted thing before her as her own. Now, in Withing's face, he saw that very look as he had dreamt it all those years ago – and it awakened in him such a pitying and sympathetic horror that he felt his stomach tighten at the sight of it.

The man approached, put a hand beneath the boy's chin, and raised him up. Withing was trembling, his face shone with a pale sweat. He looked as though he were trying to speak; his lips kept fumbling for words, but nothing came out for several moments. Then at last, his voice shaking and hoarse, he said, "Father?"

Cyrus's head reeled. Of course – this was why the stranger had possessed that odd, familiar look about him. It was because of the portrait that he had seen in the Looking Glass Cloister, the one of Lord Luke Gosselin. The man before them resembled almost an exact copy of that high-cheeked, princely face. But Luke was dead; he could not be the one who was now studying the boy's face with that same look of serene speculation. Or so Cyrus's reason insisted.

Something in Withing's first impulse to fear must have weakened, for he threw his arms about the man's neck to embrace him, but the man drew the boy away from him, holding him at arm's length.

"My sweet child." The man's voice was soft as he drew the boy away from him, holding him at arms' length by the shoulders. Cyrus saw that Withing's cheeks were shining with tears, but that he gazed at the man with a look of adoration.

He bent his head as though to give Withing a kiss, one hand firmly holding his chin as his lips fell upon the boy's throat. The gesture must have surprised Withing, for the boy gave a start, but the other hand at the back of his neck kept him still. Cyrus started forward, but the figure heard him for he suddenly raised his head and looked back at the Puritan youth and, with that same blank look, raised a finger to his lips. Silence.

The enchanted immunity from terror was over. Cyrus felt himself grow as cold as though he had caught a fever chill as the man began to smile. Withing was breathless; coughing, dazed, hardly able to stand. He faltered as the man turned again to face him. His expression was again touched with fear, but there was a hopeful quality to it as though somehow the boy imagined that all this was part of some wild dream and that none of it was really quite real save the single, unshakable fact that his father was alive again. When the man tightened his grip, Withing did not even struggle but only flinched as again the thing that looked so much like his father again fell hungrily upon his throat.

Cyrus somehow hated the thought of touching the stranger, just as he would have loathed touching a serpent; but he hated even more the way that Withing had begun to falter where he stood. Softly, he caught up one of the sacrificial knives that lay upon a nearby table. Without a thought of what his plan of action would be once he had gained the man's attention, he then seized the man by the shoulder and pulled him away from the boy. The man lost his purchase on Withing and turned to look at the one who had interrupted him.

At first Cyrus thought that something like a stream of black saliva dribbled down the man's lower lip and chin, for Cyrus could not see the man's jaw past the strip of darkness that ran from within his mouth and down past his chest. Then he saw that his lower jaw hung wide somewhere against his neck where it lay like a loose latch. The thing that hung black and squirming like a hooked worm from his open mouth looked like a loose muscle, save for the fork that cleft its lower end. The teeth that crowded above it, now that the lips were rolled back, were sharp and triangular like a shark's; but it was that wrinkled, fleshy tongue that dripped with blood, and Cyrus now noticed for the first time the trickle of crimson that ran down Withing's throat.

"My God," Cyrus whispered. "What are you?"

The tongue folded with an almost ludicrous speed back into the recesses of the man's throat. Cyrus was reminded of the tube that a butterfly might put down the neck of a flower and again felt that fluttering sickness in his stomach.

"A man, just as you – but one who will live to see your descendants after you have rotted like all the rest of mortal humanity."

The stranger seemed to have no further interest in feasting any further, but Cyrus could tell by his proximity to the ladder leading up to the trapdoor that he had no intention of allowing them to depart. Yet, Cyrus caught his darted glance at Withing and knew that, for whatever reason, it was the boy's presence alone that was required.

He swallowed his revulsion like a bitter medicine and caught hold of the man by the throat, shouting to Withing: "Get up the ladder and out of here – now!"

Withing scrambled to obey. Cyrus saw that his instincts were justified, for the man – rather than attempting to attack him – was writhing in a frenzy to escape Cyrus's hold and prevent Withing's departure. It was difficult to keep a grip on the man. Besides Cyrus's horror at the tongue that now lashed out, whipping at his face and leaving streaks of something like black oil upon his flesh and coat – besides all this, the man's skin was so soft that it was almost impossible to keep a solid grip upon it. It was as though he still possessed that added layer of fat that infants are born with. The eyes, however, for all that they widened with the exertion of his struggles, remained as expressionless as black marble and Cyrus found that he would rather watch that tongue beat and lash at him than look into that gaze. It was innocent of remorse, of any pity taught by law or nature. The creature that he held fought like a landed fish, as though its very existence depended on Withing's blood. Perhaps, Cyrus thought, it did.

Withing had made it to the top of the ladder and was now fumbling with the bolt that held it shut. He paused and called, "Cyrus, I won't leave without you!" He did not say it very courageously, for he was clearly terror-stricken and would have liked nothing more than to have left that place for good. But his eyes, for all their fear, were fixed on Cyrus with the plaintive hope that he would not have to make his escape alone.

Fortunately for both Cyrus and Withing, the decision was not left to them. The man, at seeing how close Withing was to the door, ripped free of Cyrus's hold. For his part, Cyrus sprang to the foot of the ladder, warding the creature off with the knife while doing his best to climb the crooked rungs. Close enough to touch Withing's foot, he whispered, "For God's sake, unlatch the door and open it." He turned to look for some sign of their enemy, then almost lost his grip on the ladder when he saw what the man had done.

Like some sort of insect, he had climbed the far wall and was now darting across the ceiling like an upside-down fly, straight for them. That tongue, like whipping black leather hanging past the loose, unhinged lower jaw, was a sight that Cyrus knew would never leave him as long as he lived. It was coming for them, only a foot away – Cyrus braced himself to stab at it as best he could – when he suddenly felt his arm seized from above and, out of startlement, really did lose his grip on the ladder. He thought for a moment that he glimpsed Clarice's face in the darkness above that secret chamber.

For one awful, desperate moment, he kicked out for some foothold, managing to upset a vast array of bottles that decorated the topmost shelf closest to him. Then, he was hauled up – up and through the trapdoor. The last he saw of that room below was the face of the monstrous thing below him. To his astonishment, the man was not looking at his escaped victim but rather the broken bottles that now covered the floor. A grey mist rose up out of them and Cyrus wondered if he had gone mad, for the man appeared to be trying to gather it in his hands, even as it faded out of his reach. Then Cyrus had clambered out the other side of the trapdoor and it fell shut behind him.

"Thank God we're free at last of that damned pit," he breathed, embracing the one who had lifted him free. He pulled back, assuming that he held Clarice, and then started when he saw the face belonging to the unknown hand that had caught him.

"How warm you are to your rescuer, Master Plainstaff," Childermass smiled.

"How – ?" Cyrus gazed from the blind chimney sweeper to Clarice, his own face the very picture of bafflement.

There was a vicious rattling of the trapdoor under them and Withing started with terror, but Childermass called out, "Quick! While he is stirring below us, let us run upstairs to see who is out of bed at this hour! Then we shall know him!"

It took Cyrus a moment to realize that the chimney sweeper was making a joke.

Chapter Thirty-Six: In which affairs are discussed, a new pudding is chosen to grace the Priory table, St. Aubert begs leave to hunt in his own fashion, Childermass and Cyrus once again fail to reach an understanding, and Christmas Eve comes to the Priory.

They were in a drawing room adjacent to the library, Childermass and Cyrus. Withing had gone to bed, exhausted both by the ordeal within the walls and the later horror of the secret chamber. Thankfully, the Reverend Abelin had left Feversham to stand guard over the boy before departing to inform Sir Robert of his and Cyrus's return. Cyrus, however, found his nerves too stimulated by the shocks that they had sustained in the last day and a half and preferred wakefulness, no matter how wearied, to slumber. Moreover, the sounds of the rest of the Priory awakening and making preparations for the coming Christmas Eve feast that night were hardly conducive to rest.

Childermass had followed his steps, or so Cyrus supposed, since shortly after he had entered the drawing room, the blind chimney sweeper had followed after. Well, Childermass had promised that they should have a private interview together, soon after his veiled threat regarding his knowledge of Cyrus's past. Cyrus supposed that it was in keeping with the chimney sweeper's methods to find some opportunity for his own designs in the confusion that the last twenty-four hours had created, to form some profit out of these horrors for himself.

"Why did you tell Withing that what he saw was not his father?" Cyrus asked.

"Why did you tell him that it was?"

The look on Childermass's face held no equivocation. That was the most damnable thing about him: he could tell any falsehood or any truth, both with the same cold sobriety. Whether that sobriety was derived from an honest heart or the daemonic assurance of some hidden plot, however, it was impossible to tell.

"The both of us saw him," Cyrus said at last. "And by denying what we saw, you are putting a false hope in that innocent youth's heart."

Childermass's lip half-twitched a smile, but his tone was utterly humourless. "What a corruptor I sound. You forget that I buried his dead lordship nearly a year ago. If he had been alive, I would have known it. Moreover, you forget that I am blind and therefore saw *nothing*, Master Plainstaff."

"I am not your master," said Cyrus. "Nor would I have you address me as such."

"You are a guest of the Priory – "

"But will not be mocked, as its masters are, by you!" Cyrus suddenly burst out. He covered his face with his hands, suddenly aware of just how taut his nerves truly were. When he looked up, he saw that Childermass's sightless eye was fixed upon him, his features pale and set.

"'Cyrus,' then," Childermass said. "If it pleases you."

"It would please me more if you would explain yourself more often. What were you and Clarice doing in the library at so late an hour?"

"Of all the mysteries of Laughlin Priory, Cyrus, I am the one that you should muddle over the least. However, as I have nothing to conceal, I confess that I knew where Lord Stephen's secret chamber was and intended to search it – before I realized that it was locked from the inside."

Cyrus did not bother to pursue the issue further. In this cloistered world, it seemed somehow Childermass's nature to be omnipresent. For all Cyrus knew, he and Withing might still be trapped in that hellhole if Childermass had not been there to give them a hand in climbing up. Perhaps the chimney sweeper was right; perhaps he was striving too hard against him, rather than the real danger present.

For his part, Childermass felt himself grow restless in the ensuing silence. Forced into an unnatural darkness in which his only cues came from what he heard and felt, he sensed himself under a scrutiny that he was unable to return and the very thought maddened and dismayed him. He circled the chamber until he knew that he stood behind the chair from which he had heard Cyrus speak. There, he rested his elbows and leaning down, murmured, "Forgive my unwonted familiarity, but I would prefer that we converse in words rather than looks, when it is possible."

"Of course." Cyrus understood the chimney sweeper's impulse, only wishing that he did not feel a vague discomfort at the thought of

Childermass's pale eye burning at his back. It should have helped that he knew the light in this eye had been quenched, but of course – like all unreasoning fears – it did not.

Across the chamber, a long, uncurtained window disclosed a world of blinding white. The snow had begun to fall again, thick clouds of crystalline ice burying themselves in the eaves and outdoor alcoves of the Priory. It was carried along by a gale that often turned its direction and buffeted at the panes of the south-facing windows, having them groan beneath its pressure. Cyrus thought of his dream of St. Aubert and Childermass – of the thing that had tapped upon the window like a wind-blown branch – and shuddered.

"Are you afraid, Cyrus?" Childermass asked. His voice was soft, even gentle, but his eye had a keen edge to it.

"Only remembering."

"Of course." Childermass paused. "And do you happen to remember whether you found a signet ring during your exploration of the hidden chamber?"

Cyrus hesitated. His first impulse was to tell the truth, but then he considered to whom he spoke and wished that he could deny it. It was, however, too late to plausibly lie, and so he said, "Yes, I did."

"And do you have it still?"

"I should return it to Withing."

"Yes, that would be the right and proper thing to do, if I did not already want it for myself."

"And you think that I will give it to you because of what you know of my history?"

"Yes," Childermass said, again gently. The fury that Cyrus felt at the chimney sweeper's treachery was somewhat dampened by the lack of satisfaction that Childermass seemed to derive from this victory. There was no use, however, in resisting. Cyrus had heard already of St. Aubert's invasion of the Priory and felt it only a matter of time before he was found. It would hardly help matters if his own hosts lent their aid to the Marquis's tireless efforts. In fact, were it not for Childermass, there would not even have been a search launched within the Priory for the murderer; it would have been merely assumed that he had killed and then gone his way.

Cyrus pressed the ring into Childermass's hand. He expected the chimney sweeper to instantly pocket it, but instead Childermass ran his index finger over its surface, tracing out the branches of the silver tree, before at last putting it away in his coat.

"Thank you," he said with a faint nod. "Now I must be gone."

The grim music in Childermass's voice again caused Cyrus to recall that terrible dream again – yet this time, he felt an odd flicker of pity rather than horror for the chimney sweeper. He half-turned in his chair, even though it was against Childermass's wishes, if only so that he could be assured that he heard the voice of a solid presence rather than a specter.

"Childermass," he said, and his voice must have reflected something of the ambiguity in his heart, for the chimney sweeper turned his sightless gaze in his direction with a look of surprised curiosity. "Childermass, what do you want the ring for?"

And Childermass replied with a frankness that was unwonted in him, but perfectly safe in his view, considering that Cyrus dare not betray him: "Why, this Priory is a puzzle and what you have given me is only one of the keys to its unlocking. I cannot expect you to understand what I mean – nor do I believe I wish you to, yet." He smiled with a cold mirth, as though suddenly aware of his own mystery and darkness and somewhat amused by the frustration that it must cause. "You have seen some of it though already, haven't you, Cyrus? The hollow walls, the secret chamber. Some of it. I wish I had all of it."

"What?" Cyrus was utterly bewildered now. "What can you mean, 'all of it?' The Priory belongs to the Gosselins. What do you care for it?"

"What indeed? Yet before Withing and his family returned, I was here. I dwelt here, with the kind permission of Thomas Stoddard, and the place was mine. I read all that its libraries contained. All that the Gosselins know and more, this memory of mine now holds. When they hung Mr. Stoddard from the highest chimney of the Priory, Sir Robert wished me to watch, though his son Luke said I was too young for such a sight. Then I saw the lords go inside and I stood without, at the base of the tree that they now call the Tree of the Gosselins – though it was not always so named. It seemed like a dream. I thought I would wake and my friend would be alive and the Priory would be ours again, as before. But then I was made a chimney sweeper and a servant again, as I'd been before I came to the Priory, and I saw that it was no dream. The golden-haired youth was the one who possessed these stones now and my only reason to exist within them was to obey him."

"Withing happens to believe that you are his dearest friend," Cyrus put in, speaking softly for he felt that though Childermass spoke with a swift calm, this mood of his could worsen under the slightest encouragement.

"And did I not set his heart at rest?" Childermass enquired, tilting his head, charmingly callous.

"Yes, but with a lie. It is his dead father who haunts this Priory and who is now gaining sustenance on the blood of his victims."

"Perhaps. But you see why it is that I must have this ring – this ring that opens doors within walls and lets a man move invisibly in darkness."

"You wish to have again what you lost. The Priory."

Childermass grinned then, with a real humor that surprised Cyrus. "You mean as a usurper? I, a chimney sweeper, acting as some sort of wicked Richard Plantagenet, murdering my tender nephews? O, Cyrus, you do me a great compliment in thinking that one so humble could be capable of rising to so lofty a station."

"Though I am not sure that you are capable of murder, I would not put such naked ambitions past you."

"I am glad." Childermass had regained his sobriety, though a certain wryness lowered the corners of his lips. Cyrus found that when the chimney sweeper chose to be frank, it was difficult not to feel to a certain degree complicit in his schemes. It made him feel rather uncomfortable and he nearly wished that Childermass had not chosen to be so candid.

"I have only one request," Cyrus said. "Please tell Withing the truth about his father. You, who never had a father, cannot understand how terrible a thing it is to inspire a false hope, only for it to be later proven untrue."

"But it is not untrue, Cyrus. You simply did not see Lord Luke Gosselin down there. It was another man."

"And how in God's name can you be so coldly sure when you hadn't the slightest glimpse of him?"

"I will tell you after tonight," Childermass replied, turning to the door. Clearly, in his opinion, this interview was at a close.

"And what will happen tonight?" Cyrus called after him.

"Have you forgotten? The performance of my play."

***

The Marquis St. Aubert awoke from a wilderness of troubled dreams to the sound of fluttering wings and the smell of feathers. The girl Jennie had spoken the truth when she had told him that there was a separate tower adjoining the sixth floor of the Priory – a tower that had remained unvisited for as long as she had been employed by the Gosselins. Its glassless windows were ornamented by the straw of nests; its floor, a carpet of pigeon feathers. Outside, the world was white with snow and cruel with the sting of driven ice, and in that hearthless chamber he may as well have sheltered in the very heart of the blizzard. But what was any reward without suffering?

He rose, his crimson mantle eerily rich against the forgotten neglect of that chamber. In spite of the roughness of his surroundings, the Marquis believed that he had done right in rewarding the girl with a swift death for the help that she had given him. No soul would disturb him in this citadel; it was as private as though he had been awarded his own chamber from which to better conduct his bloody office. Not that he suspected he would be much opposed, were his purpose discovered – but then his work would take on an altogether different color, would become a public spectacle rather than a private execution, and all the joyance of the hunt would have gone to waste. St. Aubert loathed the thought; once a similar thing had happened in Paris, when the man whom he had been meant to destroy had been captured and drawn and quartered before he could reach him. He had found a stranger later that evening and done things to him that still burned in his memory – but ordeals performed in a thwarted heat were nothing to those done properly, in good measure, after they had been dwelt upon thoroughly – deliciously – in the imagination. And St. Aubert knew no one in the Priory besides Cyrus – no one save, perhaps, the chimney sweeper who intrigued him but whom he knew nothing of. Well, if all went ill, the chimney sweeper would do as a substitute sacrifice – or perhaps that dark-eyed girl whom he had seen following the sweeper so closely. But why plan for failure, he thought, when all had gone so happily thus far? He could have his pick of all of them if he so chose and none would be the wiser as to where he laid his head at night. He had seen them search the Priory and had absented himself from the place, keeping amongst the noble guests who had newly arrived – and he doubted that they would trouble to search this rotted tower a second time.

The silver surface of the chest shone from where it lay beneath the window. He went to it and let his eye wander upon its contents – the shafts of sharpened silver, the needles, the colored bottles of glass filled with liquors and poison (none of which killed, but instead induced deep and death-like swoons from which the victim recovered only after he had been safely spirited away to some more convenient place of torment), the nets, the cords, the chains, the ropes with which to detain and hold, the lancets that could be unfolded to twice or even three times their original length, and obscurer instruments such as hollow tubes of curved glass which he had never used, but which existed for a future hour. He had only to discover a victim worthy of their use, one whose deserving temperament could not help but produce a response that merited remembrance.

After choosing some few of these objects with which to prepare himself, and after a final glance towards a portrait of a lady concealed within the lid of the chest, he departed the tower. He thought as he left that he spied something out of the corner of his eye. It was a flash of white, like the corner of a cloak or perhaps a bare foot; in the split second that it took for his gaze to turn fully upon it, it was gone. It did not trouble him the way it would have done Cyrus; but it did somehow, in a vague and gentle way, remind him of the troubling dreams that had filled his sleep that morning.

Once he had gained the first level of the Priory, he passed through the Great Hall and into the north transept, where all the guests were gathered. It was chillier than the other parts of the Priory; no chimney or hearth burned here and the only warmth that rose in that circular space came from the steam that poured from the mouths of mugs. Nobles and gentlewoman stood by, sipping their foggy brews out of flagons, their faces pale and wary. The anteroom shaped into a whispering gallery, throwing disjointed words spoken in private into the ear of a stranger.

"Uneasy dreams – "

"Woke to the face of a strange child by the foot of my bed – "

"Will the storm outside ever cease? There seems a stifling closeness in these – "

And, repeated several times, by various voices:

"Where the devil is Sir Robert?"

St. Aubert had been wondering this himself. A whole day had passed and still the Lord of the Priory had not shown himself since the hunt. It was decidedly odd – though certainly not the most pressing circumstance in these walls, he allowed, with his usual gentle smile. The most pressing was whether young Withing – and more importantly Cyrus – had been discovered again. He knew from the rumors that had travelled the Priory the evening before that something had spirited them away and that no search of the castle had revealed their whereabouts. Now he was in earnest to know whether they had been found and – if not – to begin the scenting of them himself. He would not have the rats and worms prise this Cyrus Colkins in his stead.

At last, he found the face that had brought him to this particular room.

"My dear Gomershall," he said, advancing towards the man with a smile. "I hardly expected to find you in this place as well." It was a lie. He had seen Lord Gomershall as one of the Priory's guests the night before and had simply not bothered to address him before. "'Tis a providential surprise, Monsieur."

Lord Gomershall, who had been watching the falling snow out the nearby window with a black look, started at the sound of the Frenchman's voice. He recovered himself moderately well, however, and gestured for St. Aubert to take a seat beside him at a stone table, though his visage still reflected a certain discomfiture.

"Methought that you still had the son of Ephraim Colkins to dispose of," said he with a raised brow. "I am surprised to see you so far north."

"And so am I," the Marquis replied, smilingly taking up a crystal glass and drawing from it the lightest of sips before setting it down again before him. "But where do you imagine my quarry has gone to ground, Monsieur?"

Gomershall stiffened. "You cannot mean that – but I have not seen him among this company. Surely you must be mistaken."

The man beside him, eyes as bright and candid as a child's, merely shook his head. "No, Monsieur, I am not mistaken. Cyrus Colkins is hidden somewhere in this Priory."

Lord Gomershall's features relaxed as his lips assumed a smile of grim relief – a wolf who has felt his victim's breath at last grow still between his clenched jaws. "Well, then," said he. "It will be little trouble for you to enquire after his whereabouts. If he is one of the two youths who lost themselves earlier, they have been found and you may learn where he is from one of the servants."

"Oh, but it is not so simple as that. I fear that it is not my custom to simply have my subjects handed down to me with a formal arrest warrant. Then, Monsieur, there is the unfortunate business of the pretty kitchen maid whom I made away with yesterday morning. The English lord of this castle would not, perhaps, look kindly upon the liberties I have taken with his wenches."

“Then you intend,” said Gomershall, his face set and unmoving. “To continue hunting after Colkins’ son by stealth rather than simply bringing this matter to an end.”

“Surely, Monsieur, when you employed me, it was not so that I might fulfill the role of a common assassin. Methought that you hated the Essex farmer and his son too much for that. And anyhow, I should be insulted if I thought that you presumed me so cheap as to be satisfied with mere destruction.”

Gomershall drained his glass and finally returned the Frenchman’s kindly smile with an ironic uplifting of the lips.

“What provoked you to kill the kitchen whore?” he asked.

“Ah, that.” St. Aubert’s eyes shone with a regretful, fond remembrance. “My own preservation, rather than enjoyment I fear, Monsieur. She fancied me well enough to allow me into the servant’s quarters and charmed me with a few sweet tokens of her affection. I believe that she thought me a foreign trader who had lost his way and thought to take me in as something more.” A look, amused and implacable, warmed his eyes all the more. “But of course, Monsieur, I could not let her live if I hoped to keep hidden, could I? Before she died, however, she told me a most curious thing. Did you ever hear, Monsieur, that there are certain walls within this Priory that – ?”

Before the Marquis could finish his sentence, however, he became aware that someone was standing quite close to the place where he and Lord Gomershall were seated. Both the English lord and the French marquis raised their eyes to see Clarice Abelin standing beside them.

Clarice had been watching the two of them, waiting for a chance to make an interruption. One of the men was broad-shouldered and cloaked in a mantle of fur, his face and his complexion darkened with a look of humorless attention as he inclined his ear to his companion. This companion was a gentleman of a fresh and roseate complexion, golden-haired, and possessing eyes that conferred upon whatever fell beneath them the same sweet regard. It was this second gentleman’s presence that gave the young woman courage to approach them, for had she seen Gomershall alone, she would not have dared to approach so forbidding a personage. She did not fear to interrupt his gentle companion, however.

“My lords,” said Clarice. “Have you seen a chimney sweeper pass this way?”

The Reverend's niece had been watching for Childermass for some time; he had promised that he would find her after speaking first and in solitude with Cyrus. But after half an hour had passed, she began to wonder whether she had not missed his sightless searching of the Priory.

"Do you mean the young man with the marble eye whom you were with last night?" St. Aubert enquired.

"You saw us, my lord?" Clarice felt a momentary discomfort, in spite of the man's guileless face. It was never pleasant to think of being watched in secret, even by a saint-faced stranger like this.

"Indeed I saw you, mademoiselle," said the Marquis. "What is he to you? A lover?"

Clarice blushed, then laughed. "How shocked Childermass would be if he heard you speak so!"

"Oh? Is he easily shocked, this Childermass?" The Marquis smiled these last words.

"Only, perhaps, by love, my lord – as I have never heard him speak of it. And we are only friends, I assure you."

"Oh, there is more between you two than that. There must be. Did you not see how poor and unwell he appeared when he spoke to you? You make him ill, mademoiselle." Clarice felt herself suddenly grow still and cold as the Frenchman continued, "I watched you rack him up there on the landing yesternight. I think he must either love or hate you, though I wonder which it is." He paused and then continued with a thoughtful look, "What pleasure it must be to have such power over another creature and not to kill him with it. Most ordinary torments must end with the death of their object, but this – this is a most exquisite paradox: a suffering that can only increase its victim's endurance. You must teach me how you do it one day, my dear."

The Marquis had disregarded the cautioning look in Lord Gomershall's eye, but paused in his discourse when he saw that Clarice had turned as white as though she were close to fainting.

"Childermass would mock you if he heard you speak so," she said at last, her gaze defiant. "For he mocks love and would never feel it for me in the way that you speak."

St. Aubert smiled then, his eyes full of a tender apology. "Of course, mademoiselle," said he. "I spoke as a stranger, not as an authority. Some men grow pale because they are tortured by love; others do so because some quality in the air or an indisposition of the stomach suddenly affects them.

Perhaps your Childermass is of the latter sort. Now," here he leaned forward and half-drew her to his knee. "Let us put some color back into that pretty flesh. See how quickly the blood rushes to bloom the face, if one has the skill to know how to revive it?"

As he spoke, he began with a careful method to brush his fingers along her jaw from ear to chin, before moving upwards to trace the contours of her cheekbone and the lift of her brow. The care with which he performed this singular operation had a hypnotic effect upon her senses, and though she hated the manner in which he had spoken before, she could not fully persuade herself to repulse him. While her previous discomfort began to dissipate, a newer and subtler one began to stir in her heart. Perhaps it was something in the quality of his touches, or perhaps in the intensity of his gaze as he watched her flush and seemed to look beyond the curtain of flesh to the very movement and expansion of the glorious, pulsing fount itself. For whatever reason, as she felt him draw her face closer to his own and his breath touch her mouth, she suddenly wrenched herself free and stumbled back.

She expected anger to flare in the man's face. Instead, his face retained its usual composure, though a look of sympathetic amusement touched his gaze as he regarded her. "Forgive my familiarity, mademoiselle," he said. "It is just as well, for it would seem that your friend is looking for you."

Clarice turned and saw Childermass, some distance away, listening to the milling guests as though he hoped to pick out the sound of her. She offered a hurried and embarrassed expression of gratitude to the Marquis and then hastened to Childermass's side.

"A curious one," St. Aubert remarked, taking another draught of cider.

"The girl, you mean?"

"The girl, yes. And the chimney sweeper." The Marquis gave a faint shrug, though his gaze still lingered upon them.

"Were you troubled with odd dreams last night, Marquis?" Lord Gomershall enquired. His question surprised St. Aubert, but the look in Gomershall's eye was not humorous.

"As it happens, yes, I was, Monsieur. What of it?"

"I dreamt too – of Wysterly Ford."

The name sounded vaguely familiar. St. Aubert's confusion was soon put to rest when Gomershall continued, "The town for whose destruction Ephraim Colkins hated me so desperately."

“Ah, yes. The town that you offered up as a sacrifice to Prince Rupert and his men.”

At the word ‘sacrifice,’ Gomershall flinched as though he had been struck, though St. Aubert had hardly intended it as an accusation. The Marquis had spoken the bland truth when he had said that he had not the slightest interest in English politics. Gomershall’s own thoughts, however, caused him to scrutinize this particular word and find in it both an accusation and an ill omen.

“I only did as the King would have wanted,” Gomershall murmuringly insisted. “It was a mistake to side with Parliament. I merely sought to correct that mistake. How was I to know that Prince Rupert would act as he did?”

“I see no reason why you should have,” said St. Aubert, his eyes on Gomershall, his thoughts elsewhere.

“It was a sin that he committed – but it was not my sin. Then why do they continually appear before me?”

“Who?”

“The murdered. The murdered, covered in blood and knife-wounds, begging me to listen to them – listen to them tell me how they died.” He gripped the handle of his empty flagon as he spoke, his eyes dark with a hate-filled remorse.

In spite of himself, St. Aubert felt a coldness touch his heart as he looked upon the stricken English lord.

“But how do you know that they were the murdered of Wysterly Ford?” the Marquis enquired. “For I tell you, Monsieur, I dreamt of murdered men myself.”

But Lord Gomershall was barely listening to the other man’s words. He shook his head and murmured, “These dreams never came to me until now – until after I met the self-righteous Colkins and his puling son.”

“Ephraim Colkins, Monsieur, is dead,” St. Aubert smiled. “Of that, I can attest more readily than any other man.”

“I want his son in the ground as well.” There was something greedy and poisonous in Gomershall’s gaze as he met St. Aubert’s own tender-eyed gaze.

“Tonight, I intend to begin preparing for Cyrus Colkins.”

“You’ll do nothing of the sort,” Lord Gomershall said, a brutal finality in his voice that took St. Aubert by surprise. “I intend to speak with Sir Robert as soon as he appears and tell him that a Cromwellian traitor resides within his walls. I'll make that young whelp an appointment with the Shrewsfield hangman before the evening's out. I won't have his life prolonged an hour longer than necessary."

St. Aubert remembered Paris and shuddered.

"You cannot mean what you say, Monsieur," he said pleasantly. "You promised him to me, do you remember?"

"Oh, you'll still be paid," Gomershall said. "Have no fear of that."

That was not the Marquis's concern, but he could tell from the look in Gomershall's gaze that there would be no use in attempting to dissuade him with words. The guilty lord had been assailed by demons in his sleep and now only an exorcism by blood could convince him that peace would again be his.

St. Aubert hailed a passing servant and plucked from his silver tray a goblet of wine.

"As it seems that our association will be at an end soon, Monsieur," he said softly. "Let us drink a toast one last time, to the restoring of your peace."

For a brief moment, his open hand hovered over the mouth of Gomershall's cup; but the movement was too subtle for the English lord to notice.

"Aye," Gomershall said, taking the cup from the Marquis and emptying it in a swallow. "And to the ending of things."

VOLUME IV

Chapter Thirty-Seven: In which a play is performed; a mystery revealed; and three tortures, two real and one imagined, are accomplished in the space of one night.

There was a quality of exaltation and mystery to that December night, the eve of Christmas; something holy and wonderful that sent a chill of wonder even through those who had not the slightest inkling that anything either terrible or awesome was to be birthed within the Priory that night. Every star that could be seen from that portion of the world shone as clear motes of light in the firmament, unobscured by clouds, above the uprearing of the mountains that rose across the forests and moors.

Childermass stood by one of the open kitchen windows, whilst Feversham and Dagworth conversed on either side of him. Though blind, he was still of use in the intricate and labyrinthine workings of the servants' quarters and with those other two officers of that menial kingdom, completed that scullion triumvirate. While his two companions spoke freely – though in truth, as usual, Dagworth did most of the talking whilst Feversham heard him with a morose half-attention – Childermass would listen to the rough scrubbing of a maid on her knees upon the stone floor or a kitchen boy stirring soup and, were he to hear a surcease of sound, he would give the offender a silent prod with the end of his broom.

Though most of the kitchen staff were so used to their presence that they barely noticed them save as sentinels to be obeyed, there was one who always resisted their intrusion into her domain and did not bother to hide her resentment. This was Mistress Gillies, the chief cook whose reign in the kitchen was never disputed – never, save upon those feast days when the supervision of Childermass, Feversham, and Dagworth was required. And though the three rarely intervened, their very presence rankled so deeply that she made it a point to subvert every order that they directed at her charges, just so that it would be clear that she was the queen and they merely the regents in this grease-stained realm.

"Put a little more effort into that scrubbing, girl," Dagworth said. "Those stones look as filthy as they did half an hour ago!"

Mistress Gillies, though across the room, heard this edict and instantly annulled it with a shout: "Get off the floor, you lazy little chit, and help me with the stirring of this gravy! The turnips are beginning to burn at the bottom."

The poor scullery maid, torn between two tyrants, hastened to obey Gillies.

"Heaven preserve us from the rule of such women," Dagworth snarled. It was rumored that he and Mistress Gillies had once had a certain fondness for one another and that the sudden surcease of this had resulted in an interminable lover's quarrel that began afresh whenever the two were brought together.

"Out of onions," Gillies snapped. "Either you've been making away with them, or else those strangers I've been seeing about the cellar have been after them."

"Are you daft, woman?" Dagworth asked. "I've never seen a body down there, certainly not after your grubby stores."

"I can't very well help that the Master of Bitches is blind now, as well as simple, can I?"

Childermass's lips turned down in an ugly little smile at this. Dagworth gave him an open-handed blow across the face and would have followed it with another had Gillies not remarked in disgust, "Oh, there they go again – like a pair of quarrelling lovers. Fairly turns my stomach."

"Speaking of stomachs, Mistress Gillies, as we've suffered the aftermath of your ill-cooked haggis on numerous occasions, I'd fairly say that makes us even," Childermass remarked.

"Save your poison for another hour, Master Chimney," Gillies returned. "I'm too out of temper for it at the moment. Lucy, girl!" she shouted at the scullery maid whom she had last ordered to stir the gravy. "I can't manage without my onions! Get you gone and fetch some for me."

"You're going to find yourself as mad as the sick boy whom they're keeping upstairs now," Dagworth sneered. "The one who Lady Mariah found out in the woods. Mad as a Bedlamite, that one is. They're having to keep him constantly under watch, you know, because he keeps babbling about sorcery and ghosts that approach him in his sleep. If he doesn't die of his wounds, he'll certainly live out the rest of his days in a madhouse."

There was a contemptuous leer on Childermass's face as he remarked, "And I suppose, Master Dagworth, that you were not troubled with dreams yourself last night?"

"A madman is not a man who dreams, but a man who begins to believe that his dreams hold some truth in them," Dagworth returned. "If I was plagued with nightmares, then what of it? You do not find me any paler than usual upon awakening, do you? Oh, I forget – you're blind, poor sweet."

"It would be difficult to tell anyway, sir, under the dirt."

***

Lucy had never liked descending into the cellar alone. When she had first come to the Priory, she had always imagined all sorts of things in those shadows – and that had been before the first death a year ago. Now, with Jennie's murderer hidden somewhere away, she hated still more her errand.

Disobedience to Mistress Gillies, however, was out of the question. One reason Gillies hated the presence of Feversham, Childermass, and Dagworth so greatly was the fact that she could not exercise her usual methods in their presence. But Lucy knew that once they were gone, she would dole out punishments to the offenders – there was no doubt of that. So she went down upon her knees and began to diligently hunt for a sack of onions amongst the accumulated sacks and kegs of dried meat, ale, and herbs that filled that place.

A sound at her back caused her to turn and search the area with her eyes. When she saw nothing save shadows, she gave a faint, nervous laugh and continued hunting for the sack of onions. Then it happened again – that little shuffling, scraping sound. Lucy turned around again, but this time more slowly (for the hair at the nape of her neck had begun to rise with an instinctive, electrical terror) and looked to see the cause of her startlement.

It was a young man with dark hair, that much Lucy could tell by the light of her candle. But there was something lopsided in his gaze, as though one eye had been pushed out slightly, causing it to appear distended like a snail's eye, while the other – flecked with blood – was fixed on her with a lidless scrutiny. For a long moment, this young man, this creature that could not possibly be alive, simply watched her with its dead, glazed eyes; then its lips parted and it pointed with a broken finger to the dirt floor at its feet.

And Lucy, compelled by a force that had neither pity nor care for her tears or the crawling revulsion that she felt, instantly found herself kneeling on the ground to obey the rotting finger's silent direction.

***

Childermass had quitted the kitchens for the Great Hall soon after poor Lucy had descended into the cellar. He listened to the sound of Shipwash shouting directions to the Worshipful Company of Grocers, the sound of canvasses being moved, and the murmur of players attempting at the last moment to rehearse their few lines.

Shipwash, for his part, was frankly amazed at the progress that the Worshipful Company of Grocers had made in the last few days. Formerly, he had resigned himself to the idea of an evening filled with half an hour of out-of-tune caroling and a half-hearted attempt at a nativity play. Now, after a week of his own bad-tempered obstinacy and Childermass's careful direction, the Company's programme had been altered to include only ten minutes' worth of carols (still too long by Shipwash's reckoning) and a whole hour of the drama that Childermass had written out – the tragicomedy, as he had called it.

In all honesty, Shipwash loathed the chimney sweeper's masterwork. It curdled his blood as few tales had done. However, once the gloomy Crawley heard of his distaste, Crawley came out in fervent support of its performance. It was a venerable tradition, he declared, to tell tales of ghastly terror during the season of Our Lord's birth and who was Shipwash to oppose this? And the truth was that even if Crawley had not emerged in such perverse support of Childermass's creation, Shipwash had made a promise to the chimney sweeper that it would be performed and, in spite of his qualms, he was a man of his word. It was true that he had half-hoped that Childermass's blindness would prevent its performance, but the chimney sweeper's rigid single-mindedness in respect to its consummation soon put the lie to this momentary hope.

Shipwash caught sight of Childermass and said, "I have the robes for your part ready. I'll lead you to them, if you like."

"Thank you." Childermass seemed more distracted than was his custom, as though his mind and heart were hardening in preparation for some necessary yet terrible deed.

"There's still time to call this off," Shipwash remarked.

"I take it that you don't approve of my humor, sir."

"If this is the sort of thing that makes you laugh, Master Childermass, then I am very much afraid for you."

"I am afraid for myself as well, but not, I think, for the same reason that you are. Come, our audience will assemble soon. We have delayed too much already."

"Think for a moment, Master Childermass. You do not think it sacrilegious to perform such a thing before the day of Christ's birth?"

And then Childermass said the thing that convinced Shipwash that the chimney sweeper was either the maddest or the most purely wicked soul that he had ever known:

"Bless my eye, sir, it will be the holiest thing that has been done within this Priory in all this bloody year."

***

It had been fifteen minutes since Mistress Gillies had ordered Lucy into the cellar and still the scullery maid had not emerged. Too busy watching a steaming pudding to go down herself, she ordered Dagworth and Feversham to discover what was keeping Lucy so long.

"More than likely stealing some sugar for herself, the little chit," she murmured, face shining with sweat as she labored over the stove. "Go find her and give her a clout on the ears for me, will you?"

At first glance, the cellar appeared empty. Then Feversham happened to look down and see the scullery maid crouching on the floor. Her hands were caked with dirt, but she kept scrabbling at the dirt beneath her as though unconscious or uncaring of the filth. When Feversham took her by the hand and tried to pull her to her feet, she gave a little scream and looked up at him with starting eyes, her face streaked with tears.

"Stop him," she begged, her voice hoarse and deep, not her own at all. "Please, sir. Stop him. Please."

And, like a token of love, she pushed into the ostler's hand one of the treasures that she had unearthed – a human fingerbone.

"Take her out of this place," Feversham told Dagworth, his voice hoarse. "And then return to me – with a shovel. Methinks there is more work to be done here."

"Should we tell Sir Robert or Reverend Abelin?"

Feversham nodded. "When the play is over, we shall tell them. But it must be done in private. You know that Sir Robert would never forgive us if we told him before Lord Withing."

"Aye," Dagworth grunted, lifting Lucy into his arms. "He does dote on the boy more than his own health at times."

"It is not long," the scullery maid whispered. "His change is almost complete. Oh, stop him before he changes."

"Of course, sweetheart," Dagworth grinned, giving her a kiss. "We'll keep that in mind, won't we, Master Feversham?"

***

By the time the Marquis St. Aubert departed from Lord Gomershall's chamber, his gloved fingers still slick with sweat and blood, Childermass's play was already well underway. He could hear the deep grind of the organ bass, breathing out a slow two-note plainsong and the chimney sweeper's voice resonating from the Great Hall. Even three floors removed, St. Aubert could discern a dark quality to the chimney sweeper's voice, heightened all the more by the echoing response of wordless sobs that occasionally interrupted the progress of his speech.

After the last hour spent with Gomershall, the Marquis looked as flushed and exhilarated as a child who has been allowed to stay up past his accustomed hour; but his memory of the body that had only ceased at last to shudder a moment ago did nothing to decrease his curiosity. If anything, his recent exertions only sharpened his appetite for a good English tragedy, a genre for which he had a keen taste.

His right hand was still clothed in that torturing gauntlet, the five knives still extending past his fingertips. As he leaned upon the railing that gave out upon the Great Hall, they shone with the reflected luminance of the torches that encircled the stage. All other lights had been extinguished, so that every gaze could not help but be fixed upon the action of the drama.

And St. Aubert saw it. Looking down, his heart still pounding with the memory of blood, he saw the figure of Clarice bound to a wooden stake set in the center of the stage. Her dress was torn and streaks of painted blood marred its whiteness. Childermass strode back and forth before her like a tyrant before his chastened subject, or an artist before a canvas, pausing every now and then to call her attention to some better agony. The Marquis watched, fascinated by the simple brutality of the spectacle.

Cyrus, sitting amongst the audience, remembered how his father had once railed against the London plays that had been so popular before Cromwell's reign and that now, after the restoration of King Charles II, had returned to the playhouses. There were some religious and political Dissenters, Cyrus knew, who did not think such extravagances immoral and even penned their own scripts for the playhouses, but his father had not been among them. Cyrus wondered what the dead Ephraim would have thought had he seen his son sitting amongst these noblemen in their silks and furs, watching such a scene. Would he have been ashamed of his son, not only guilty of making himself audience to such a pageant, but even finding himself somewhat intrigued by the look of it? Cyrus put these thoughts out of his head and concentrated instead upon the peculiar instruction that Childermass had delivered to him several minutes before the start of the play.

"Watch the men and women around you. If there are any who rise suddenly and depart, remember who they are. I must know of them."

Now, watching the gruesome spectacle that Childermass had fashioned, he began to wonder what the chimney sweeper had meant. What meaning could reside behind the tortures and apparitions that filled his stage – what thing in all these painted visions could prompt someone to rise and leave in guilt? Horror perhaps, but not guilt.

He glanced at Withing. The boy was watching it all with a look of wonder and terror and a kind of incredulous delight as well, as though fascinated by the magic trick made of paint and mannered lines that had transformed his hero into a villain. At the beginning of the play, Childermass's character, the Viscount Cavalcanti, had been presented as a man afflicted with a wasting illness, pale and drawn, unable to leave his bed and attended only by his niece Lisabetta, played by Clarice. In these scenes, there was a closeness about the two characters that had a mesmeric quality to it: the bed-ridden lord half-veiled by the translucent curtains of his canopied bed, the figure of the young woman in white moving to and fro to fetch him medicines, and Cavalcanti telling her of his love for her. Now, the positions were reversed – Cavalcanti, upon hearing of her secret engagement to Don

Bartolo, had arranged for her to be brought back to him, compelled her to be bound, and then begun his work on her.

Part of what twisted Cyrus's stomach and fascinated Withing's imagination was the sheer incomprehensibility of Cavalcanti's madness. He seemed to derive no pleasure from the act, but continued it all with a joyless efficiency, though he offered his own enigmatic replies to her tearful questions.

"Why, my lord, must you rack me so? Why do you not either take pity or kill me at last?"

"The fruit must ripen before it can be plucked."

Clarice heard these words as she stood against the stake and watched the chimney sweeper make his way back to her. He had been plucking new instruments from off a table that stood in the same space that Cavalcanti's bed had inhabited in the earlier scenes. The one he now held to her throat was curved like a sickle and shone beneath the overhanging torches with an oiled gleam. As he did so, he uncapped a vial of water that he had kept hidden in his sleeve, and let a few drops of it fall to the floor, murmuring something in Latin.

"Is the ritual almost complete?" she whispered.

"Yes." He knew that his audience was too transfixed by the running current of painted blood that now ran down her throat to notice their exchange.

"Did I say the words right during the first half hour?" she asked.

"No reverend could have done better," he said. "And now we are nearly at an end."

"Will it work, though? Perhaps you should have had my uncle bless the water instead of doing it yourself."

"We performed it in the sanctuary of the Priory like good Christians, did we not? Let that be our concession to orthodoxy." In a raised voice, again in character, he said, "Ah! She leans against her bonds, with the warmth running out of her, flooding my fingers. What an exquisite thing it is."

"Please," said Clarice, herself in character again. "I will give you anything, my lord, even love – if you will only save me."

Childermass took her face in his hands, his blind eye cold and implacable. Then, in a moment that held their audience breathless, he kissed her. She felt her cheeks burn and her stomach tighten almost to sickness with the excess of conflicting emotions that she felt. On the one hand, she could not forget that this was hardly a real show of affection; Childermass had even, with a sneer, described this kiss as the crowning horror of his masterpiece. But she could not help herself; perhaps it was the mad excitement of the evening, her growing fascination with the chimney sweeper, or even those strange, enigmatic suggestions that St. Aubert had smilingly put to her. Whatever alchemy of thought and sense had worked this enchantment within her, she felt its joyance course through her; it brought her up breathless and made her press her lips against his, in a reaction that surely elicited a certain horror from those in the audience who caught what seemed to them an unnatural fervor for a heroine to show her tormentor.

Childermass drew back. His cheeks were stained with sweat; his marble eye looked like a dirtied jewel in the torchlight; his living eye glittered with a look that could be sharp desire or sudden contempt. Then, with the index finger of his right hand, he drew the sign of the cross in the air upon that stage that had been erected where the Priory's altar had once stood many centuries before, and as he did he said clearly and distinctly, "Lux fiat."

It was at once the last line of the ritual prayer that he had found in an old treatise on witchcraft in the Priory's library and the last utterance of the play, before Cavalcanti drove a nail into his victim's skull. The audience sat in stupefaction, feeling far too unsure, far too uncomfortable to clap, but still too riveted to scorn its joyless and perverse conclusion until they were certain that the play was truly at an end.

Childermass was straining his ears to catch the sound of something – anything – that would tell him that the secret exorcism that he had performed in the guise of a play had not been in vain. He knew that the holy ritual that he had carried out was meant to ward evil, repel it, and in so doing somehow reveal its presence, in spite of whatever pains its practitioners had suffered to keep it in shadow.

It was while he stood there, turned to the audience, that he began to feel a change come over him. It felt like a tremor erupting from deep within his skull; even though his mind remained remote and calm, he felt himself begin to tremble as though all his nerves had begun to twist and writhe beneath his flesh at once. He heard cries of horror around him; something told him that what was happening to him was far worse than he could tell, locked away in the fastness of his sightless brain. Clarice had somehow freed herself from her loose bonds and was holding him by the shoulders, but she could do nothing to stop his convulsions. Childermass, gasping for breath, wondered with a distant fascination whether this was what it felt like to die. At the tips of his fingers, he felt a spreading coldness like dripping water. In his mouth, his very breath seemed formed of airy ice.

The thought also came to him that perhaps he had gone too far. Perhaps this was the punishment for resurrecting an ancient ritual – prayer though it was, perhaps he had been considered impudent for even attempting it himself, without the aid of someone holier, more adept than he. But what holiness was required that he did not already have some portion of? If he sinned, did he not also have a measure of grace?

"Christ," he gasped, for it was a struggle even to speak now. "Oh, God! Save me – "

And then, in a thunderclap, he knew what was happening. He was no blasphemer at all; he was only paying off his final debt to Ephraim's ghost.

The Marquis St. Aubert understood better than the rest of the audience, Cyrus included, what Childermass had realized at last. He saw the chimney sweeper begin to falter and he gripped the balcony railing, watching with a keen eye to see what would happen. And then the miracle occurred.

St. Aubert often regretted that once his victims were lost, he could never again recover the transfiguration that he had wrought in them. But when he saw the blood begin to flow from Childermass's mouth and his fingers lengthen and drip as though they had turned into streams of blood, as though his hands had been severed at the wrists; when he saw these marks, he knew that it was the very suffering of Ephraim Colkins resurrected in the flesh of the chimney sweeper. The neck was crooked, bent, as though the stem of bone joining the skull to the body had been broken.

"Cyrus," Childermass said in a voice that did not belong to him. "Be warned, my son. My murderer is within this very room." The chimney sweeper turned eerily to face St. Aubert who, in spite of his curiosity, withdrew into the shadows. He saw Childermass lift a finger and point to him, his sightless eye fastened upon him, and heard the chimney sweeper speak again in that unearthly voice. "There."

The message had been delivered. Like a discarded letter, Childermass fell to the floor of the stage. But he was now laughing – laughing in a way that seemed most peculiar for a young man who had been possessed by a dismembered ghost only moments ago. And St. Aubert could see from the glitter and movement of his living eye that he was blind no longer.

The Great Hall was an absolute chaos by this time. Fingers were pointing in the direction of St. Aubert; ladies and noblemen were alternately swooning and babbling that what they had seen on the stage was no more than a trick of light or paint; some were saying that Sir Robert should expel the chimney sweeper from his service, others that it was the most accomplished tragedy they had ever witnessed. Only St. Aubert, far above them all, clapped with a fervor wholly unironic.

Looking down, he saw Cyrus and Withing struggling to evade the mob of panicked nobles; saw Childermass standing like a grim sentinel upon the stage, looking out into the darkness of the audience as though expecting an encore of the horrors that he had so gleefully performed. This was not a time for a man like the Marquis to emerge; he already saw that some of the guests were pointing after him, shouting that he should be brought down and hung – the same persons who, only an hour before, would have applauded his mission. But it was passion, not politics, that inspired them now. They would see him as a monster rather than an assassin and would only later realize that they had defended the son of a Puritan against the agent of a fellow Cavalier. He had dealt with men like these before and knew that their consciences came and went as easily as birds. They would soon be themselves again, but he could not be sure if this would happen before or after his death. For a split second, he fancied that he caught Childermass's eye and that the chimney sweeper gave him the slightest of nods. There was nothing gloating in the gesture; it was simply an acknowledgement. St. Aubert thought it immensely humorous that the self-made Lord of Misrule in this chamber was also the one most in possession of himself. Or perhaps it was appropriately contrary; if the world had turned upside down, putting chimney sweepers in command of noblemen, it was only reasonable to expect that even this anarchy should hold some shape and order of its own. The tail required as much direction as the head.

Someone on the far side of the Great Hall had lost himself even more wholly than the rest of the mob to Childermass's art. Choking thickly, Sir Robert stumbled past the dazed nobles and caught Withing to him. The boy called out for someone to help – someone to help his grandfather, who could barely stand on his own – who was gagging on his own blood. For some reason, even as Cyrus ran to Sir Robert's aid, he felt a curious feeling of repulsion for the old man. There was something too soft and smooth about the hand that caught his own; something too sweet and foul in the breath.

Sir Robert's grip on Cyrus's hand suddenly loosened. He was on all fours now, his whole body convulsing, his face turned down to the floor. Withing knelt by the old man's side, but Childermass – who had leapt from the stage and made his silent way unnoticed – took the boy by the shoulder and pulled him away with such violence that Withing lost his balance and stumbled to the floor at Childermass's feet.

The chimney sweeper barely noticed. He approached Sir Robert and before he spoke, gave Cyrus a look that told the Puritan youth that it would be better to keep a distance. Cyrus, though he hated to do so, obeyed the command in that pale eye. He knew, somehow, that something ruthless was to be done and that he had no business in it.

"My lord," Childermass said.

The head jerked up. Cyrus flinched at the wrinkled face, with its mottled mixture of blood and saliva that still dripped in a half-congealed glue from the chin and lower lip.

"Still submissive in tongue, if not in spirit, are we?" Sir Robert murmured. "You believe that your blasphemous ritual reduced a poor old man to this state. How can you know that what you have done has not offended God as well as the Devil? Mixing the profane with the sacred cannot be done."

"My lord, with all due respect, you did so yourself with some rather potent results."

"You search for an enchanter with the secret to youth, not a broken ancient. Put that crucifix that you doubtless stole from some altar to my forehead. See if it is not so, chimney dust."

"Do it, Childermass!" Withing cried. "You will be proven wrong."

Childermass's fingers twitched about the heavy iron cross that he carried. Then, with a shrug, he touched it to Sir Robert's brow.

Withing gave a cry of joy. The old man was unaltered by the touch. But Childermass held the boy back.

"What now, chimney sweeper?" Sir Robert demanded. He had risen again and now faced Childermass with a look of scornful amusement. "Do you hope now to avoid your chains by prolonging your insult? Is that your game now?"

"Grandfather," Withing protested. "Childermass meant no harm in particular to you. He only sought to – "

But Sir Robert raised his voice above the boy's. "Come away from him, child, and come to me. Or would you side with a common servant against your own blood?"

Withing paled and actually wavered for a moment between Childermass and his grandfather. Finally, it was Childermass's faint nod of permission that caused him to cross over to Sir Robert's side. The look was not unnoticed by Sir Robert and the very fact that Withing had waited for such a sign caused an expression of pure malignance to overcome the old man's countenance. Putting his arms about Withing, he called for Dagworth and Feversham, who at that moment had entered the Great Hall from the servants' quarters, and said, "Take this young man away from here. We shall see him hanged tonight from the same tower as his old master Stoddard. Our murderer has been found at last."

"He is innocent!" Clarice cried.

Even Dagworth appeared doubtful of this order. "My lord, Master Feversham and I found more bones in the cellar of the Priory."

Sir Robert curled his lip. "Of course – more of his victims."

"What proof do you have that they are his victims?" Cyrus asked. "Besides your own hatred of him."

Sir Robert turned on his with an empty look that was somehow more terrible than actual hatred. "Keep out of this."

Chilled, Cyrus recoiled from the man. He found his hand going to the dagger that he kept hidden in his coat, his fingers curling sweatily around the handle, his throat tight. Montrose, who was standing by, met his eye and gave him a look of mutual disquiet. For once, Cyrus was glad of the man's presence.

"What are you hesitating for, Master Dagworth?" Sir Robert demanded, impatience now coloring his voice. "You've flogged him before without any compunction. Put him in chains and take him away. Or do you actually believe, after all that he has done, that he is no monster?"

Dagworth laughed dryly. "I never said that he was no monster, Your Lordship. 'Tis only that I am not certain that he is the monster you're after. However," he added, taking Childermass by the shoulder, "if it pleases you…"

"Wait a moment," Childermass said, as the Master of Hounds held him fast and Feversham began to tie his wrists together with a coil of coarse rope. "Give me a chance, Robert Gosselin, to try your innocence one more time."

"And continue this revolting farce? I will not be touched by you again, chimney sweeper, and by God's blood I'll see your choked corpse within this hour."

"Yes, you could not endure a second touch from me," Childermass said.

"We shall see how well you endure the hangman's rope. Or perhaps the disease that compelled you to torture young men will cause you to enjoy even that. One can only hope, though not expect, that you shall suffer a little on earth before passing into the Devil's hands."

"What a princely heart to take such pains for my pleasure," said Childermass, his voice thick with mocking perversity.

"No!" cried Withing. Tears were flooding his own eyes, but his voice was made uncommonly steady by its desperation. "Childermass, tell them you are innocent!"

"They already know it, my lord."

Clarice watched, mute with despair, as he was led out of the Great Hall. Cyrus, however, felt himself compelled to follow and approach Childermass one last time.

"Have no fear, Cyrus," Childermass assured him as they ascended the winding stairs that gave onto one of the Priory's towers. "Your secret dies with me. Unless, of course, your father's murderer intends to put the rumor about. You must be careful of him, Cyrus, at least for my sake. It would be an unholy waste for me to have been blinded and possessed by your cursed father's ghost, only to have you murdered in spite of it all."

"Thank you," said Cyrus, feeling rather stupid.

They had reached the top of the tower by this time and had now emerged into the bracing night air of the battlements.

"You have no reason to thank me. I would still use your history to my own advantage if I were not soon to die." Childermass gave him the familiar, sidelong look that occasionally shadowed his countenance and made it a thing of darkness. "There is one last thing I would ask of you, though. Find the cross that I used upon Sir Robert before I was made captive. Keep it with you and search him out again immediately. I do not think that Withing is safe alone in his company tonight."

"I will," Cyrus said. "Farewell and – God bless your soul."

"I am not lost to hope yet," was Childermass's only reply.

He waited until Cyrus had left before allowing himself to be sick over the side of the wall.

Chapter Thirty-Eight: In which one horror is extinguished only to be replaced by another.

The Great Hall was a whispering gallery of rumors and suppositions, shaken guests trying to make sense of the double horror that they had witnessed that night. Cyrus moved past them to the staircase, forcing his mind to concentrate on the spectacle of Sir Robert rather than his memory of Childermass. He was ashamed to admit it, but it was the chimney sweeper as he had been on the stage, possessed by Ephraim, that occupied his mind most. He kept recalling new details of that vision that had not fully impressed themselves upon his vision at their first sighting. He had imagined at first that his father's lips (through Childermass) had moved along with his speech; but now that he thought back, he realized that only blood had flowed from that mouth – the same thick, dark flood that had gouted and spurted from those wrists. With that memory, he knew at last what had been done to his father. He had been shorn, pared down to a body without tongue or hands, and then after this outrageous robbery had been committed upon him, he had been hanged. The indignity of it changed the way that Cyrus saw his father's death. He had imagined it before in so many ways and the very vagueness of these nightmares kept him afraid. Now that he had seen the bland mechanics of dismemberment and death, the condition of his heart had somehow altered. Horror is a wintry emotion, shocking and freezing the soul with its constant, pricking needles, its snowy, rictus smile, so that the victim can hardly move for fear of some further agony. But the thing that gripped Cyrus's heart now was hot and fierce and he felt himself refashioned under its influence. When a hand fell on his shoulder, he nearly struck out at its owner.

"Cyrus, are you well?" Montrose was eying him with some bemusement. The Earl recognized, perhaps better than most, the telltale signs of a heated temper, but he had never seen such an emotion possess the Puritan youth before.

"I have to go after Withing," Cyrus said. It was only when he spoke that he realized how out of breath the last few minutes had made him. "Can you tell me where he and Sir Robert went?"

Montrose gestured upwards, the emerald on his finger glowing as greenly as his eyes. "What is the trouble? Can you tell me?"

"I'm not sure myself. But I would be very grateful if you would look after Childermass. Don't let Dagworth and Feversham hang him, if you can help it."

Montrose sighed. "Knowing Dagworth, he'll prolong the whole affair into some game that will last into the small hours of the morning – but if you are really concerned, I suppose I'll oblige you. I hardly owe Sir Robert anything after he chose to side with Squire Toby in that last financial dispute of ours." He added with a confiding smile, "And it's rather thrilling to be on the wrong side in all this."

For a moment, Cyrus felt a little befuddled. Then he realized that Montrose spoke, in a certain sense, correctly – any court of law would frown upon such an intervention against the Lord of the Priory's word. For his part, Cyrus was trying to evade a fate that any jury of Cavaliers would have considered him fully entitled to. From a different perspective, he supposed that he might be reckoned as much a villain as St. Aubert. No one had ever asked him to explain himself, however, and it was hardly the time to rehearse a self-apology now.

"As you say, Your Grace," he said and continued upwards, into the higher regions of the Priory.

***

"Your great uncle Stephen was not merely a secret Catholic. He was a soul on fire with a desperate fear of death itself and he soon convinced himself that his only escape could be found in a study of the occult."

In his mind, Cyrus turned over those words that Childermass had spoken, and rehearsed in his memory the tale of Lord Stephen and his quest for immortality. What parts of the narrative were mere nursery tale trappings it was difficult to tell; yet Cyrus felt that at its heart, there must be some truth to it. Like all the best tempters, Childermass rarely told lies; only those truths most convenient to his obscure purpose.

It was ironic that Cyrus – the stranger, the wanderer – was to be the spectator of this last act. He had not heard the howls of the strange beast that prowled the Priory by night himself, nor had he endured the last year of secrecy, terror, and murder. Most of what he knew was either through hearsay or the scraps that Childermass had so carefully divulged. Yet in spite of his secondhand knowledge, he was to interrupt the conclusion of a tale that had begun years before his birth, with the ambition of one Lord Stephen. He felt a shudder pass through him at the thought. *The word made flesh*, he thought. The phrase, summoned to his mind in that dark hallway several feet away from the door of Sir Robert's bedroom, now made his own flesh crawl.

He heard voices behind that door and forced himself forward. The iron cross that Childermass had stolen was heavy in his hand; he could still feel the chimney sweeper's sweat covering its lower part. Was it fear or anticipation that had made Childermass's palms grow wet? Cyrus put the thought out of his head and entered the quarters of the Priory's lord, holding the cross before him like a shield and trying not to feel foolish or afraid.

He found himself in a hallway that gave out into an anteroom, bare of all furniture save a short table. A sable wolf pelt lay in a folded heap atop it next to a candle that bowed and flickered in Cyrus's wake. It was from the door opposite the hallway that the voices came, penetrating the darkness with their sibilances and silences. Somewhere below, far, far below in the Great Hall, someone had begun to minstrel a carol; the sounds came, half-heard and pensive, in the shadowed horror of that chamber like echoes of Heaven heard in a hollow cavity of Hades.

"It is too soon, my lord." It was Reverend Abelin. "Four days must pass before the ritual is made complete."

(Carefully, every muscle wracked under the strain of keeping silent, Cyrus pushed the door open and leaned inside.)

"Christmas Eve is as holy a night as the Feast of the Innocents. The difference of four days will mean nothing to the work that we do. Tonight they shall all see the change in me. Their looks of wonder shall be all the christening I require."

"My niece will not forgive the death of Childermass," Abelin remarked. The lower half of his face was covered in shadow, but his eyes burned as they lifted to Sir Robert's face.

"I have suffered the chimney sweeper to live as long as I have, for the simple reason that to have slain him sooner would have drawn attention to the rumors that he sought to spread of me. Such concerns are no longer of any consequence now. He shall die tonight – as shall you, Master Plainstaff."

Robert Gosselin's gaze turned on him so suddenly that Cyrus flinched, the cross nearly dropping from his hand.

"Oh yes, Cyrus, you shall die. Why did you hearken to the chimney sweeper and come hither? Why did you not remain with the rest of the guests? You would have at least shuddered in safety there."

"I came for Withing."

"Then by all means, join him."

Sir Robert stepped back and Cyrus saw the table, the candles, and the chains. When he saw the boy lying there as well, he felt a sudden, incredulous laugh begin to rise in his throat and felt certain that he would be sick.

For it all seemed so right. It was the final set of a tragedy, it was the dark room of his dreams, it was the feast of human flesh that his nightmare of several nights ago had prepared for him. There was no Childermass to awaken him now, however, and it was not his father's head upon a platter that lay before him. It was Withing, the side of his face black with blood, his body stilled by the swoon that the shock of some blow had dealt him. His expression beneath the blood was calm; Cyrus doubted that he had even seen the hand that had struck him. The fetters at his wrists and feet seemed redundant, constraining limbs that had already been shocked into repose.

"You would murder your own grandson." Cyrus spoke without the slightest inflection of amazement. Nothing could astonish him ever again, he thought. Nothing could be so wicked or so unnatural that it could shake his soul. He could have watched doves devour their young whole without even batting a lash. He underestimated, of course, the heart's capacity to accommodate itself to more suffering – but the thought gave him an unreal sense of comfort and unreality at a moment that might have shaken his sanity, had he troubled to recognize the truth.

"You thought that I was my dear son Luke when you first saw me, didn't you, Cyrus?" Sir Robert said. The folds of flesh at the corners of his lips deepened smilingly. "But of course you would. He always favored me – or the way I once looked, when I was a young man." He nodded towards Withing. "It is a very little thing to kill one's grandson when one has already slaughtered his father."

"And you will help him," Cyrus said, turning to Abelin. "You, a man of God."

"The men of God in London have done worse than I and never blanched, knowing that it is all in service of a...higher cause," said the Reverend Abelin. He spoke in a tone of empty comfort as his hand gestured airily upwards, causing the candles to flicker, his smile undercutting the dull logic of his words. There was a way in which the two of them were relishing the interruption that Cyrus's intrusion had created – the explanations that they proffered him, gloatingly banal, were as much for their own ears as his. He wondered how often, when they had heard a tortured victim's weeping questions, they had turned to look at each other with those very same enigmatic smiles upon their lips. There was even a pleasure that they took in the idiocy of their replies. They knew as well as he that this evil that they had created together ran so deep that any attempt to put it in words could never do it justice. If they had been artists as well as destroyers, perhaps they would not have bothered to speak at all and merely allowed the table between them to speak dumbly for itself.

Abelin began to approach him then and Cyrus backed away until he saw the musket in Abelin's hand. The Reverend took the cross from him and, with a sudden start, dropped it as though scorched. Then with a smile, he lifted it again, remarking, "Dear me, that wasn't quite right, was it? Well, we shall remedy that." In a swift arc, he brought the cross down upon Cyrus's head.

The pain was so staggering that Cyrus barely felt the stone floor strike his face as he fell against it. Strangely, though the agony of the blow forced tears from him, it was really his inability to discern just how serious the hurt was that truly frightened him. His brain had gone cold and felt loose and dizzied; his stomach convulsed; he felt where the edge of the cross had struck him and when he brought his fingers away, saw that they were grimy with blood and hair. The edges of his vision were dimming and bright lights were exploding behind his eyes. He did not try to sit up any longer; he let his head fall again on the floor of that dark room and felt his broken head stain the stones.

He knew that if he lost consciousness, that it would all be over. They would kill him in his sleep and he would never even have the chance to put up a pretense of resistance before their knives found him. The thought sickened him even more than the idea that his skull had been battered open. He forced himself to concentrate on the sound of their footsteps, the rippling echo of Abelin's laugh. His nostrils bridled at the smell of fresh incense; he heard the scrape of a knife against stone and felt his scalp rise as though by reflex. The desire to sleep remained horribly close, like the darkness that had closed on his vision when Abelin had first struck him down. It terrified him even more than the thought of Sir Robert and his knives.

He knew that he had drifted off momentarily when his eyes started open at Abelin's singing. The man was chanting something in Latin; he saw Sir Robert circling the table while the Reverend stood by Withing's head, holding a large, leatherbound volume open before him. When Abelin's voice would rise to a certain high note, the Lord of the Priory would take up the knife that he kept sheathed at his side and bury it in Withing's flesh – deep wounds but not mortal, enough to harrow the nerves and draw blood but not grave enough to endanger the boy's life. The time for mortal wounds would come later. For now, this was outrage enough.

They had thrown the iron cross in an out of the way corner of the chamber. The lamp that stood on Withing's table threw a quivering shadow over it, elongating its angles and making it seem like some dark, diminished thing. Beside it, a castaway dagger lay, perhaps too blunted for the subtle uses that were required of it. Cyrus crept on his belly towards it, moving inch by inch and keeping his gaze ever upon Sir Robert and Abelin, praying that they would not mark his progress. They were far too bent upon their own labors, too sure that the young man had already been beaten close to death, to trouble after him for the moment. But that could change in an instant if he grew careless; if the dizzied pain that he felt caused him to forget himself and move too quickly so that their gazes moved from their victim to him, it was finished. His limbs shook with tension and for long intervals in between his groping movement, he lay upon the stone floor, drawing breath as quietly as he could.

Cyrus supposed that it had been during his momentary swoon that Withing had come awake. He wondered how long the boy had pleaded with his grandfather, sued for mercy, before giving himself up as a lost cause. How many twists of the knife had it taken to reduce the boy into the creature who now lay bound to that table, who when he was not screaming out as a fresh, glistening inroad was made into him, lay there softly crying? This last sound was somehow the worst. It gnawed at Cyrus's heart as earnestly as did the motionless, wrinkled face of Sir Robert, the bell-like singing of Abelin, or the soft sound of the knife as it forced its stubborn way through skin and muscle. There was something terrible about those sobs that filled the space between the screams; something pitifully mindless, as though the reasoning part of Withing, the part that was his spirit and soul, had retreated from the body on the table and all that was left was his flesh, sorrowing and shrieking at its own defilement. Cyrus felt his stomach wrench at the thought.

Abelin suddenly ceased in his chanting and the Puritan felt his brain ache with the sudden surety that he had been seen. He was only a finger's length away from the dagger by this time. If they did make for him, he told himself that he could still have time to catch it up and plunge it into them before they had killed him. He had that hope at least to calm him.

But it had not been Cyrus that had interrupted them. As he lay there, eyes closed, muscles tensed but motionless, he heard Abelin and Sir Robert hold a whispered conference; heard Sir Robert question the Reverend and Abelin answer in a doubtful tone.

"I will see, though I do not know how anyone could have entered this apartment without our knowledge," Abelin at last said and forsook that narrow chamber for an anteroom to its right, closing the door softly behind him.

Cyrus forced himself to remain still, opening his eyes as much as he dared, to see where Sir Robert now stood in relation to himself. The man was standing by the lantern, in the little hollow of light that its flame created between the table and the right wall of the room. One eye bore the full brunt of the light; the other, save for the lashes which were gilded gold, was lost to darkness. And in that moment, Cyrus saw the Priory as a honeycomb cut crosswise – saw the whole Priory from crypt to ceiling, revealed in one instant, with the noose for Childermass at its steeple, the barren coffin of Luke Gosselin at its feet, and this crouching being at its center: the eye of the wheel around which all the other horrors merely revolved from separately conjoined spokes.

Withing's body was trying to slip into a swoon; Cyrus could tell from the way that his breathing would occasionally grow more even until Sir Robert's fingers prodded him into wakeful suffering once again. A sound, soft and indistinct, filled the room at intervals, like the skin of a snake rustling in a heap of leaves. Cyrus, in spite of the danger, glanced up at Sir Robert. The man was whipping his tongue back and forth along the dry line of his lips, as smartly as the back and forth of a lady's fan, leaving a gleaming coat of spittle at his mouth. Cyrus closed his eyes and as darkness replaced this eerie vision, he was sure, for one dreamlike moment, that what he had seen could not have been real. But he did not look back to confirm this fancy.

Perhaps five minutes passed – perhaps an hour; Cyrus could not tell. But it was long enough for Sir Robert to begin to grow restless and wonder aloud at what delayed the Reverend's return. He started towards the door and it was that momentary distraction that made Cyrus reach at last for the hilt of the dagger.

It was a mistake. Somehow, with an instinct more like that of an animal than a man, Sir Robert jerked his head in the young man's direction and saw in an instant what he was about. Cyrus's fingers closed on the knife at the same time as Sir Robert had him by the throat. The young man struck out and found the flesh of the nobleman's throat, burying the dagger hilt-deep inside him. Not even a murmur escaped Sir Robert's lips; with an unimaginable strength, he instead flung Cyrus across the short width of that chamber and stood there for a space, watching him.

Cyrus struggled to breathe regularly, still somehow grasping the knife. When he looked up, he saw that Sir Robert was pointing a musket directly at him.

"One step closer and I shall kill you," said the nobleman. "Now put down the knife, Master Plainstaff."

For a moment, in spite of the weapon trained upon him, Cyrus faltered. The idea of giving up his last hope of defense and making himself helpless once again before this man was revolting. Then he saw the place where he had stabbed Sir Robert; saw that the dark blood flowed and yet the monster still stood there, eyes undimmed, showing neither pain nor frailty in the face of a wound that should have been mortal. As Cyrus let the knife fall from his hand and saw Sir Robert's slow smile, he knew that he had been required to disarm not because of any harm that he could have done to the man, but merely as yet another act of humiliation.

"Open that door." Sir Robert's finger was trembling as he pointed to the door through which Reverend Abelin had disappeared. Cyrus wondered at what could frighten a man who could endure a knife wound. But he had no other choice save to go where Sir Robert indicated, put his hand to the doorknob, and begin to turn it, with the musket pressed at the back of his head.

A groan of agony broke the silence, chilling Cyrus and causing Sir Robert's finger to tighten reflexively about the trigger.

"Please," he heard the voice of Abelin whisper. The man was speaking with difficulty, as if through tears or clenched teeth. "Please do not open that door any further, my lord, I beg you. My…life depends upon it. Oh, Christ," he gasped and then Cyrus heard him begin to openly weep.

"This is all a trick," Sir Robert whispered, though Cyrus could feel the man's rapid breathing at the back of his throat. "Some blackmailing ruse. Open the door, Cyrus. Whoever is holding Abelin captive will not be able to fight me."

Cyrus hesitated. He had felt someone holding the door back, a gentle but definite pull, and did not relish the idea of being the one to first meet whatever stood behind that door. But he had no other choice – not with that musket at his neck. In a single motion, he forced the door open. Sir Robert saw what was inside and cursed. Cyrus only gazed with a silent, wondering horror.

Something fell wetly to the floor at Cyrus's feet – something soft and moist and attached to a long coil of wire. A hook curved around it and it throbbed and spouted on the floor; for one mad moment, Cyrus thought it was a landed fish. Then he saw Abelin standing there, held upright by cords that bound him to a post in the center of the room. There was a ragged crater where his chest had been; his mouth hung open, willing to shriek but able only to expel an odd whistling breath before he slumped against his bonds, mouth slack, dead.

Cyrus's gaze fell once again to the hook embedded in the human heart at his feet; then looked to see where the wire was harnessed to the knob of the door. His tongue tasted dry and acidic and, in spite of Sir Robert's probing musket, he stumbled to his knees and crouched there for a moment, trying to hold back the sickness that threatened to overwhelm him.

The room was even more narrow than the chamber in which Withing lay – more of a cupboard than a room, really, with shelves of stone lining the side walls and a single wooden door standing behind the post where Abelin had been bound. A lantern hung from the low ceiling, rocking slightly in the draft, making the shadows at the corners of the room quiver. Sir Robert prodded Cyrus forward with the shaking nose of his musket, towards the door at the other end of the room.

"Whoever did this," he murmured, "he is in that other room. There would be no other place for him to go but there."

"We should bring help," Cyrus began.

"You *are* my help, fool," Sir Robert hissed. "Do you think I would risk having a stranger enter here before finishing with my grandson? No, you will go in there alone and see who it is that did this and if he kills you, then I am well rid of you. But if you are clever, you will lead him out and then I will shoot him down like a beast. So you see, Master Plainstaff, if you wish to live, you must use whatever wit you have."

Somewhere at his foot, Cyrus saw something glitter against the dull stone. He stooped and picked it up, turning over the crystal dove, marveling at how numb his fingers were. He could barely feel Sir Robert's musket, nor his own hand on the doorknob as he turned it. In several seconds he was inside that cavity of darkness and the door had closed behind him. He wondered whether all men who found themselves walled up alive in their own tombs felt the same as he did – weary and suddenly, exquisitely cold.

Chapter Thirty-Nine: In which Sir Robert Gosselin exchanges one skin for another.

The Marquis St. Aubert stood against the far wall. The white of his coat and gloves were stained with blood – deep smears that at the center were almost black and at the edges petaled into red. His cheeks were heightened with color; his eyes had the look of starlight about them, emptily ethereal; when he saw Cyrus, he froze with the expression of a dead saint who for a moment imagined that he had explored all of heaven's galleries, only to turn a sudden corner and find an unexplored hall.

"He stood like that, with the hook in his breast, for nearly half an hour before you pulled his heart out." The Marquis had not drawn a breath for almost a full minute before he had spoken; Cyrus could tell by the sharp way in which he inhaled before continuing, almost wonderingly, "Can you imagine it? How long do you think you shall stand, Cyrus, when I have done with you?"

This room was as circular as the last room had been rectangular. Wolf pelts hung from ceiling hooks at certain intervals and beneath them, like whitened seashells, lay an ocean of bones. Cyrus heard them snap and splinter beneath the Marquis' approach.

"Do tell me, Cyrus," St. Aubert continued. "Will you try to stay alive as long as you can while it is happening or will you try to provoke me so that I shall be forced to kill you early?"

"I – cannot say," Cyrus said. He was amazed that his voice shook; he felt perfectly calm inside, or so he believed.

"You will. It will be all you think about for some time, I assure you."

The first shock of joy had passed from the Marquis's face; now a look, almost cunning save for its tranquility, had come over him.

"Why did Sir Robert force you here? What does he hope to gain from giving you to me?"

"He is afraid of you," Cyrus replied. "You can well imagine why."

"And he wishes you to…?"

Cyrus found himself coming to several conclusions all at once. The first was that he more than likely would not survive this night. If Sir Robert's musket did not bring him down, then St. Aubert's knife would. The second was that the only thing that mattered to him at this point was Withing's life. If St. Aubert gained the upperhand in this encounter, then Sir Robert's ritual would be ended and the boy would be safe. The Marquis had no interest in Withing, only Cyrus. If Sir Robert prevailed, however, then both Cyrus and Withing would die. It was as simple as that. Still, he had to be certain.

"You will not harm Withing, will you?" Cyrus whispered suddenly.

The Marquis paused and then said, "If you mean the boy on the table, then I shall keep him safe – so long as you do as I say until we are safe from here."

"I will." Cyrus, naturally, had no intention of honoring this promise, but he had to trust that his father's murderer held a greater respect for the common laws of gentility than himself. It was all, he realized, that he could hope for at the moment.

"What is he doing in there, this murderer?" St. Aubert asked. He did not sound afraid, but there was a cautious edge to his voice. Perhaps even this bloody Marquis, surrounded as he was by the frail refuse of rotted corpses, could not look on this chamber and keep his soul from shuddering, even if the motion was only reflexive.

"He is waiting for me to lead you out so that he can shoot you."

"What would you suggest that I do in order to prevent him, Monsieur?"

Cyrus forced down the thick lump in his throat, driving away the image of Abelin and the hooked heap of pale flesh and throbbing tissue – or, worse, the possessed Childermass with his bleeding mouth and wrists. It did him no good to recall what the man beside him was. The main thing was to use him as he would a savage dog until Sir Robert was at last finished.

"He'll kill whatever leaves this room."

"Then it is to my advantage, Monsieur, to already be dead."

"How do you intend to manage that?"

St. Aubert smiled at him, his gaze alive with a clever secret. "By insisting that you kill me."

***

Sir Robert had waited a full two minutes before he heard the beginnings of what sounded like a fierce fight. He stood there, fingers knotted about his musket, until a silence fell again within that chamber. When the door began to open, he pulled the trigger and blew a ragged hole through the wood.

"Christ, my lord, I beg you to hold your fire!" Cyrus cried out. "The Reverend's murderer is dead."

Sir Robert did not lower his musket, but he saw the bloodied knife that the Puritan held and the motionless figure lying upon the stones at the far side of the chamber.

"How did this…happen?"

"He tried to kill me. I managed to wrest the knife from him and…well, you see what has been done to him."

"Put the knife down."

"But, my lord – "

"Now." It would have been a scream, had it not been so hoarse. Shaken, Cyrus let the knife fall from his hand.

Sir Robert went to St. Aubert and knelt beside him, searching for some certain proof of death. He felt the man's clothes, slick with the late Reverend Abelin's blood, and looked up at Cyrus, grinning with amusement.

"What a sick creature you are, Master Plainstaff. You've made a revolting mess of him, did you know that?"

He had hardly finished his sentence before the silver knife-fingers came alive. They flashed and found the wrist of his musket hand. His fingers spasmed for a moment, struggling to pull the trigger, but the nerves and arteries that bound his hand to the rest of him had already been severed by the Marquis's own intrepid thumb and forefinger. A look of astonishment, surpassing even the rage that had been surprised into his eyes, now came over him. He managed to pull away and stumble back, but it was too late. For someone who could sustain a stab to the heart, his flesh appeared to at least be as vulnerable as any other man's. Now, with his hand hanging by a tendon to his wrist, he backed towards the door. His whole body shook as though he were going into shock; he groped out as though blind, the fingers of his left hand clenching about one of the wolf skins that hung from the ceiling.

Cyrus bent to pick up the musket, but St. Aubert put a gauntleted hand on his shoulder, pulling him away.

"I cannot have you taking that," he said, his gaze a gentle reprimand.

Now was the time, Cyrus thought, his heart burning. It was life itself that he was fighting for, nothing less. Life and the memory of his father's suffering. God help him if he failed.

And so, with St. Aubert's murdering fingers still upon his shoulder, Cyrus took up the musket. In his mind, the action was an incredibly slow one, but in reality it took only a second. And, in another second, he had broken free of St. Aubert's grip and struck out at the man with the butt of the musket.

Again, Cyrus underestimated the strength of his own terror. The force of his blow staggered St. Aubert, causing him to lose his footing and fall back. The man did not look angry, only surprised, as though pain was too great a novelty to be taken as an offense. He barely seemed to acknowledge the wound that had opened his lower lip, save to trace a finger speculatively over it.

"Your promise," he said, gazing at Cyrus. Then, without waiting for a reply, he made for him.

Cyrus fired, but his aim was dreadful. He took the Marquis not in the breast but above it, blowing away half his left shoulder. The young man did not spare a moment to stare at the fresh mutilation that he had created in his pursuer, nor the look that suddenly darkened the mild blue of those eyes.

"You will not leave me alone here, Cyrus," he said. "You could not."

Sir Robert had wrapped one of the wolf skins about him. It rippled about him the way cloth moves when it floats on water and Cyrus thought for a moment that he saw it stretch and expand like the filmy sac that covers a newborn horse. He did not know what he was seeing, could not imagine how great a horror it would be to wait out whatever transformation was taking place in the nobleman.

And with this dark uncertainty, Cyrus stumbled out of the room and shut the door behind him, bolting it fast.

Let them tear each other apart, he thought as he raced through the darkness for Withing. Let them be damned together. Let Heaven give them their own blood to drink. *Their own blood.*

He realized several seconds later that he was repeating this last phrase aloud under his breath over and again like a prayer and felt giddily sick.

***

The air around him seemed to howl. He could not be sure whether it was his own hearing that created this illusion or a palpable sound, but it gave his ear a humming that he could bend to more easily than what rose from behind the locked door. Something inhuman had begun to scream in there; if the Marquis was crying out for help still, Cyrus would not have been able to hear him over the animal sounds that filled that wretched room.

The musket felt slimy in his hand and he felt his fingers beginning to wrinkle with sweat, but he held it and thought wonderingly that he had shot at his father's torturer with it. Then he thought of the wound that he had made and felt a fresh wave of revulsion mingled with relief. If only he had thought to shoot at Sir Robert as well, perhaps cripple them both. But there was still time enough – time enough, if he acted quickly.

He found his way to Withing and began to fumble with the cords that bound him, making short work of them with one of the knives that he found in that room. Withing was awake enough to begin crying at the sound of a stranger, but when he recognized Cyrus's voice, a look of ecstatic relief covered his face.

"My grandfather – is he near?" he asked, his face going wrong for a moment with terror. "What are those awful sounds?"

"Never mind," Cyrus said shortly. He helped the boy to stand, looking towards the hall that led away from that chamber. "Come, let's leave this place."

Withing followed, his face pale not only with fear and exhaustion but also from loss of blood. After several steps, he stumbled to his knees and crouched there, gasping for breath.

"I can't go on," he said, an edge of panic to his voice. "You have to leave, Cyrus."

"Shut up," Cyrus snapped, uncommonly vicious. Supporting the boy as well as he could, he half-dragged Withing down the hall to the door that led from that suite to the outer world of the Priory. Somewhere at their back, he heard the sound of splintering wood. With a desperate twist, he tried the door – and found it locked.

His first thought was that this was impossible. How could the door that he had passed through only an hour ago have been locked? Of course, Sir Robert or the Reverend Abelin would have had many chances to lock it after they had struck him down, but this thought did not at first occur to him. It seemed, instead, a cruel trick of fate – they had come so close to escape only to find themselves blocked at the last moment. He struggled with the locked door for several seconds before giving up with a groan of pure disgust.

"Stay here," he ordered Withing. "Keep yourself hidden in the shadows and, for God's sake, keep quiet."

He returned to the chamber with the bloody table. There were still the sacrificial knives gleaming in the lamplight. Cyrus chose one and sent the rest scattering down the hall – there was no reason to leave them for his tormentors.

He heard a movement in the room adjacent; something softly coming for him by way of the bloody chamber that held Abelin. He waited for it, wondering whether somehow St. Aubert had survived and knowing somehow that nothing earthly could have withstood the power that rippled beneath that wolf's skin. And if the Marquis St. Aubert, with the edge of his knife and wit, could not withstand it, then what hope did Cyrus have?

Sir Robert had lost most of his former self in those few minutes that he had spent out of Cyrus's sight. The bones and muscles were out of joint, striving and straining into places and postures for which they had not originally been formed: the upper arms straining to touch the ground, the nails distended and grown long as a wolf's teeth, and the flesh covering a mass of knotted muscles that writhed as Sir Robert approached him, panting with a breathlessness that seemed borne less from fatigue than hunger.

Cyrus gripped his knife, his vision suddenly blurred and dizzy with terror and revulsion. An odd impulse seized him for the briefest of moments; an impulse to throw away his weapon, close his eyes, and allow this monster to take him, if only so that he would no longer have to look upon the contours of its being. Reason shook him awake a second later, but the impressions of this desire remained in him as well as an opposing impulse that held his brain in thrall at the same time – namely, to swallow the horror with his eyes, staring at it until he had committed every wolf-like motion and every blood-stained nail to memory, until ultimate knowledge and ultimate apathy at last united.

The thing sprang for him and he raised the dagger, hoping that its weight collapsed upon the point would be enough to murder it. But it managed to avoid the weapon, throwing him heavily to the ground and jolting the knife from his hand. He found himself suffocating beneath it, groping about for something – anything – to grip so that he could pull himself free. His fingers clutched cold iron; he struggled breathlessly to draw it closer and as he did, he happened to drive his elbow into the wrinkled face that leered and slavered above him.

Something went wrong then; something in the shape of Sir Robert's face had gone awry, like a child's mask that has been knocked crooked in the midst of a game. Even Sir Robert, lost as he was to the human part of his soul, sensed this new change with an animal's instinct, for a long-nailed hand went up immediately to his face. But this new movement only served to complete his undoing; the mask of old flesh fell away from him and Cyrus saw above him the smooth, young face of the monster that he and Withing had beheld in that secret chamber beneath the Priory's foundations – that unearthly, infantile visage that had, save for the eyes, resembled so much the portrait of Lord Luke Gosselin.

How long, Cyrus wondered, had Sir Robert kept the castaway of his own old, molted flesh as a shield to cover the miracle that his experiments in sorcery had wrought beneath it? It was impossible to tell, but the crude disguise had worked wonderfully enough to where it could have been kept up for months without notice. Now Cyrus had upset it and he was amazed at the look of hideous vulnerability that hovered in those blank eyes for the briefest of moments. Then the jaw went slack and the tongue curled out, soft and wrinkled, to throttle and suck. And where it fell, his nerves screamed.

Trembling with agony, his hand flailed out at the maskless thing with the first thing that he could grab hold of, striking it full in the face with Childermass's cross. He nearly choked at the smell of smoke that rose from the nobleman's flesh as the iron touched his flesh. Now he understood. Of course the cross had done nothing when the chimney sweeper had touched it to Sir Robert's forehead earlier; he had been touching a castaway molting rather than the actual flesh. Now Cyrus saw Childermass's vindication in the blistering wound that covered the nobleman's forehead and made raw his cheek.

"You bloody, self-righteous bastard," Cyrus whispered. "You wanted Childermass branded a monster only because he was so close to knowing what you truly are."

The smile on Sir Robert's face was made the more awful by the fresh wound that now accompanied it.

"Oh, but it would never have been so easy, Cyrus, if he had not been something of a monster already."

He seized Cyrus's arm, twisting it, but the young man kicked out at the man with all his strength. There was nothing even remotely human in the face that bent over him now. It was just a crater of gnashing teeth and the gleam of two black eyes. His fangs were clenching so close to Cyrus's throat that the boy could feel the hot wetness of them. He struck out harder than he realized and the iron found its way beneath the man's chin. Something cracked, then; the neck went suddenly limp and elastic and the thing's head lolled back between its shoulders at an impossible degree.

But Sir Robert still came for him, mindless of his snapped neck. His claws raked across Cyrus's face, bloodying his cheeks; his nails narrowly missed taking out the young man's eyes. Cyrus's heart felt trapped somewhere between his throat and his lungs as he backed away. The cross still burned the nobleman's flesh every time he struck at him, but Sir Robert seemed impervious to the pain. The smoke of his flesh filled the air, but only Cyrus choked on it while his adversary continued silently to tear away at him.

Cyrus dropped the cross and backed away to the other side of the table, away from the loose-headed thing that had once been a man. Its tongue was still whipping back and forth between its teeth; he avoided its scalding spittle and seized one of the torches that hung from the wall. The fire caught easily to Sir Robert's black robes, rising in a curtain of flame to swallow the distorted flesh within. Cyrus watched him blacken and then fall apart as softly as wax, while the tongue like a separate organ continued to work steadily back and forth until the fire reached it too and turned it to crumbling powder. The only solid thing left of Sir Robert Gosselin was the ring that he had worn on his left hand, bearing the seal of the Gosselins.

For a moment, the room was raining human ash, soft and gentle, upon Cyrus's arms and eyelashes. Then a blinding light filled that space for a quarter of a second, accompanied by a ringing silence, and the fragments of soot scattered with a deafening explosion, ash transformed into blood. It dripped down the walls and covered the floor with crimson filth while the torches' flames burned high and blue. A sweet scent choked the air and a lungless scream rose, so exquisitely hopeless that Cyrus felt tears flood his eyes at the sound. Then all was darkness and silence.

Groping the way he had come, Cyrus made his way to where Withing lay in a fainted heap by the locked door. How he hoped that it was all over at last.

Chapter Forty: In which Childermass is creative in his own demise.

It took an hour for someone to finally unlock the door to Sir Robert's suite and even then it was only due to Feversham's conscience over a technicality. This, in turn, was largely owing to the bungled mess that both he and Dagworth had made of Childermass's execution – a mess that he hoped they could extricate themselves from with minimal embarrassment.

It had begun with Childermass's sudden and rather implausible confession that he was a Catholic and that he had come to the Priory all those years ago for the sole purpose of disseminating Jesuitical pamphlets.

"Well, what of it, then?" Dagworth asked. "We always knew there was something off about you. All the better that you're about to die, don't you think?"

"It's hardly proper to hang a regicide, Master Dagworth," said the chimney sweeper. "And I assure you," he added with a leer. "That every one of those pamphlets called for the King's assassination."

There was not a man among them who did not know the fate of a regicide. It was the most feared death sentence of all, to be drawn and quartered; and though none of them in that remote area of Scotland had ever actually witnessed such a thing, their imaginations had already painted vivid depictions of what a man must feel and look like after he has been tied to four wild horses by four separate limbs.

"Are you saying," Dagworth said, his cruel eyes suddenly incredulous. "That you wish to be drawn and quartered rather than hung?"

"I think that one's own private wishes are irrelevant in such a matter, Master Dagworth," said Childermass, with a sanctimonious pursing of the lips.

It was a situation made all the more awkward by the fact that a small crowd of the Priory's guests and the grocers had gathered upon the battlements, mugs of ale in hand, to watch the chimney sweeper's hanging. Every last one of them naturally heard his pronouncement and most of them were muttering in favor of a more stimulating amendment to his sentence. Some of them even began to loudly demand it. Feversham's long features grew more despondent than usual; Dagworth appeared suspicious; Childermass merely shrugged his shoulders as though to say, "You see how it is?"

By the time Montrose arrived in order to rescue the chimney sweeper, he found himself bullied back into the courtyard of the Priory by a crowd eager to see the outcome of this execution. He could barely make out the chimney sweeper amidst the froth of humanity that surrounded him; he could, however, occasionally overhear snatches of his suggestions to Dagworth and the crowd and they were of the same pretty vein as his earlier one.

So when Feversham finally stood before the door that led to Sir Robert's abatoir, he first called, "My lord, may we have permission to make use of four horses and melt down one of the gold ingots in your storeroom?"

"Feversham, for God's sake," came Cyrus's voice, "open this door! His Lordship Withing has been gravely injured."

The ostler fumbled with his keys and made free at last the Puritan and the young lord. As the door opened, he raised his eyes to the tapestry of blood that spattered the walls of that place.

"Is His Lordship well?" he asked, pale.

"His Lordship is dead along with the Reverend Abelin," Cyrus said shortly. "After nearly murdering his grandson."

Feversham nodded shakily; this was all too much for him and it seemed easier to take the Puritan's word as proof enough for now.

"And what could you possibly need horses and melted gold for at this hour?" Cyrus asked as the two of them struggled to lift Withing between them.

"The four horses for the drawing and quartering," the ostler panted. "And Master Childermass did insist most vehemently that we pour melted gold into his wounds afterwards. He was most insistent, in fact, on that point."

***

The horizon had begun to lighten with dawn by the time that Cyrus came to the Priory's courtyard. He had not realized it in the darkness of the corridors, but now in the grey open air he saw that he was covered, head to foot, in blood. He threw off his coat, but the white cotton of the shirt that he had worn underneath was soaked as well. It was impossible to tell how much of it was his own and how much Sir Robert's. It was all the same dye.

The crowd of guests had lost interest in Childermass's execution as quickly as they had been seized by it. After it became apparent that nothing would come of the chimney sweeper's suggestions, most of them had scattered with only a few still standing by. They were laying bets as to whether, in the midst of his torments, Childermass would prove blasphemous or penitent.

"I'll wager he's a blasphemer," remarked one of them that Cyrus passed. "I saw a man hanged a month ago in Shrewsfield. Had the same philosophical look upon his face at the start, but when he saw the rope he began to say things that would have curdled the blood of a heathen."

Childermass, who was sitting at the edge of a well and watching the mild December sky, was the first to notice Cyrus's approach. He stood and the rest of the courtyard, sensing a change, followed the direction of his gaze.

"Sir Robert Gosselin is dead," Cyrus told him. "And the Reverend Abelin with him. They were sorcerers, the both of them. They killed Lord Luke Gosselin and would have killed Lord Withing if I had not prevented them. As it is, they murdered one other man in that upper chamber…whom I did not recognize." He knew by the look in the chimney sweeper's gaze, that look that suggested that something behind Childermass's eye had been tickled into life, that it was well understood who this other man had been. Then, turning to the crowd, Cyrus continued, "It was they, not Childermass, who were behind the deaths of the villagers. Now, if you will but release him, I will ride out and fetch a doctor for Withing."

"But he confessed himself a secret Catholic," Dagworth said with a sour look. He looked like a man who had always half-expected to lose his end of a bet but still felt cross about it.

Cyrus managed a smile then at Childermass. "It would serve you right well if you did end up drawn and quartered at your own suggestion."

"Better my own than another's, Master Plainstaff," Childermass replied.

Something had changed in the air. The snow was falling but the air felt warmer and lighter. Cyrus found himself stumbling suddenly to his knees, but the pain in his head had disappeared to be replaced with a wonderful, floating kind of relief. Dagworth had caught him by the shoulders and was asking him if he was all right; Childermass, hands bound behind his back, watched him with a look of mild mystery. Then even these faces flickered and sank beneath the coming darkness. But this time Cyrus welcomed it.

Chapter Forty-One: In which Childermass takes to himself a secret joy and Shipwash finds a new horror in an upstairs chamber.

In the end, it was Feversham, Childermass, and Dagworth alone who returned those bloody chambers to something like their former state. They were not able to clear it of that sweet, rusty smell; nor was there much that they could do for the more stubborn stains. But they buried all the bones, both animal and human, burned the wolf skins, and washed the stones with lye and water. While the rest of the servants stood outside those rooms with a kind of superstitious repulsion, the triumvirate worked on with their usual mechanistic efficiency. Dagworth was so utterly unaffected by his surroundings that he even found time to complain of the botched execution of several hours past.

"Here we are, scrubbing floors together, when you were to be drawn and quartered," he remarked whimsically, scratching at his ear. "Lord, what a waste."

"One must leave something for the future, Master Dagworth," the chimney sweeper reminded him. "I still pray every day that one of your curs will find the wit to sink his teeth into your crotch. But Providence does not move according to our poor mortal wills. Alas."

"Will the two of you hold your tongues for a moment?" Feversham said. "Master Plainstaff said that another man was killed, did he not? But I can find nothing here save blood."

"Well, there's your answer then," Dagworth sneered. "Ate him up, bones and clothes, Our Lordship did."

But both he and Childermass followed the ostler anyway into the chamber in which the Marquis St. Aubert had been locked away with Sir Robert. And both of them were silent as they saw the peculiar emptiness of that room.

After a space, Dagworth shrugged and turned away. But Childermass still stood, looking at that room and wondering what about it made him feel cold and uneasy, made his heart beat faster as though he had drifted into the middle of a frozen lake. Then he realized what it was and could have sworn that at that moment of realization, his heart ceased altogether while a smile shuddered its way to his lips.

For none of the blood in that room had changed color. There was no hint of congealed rust or dryness about it. It was still the same dripping crimson that it had been when it had first flowed and when Childermass, with a trembling finger, put it to his tongue, it was as fresh as if it had spurted from his own thumb.

***

Cyrus woke to find himself lying in bed. The sky outside his window was twilight blue verging on black; by the crackling fire, he saw Childermass reading a book of chivalric tales. When he started up, the chimney sweeper laid the volume aside and came to his side.

"Better, Master Plainstaff?" he asked.

"Is Withing well?" Cyrus looked about as he spoke; the quivering shadows by the hearth made him nervous.

"Dr. Erskine himself has been with His Lordship since this morning. His wounds are grave, but not mortal."

"Thank God." Cyrus fell back upon his pillow, suddenly aware of the blinding pain in his head. Somehow sleep had dulled it, but waking had brought it back along with the memories.

"Will you be able to come down for Christmas supper, sir?" Childermass asked. "Or shall I bring you something."

"Are you well yourself, Childermass? You look different somehow."

"Different, sir? How?"

Cyrus wondered why Childermass appeared so unsettled by such a simple question. In truth, he could hardly answer the chimney sweeper's question for he hardly knew what difference it was that he sensed. If anything, Childermass seemed more himself than he had ever seemed before, if such a paradox made any sense. Everything that was fundamentally Childermass – the high, narrow arch of the shoulders, the divide between the speculative winter of one eye and the dead marble of the other, even the lank fall of his hair – all seemed magnified in some subtle and peculiar fashion, as though held beneath some psychic glass. Cyrus gazed at him for a long moment, trying and failing to determine what difference created this shining copy of the original.

A hard smile now played on Childermass's lips. He seemed far less uneasy now, as though he sensed the other's confusion and it somehow dispelled his disquiet.

"Tell me, Cyrus," said he. "How fare you, knowing as thou dost that thy father's murderer is dead and that none now know thy secret name?"

"None saving you," said Cyrus.

"Surely you do not consider me as you did St. Aubert."

"That depends on how you choose to use your advantage over me," the Puritan said. He was too weary to follow the rules of Childermass's cruel game and deliver an appropriately anxious reaction. "It matters little to me one way or the other."

"Shall I leave you then?" the chimney sweeper asked after a moment, palpably disappointed in Cyrus's apathy.

"No, I shall come down."

As Cyrus spoke, he struggled to his feet and Childermass caught him as he faltered.

"Begging your pardon, sir, but you hardly seem strong enough," the chimney sweeper remarked.

"It's only my head," said Cyrus, waiting a moment for the dizziness to dispel before shouldering his coat on. He looked at Childermass then and was amazed again at how forthright the chimney sweeper's gaze turned whenever they found themselves unsurrounded by others. It was as if Childermass was so close to solitude when they were alone that he did not bother to adopt his usual masks.

"What was it that I saw last night, Childermass?" Cyrus asked suddenly.

"Would that I had been there to tell you. I chafe more than you know at having been absent in that hour." He wetted his lips then and his mouth went wrong for a moment, as though he somehow tasted the next word before it left his lips and found its flavor bitter. "Please – tell me what you saw. Leave nothing out. I must know how it was."

And so Cyrus told him of the ritual that he had found the Reverend Abelin and Sir Robert in the midst of performing; of the wrinkled tongue that fell from Sir Robert's mouth and that he used to spit and suck at his enemies and victims; of the way that he had drawn a wolf pelt over his shoulders and suddenly begun to shiver and transform into as much of a beast as his twisted muscles could mimic.

Childermass listened without interruption until Cyrus ceased at last to speak. Then he stood and went to the window, his eye rising to the moon.

"That such things can be!" he said. "And you've not only read of them in books or heard of them in taverns as I have – you have seen them, been touched by them."

"And I wish to God I hadn't."

Childermass turned and stared at him. "Of course, I wish you had not either. It must have been a hideous ordeal."

Cyrus took courage from the fact that the chimney sweeper had finally said something prosaic to say, "But was Sir Robert a monster?"

"Not in the physical sense. He was a sorcerer and what you saw were manifestations of his great power. I always suspected that our murderer was of that sort. The bloodless, shriveled corpses, the howling that I heard on those nights before a body was found, all made me sure. And he certainly concealed his tracks neatly, the cunning bastard. Do you recall, Cyrus, how many dead victims had the marks of torture about them? He had to do that in order to have them say those words, the words that the wounded boy that Lady Mariah found in the forest was repeating. Caelum te nego, ave terra. I renounce you, Heaven. Hail, Earth."

"I don't understand."

"If you were a sorcerer and you dealt with spirits as often as with mortals, Master Plainstaff, wouldn't you fear them as much if not more? Now why would you have your victim say those words before he died?"

Cyrus felt a chill. "So that his ghost could not leave this earthly sphere?" After a pause, "But what good would that do him? If he feared their spirits, wouldn't he want them kept away from him?"

"No, sir, he would want them kept trapped and out of the way."

"But how could he do that?"

"Do you remember the secret chamber beneath the library – the one that you and Withing stumbled upon?" Childermass smiled. "I often wondered what those bottles that I saw down there were – the ones you so clumsily broke in your haste to leave and that made the place so murky. Didn't you ever wonder yourself?"

Cyrus felt sick with loathing. "What man would do such a thing?"

"A man unlike you or me, it is true, Master Plainstaff, but still only a man nonetheless with a man's usual frailties. I fear that Sir Robert took very much after his brother Lord Stephen, the one who was so afraid for his flesh and its continued wellbeing, but clearly went much further in the study of witchcraft. I think, too, that we now know what the final rite was that Alison Mackenzie or The Mistress – whichever you wish to call her – asked him to perform, the one that made him renounce the black arts forever. That thing that you saw, the shriveled tongue, must surely have been what the old gossips called the 'tongue of Satan' – and oh, how it took root and grew once Sir Robert found it in Lord Stephen's secret chamber and decided to put it beneath his own tongue! It must have been what gave him the thirst to drink blood, don't you imagine? And that blood worked the wonderful alchemy that you saw in him. But he could not have his new youth discovered and so he kept a molting of his old skin to cover his face until the work was complete. Can you imagine it?" Childermass shook his head with a kind of simple marvel.

"You brought him down," Cyrus said. "He would have done as he pleased if you had not told me what to do."

"*We* brought him down, Master Plainstaff. But I only did my duty to the Priory. It was noble of you to prove so considerate towards us." His tone was too dry for Cyrus to determine whether any of this was said sincerely or ironically. Knowing Childermass, he could easily believe that its spirit contained a convoluted mixture of both.

"Do you ever wonder, Cyrus," Childermass continued as they stepped into the hall. "About the death of that child Nat? He was found in pieces in the treetops, too high for any creature without wings to have reached. What enchanted mantle do you think His Lordship put on that night and how do you think he looked after it changed him?"

"I thank God," said Cyrus, "that I do not know."

And Childermass who did know (for he had heard it from Nat himself) felt an unnatural impulse towards mercy and so kept silent.

***

To Cyrus Colkins, there was something familiar in the air, some quality of mood or circumstance that reminded him of the first night that he had spent in the Priory – that night when, after a long day spent in sleep, he had descended into the Great Hall and found its inhabitants at supper. He had been alone then and had found an unquiet table, silent and restless after a year of horror.

Now he came with Childermass at his side to find a room mostly filled with strangers, save for one table at which Withing, Mariah, and Clarice sat alongside Lord Montrose and Squire Toby. Withing looked pale and ill, propped up in his chair with pillows and blankets; but his eyes had a sparkle that, for the most part, was innocent of that listless melancholy that had plagued him ever since Cyrus had known him. When he caught sight of the Puritan, the boy immediately sat up and cried out, "Cyrus Plainstaff!"

The room fell silent as Withing said simply, "You saved my life." Tears shone in his eyes for a moment before he looked down and away, embarrassed by the stupefaction on Cyrus's face.

Mariah saved the moment. She stood and said, "Hail the savior of the Priory's new lord."

And the rest of the guests, relieved at understanding at last the meaning of this scene, all stood and took up the cheer as well. When it finally died away, Cyrus said, "And hail its second savior – Master Childermass."

The guests had felt perfectly correct in clapping for a fellow guest, but the idea of clapping for a chimney sweeper was foreign to them. A few scattered claps came from the grocers, mostly those who knew him from his visits to Shrewsfield, and Withing and Clarice applauded him. Childermass sardonically clapped for himself and then nodded to Cyrus saying, "Methinks it is your night, Master Colkins, and I don't begrudge you of it. We all have our times and places, sir."

And Childermass took leave of him and went to stand with Dagworth and Feversham, remote and strange once more.

The Great Hall was filled with the winter's chill, for the tapestries could not keep out the wind-blown snow. Cyrus sat between Withing and Mariah and felt the boy press his hand warmly, heard the wassailers as they began an out-of-tune rendition of 'Personent Hodie' and wondered if what he felt at that moment was finally peace. He had felt many things since he had fled to the Priory – relief, happiness, fear, and now this. Heaven grant that it would last.

For it was Christmas night and Cyrus felt that he had reached sanctuary at last.

***

The Great Hall was still filled with guests when Shipwash retreated to the staircase, hoping to find a moment's solitude. The evening's ale had made him warm and unsteady, as though an invisible cloud hovered between himself and the world. It made even his sorrow (now more faded than fierce) and his relief at Sir Robert's discovery and death seem as light and airy as snow or steam. There was a relief in this lightness, even though Shipwash knew that it would fade as soon as the ale had passed through him. The days had been too heavy, too unrelenting for him to feel anything save their weight; drunk, he at least exchanged numb sorrow for sedation.

Shipwash was no fool. He had dreamed of Sir Robert's victims just as the rest of the guests had when Cyrus had upset the glass bottles that had imprisoned their souls. And because he was no fool, he could not dismiss those blood-stained visions as the morbid toilings of his own brain. Not after he had seen Nat in them, had felt the boy's hand in his own, and heard his voice. Nat, alive, had barely spoken to him; he had been too busy drowning beneath the death of his parents. Now dead himself, he could do no more than plead, as he had done before with the merciless Childermass, for protection. Hearing the boy speak again, while covered with those terrible, dismembering wounds, Shipwash knew that no imaginative power or memory could have brought that voice back to him. It was Nat in truth, begging the grocer for an aid that Shipwash did not know how to give him.

He climbed higher until he reached the second floor of the Priory, until he stood where Cyrus had stood before he had gone farther on into Sir Robert's chambers; where Childermass, before Luke Gosselin's death, had sometimes stood to listen as the Priory settled above and beneath him for the night. One door at the end of the hallway, he noticed, had been carelessly closed. The slanting line of moonlight that fell from the crack between the door and the doorframe was pale and steady and Shipwash, mostly because he little knew what else to do, moved towards it through the darkness –

***

– at the same time as Childermass, alone in the Priory's deserted kitchens, held a thimble-sized vial of glass to the light of a moonstruck window. It shone crimson in the silver light, pregnant with a few drops of blood. They were as fresh and running as they had been the moment that the chimney sweeper had caught them trickling from the walls of Sir Robert's chamber.

Childermass stood there, as though in silent thought, for several minutes. Then, almost tentatively, the way a man might put his hand into a tame snake's cage, he put a finger into the vial and touched a drop of the blood to his tongue.

This time, he was prepared for the change. His nerves and heart were ready for it. Before, he had been so overwhelmed by it that he had fallen to the floor; his attempts to regain control of his nerves had ended disastrously, almost driving him mad with pain. When he had at last surrendered out of necessity, his invisible conqueror had rewarded him amply. Once he knew what it wanted of him, he lost the impossible desire to fight it.

It wasn't really Sir Robert's blood or St. Aubert's. It was something that had flowed through Sir Robert's veins, yes; but it had not belonged to him. That much was evident from the way that it continued to live even after its host had been reduced to ash. It was still ready to fill and remake whatever living chalice chose to hold it.

Childermass had not had enough of it for any true change to be wrought in him. Theirs was a courtship, not a marriage. He took it into himself, let it agitate and possess him; fill his mind with visions that twisted and sighed like speaking shadows; satisfy him without leaving any true mark of itself upon him, save perhaps that peculiar look that Cyrus had noticed in him earlier that evening – that look of curious completion. He felt himself the hero who had slain the dragon and devoured its heart; who understood what it was that the birds sang above him in the trees. It was not an abomination that he treasured. It was his glittering trophy, his by right of conquest.

He looked again at the vial. It seemed as full as when he had first filled it, warm and vital in his hand. He wondered if it hated him for loving it. The thought made him smile.

He uncapped it again. This time he was in no mood for a mere taste. He put his lips to it and threw his head back, taking it in one draft. Then he sank to the floor, setting it against himself, willing it to try and undo him once more.

***

At first, Shipwash thought that someone had upset their dinner upon the floor. The air of that chamber was heavy with an organic, almost animalistic scent. He brought his hand away from the doorknob and rubbed his fingers together, incredulous at the strong-smelling glue that now clung to them.

The moonlight was too stark for clear seeing. A man was lying on the bed – he could tell that much. His four limbs were straining towards the bedposts at his head and feet, for they had been forced into that position by ropes, now blackened with blood. A white bedsheet, colorful with his spoiled entrails, had been thrown carefully over his face and torso.

Shipwash watched his hand go out as though it belonged to a stranger – watched it take hold of the sheet and throw it back – and looked down into the dead face of Gomershall, the chest and stomach that had been parted so neatly down the middle, opening into a crude, sidelong mouth, and the steel stakes, thin as needles, long as pokers, that had been lanced through his slit until he had died of them. But it was the thing of crystal, resting by the dead lord's cheek upon the pillow, that Shipwash's eye caught and held.

He had seen it once before, in a boy's hand – Nat's hand. He remembered asking the child where he had found it and how Nat had said that it had been given him by one of their company, the strange Frenchman who would later save them from the witch Mackenzie and her brood. And as Shipwash lifted the glass dove and turned it over in his hand, watching as it magnified the horror on the bed in its crystalline breast, he heard the sound of someone entering that chamber and knew, even before he turned, whose face he would see.

***

The blood had given up presenting him with mere shadows. It was now taking apart his vision and letting him see his world, reconstructed in blood.

Childermass wandered down the Priory's corridors and saw that the walls were now made of flesh as well as stone; when he touched them, they gave a bruised sound that made him shudder. The stained-glass windows shone like the outer membrane of a human eye and the winter drafts floated past him like successive breaths. It was as though he had been reduced to something less than an atom and now wandered through the chambers of the Priory's heart, picking his way through its body like some adoring parasite.

He knelt for a moment as though in reverence of the living walls that enclosed him and that was when he felt it shudder. There was something wrong with this sensation, something that disturbed even his fascinated rapture. He looked about, whispering for it to tell him what he could do to relieve it. And as he pleaded, he saw what it was in an instant, as though the Priory had opened up to him its folded walls and shown him the inner secret of its canker.

The frank and practical side of Childermass knew that what he saw was an impossibility – that the man or spirit that he saw was dead and that no earthly power could have brought him back. And so, with the same cold logic, he determined that he must be done away with in some manner necessarily peculiar but not inconceivable.

The world of flesh and stone pressed against him on all sides. He gazed a moment longer at the luminous face of the newborn horror, its finger-blades spreadeagled fanlike out of its left hand, and then put a shaky finger down his throat, coughing up enchanted blood.

He awoke, sticky with his own sweat, but wholly on solid earth again. One thought floated madly within his otherwise tranquil brain, raged like a bird beating its wings bloody against a cage. The Priory was calling for his help. It was not calling its lords, its ostlers, or its noble guests. It was calling him, him, him – Childermass, the Master of the Chimneys, the one who had looked at it from a distance and loved it before he had ever really known it, the one who had stolen away one of its signet rings, who had tasted the blood of its lord.

"Oh God," he said breathlessly. "That such things can be!"

Then he was running out of the kitchen, through the Great Hall and past the Christmas guests, deaf to the cries and questions that followed in his wake, up the stairs and into the darkness.

***

Shipwash's legs backed him away towards the window, but his eyes remained fixed upon the man who now approached him – the man who he was certain was the author of the tortured tableau on the bed – the man who had saved him from the witch and her sons by proving a greater monster than they – the man who Shipwash did not know as the Marquis Antoine St. Aubert.

But oh, what a change had been wrought in him since last they had met. Shipwash could not have known it, for he had not even realized that St. Aubert had found his way into the Priory, making himself at home in its forgotten towers; he could not have known of how the man who had blinded animals and scourged them ahead with the ease of a devil had been reduced to a blinding agony himself within that narrow chamber into which Cyrus had locked him away with the ravening Sir Robert Gosselin. The futile struggle that St. Aubert had put up against his attacker had lasted only a moment. Then Sir Robert's teeth and claws had found their way into his throat and he found himself choking on his own blood, felt his vision dim, and realized incredibly that something in him was loosening, some hold that he had on himself that he had thought was so sure was beginning to relax. He had felt distanced from the atrocities that were being done to himself, had found himself able to notice the way in which his body could not decide whether it was suffocating or drowning, that something inside him had gone cold, had turned to ice, that his body was trembling from the cold, and that the world was darkening into a midwinter night all around him.

He had then wondered if he looked like the men and the women whom he had put to sleep himself. All their faces from the first to the last passed before him, from the girl who had once been so joyous to call herself his bride before the shadow of his soul had covered her, to the kitchen maid in the Priory who had loved him to her own destruction. Then there were those in between – the faces, like stepping stones, that marked in blood the progression of years that had taken him from then to now. Now it was his own blood, his own suffering, that stood as a final stone to mark the end of his course. Another man might have felt the irony of it. All he could feel was a kind of amazed disbelief. And then his body could suffer no more and his spirit had fled his flesh like a burning house.

"Did you do this?" Shipwash asked.

St. Aubert looked down at what was left of Gomershall. His smile was movingly radiant.

"Oh, yes."

After a pause, the grocer said, "Why?"

"I did not see you affected by the blinding of the witch's goats, Monsieur," the Marquis said. "And this man was less to me than them."

"And that is why you killed him?"

"I did so because he would have betrayed a promise – a promise very dear to me. Does this answer satisfy?" He asked this last with an amused sort of gallantry. Shipwash then heard with a preternatural clarity the sound of his mantle as it brushed past the bed; as he began to come closer.

There was something different about this man. Shipwash did not know how, in that awful moment, his nerves could stand to notice such a subtlety, but they did. His senses were alive with the difference. It was like a visible fever that spread through the Frenchman; Shipwash almost felt it reach out and touch him as he stumbled back, his feet proving treacherous and nearly tripping him as he tried to circle the bed, tried to keep it between the Frenchman and himself.

"I met the man, the man who killed little Nat," St. Aubert murmured and this mention of Nat riveted Shipwash in spite of his fear. "The monster, the *cauchemar*. I thought to kill him, but he slew me as well, Monsieur. I know he did, for when he had done with me, I felt my spirit rush out of me and alight in darkness. I could hardly see where I was, but it was as though I were running down the walls with my own blood."

"If you died," said Shipwash. "Then why – "

"Because I was made whole again. Something made my flesh and blood come together again, do you not see, Monsieur? But I cannot say what it was. Please tell me, if you know. I am innocent of the powers in this Priory, though I know they must be great. And I wish to learn of them."

There was something almost touchingly inquisitive about the look of him; Shipwash could almost forget the tortured body on the bed, forget his cruelties and his relish of them, in the chill of wonder that both of them shared in that space. The old Shipwash, the Shipwash before Nat's death and his coming to the Priory, would have laughed at such an account. But Shipwash had changed too and he knew now why St. Aubert had appeared so differently. There was a gleam to the gold of his hair as though it were still wet with its afterbirth; the same blue was in his eyes, but their clarity had been born scarcely several hours ago. His was a new and perfect flesh and Shipwash felt worn and dirty next to it. He thought, so suddenly and earnestly that it made him giddy, that he wished that this miracle could have been performed upon Nat – that if he had learned the secret of it, he would have made it happen to the child. And so, overcome with awe and a kind of poignant wonder, he made a mistake.

"If what you say is true…" (He said this merely as a formality; his own eyes and intuition confirmed the truth of St. Aubert's resurrection.) "…If it is true, then I cannot say what brought you back." He would have said more, but he still feared what this man was. His resurrection was wondrous, but it was a miracle done to a monster.

Shipwash then looked down at the remains of Gomershall, his vision suddenly overcast with tears. He saw again the ravaged body of Nat, remembered the pieces of him in his arms, so terribly light, and suddenly looked up to find that St. Aubert was beside him.

"I saved you once," the murderer said, his voice so soft that Shipwash almost imagined that it came from within his head. "Do you think that I shall save you again? Is that why you do not fear me, Monsieur?"

"Oh God, forgive me," Shipwash said breathlessly. He knew only too well why he had stood there so fearlessly in spite of what would come. Perhaps he would have fled if he were not numb with ale and sorrow; perhaps he would have been stronger if he had not seen this man resurrected while an orphaned child's grave lay covered in frost. All he needed at that moment was the voice of someone, anyone – even old Crawley's dull pedantry – to call him from his deadly station.

"Why do you not speak to Him face to face?" St. Aubert asked. "I can bring you closer to Him than any priest."

Then the darkness broke and Shipwash saw Nat himself, standing by the door to the chamber, his face distraught with terror. And Shipwash flinched, for he knew somehow that the boy's terror was for him – a warning come too late.

Then the door flew open and someone else was standing there where he had fancied that he saw Nat's pale face: a young man of soot-smelling clothes and a single livid eye. Something in that eye seemed to falter when it met the pathetic voiceless look in Shipwash's own gaze and the man knew then that he was very close to death. Yet St. Aubert followed Shipwash's look and something about the sight of Childermass caused his murdering hand to pause and in that blessed moment, Shipwash found the strength to do what he could not do before: to run.

***

As St. Aubert heard Shipwash stumble blindly from that chamber of death, he continued to gaze at the creature that had come to put a rude end to his pleasure. For one burning instant, they merely looked at one another – the chimney sweeper and the Marquis. Then Childermass smiled, and his smile was provoked as much by the fact that he had at last seen the monster of Cyrus's tale as by the knowledge that he had redeemed Shipwash, in his own peculiar way, from the lingering death that St. Aubert would have wished for him. There was enough that was human in St. Aubert to revolt at that smile and as he took a step back from the body of his freshest victim, the blood-spattered Marquis felt that same sense of revulsion and horror for the chimney sweeper that he had experienced when he had first laid eyes upon him. He could not have dreaded the young man more if he had been the ghost of one of his victims.

The Marquis was no fool – he read in those looks a great portion of the chimney sweeper's soul and what he saw intrigued and repelled him. The extent of Childermass's disease, that devouring curiosity, of course, remained unknown to him; but that look of grim interest still betrayed the chimney sweeper's heart and opened it to the last person in the world whom he would have wished to read it. In a flash of insight, half made of intuition, half of imagination, St. Aubert saw Childermass for a cruel huntsman who would readily plunge his dirk into the breast of the nightmare that his curiosity had drawn him towards, if he saw in it some challenge to a greater and still more obscure desire that animated him. Only such a perverse warring of motives could have produced a countenance such as Childermass's, at once callous and impassioned. It was the most refined mixture of antagonism and affinity that St. Aubert had ever seen and he found himself fascinated by it, even as he acknowledged that this chimney sweeper might very well attempt, in his own perversion, to destroy him for his violation of the Priory. It would be in keeping with a nature such as Childermass's to twitch that cruel little smile of amusement upon some new horror, before quelling it with his own suffocating craft so that it might not rise ascendant above his own.

The old, familiar impulse rose in St. Aubert, fountaining his heart like the blood that ripples so generously from an opened throat. Thoughts flashed before his eyes in swift succession, like the images of some magic lantern show, each one contradicting the other in turn. One stood above the rest – that he must martyr this young man quickly or else his own life would be forfeit. But where this conviction sprang, or why the pure single-mindedness of Childermass's countenance formed in him this separate resolve, he could not tell.

***

Then the chimney sweeper looked down at what remained of Gomershall, something piteous flickered in his eye, and the spell was momentarily broken. He was only another trespasser, another thoughtless intruder who had destroyed a moment of grace, and St. Aubert longed to destroy him as he had Gomershall. Without a second's delay, he caught Childermass to him by the throat and held him like that, letting him choke.

"Did you…" Childermass gasped. "Did you do this to your wife? Is that how she died after all those months? Had you finally had enough of her blood when you…strangled her…? Was that it?"

Revolted, St. Aubert threw him down on the bed beside the opened body of Gomershall. His hands were moving quickly, drawing out the black cord that he always kept in a coil inside his coat pocket. The chimney sweeper was coughing, but his eye sparkled with a kind of cold relish as he saw how well he had disquieted the Marquis.

"How do you know of my lady?" St. Aubert murmured. "Did Cyrus tell you?"

"Not willingly, my lord."

"Then how?"

Childermass swallowed. He did not feel afraid exactly, but he also did not feel as immune as he had before. In a moment, he could be as dead as Gomershall. A calculating desperation began to grow large in his brain. He had been sent here as the Priory's messenger-boy-turned-assassin and now found himself feeling far less sure of his errand. Had it been the Priory's will that he die here as some kind of sacrifice? Would his death be the necessary catalyst to bring down the monster St. Aubert? Childermass spit out the thought and cast about for some means of escape.

"I simply knew," he said. "I can sound a soul as easily as some men do a well and I knew Cyrus's history and, by it, yours. Just as I know who murdered you and the powers that he possessed. The powers that brought you back to life."

St. Aubert had intended to knot Childermass's wrists together and bleed the precocious young monster to death, but these last words stilled him. It felt as though fate was coming together for him, just as his ravaged flesh and bone had. His vision was altering along with it as well. There was still something that disgusted yet fascinated him about the chimney sweeper, but now there was a practical need for his continued existence as well. Of all the Priory's denizens, he seemed to St. Aubert the most likely and willing to talk.

"You know what has happened to me?" he asked, after a long pause. "You know of my resurrection?"

"Who does not?" Childermass replied. "It is the greatest miracle that I have ever witnessed."

"You understand, then, Monsieur," the Marquis said, with a kind of tender relief. "You understand what a transfiguration has been fulfilled within my flesh. I can see that by the look of your face. That is why you are not altogether afraid of me, is it not? Please tell me, kind Childermass." His coat was stained with Gomershall's blood, his fingers still held the tight little coil of rope, and his eyes were bright with moonlight and anticipation. "Please say what has happened to me."

Childermass felt fear tighten his throat. He knew that if he did not give this man what he wanted, then his life was over. When the Marquis, impatient with his speechlessness, struck him across the mouth, Childermass decided to say something that he knew would earn him St. Aubert's full attention.

"Please don't hurt me," he whispered. "I will tell you everything, truly I will. Only promise that you won't kill me."

"Very well," the Marquis said, eyes sparkling. This was an exchange that he was well acquainted with.

"You must promise," Childermass said. "Swear it."

"I swear by the holy church that you will not die if you tell me what I must know."

The corners of Childermass's lips turned down and he shook his head slowly. "Swear by the name of your wife."

Something darkened even St. Aubert's brightness for a moment, but he said, "I swear by her name."

"Say her name."

For a moment, the Marquis turned pale with hatred, as though a light somewhere within him had flared. Then he relaxed, like a serpent slowly uncoiling itself. He sat upon the edge of the bed, leaning forward, knife in hand, and let the edge of it cut into Childermass's cheek.

"Columbine," he said into that hungry ear. He leaned back then, his gaze full of smiling contempt. "I suppose you know that if you do not fulfill your end of our agreement, that you shall die."

"That is, after all, our agreement," said Childermass.

The chimney sweeper's own smile looked longer, somehow, with the line of blood along his cheek.

And he was thinking, *of course, Columbine is another word for dove, and now it all begins to come together.*

But there was still, he knew, so much more to know.

Chapter Forty-Two: In which Cyrus bears witness to a most wicked miracle.

"Cyrus? Are you well?"

He came awake, out of what seemed an interminable dream that he only half-remembered, and blinked at Mariah. She was smiling at him.

"Too much ale?" she asked.

"It always makes me a little drowsy," he admitted.

He let his gaze float up to the ceiling and instantly wished that he had not. The angles had vanished and the Priory's scaling walls leaned down upon him, dizzying him with their lowering weight.

"A little sick too," he added.

"I'm afraid we haven't the best ale to offer our guests," she said. "Though Toby and Montrose appear to be making the best of it."

Cyrus could see the two lords sitting at a separate table. Cards were floating in a shallow puddle of wine at their feet. Disjointed phrases of their conversation came to Cyrus intermittently – something about horses, whores, and debts.

"I fear that I've been so intent upon our own troubles that I've never ventured to ask after your own." She smiled a little sadly at him and Cyrus caught, as he had a few times before, the glimmer of a question in her eyes. He felt strangely unsettled, as though something were expected of him, something rather obvious, and he had mysteriously forgotten it.

"Have you a home of your own, Master Plainstaff?"

What did she expect of him? He knew that she wanted to hear the tale of a nobleman, probably one whose home had been seized by Parliament's troops, whose father had suffered for the King. Cyrus could feel the lie rise to his lips already. It would be so easy to tell – he had rescued Withing, ended the murderer. No one would ever question the legitimacy of his claim, no one would ever know. No one save Childermass, and Cyrus knew that the chimney sweeper would never tell unless he felt threatened by him. It was too rich a thing to hold the secret to himself.

He looked at Mariah's expectant face, the calm of her grey eyes. He knew that the truth of what he was would repulse her, would perhaps even turn her and the rest of the Priory against him. And perhaps it was best that way. His father's murderer was now dead and what reason had he to live under this roof as a lie?

Cyrus rose a little unsteadily, eyes lowered to the table. Mariah started up immediately after him, came to his side, and took his hand.

"You are still in shock, still hurt after last night," she said. Her fingers were cool against his brow.

"I am well," he said. "Only very tired."

"Cyrus." Mariah's voice was suddenly sharp with fear. He turned again to look at her. Her face had gone very pale. "We have assumed much of you since you came here. But you are not really as we imagined at all. You are something very different, aren't you?"

As Cyrus paused, unwilling to deliver the answer that she expected, Shipwash entered the great hall. Among the sea of flushed revelers, his face appeared as white as a dead man's. When he met Cyrus's eyes, the Puritan felt a sympathetic shudder run through him.

"He is alive," he said. "*Alive*." And Cyrus somehow knew who it was that he spoke of. "And Childermass is with him."

"Warn them," Cyrus whispered, nodding to the throng. "They have no inkling of what wickedness it is that you saw."

And then without another word he was struggling through the crowd, to deliver Childermass from his assassin.

***

The silence in the Priory's upper floors was incomplete, fragmented by the sounds that spilled from the Great Hall. The windows were filled with moonlight and the shadows of wind-blown tree limbs. These shadows moved as though they were underwater, casting new shadows that writhed on the hallway floor.

Voices moved somewhere in the hallway ahead, vague and indistinct as the shadows.

"The blood caused you to come alive again. It put you together. It does the same to me when I drink it. I can feel it giving to me what I want."

"And what is it that you want?"

Cyrus followed the voices until he stood close to the half-open door of a bedroom. In the darkness, he looked in to see who spoke, knowing already the faces that those voices belonged to.

Three men were in that room, two alive and one lifeless. The dead man was stretched out on the bed, as though asleep: face bloodless, eyes dark.

Silver lancets sparkled from his body. The face was one that had haunted his dreams constantly, only a little less than St. Aubert's – the face of Lord Gomershall. There was no smile of coercion or look of grim hatred in him now, though – only cold limbs and a remote grimace of agony. Dark and sprawled upon the bed, he looked like some enormous, pinioned insect and Cyrus felt a chill of dread for him even then.

Childermass was seated in a chair by the bed, speaking of blood in the same soft monotone that Cyrus had overheard before. It occurred to Cyrus that he had never seen Childermass afraid before. But the chimney sweeper was pausing only long enough to swallow and, occasionally, to draw a long breath; he talked as though he feared that something wonderful would end or something terrible begin if he stalled. His lower mouth and chin were dark with blood, where he had been struck; his hands were tied together with a piece of black cord and fastened behind his back to the chair. There was a kind of dead electricity in his living eye; it followed the man who stood before him, at the other side of the bed, with a look unfathomable.

A triptych from Hell: the light streaming in from the high window, illuminating the tortured remains of Gomershall as its centerpiece; Childermass to the right, mouthing of Sir Robert's blood; and to the left, St. Aubert.

Cyrus knew that he did not dream, but he could not understand what he saw before him either. At once, he saw the dead remains of the man who had ordered his father's execution – and, standing over them, alive again, the Torturer himself.

He stood in the shadows, but somehow St. Aubert sensed his presence in spite of the darkness.

"Cyrus!" he cried, causing Childermass to fall silent and look in the direction of the door as well. "How glad I am that you could join us. Do you not see what I have done to the man who wished your father's death?"

There was no irony in the Marquis' voice. The man genuinely expected some show of gratitude.

"Oh God," Cyrus murmured.

St. Aubert was now standing behind Childermass's chair. His hair was no longer confined to the powdered wig that he had once been fond of; its gold was as wet as an insect broken out of its chrysalis. His face, likewise, had the same look of slick, enchanted life, as though a fire had been kindled beneath his flesh, making it sweat and shine.

"Do you know why I killed him?" the Marquis enquired. "It was for you. He broke faith with me; he at first promised that I would have the honor of bringing you to ground and then, at the last moment, threatened to have me change places with the hangman. But what did you do the night before, Cyrus? Did you not also break faith with me as well?"

"You truly expected me to honor a promise that would lead to my own destruction?" Cyrus asked. "Can you really be so blind? Look at what you have done to Gomershall, who never meant you harm, who thought of you as his accomplice. You destroyed even him."

"I never desired any man or woman's destruction – not at the beginning," the Marquis said. "But why should I explain myself? Even this chimney sweeper, who never saw me until tonight, understands what I am better than you. Now let me think, Monsieur. The both of you made a promise to me – you, to let me kill you if I spared Lord Withing's life and you," he said to Childermass, "to be spared if you only told me what I wished. One of you betrayed me, the other fulfilled his promise. But, alas, I have always meant to kill you, Cyrus. So how best to settle your debt to me?"

Childermass could guess where this was going. He knew even before St. Aubert pulled his head back by the hair and set the knife against his throat. He had hoped…but he should have known that he had gone too far with his cruel game when he had made mention of the Marquis's lady. The urge to learn her name and also – why pretend? – to see St. Aubert's face when he had been forced to utter it had been too compelling. But Childermass still caught his breath when he felt the edge of the blade and his vision darkened dizzily for a moment: a kind of rehearsal of death.

"Shall I kill him before your eyes, Cyrus?" St. Aubert asked, his gaze weighing the young man's reaction. "Then we shall have both betrayed a trust and our accounts shall be most happily settled."

A dark spill of blood fell down Childermass's throat as the knife pressed deeper.

"Do not loathe yourself, Cyrus," said Childermass matter-of-factly. "He meant to do this to me all along. You were only a convenient excuse."

St. Aubert's blood had been up for this. Nothing could have satisfied him more than to slaughter Childermass with the artless efficiency of a butcher. But these last words cancelled his abilities. He had meant to slay the chimney sweeper as an animal. Now he would die a martyr, at least in Cyrus's eyes. A martyr. The creature who had smiled at Columbine's name.

"Devil," St. Aubert said, drawing back from the bound captive.

Childermass's lips were pale and set, but there was a smile in his living eye.

Cyrus watched their interchange as though the two spoke in foreign tongues, unable to follow the process that had brought Childermass from death to momentary safety.

St. Aubert glanced back at Cyrus with a look both baffled and furious. Then he knelt to the level of Childermass's ear and said, "You have only prolonged your death. Think of yourself, my friend, as only a poor, lingering ghost who has not been sent to Hell yet. I shall be the one to finally damn you."

Childermass met his gaze and believed it. But this assurance could do nothing to rob him of the satisfaction that he felt at the Marquis's look of provocation. Beneath his look of terror lay a sense of dazed exultation. He barely felt the man's grip on his throat. All his feeling had rushed to his heart and he was left entirely numb elsewhere.

St. Aubert held Childermass by the throat, until he saw his eye go dark. Then he rose and looked at Cyrus.

"Not tonight," he said. "But soon."

"Why do you delay?" Cyrus asked, shaken by both fear and bafflement. "Why do you not kill me now? It's what you've wanted all these months, isn't it? My life?"

"Yes, your life," said St. Aubert. "But that I can have whenever I wish it. My present state is not as my former one. Now I strain after higher stakes. This Priory is mine now and all within it. It is the inheritance of my blessing, my resurrection. Name one soul who can stand against me now, Monsieur."

Cyrus had slowly unsheathed his own dagger and now, with a sick convulsion of the heart, he drove it into St. Aubert's throat.

"I am glad that you attempted that, Cyrus." It was horrible to hear how thick and soft his voice came, between the little spurts of blood. "I want you to see how hopeless it all is."

The Marquis drew the knife out and let it fall, then looked down at his bloody hands with a speculative glance. Already, his throat had begun to close up, overgrown with new flesh. A quick convulsion, the sound of sucking air, and he was whole again.

"And now for you."

Chapter Forty-Three: In which another miracle of horror is wrought within the Priory and in which Childermass's prophetic soul is not enough to save him from his wicked curiosity.

Cyrus woke, head sore, muscles aching from their long, ungainly repose on the rough floor of Gomershall's chamber. He wondered how long he had been unconscious since the Marquis's final blow sent him reeling into darkness.

The moon was submerged almost wholly beneath the treeline; it sent a fragmented light into the room over the very edge of the windowsill, illuminating a dead finger, a spill of blood, a bedpost.

Childermass was still sitting trussed to the chair, his left cheek resting languidly against his shoulder. He had the same dead look that he had possessed when Feversham had carried him into the Great Hall one chilly morning, not many days past – the morning when he had awakened blind. It was an odd, grotesque kind of swoon that he had fallen into, an unbreathing trance, as though the spirit had completely vacated the flesh, leaving it in a state of temporary isolation. One eyelid flickered slightly, but it was only a draft of wind, not a dreaming nerve.

Gritting his teeth, Cyrus hauled himself upright and went to the chimney sweeper. The movement brought Childermass awake with a start. When he looked up at Cyrus, he smiled a little uneasily.

"I thought you were him for a moment."

Cyrus cut Childermass loose with his knife and the chimney sweeper slowly began to rub life into his hands. As he did, he looked again at what was left of Gomershall.

"Horrible," he said, voice flat, his gaze too dazed to show any emotion stronger than bruised curiosity.

"Yes," said Cyrus. They looked at each other, both wondering at the silence that pervaded the Priory. Not a sound came from the other side of the door.

"If we were the only ones left, I would say that we should stay here," Cyrus admitted a little shakily.

“He is hoping that our friends will draw us to him.” Childermass was still tracing the length of Gomershall’s corpse with his eye. His thoughts tended less towards his own promised destruction than the image of Clarice or Withing, made in the image of the rest of St. Aubert’s victims. “He does not wish us to die here.”

He stooped to the floor, as he spoke, and traced the blood that had fallen from St. Aubert’s throat when Cyrus had stabbed him.

“Strange,” Childermass said.

“What?”

“It has turned dull as rust.”

“It usually does, doesn’t it?”

“Well, Cyrus, I suppose it depends on the quality of blood.”

***

They went to the landing and looked down into the Great Hall. At first, Childermass thought to himself, this was only one man against many. And then he thought: no, not a man, but a newmade creature. Whatever ran through Sir Robert’s veins, it transformed the flesh and turned it into the substance of angels. This new flesh did not have any care for whatever spirit inhabited it. It could have been a saint, it could have been a Nero.

Whatever Shipwash had told the revelers, it had not been enough to save them. Childermass saw a boy, one of the wassailers, lying with a cut throat, face cobwebbed with blood. He was only one of many. Most had fled at the start of the Marquis’s assault, perhaps wisely seeing that resistance was not an option, but some few had stopped to help their tortured friends and these two made up the silent company that lay below them.

“Why did he attack these?” Cyrus asked.

“He wanted to clear the Priory of everyone except ourselves, I expect. And to show us his strength.”

They descended to the first floor, moving past the blood-spattered sleeves and pale faces. The doors that opened into the courtyard were open, letting in drifts of snow. Together, Cyrus and Childermass managed to haul them closed and bolt them. The Priory echoed again and again with their joining.

They knew what they had to do next. For the next several minutes, they turned over the bodies of the dead, looking into the slaughtered faces for some recognizable feature. Childermass's heart stopped for a moment every time he saw a young woman, dark hair fanning the floor in motionless ripples, or a boy of Withing's age. He continued, though; methodical in the midst of his stomach-turning routine. He looked up momentarily at Cyrus and saw that the Puritan had slumped into a chair, too sick to continue.

But Withing, Mariah, and Clarice were not among the dead. Whether they had escaped from the Priory with the rest or had been murdered elsewhere was another matter, but they were not one of the poor creatures who lay at their feet.

Childermass knelt at the base of a marble angel, and gazed up at the rafters for a long while, silent and expressionless. He thought of when he had lived in Houndswick as a boy; when he had climbed to the top of a tree and looked across the forests at the towers of the Priory and imagined himself inside. Then he looked at the dreamless sleepers around him and something in him melted.

Cyrus had never seen Childermass like this before. He had seen Childermass the deceiver, the torturer, the one who knew how best to save the Priory and how best to put terror into the heart of whoever caught his eye. Indeed, Cyrus had always believed in two things – the young man's knowledge of the Priory and his endless capacity for cruelty. There was something disquieting in having this image, however unflattering, altered.

Childermass wiped at his cheeks, tears and soot streaking a bruised line along his cheekbone. He glanced at Cyrus. His gaze, in spite of the tears, was eerily distant: for a moment, his living eye was the twin of his marble one.

"I think we should go out to the stables," he said. "See how many of the horses are left."

"And then?"

He smiled. "What do you think we should do next?"

"How long will it take us to search the Priory for our friends?"

"A day, to search the places that they know, if we go together. Half that, if we search apart. There are many hidden places they could not possibly find."

"Do you think that we should search separately then?" Cyrus asked.

And Childermass, with a shaky grin, said, "Not if we can help it."

***

Up staircases that wound like centipede coils, giving out onto floors of yellow dust and shadow; down cellars and unlighted passages, cold as tombs; ascending once again into levels of dim light before turning into windowless chambers; so Cyrus and Childermass toiled their way through the Priory's mazes. Morning came, the dawn of the day following the feast of Christmas, but the world outside the Priory had darkened with a fierce winter storm; all they knew of it came through the flashes of lightning and the hollow keening of the wind that occasionally filled their ears as they passed by shuttered windows.

They found no one in their wanderings, not even St. Aubert. The Marquis had hidden himself as well as had his victims. That is, if their friends had even remained in the Priory. Their search of the stables had revealed that most of the horses were gone, spurred by the fleeing guests. Had Clarice, Withing, and Mariah been among them?

It was nearing twilight by the time they returned to their starting point in the Great Hall, spent and cold. Childermass stirred awake a fire in the hearth and they sat by its flames, too exhausted to speak. It had been a relief not to find their comrades dead, but their inability to find even the slightest trace of their whereabouts instilled a new kind of strain in them. It was as though they were neither alive nor dead: unreal.

"One of us should sleep for an hour or so while the other keeps watch," Childermass said.

Cyrus looked as though he could barely keep his eyes open, but he asked, "Which of us shall go first?"

"I have no desire at all for rest. You go first and I shall see that we're not murdered in our sleep. Perhaps by morning, the storm shall have passed and we can make our way to Houndswick."

"And abandon the Priory to the Marquis?"

"What else can we do?"

Cyrus made a pillow out of his coat and collapsed upon the straw beside the hearth.

"He wants us to feel that there is nothing we can do to prevent him," he said suddenly. "That's why he didn't kill us with the rest of them. He wants us to die thinking that there was nothing that we could do to help ourselves. But I don't believe that, do you, Childermass? Even if he did come back from the dead, even if he is some sort of hellish Lazarus, he is still able to be destroyed."

"I think you speak more truly than you know," said Childermass gravely.

"What do you mean?"

"I mean that his power is not even as great as Sir Robert's. Sir Robert's blood remained wet and red hours after its shedding. St. Aubert's blood is like our own – congealing and mortal."

"What does that prove? He can still withstand a knife to the throat."

Childermass's reply came in a whisper. "Whatever process changed Sir Robert's blood into something wholly unearthly, that process has not occurred in St. Aubert – at least not yet. I think that may mean that he is not so powerful. He thinks that he is immortal, in a sense perhaps he is, but he lacks Sir Robert's power.

"Sir Robert was obliged to sacrifice his son and attempt, at least, to do the same to his grandson in order to transform his flesh utterly. The same holds for St. Aubert. If he does not do something, he will go back to what he was before."

"But what must he do?" Cyrus asked.

"Perhaps his own flesh will tell him. We must hope that he does not learn before we have the chance to destroy him."

***

It was only when Cyrus's breathing had grown regular that Childermass dared to draw out his vial of enchanted blood. Even then, he kept stealing glances towards the sleeping young man as though he expected Cyrus to start awake at any moment with another question. He had supplied the Puritan, he supposed, with a clever and soothing enough tissue of suppositions, good enough to help him sleep – but perhaps Cyrus would think of some contradiction that had not occurred to him.

The truth was that Childermass was not at all as certain as he had pretended that St. Aubert could be opposed. The man had taken on the flesh of angels. The thought staggered the chimney sweeper. He could hardly see past it to the more practical questions that surrounded it, such as how long this change would last and whether there was anything that could be done to reverse it. He had compared St. Aubert to Sir Robert. The analogy was dreadful. Sir Robert had been a sorcerer who had somehow, by taking in the blood of victims, created a holy spring in himself that fountained its immortal essence through his flesh. St. Aubert had been recreated out of the eruption of this font. His very flesh was its product. How could the two cases even be compared?

Childermass was shaking. A flickering shadow thrown by the fire made him start as though struck; every sound that echoed through the Priory fell on his ears with the exquisite torture of a continuous drip. He looked at the vial of nightmares that he held and wondered what kind of compulsion it was that made him wish to drink it. Sir Robert had always believed there was something wicked about him; had said as much before his hanging. For a moment, Childermass wondered very much about himself. Then this moment of introspection winked out and the chimney sweeper returned to the business of leaving the world.

He had the vial to his lips when a voice spoke his name, causing him to start and nearly spill its contents. It was Nat, solemn and blood-stained as always.

"Christ," Childermass murmured. "Shouldn't you be in Heaven by now? The spell keeping you back has been broken."

"Please don't be angry with me." The boy was tearful. "I only wished to help you."

Childermass shook the vial under the ghost's nose with a cruel, twinkling-eyed humor. "Only trying some of the simon-pure stuff for myself. What do you think of it? Your blood helped produce it, after all."

"It was never meant to be born here," Nat said. "The new flesh. It's not supposed to belong to you, Sir Robert, or anyone."

"No, no, of course not," Childermass agreed pleasantly. "What do you think should be done about it?"

"I don't think that anything can be done about it," said the ghost.

Childermass found that he had begun shaking again; spasms that came and went every few seconds. He was sick with fear.

"When I take this, what does it do to me?" he asked. "It doesn't remake my flesh."

"You don't have enough for it to do that."

"Then what does it do?"

"It shows you…places."

"I saw the Priory, but it looked very different. It looked alive."

"It likes to frighten you."

"What does?"

Nat was trembling himself now. "I don't know. But I don't want you to die, Childermass. Not like Master Shipwash. Please listen to me."

He heard these last words as he drank down the blood; heard them as though they came from somewhere far above him. Then Nat and the rest of the world around him disappeared, leaving him alone with the blood.

The Great Hall was cleared of everything: bodies, tables, and even windows. It was a vast, doorless space of stone. Somewhere in the darkness of the rafters, there hung the beginnings of a rope, but Childermass could only see the end of it, where it looped into a noose of thorns.

Nat had said that it liked to frighten him – whatever *it* was. Perhaps it sensed how close he had come to that particular death.

"But I cannot be afraid," Childermass said, raising his voice to the darkness that pressed like a vast sheet above him. "I am too fascinated by you."

The walls shifted around him, grew like expanding flesh. He went to the noose of rope, took hold of it, and after one cold moment, put it around his throat. He felt its writhing knot tighten around his throat, felt it try to stop his breath.

"Show me what I wish," he managed hoarsely.

Like in a dream, he saw the floor disappear beneath his feet, heard the snap of bone as his neck broke, tasted the trickle of blood. He knew, as one sometimes knows in a dream, that it was not real. But he still felt a jolting terror as he saw and felt himself hang, dead and helpless, over an endless darkness.

Then below his twitching feet, a light shone and he saw the Great Hall – the real Great Hall – as it was before he had taken the blood. And through the walls, as though they were made of grey glass, he saw the Marquis St. Aubert. The man shone with a heavenly luminance, teeth and eyes. Something beneath the cloth that covered his left breast glowed like a star.

Childermass did not know how he knew it at that moment, but the sudden realization came to him that he was not having a nightmare. The enchanted blood had worked him up into a state of exhilarated terror, controlling his vision with images and sensations that corresponded to his own worst fears, but perhaps it was all for a dispassionate purpose. Perhaps he had mistaken its motives for intelligent malice, when all the while it was instead as practical-minded as a parasite, inducing a certain state in him so that his heart would race and his frenzied blood could mingle with it, giving it access to his flesh. Perhaps it wanted him as much as he wanted it. He wondered that now, as it tortured him, changed his vision, and let him see through walls. Perhaps it did not recognize what it did to him as torture, any more than would a disease have thought of its work as an invasion. It only meant to tear the scales from his eyes in every way at its disposal. There was a cold comfort in this avenue of speculation, but Childermass could not be certain whether it was the truth or a solacing lie.

Childermass gazed long at the shining light at St. Aubert's heart, wondering what it meant. The blood could let him see more clearly, but it could not or would not tell him the meaning of what he saw. He tried to concentrate upon it, tried to think what it was that he saw now that he could not see without the blood; but the world had begun to sway and rock, making it difficult for him to focus upon it. The rope upon which he hung suddenly broke loose and he fell to the floor of the Great Hall.

Childermass started awake, dizzy with pain and clammy with sweat, to find Cyrus shaking him awake. He stared at Cyrus and the young man recoiled from his gaze.

"What happened to you?" Cyrus asked. "You looked as though you were awake and having the worst sort of nightmare."

Childermass looked at him for a long while, without replying. His eye held an enchanted light that struck Cyrus as repellently fascinating; the glamour of a pale liquid held to light, something to prove either mithridate or poison. It was too bright, too intense for Cyrus's own gaze to match. He quickly looked away, preferring to show unease rather than feel himself swallowed by that depthless eye.

"I was keeping watch on St. Aubert," Childermass at last said in a low voice. "I think I know how he can be…prevented."

The chimney sweeper stopped in the middle of his speech. The blood was trying to take hold of him again, trying to stimulate his nerves so that his heart would beat again for it, letting it flow through his own, ordinary blood and change the way his flesh worked. Now it was turning Cyrus's face into a thing of nightmare, like the mutilated bodies on the floor beside them. He gazed wonderingly at the horror, knowing it to be unreal and feeling himself tremble before it nonetheless.

"What has given you an idea?"

Childermass watched as a maggot squirmed under the skin of Cyrus's cheek.

"Call it inspiration," he managed with a sickly sort of smile.

***

"His flesh remakes itself?" Childermass asked rhetorically through clenched teeth, his face gleaming with sweat as he brought a torch down and handed it to Cyrus before taking one of his own. "Then try burning a hole through it before cutting it up. Fire worked well enough with Sir Robert. We can only hope the same is true for what was born out of his blood. Oh, and Cyrus," he added, "Try for the heart. I think it may be the frailest part of him."

"Why?"

"If only I knew."

Childermass's eye had lost all method and calculation – it looked naked, flayed, as though something had hauled down every veil and wall, unclothing the mass of squirming, raw nerves beneath. He occasionally looked at Cyrus with an incomprehensible expression of horrified wonder and Cyrus, who could not know of the ordeal that the chimney sweeper was enduring, returned these looks with an understandable amount of bewilderment. How was it, then, that Cyrus could look into the chilling grey of that eye and feel convinced that the brain behind it had solved how to save them? It was Childermass's voice – that low, changeless voice – that made him trust what he did not understand. Above the lifting of the tapestries in the winter wind and the settling of the Priory, its sweet music came with a promise of escape and Cyrus believed in it. His fingers tightened around the handle of the torch as he heard Childermass say, licking his lips, of how he thought St. Aubert might be stopped – and, for the first time, he did not feel like a farmer's son hunted down by an assassin but rather like a knight set to vanquish his foe.

"We can leave the Priory tonight, but only if we are very careful about it," said Childermass slowly. "He will take us out in spite of our struggles, but only if we are stupid enough to let him catch us together. Divided, he cannot hope to ensnare us all, for there are too many of us."

"What are you saying?"

"I will go out to the chapel and bring some of the horses with me. You will find the others, if others may be found, and bring them to me. I don't know if the storm has ended, but perhaps we can ride as far as a nearby farmhouse and find shelter there."

"Wonderful. And draw him out of the Priory so that he can murder more innocents."

"What else, then?" Childermass asked.

"We need to wall him up," Cyrus said. "Here, in the Priory, in some room that we catch him in. It's the only way."

"He is very strong."

"And yet the one thing he doesn't seem able to do yet is walk through walls."

***

They began by locking and bolting all the doors and shuttering every window on the lowest floor. Then Childermass gave Cyrus a silver whistle and told him that when he found the Marquis, he was to blow on it as loudly as he could.

"I will do the same if I find him. It's clumsy, but the only way. We cannot search for him together because our plan requires that we corner him. I will search the Priory starting from the top floor and you the bottom. If we meet in the middle, we will decide that our quarry can walk through walls and devise a new stratagem accordingly."

In the dim light, Childermass's smile had almost the plaintive sweetness of Withing's. It made the dark cynicism of his words seem both touching and grotesque. They had locked themselves away in this world of stone and ice with a man bent on destroying them both and it felt as though they were the only two who could prevent his evil from touching the rest of the world. Cyrus had always known that the time would come when he would have to face his father's murderer, but he had never dreamt that it would be like this. In a sense, the reality was more terrible, for St. Aubert had been made as deathless as a nightmare; but Cyrus was not alone to endure it. That was another difference.

For Childermass, it was the logical outcome of all that had happened in the last year, the inevitable offspring of the monstrous union that he had envisaged betwixt Sir Robert's sorceries and St. Aubert's killing presence. It was as unpleasantly reasonable as the knowledge that if you turned a screw, the agony would be doubled rather than eased. But the utterness of the Priory's collapse shocked him. He had come to Laughlin Priory as a boy; it had helped him escape the death of a Houndswick chimney sweep, had let him see inside itself, had changed his world from the open moors to its own closed, vast interior. Now it was bleeding at his feet, begging him, its slave, for succor. He had heard it groan – or hadn't he? Had that vision only been a product of the blood's enchantment? And if so, what was the source of that enchantment? Childermass would have given his life to know yet he also dreaded the knowledge.

They had stood there for a long while, silent. Neither felt a great desire to separate, to begin their explorations apart.

"We should start, I suppose," Cyrus said finally. "Before he escapes us."

"Oh, Cyrus, what I think you mean to say," said Childermass. "Is that we should start before we return to our senses and realize how foolish this plan is in the first place."

***

From where he held dominion, the Marquis St. Aubert could see the two as they plotted against him; knew the fate that they wished upon him, the life-in-death in a sealed chamber. He might, perhaps, have even felt some fear that their designs might be accomplished, were he not too overcome by the thought of what had already happened to him, and of what was happening still. It was something wonderful, miraculous – but there was something terrifying about it as well. A man cannot help but love what gives him life, but he cannot help but ask himself what its motives are as well. It was this – this, and the peculiar feeling that the blood had left him with – that now consumed his thoughts. The Marquis heard Childermass begin his ascent into the Priory's towers and wished that the chimney sweeper had known more of what Sir Robert had accomplished with his alchemical experiments. There had to be more to his resurrection than the spilled blood of young men – St. Aubert was certain of it.

An hour passed as he stood there, alone with his thoughts, and listened to the steps of Childermass as the young man began his revolving descent down staircase after staircase, drawing ever closer to the Marquis's own floor. Something in Childermass's eye had told St. Aubert that the chimney sweeper was more expert in his knowledge of Sir Robert's blood than he had before admitted. But he could not bear the thought of begging Childermass for the knowledge. Better to wander the world, immortal and ignorant, than give the chimney sweeper the pleasure of knowing that he had once again had St. Aubert at his mercy.

He held out his hand, looked at the reflected gleam of the silver knives at his fingers, and waited. His flesh was different, reborn and new; every hair and particle of his being was that of a completely new creature that, though identical in appearance to his old flesh, was still not the same. The soul within, though – that had not altered in the slightest, nor had all its old desires. Still within him, like a thread of color through clear stone, as constant as it had been on the day when he had held his lips to his lady's pricked finger, that longing remained. It made him wait, minute after minute, as motionless as a hawk, while he waited for Childermass to come for him.

At last, he heard the chimney sweeper arrive at the second floor and, as St. Aubert had guessed, Childermass paused for a moment before the door of Sir Robert's chamber. It was locked. Childermass must have known that there was no chance that the Marquis could be inside. And yet presently, there came the soft grinding sound of a key turning in the lock. It had been just as St. Aubert had hoped. The chimney sweeper could not resist a look.

With an unhurried craft, St. Aubert roused himself at last from his place of waiting and went to meet his quarry. He saw Childermass standing in the doorway, torch in hand, as though he were listening for something. The Marquis stood there for a space, knowing that he could put an end to the stillness of the moment, but choosing not to do so at once. There was a kind of power in delaying as well as acting.

Finally, deliberately, the Marquis took an audible step closer. Slowly, Childermass turned about. His living eye was wide and bright; as he turned, his torch erupted into a brighter flame, fed by the draft of sudden motion. Its brilliance made his marble eye look eerily alive as well. He was carrying a dagger and a cross, both clenched in his right hand.

"Which do you intend to use on me, Monsieur?" the Marquis enquired. "The fire, the blade, or the holy cross?"

He saw Childermass's throat move with a convulsive swallow.

"I have made your position rather difficult, have I not?" asked St. Aubert. "You wish to back me into a chamber and whistle for your young friend. But I have you now as you wanted me."

"No," said Childermass, retreating a step, still holding the torch before him. He had tucked the dagger and cross under his arm and was fumbling for the whistle.

Before he had it to his lips, St. Aubert rushed for him. Shakily, Childermass forsook the whistle and brought the torch and dagger up again. By this time, he had backed into Sir Robert's sacrificial chamber. The table on which Withing had been bound now stood behind him.

"Are we to stand here forever, Monsieur?" St. Aubert's gaze went from the torch to Childermass's eye, an enquiring smile on his lips.

"Cyrus will come soon and we will seal you up together."

"You wish to trap me at the site of my resurrection? Even for you, chimney sweeper, there must be something surpassingly loathsome in the thought. Or can even that not affect you? Is it really your wish to dam me up here? Even before I have learned what has become of me? I am still so much in the dark – I long to know more of the miracle that was done upon me. But locked away for eternity, what else will I do but suffer and wonder?"

St. Aubert knew that there was nothing Childermass could do against him – knew better than even Childermass how hopeless his circumstances were. But he wanted to see, before it all ended, just how thoroughly depraved the chimney sweeper was. It was fascinating, to put a kind of false power into the young man's hand, and see how it turned his head.

And then a peculiar thing happened. A look of sympathy, however unwilling, entered Childermass's eye and the torch faltered for a moment in his hand. But as his eye softened, a draft shook the flame of his torch, so that its shadow quivered across his face and scattered the darkness at his back. It contorted his expression, caused his eye to appear as though it burned with a livid fire, and turned his face into something gloating and inhuman, when it was actually at its most pitiful. St. Aubert's heart turned to ice at the sight.

"What are you?" the Marquis murmured. Childermass raised the torch against him as he approached, but the Frenchman took its blazing head in his hands. The revolting scent of burning flesh filled the air, but St. Aubert did not cease until he had wrenched the thing out of Childermass's own fingers and thrown it behind him, to the far side of the chamber.

Childermass felt for the whistle, fingers slick with sweat. His eye was fastened on St. Aubert's hands. They were smoking, a mess of ash and burned flesh, but already a wet growth was appearing at the ends of those stumps; the vague semblance of expanding muscle and skin. Shakily, he put the whistle to his lips and blew.

Two seconds and St. Aubert was upon him. He managed that many seconds' worth of a whistle before the breath was knocked out of him. Then he felt those wet, rudimentary fingers around his throat; felt himself lifted clear of the floor. Choking, he struck out with a vicious accuracy at the man's eyes, so that St. Aubert lost hold of him for a moment. Childermass then backed away, dagger in hand. His gaze was fixed on the Marquis' heart. If he could only put the knife through it, know what it was that the blood had shown him shining there –

"I doubt Cyrus heard so little a sound." St. Aubert was coming for him again, hands whole again. He lifted his silver knives from the floor, put them over his left hand again, and beckoned to Childermass with a charming smile. "Do it again, Monsieur – I am certain that you can do better."

Childermass made a movement to bring the whistle to his mouth and when St. Aubert again came to prevent him, the chimney sweeper's other hand lunged up to hook the man's heart out. But the Marquis had seen where Childermass's gaze had lingered. He caught the hand and twisted the knife out of it.

"Good lad," he said. "You've tried the fire and the dagger. Now let's see you with the cross."

He stood back, letting Childermass retrieve the crucifix that had fallen to the floor. Childermass knelt and picked it up; before he could do anymore, St. Aubert took the other end of it, pulling him to his feet, forcing him against the wall.

"I am not Sir Robert," St. Aubert said. "I have performed no black rituals, sacrificed no innocents. You would not use a cross against a mere assassin, would you, young man?"

The Marquis took the chain that the whistle hung upon, snapping it cleanly and throwing it aside. Childermass watched; for the first time, he felt unable to breathe, to think. He dreaded the man's reluctance to kill him. It could only mean the worst.

"You know me well enough already to anticipate what I shall do with you now, Monsieur."

Childermass's tongue was thick, inarticulate with horror. Somehow, he managed to speak. "You haven't the time. Cyrus will find you too soon."

"But not in here, not in these locked chambers, where no sound can escape. We are safe from the world for as long as I choose. Why, you seem suddenly very affected, my dear Childermass. Can it be that you are finally afraid of me?"

Before Childermass could reply, the Marquis gave him a swift, brutal blow to the chin. All the terror drained out of the young man's face; he fell gracelessly into St. Aubert's arms. He would be senseless for at least an hour. The Marquis had dealt with enough victims to know that it was best this way, at least while he made arrangements for whatever ordeal he had planned for him. Too many tried either escape or clumsy attempts at suicide. They never succeeded, but they still spoiled the mood of helplessness that St. Aubert wished to sustain. Now Childermass was safe from both of these temptations, preserved for whatever suffering St. Aubert had set his heart upon.

Chapter Forty-Four: In which Childermass and the Marquis understand one another perfectly.

Childermass awoke to find himself lying on his back, head pillowed by cold stone. Though his senses were still confused, he knew by the lingering scent of lye where he was. It was the third and last chamber that he, Dagworth, and Feversham had scrubbed clean – the one filled with human bones and hanging animal skins. Now it was bare and shining. The torch that he had brought had been rescued before sputtering out and burned from a niche in the wall above him.

Childermass tried to move, but the cords that bound him were too tight to admit even a slight change of position. They were coiled and knotted completely about him; had they been drawn any tighter, they would have bitten into his flesh. Other ropes were attached to those that constrained him, at his feet, his waist, his shoulders; they hung from the hooks in the ceiling like the loose threads of a web, anchoring him to the center of the chamber. Childermass gazed at these wonderingly, a tear threading its way across his cheek; otherwise his eye remained bright and removed. He looked like a seer, gaze fixed on the closed-off heavens above, trying to read his fortune in the constellation of chains that enclosed him.

An open chest made of gilded silver stood in a corner of the room. Its contents shone in the torchlight, flashes of glass and steel. Childermass turned his eye to these, transfixed by the half-seen shapes that he saw within. They could not all possibly be intended for him – all those hooks, lancets, knives, pokers, nails. There was only so much that he could suffer before death intervened. He had that thought, at least, to sustain him.

A painting done in oil ornamented the inside of the chest's lid – a woman's face, faded but still poignantly lovely in the sweet mould of the lips and the tender sympathy of the gaze. What look had that face worn at its last moment of suffering? Had blood fallen from those lips, and tears from those eyes? Childermass gazed at the poor victim, a victim now himself, and wondered how he would seem at the hour of his death; at what transfiguration would take place in him this night. How many specters in legend were the spirits of the tortured rather than of the torturer – the tongueless woman, the walled-up nun, the forsaken lover? What was there about a victim of some hideous crime that was so particularly horrifying? Was it that they still existed, but only as a shadow of what they once were – only to suffer and to inflict suffering? He did not know, but he imagined himself as one of this pitiful host and his lips twitched at the thought.

A shadow darkened the doorway of the chamber and St. Aubert entered. He shut the door carefully behind him and then went to Childermass, kneeling beside him, a look of peculiar expectancy in his gaze.

"Forgive my absence, Monsieur," he said. "But I was obliged to know where your young friend was, so I could know how best to proceed with you."

"Have you murdered him?"

"No," St. Aubert smiled. "But he is far down in the library, perhaps looking for the rest of your friends. He will be a long while coming. I fear that you will be dead when next you are seen by anyone after myself."

"Then there is a limit to how long you can have me suffer," Childermass said.

"Oh, you shall suffer as long as I wish. Touching that, I pray you set your mind at rest."

He rose then, gazing down at the chimney sweeper with a speculative eye. Perhaps he wished to remember the way that Childermass appeared now, helpless and whole, so that after his work had been accomplished, he could recall it and compare it to the finished product. Childermass felt his own nerves tighten and brace beneath that gaze. His hour had come at last. He prayed that he would not abandon all reason and spend his last moments either mad or begging this man for mercy. It was well that he could not see himself at that moment, for then he would have seen the silent, imploring look that he fixed upon his torturer. St. Aubert, however, did see it and a smile of unaffected sympathy played on his lips. It was peculiar, how all the earlier enmity that had animated the Marquis had now utterly left him. His old, courteous nature had returned; but Childermass knew that there was no genuine pity in that gallantry. There never could be, in such a heart as his. No surfeit of Sir Robert's enchanted blood could have remade that soul. Only its own will and that was as rigid and inflexible as Hell itself.

"In most cases, I have had to make use of these." St. Aubert held up a brutal gag in his hand, made of leather and iron. "But in your case, I hardly think it necessary."

Every word fell like a blow on Childermass's heart. His brain was running madly ahead of itself, devising torture after torture, each worse than the one before. Ignorance was already tormenting him with its cunning, shadowed suggestions.

"Why?" he asked.

"Do you know how I determine what I will do with a man or a woman, Monsieur?" St. Aubert replied. "You know so much of me – I, so little of you. Tell me if you know enough to guess this."

"Blood," Childermass said. "It is your…obsession."

"Very good. But do you imagine that I will uncover it in the same way every time?"

"No."

"And why not?"

"I cannot tell," Childermass murmured, beside himself with anguish and anticipation.

St. Aubert reached up and took hold of the chains knotted to the ceiling hooks, pulling them taut. Childermass felt himself lifted clear of the ground, heard the groan of chain as it raised him to the level of the Marquis's shoulder.

"Are you comfortable? I would not wish any minor discomfort, Monsieur, to distract from what it is that shall be done to you." He smiled at Childermass and put a hand upon one of the hanging cords that suspended him horizontally, studying the spectacle of him. "With Cyrus's father, I fear I was crude – I shall not hack off your limbs or rip out your tongue. Nor shall I tear your heart out as I did the Reverend Abelin. You see, it all depends upon the quality of the material. And for you – for you I have something very particular in mind."

He withdrew a hollow tube of glass, shaped in an arc. One end of it was attached to a black ribbon, the other to a hollow needle.

"I had a friend, a very learned doctor in Paris, devise several of these for me. Methinks that this particular one shall fit you quite prettily."

Childermass looked at it but his mind remained closed, an utter blank.

"You still do not comprehend your fate? This tube of glass will go into the vein below your heart and draw your blood out with every beat of that organ. But I abhor a waste of good blood. Its end I shall place here between your lips. What goes out shall return once more to you."

The Marquis saw Childermass's gaze begin to darken in a swoon, but he merely took him by the feet with a practiced hand and held his victim at an angle so that the blood rushed to his head and he remained fully conscious. Then, once he was assured of Childermass's recovery, he began to unfasten the young man's shirt until his breast was uncovered.

"Now, you must not feel ashamed, Monsieur," St. Aubert was saying. "Of anything that you are compelled to do. I know many to whom the greatest torment of all is feeling that they have lost all dignity at the moment of their death. But please, weep and struggle as much as you wish. I shall hardly think less of you. This," he pressed a helpless vein that pulsed at Childermass's throat. "Is all my concern. Do you understand?"

The Marquis then held up the glass device and unraveled the black ribbon before bringing one end of it to the chimney sweeper's lips.

"And now," he said. "Have you anything to say before we begin?"

Childermass looked as though a single touch would have melted him to tears. And, in spite of his desire to open the young man's vein, St. Aubert held back, not wishing to miss a single plea or entreaty.

Never had two antagonists been so horribly aware of the role that each inhabited, so peculiarly conscious of what was expected of himself, of the other. Childermass's lips parted and he spat hotly into his torturer's face; St. Aubert raised his hand to strike him – then caught himself with a peculiar suddenness. He wiped at his cheek and looked down at the young man, his gloved hand now wet with his spittle. There was no condemnation in his gaze; it seemed to say, "You could not help yourself, could you?"

Then he gripped Childermass's face with one hand while with the other he drove the needle at the end of the glass device into the vein at his victim's breast. Blood, red and living, flew up the arch of the glass, some of it escaping to stain the victim's breast and throat. This sight threw St. Aubert into a paroxysm of delight; his eyes burned and his breath came faster as he worked to force the glass between Childermass's lips. His victim resisted but, bound and suspended in chains, what could he do to prevent the Marquis from having his will? Once the black ribbon was tied about his head and the hollow flute of glass forced down his throat, he knew that it was over. He was a lost cause that had only its own demise left to hope for.

St. Aubert drew back a few paces, contemplating what he had created, taking it in with his eyes. Every detail fascinated him; he sucked on the tips of his fingers, eyes glistening.

Childermass was already choking on the red, irrepressible fountain. It was appalling how helplessly mechanical his body had become; he could no more prevent the tears of anguish that chilled his cheek than could he check the flood that breached his throat. A series of shudders began to convulse him as he rapidly went into shock, swallowing in forced gasps all that he lost.

The Marquis gathered up his tools and went to the door, but not before turning for one last look at his handiwork. Childermass, in the midst of his suffering, saw the look; even in extremis, he comprehended its meaning. His death was not to be one of ignominy; it was to be a performance of pathetic energy, recalled and commiserated by its only author and audience.

The world was growing darker and darker; his mouth and throat, sinks of blood. He did not see when the Marquis lifted his hand like a stage director hastening the fall of a tardy curtain and turned his back at last upon the dying sufferer.

Chapter Forty-Five: In which Cyrus ingeniously starts one flood and stops another.

Cyrus had only just reached the second floor when he heard the low, lucid call of Childermass's whistle somewhere above him. He hastened up the stairs, taking them two at a time, and again it sounded, still several levels above.

"Childermass!" he called. "Where are you?"

His only reply was another drawn note, like that of a trapped bird in a chimney. Wiping tears of exertion from his face, Cyrus continued his climb.

He had ascended to the sixth floor when he heard it a fourth time. There was no doubt now that he was on a level with the source of the call. He called Childermass's name a second time; his only answer was silence.

The sixth level was the most abandoned of all the floors that Cyrus had found above the ground floor so far. The windows were glassless, uncovered with tapestries. Snow and leaves were scattered across the stone floor. A sleeping pigeon started awake as Cyrus paused to fix his torch into a niche in the wall. Its echoing cry reverberated against the walls as it fled for the darkness at the end of the passage ahead of him. And then, out of that darkness, St. Aubert came forth. The chimney sweeper's whistle hung from his fingers.

"What have you done to him?" Cyrus asked.

"I left him in the care of Sir Robert's locked chambers," the Marquis replied.

"Dead?"

"He was alive, Monsieur, when last I left him. Whether he still is or not, I cannot say, though I hope so. It would be a pity, after all that I have done to him, for him to enjoy it all in so short a time."

So Childermass was dying a tortured death below them – just as Cyrus's father had died, shorn of limbs and tongue, and just as many more souls would suffer before at last being put out by this man.

"You, I think, will not waste time in questioning me, as poor Childermass would have, had I let him. Our chase has lasted too long for that."

"You murdered my father," said Cyrus. "There is nothing left to say."

"Yes, Monsieur," St. Aubert replied. "I murdered him. As I shall you."

"If your strength is greater than mine. I shall fight you first."

"If you insist," the Frenchman replied, politely indifferent.

"But let me go to Childermass first."

"You have a good will, Monsieur, but he is beyond you altogether by now, I should think. I left him quite a banquet to exhaust and I expect that its enjoyment has already finished him."

Cyrus, white-lipped, made a move for the staircase, but St. Aubert caught him by the coat, staggering him against the wall. There was a brutal urgency in the man's fingers and when he spoke, all the softness had left his voice.

"Poor creature, do you think that I will kindly wait for you to fly and save a corpse when I have put myself to so much trouble to find and make a corpse out of you?"

Cyrus wrenched himself free of the Marquis's grasp and backed several steps away, readying the cross in his right hand. St. Aubert laughed then, and paused for a moment to study his intended victim. In that windswept corridor, the moonlight caught his hair, making silver out of gold. There was that same touch of sympathy in his eye, that look so at odds with his disease, that made an innocence out of his deformity. Cyrus wondered whether the man before him actually realized the full horror of what he did or whether he was so caught up in the vision of blood before him that he did not perceive himself so much its maker as its audience. It was little wonder that Childermass's own ravenous eye had comprehended the man so well; just as it was little wonder that the chimney sweeper had been so amazed by his own peril that he had failed to save himself from it. But Childermass for all his peculiarities was no monster; he had tried to save them all and had only succeeded in losing himself. If Cyrus did not keep his head, he would soon follow after.

"You have only your cross," St. Aubert remarked. "Your friend, at least, was wise enough to arm himself with a blade."

"What good would it do?" asked Cyrus.

The Marquis unsheathed a knife, long and thin as a physician's scalpel, and threw it to the young man. Cyrus fumblingly caught it.

"There, now. I have made you more equal to me than was your father when we met."

"No," Cyrus shook his head, letting the knife fall. "You know already what little effect it has upon you." He then stood the cross against the wall at his back. "I am as unarmed now as I was before."

The gaze of the torturer flickered momentarily. Cyrus knew that this was not how he had anticipated their encounter to resolve itself. He was now adjusting to a new vision, a new comprehension of what he must undertake.

"You are right," the Marquis said at last. "You will die because it is in the nature of your flesh – as I will live for it is now the nature of my flesh. We must all live and die according to our natures.

"Methought that a vision of heaven came to me as I worked upon your friend. I thought of my lady and of how she looked when she bled for me and what a pity it was that she slipped through my fingers so soon. What would it have been, Cyrus, if I had known this proof against decay – if that flesh and blood that I contorted could have refreshed itself, remolded itself, forever? She, incorruptible, eternally in my eye."

"To eternally hate you?"

"Hate? Oh no, Cyrus, not she. She loved her unwilling murderer to the last, he whose very approach brought her to tears. I know there must be a God in the heavens, for who else could have formed such an angel as she? It was these careless hands that let her soul escape their lovely prison, but it was not my will."

The storm without the Priory had stilled to a whisper of its former self. The sky had lightened from black to a wan grey; the hour preceding dawn. The leaves in the hallway stirred, draft-driven; the north wind's howl had lowered to a breath, muted, inconsolable. Cyrus's body ached with weariness; the man before him looked as though he could never know such a complaint even had he wished it. He was smiling again upon Cyrus; only his eyes held an aftertaste of their former melancholy. Nothing, not even the memory of her, could prevent him from taking pleasure in what he was about to see and do.

He crossed the space between them and took Cyrus by the shoulders, standing him against the wall by the window. There was a thinness about his lips now, a kind of austerity to his resolve, as he clamped a manacle to Cyrus's left wrist, raised it to the wall, and hammered it into the stone. With Childermass, there had been something joyously improvisational in the spirit of the act; he had drawn his inspiration from both his victim's lurid expectations and his own imagination. With this, however, he was undertaking a thing that he had devised and dwelt upon for weeks. It little mattered that Cyrus made no effort to prevent him. He was not seeing the youth as he really was but rather as his mind's eye had painted him before.

Clouds of powdered stone fell as the Marquis finished setting the clamp into place. A dark line of blood ran down Cyrus's arm where the teeth inside the manacle had bitten into his wrist.

"There is something in my pocket," Cyrus said suddenly.

St. Aubert watched as the young man fumblingly felt in his coat and then drew out a thing of glass that shone in spite of the clots of blood that covered it. Smilingly, the Marquis looked at the crystalline dove and said, "Please, Monsieur, I insist that you keep it. It was a gift."

Pale, wondering if his hand shook as much as his nerves, Cyrus began to return it to his pocket. In the split second before his fingers emerged again, he knew by the look in St. Aubert's eyes that the man realized what he was about – realized it even before Cyrus's hand emerged with his own dagger that he had kept hidden all the while. Cyrus could not tell what it was that caused the Marquis to hesitate momentarily – perhaps he was so sure of his resurrection that he could not contemplate the knife with the same fear that he would have before. By the time he chose to act, Cyrus had already made a wild strike at his heart, driving the dagger hilt-deep into his breast, where Childermass had told him to go.

A trickle of something white and liquid fell from a corner of the torturer's lips. Slowly, he looked down at his transfixed heart.

"What good was this?" he asked. "Do I not still live?"

He took hold of the dagger and pulled it free of his flesh. It was slick with the same thick, sluggish glue that had trickled from his lips. With the blade loose, the fluid began to flow more copiously. Where it touched St. Aubert, his flesh began to melt and run. He tried to wipe at it with a cloth, to prevent its spread, but there was nothing that he could do. The skin of his breast was the first to go. It fell back wetly, uncovering his breast and a torn sac, swollen and sagging, that throbbed where his heart should have been. If that was the source of the resurrecting fluid that the blood had created in him to keep him whole, it was as destructive to him now as it had once been restorative. It was eating him from the inside, collapsing his flesh and bone together.

Cyrus could barely look at him. The resplendent gold of his hair was dripping with it; half his face was lost, his smooth cheek eaten away, revealing the raw line of his jaw, gummed with blood. His breast was open, the white ribs curved and spread like the legs of an enormous centipede. The Frenchman looked down at himself, at his melting parts, and then met Cyrus with a look of bewilderment. He had never understood what change had occurred in him to make him alive and keep him whole; he understood still less now his own destruction. But one thought still possessed him. He dipped into the font of his opened heart and came at Cyrus, finger dripping, his other hand tightening about the youth's throat. Desperate, Cyrus kicked out at him with all the force that dread could conjure.

Then the sac of fluid at St. Aubert's heart broke open and a spray of it flew through his lungs, up his throat, and over his chin. His head fell back; he groaned as it covered him, as it took away his lips, his nose, his eyes, and the perfect flesh of his face. With a soft sound, half a sob, half a sigh, he fell at Cyrus's feet, a wash of floating bone and melting flesh.

Cyrus was struggling with the manacle that held his left arm captive, all the while keeping as far against the wall as he could to avoid the dissolving dew that had settled on the stones beneath him. Gritting his teeth, he pulled against the manacle, disregarding the pain of it, until he had wrenched it free of the wall. The keys to Sir Robert's chambers had fallen beneath the Marquis' mantle; Cyrus caught them up, along with his torch. The smell of that human lake was still in his nose as he fled down the hallway to the stairs.

***

There was no sound that came from the second floor, but if there had been Cyrus would not have heard it above his own heartbeat and racing steps. He unlocked the door to Sir Robert's chambers and went ahead, calling out and receiving no reply. If he had not taken his torch, he would not have found his way for it was as dark as a closet in those candleless depths. The walls shone sweatily, like the moist interior of a well or sewer. The place was utterly silent.

He found Childermass in the last room, still suspended in chains, hanging motionless in the center of that lightless space. There was broken glass on the stones beneath him. In his agony at drinking down his own substance, he had managed to bite through the hollow flute, the current washing over his breast and chin. He must have striven long in the darkness, for there was blood running down his legs from where the chains held him.

There was no anguish upon his face now; he was still, his living eye lightless and open. The tears that ran across his face had dried, mingling with the blood that stained his mouth and cheek. Cyrus thought of how Childermass had been before and felt a chill when he saw the pale, unbreathing peace of him now. Sick at heart, he touched his hand, offering up a silent prayer for the chimney sweeper's soul.

And then just as he began to plead for Childermass's eternal peace, he heard a hoarse attempt at a cough. At first he was too bewildered to know what to think; but when he saw the light of life once again flicker in the chimney sweeper's eye, tears of relief choked his throat. With trembling fingers, he unhooked the hanging chains and lowered Childermass to the floor, unknotting the ropes that bound him. Childermass was coughing up gouts of the blood that he had swallowed, was shaking and cold as ice, but he was alive. He was alive.

Had Cyrus's mind not been so filled with the wonders and horrors of the past night, he might have wondered at the chimney sweeper's miraculous recovery. He might have wondered at what immortalizing power pulsed in those pallid veins, causing Death itself to turn the sufferer away and let him draw breath in spite of all that had been done to him. But Cyrus did not know of Childermass's secret store of Sir Robert's blood; he did not know what it was that the Childermass had imbibed that had repulsed even Death's appetite and kept him alive to draw breath for another day.

Instead, it felt as though a light had dawned somewhere within Cyrus's brain. He embraced Childermass with a sudden, almost wild affection that took him by surprise as much as it did its object. But Childermass did not stiffen or repulse the gesture. They had been many things to each other since the duration of their acquaintance; at times even enemies. Their conflict had never been addressed by either of them directly; it seemed fitting then that when their friendship began, it was a thing known and acknowledged, not through mere words but within the silent communion of their souls.

"The Marquis St. Aubert is finished now," Cyrus told him. "He can do no harm to the Priory or anyone else in this world any longer."

"You destroyed him, Cyrus," Childermass said simply.

"We destroyed him. With the help of Heaven and whatever marvelous intuition it is that you possess."

Childermass could not help but smile at the thought of whither that intuition came. But he had lost much blood and when he tried to stand, the world grew dim and his balance faltered.

"Hold on a moment," Cyrus said. "I think I know what can be done about that."

He left the chamber and returned a minute later. In his hand, he held Childermass's broom.

"God save you, Master Plainstaff," said the chimney sweeper, wiping at the blood on his lips with the back of his hand. "I think you may have found a useful purpose for that thing at last."

Chapter Forty-Six: In which a castle is, most disappointingly, not burned down.

Shipwash's warning had not been enough to move most of the Priory's revelers, but those who had been more closely acquainted with the recent horrors of the past year took heed of what he said. It had taken them several hours to ride from Laughlin to Houndswick as the winter storm began; they had spent the whole of the twenty-sixth of December within one of Montrose's parlors, praying for the ceaseless storm to abate; and now with the dawn of a new day approaching and the blizzard's rage at last diminished, they were still discussing what was to be done about the Priory problem. The upshot of it all was that neither Montrose nor Squire Toby, having escaped the bloody carnage of a few hours ago, were particularly eager to return to Laughlin and encounter St. Aubert a second time. Mariah, the one person in that company of escaped grocers and nobles who was more indignant than afraid of this newest outrage, had mentioned several times that the best thing to be done would be to visit the Lord Mayor and have him organize a party of militia to storm the Priory and take this newest murderer prisoner, but both Montrose and the Squire had both objected to this course of action.

"My dear lady," said Montrose. "What do you propose that our militia do against him? Short of skewering the man like some insect to a hopefully unmovable object, there is really no way to deal with such a creature."

"And so you are content to leave Cyrus and Childermass to face him alone."

"I hardly think that 'content' would be the word. Call it a melancholy resignation."

Mariah looked hopelessly towards Feversham and Dagworth, both of whom were leaning against the wall, looking uncomfortably out of place in that vast apartment. The Master of the Hounds gave a shrug of his broad shoulders and said, "Well, Miss, seeing as how Master Plainstaff was a stranger and Master Childermass was, well, himself, then I suppose it is up to you and young Lord Withing to decide what's best done for them."

Feversham, roused out of his shocked reverie by Dagworth's voice, murmured, "Aye, Childermass can look to himself and as for the other boy, he's more than likely been a corpse for hours already."

"But now that I think on it," Dagworth continued to the ostler in a half-whisper. "If we find Childermass's body soon enough, I'll have the chance to bury him out back with the rest of the dead curs as I always promised him I would."

"And have his spirit haunt us for the rest of this mortal life?" Feversham muttered guardedly. But Mariah leapt on this chance and said, "Then you will both go with me to the Priory?"

Dagworth gave another shrug and a nod. "If we can bring a larger company with us, of course, my lady."

"Then I will go and speak to the Lord Mayor myself. If none of you noble gentlemen will accompany me." She had grown weary of Montrose, Squire Toby, and their indifferent cowardice and furthermore felt that if she saw Mrs. Leaske circle the room one more time with a silver platter of chocolate cordials, she would shriek. Already she had wasted an entire day attempting to rally the two stubborn men to her cause. She glanced at Shipwash and Crawley whom along with ten other grocers, had managed to escape as well. "Will you come with me or no?"

"Lady," said Crawley. "You talk of rescuing your Priory and friends, but I see no other course except to simply burn the place to the ground. If you decide on this, we are with you."

The other grocers, blood-spattered and exhausted, nodded their agreement with this sentiment. Even the gentle-hearted Shipwash bowed his head in hopeless assent.

"Very well," said Mariah, her throat tight. She looked to Withing who was sitting forlornly beside Squire Toby. "What do you think, cousin?"

And he looked up at her and said, "Very well. But only after we have made certain that Cyrus and Childermass are no more."

His lashes were dark with tears, but his voice was steady with a despair, deep and transcendent. He had already lost his father and his grandfather. It was obvious from the grey look of his lips that he fully expected to receive the death of his two friends within the next hour.

"Then let us not delay any longer," said Mariah. "Let us put an end to this once and for all."

***

They could see the Priory as they came upon it half a mile away, towers and battlements stark and black against the sky, rising above the trees that skirted the moors, shadowing the forest. It looked lonelier than the mountains, for they had each other for company; save for the watch tower that stood a little distance from it, the Priory stood like a crown upon the bare stone head of a hill, its battlements higher than the tallest mountain. Soon the flames that would rise from it would make it stand brighter and taller still. And when the fire died, when the smoke cleared and mingled with the woodland mists, when every stone was scorched and every chamber looked like the inside of a cold abandoned furnace, it would still be there. It would always be there; even if one were to take it apart stone by stone. There were all those endless levels beneath the foundation that ran in spirals beneath the hill; there was the watchtower and there the springs and wells that watered its gardens and its inhabitants. They would all be forgotten by men in time, like the Roman ruins that still could be found in country glens and fields; places only visited by strange spirits and those men who sought after them. And while it all fell to ruin, they would be safely away, she and Withing and Clarice, in the bright walls and carefully-kept gardens of an English estate; and perhaps after many years, their memories of this year and its horrors would fall as well to ruin. Perhaps she would forget Cyrus's face and Childermass's grim, sly looks and perhaps their voices would only come back to her in the early morning hours when the mist turned English fields to Scottish moors.

And then she turned her eyes from the torches and saw that above the Priory's towers and chimneys, a smoke had begun to rise.

"Dear Christ," she murmured. "He has already set fire to the place. And Cyrus and Childermass are still within."

She spurred her horse forward, galloping ahead of the Houndswick villagers. She had thought that the murderer would only want to keep the Priory for his own, but now it seemed evident that he wished nothing less than to claim its destruction for himself. Clarice and Withing, both of whom had taken in at once the change in Mariah's manner, followed close after on their own horses. The rest of that party, footbound, could do no more than quicken their pace. Squire Toby and Montrose who brought up the rear on their own mounts, decided it more prudent to wait and watch the outcome of all this with an appropriately formidable wall of intervening peasants standing betwixt them and the Priory.

The wind, the black branches wet and gleaming with ice, the banks of snow along the path, they all flew past her as she went that last half mile to the Priory. Breathless, flushed, she was too exhausted even to feel afraid. Only when she at last looked up and found herself under the shadow of the Priory did she feel a darkness once again come to cover her soul. When she saw a motion behind the courtyard gate, an image of the sprawled dead in the Great Hall rose like a crimson prophecy in her heart and she brought a hand to her mouth while her other went to the dagger that she had hidden in her belt. She could not take her hand away, even after she saw Cyrus emerge, bruised but smiling wearily, and saw Childermass come to stand by him.

"You are safe!" Cyrus called out.

"You are safe," she managed.

Withing, riding a little behind Mariah, caught sight of Cyrus and Childermass at the gates of the Priory and drew his horse up so sharply that its hooves slid against the icy road. He dropped out of his saddle and ran towards them – then stopped short, a few feet away. The boy's eyes, all the haunted suffering and terror that filled them, wavered for a moment like darkness before a coming light. He gazed at their bloody clothes, at their shadows on the snow. It was as if he could not bring himself to believe that it was they and not their ghosts that he saw.

"Withing," Cyrus said softly. "It's all been set right now."

And the boy finally met his eyes and somehow then knew that it really was all right – that they were safe and well at last. His face went wrong with joy, for a moment, as though he were about to cry. Then he closed those last steps between them and hugged Cyrus, tightly and breathlessly. In a rush, Cyrus remembered the heady ride in the carriage when he had first met Withing after his rescue from Montrose's apartment; remembered how, when Sir Robert was ravening for them both, the boy had pleaded with him to leave and save himself, in spite of all the tortures he had endured; remembered best and most poignantly that morning the look that Withing had worn when he stood at the balcony overlooking the Great Hall and told Cyrus how much he loved and hated the Priory. They didn't come to him softly like recollections; they tore into his consciousness like fresh experiences relearned. He felt embarrassed by the tears that made raw the back of his throat, even more so when he saw the faint sneer on Childermass's face as he watched them.

Childermass's smile disappeared however when Withing, not content merely to embrace one friend, made a move towards him as well. In a crude attempt to avoid the boy's show of affection, the chimney sweeper managed to trip over the broom that he had been using as a crutch and fell against Cyrus, sending the three of them sprawling in a heap on top of each other.

"What in God's name – "

The villagers of Houndswick had finally arrived, torches in hand, just in time to catch an eyeful of this ridiculous spectacle. They looked from the young men to the castle; from this proximity, it was clear that the smoke that Mariah had noticed rising from the towers was clearly only channeled harmlessly from out the kitchen chimneys.

"Do we still burn the place down?" one of them asked, a little wistfully. They were all staring shamelessly at the dark shape that rose before them; it was the closest that most of them had ever come to the Priory. The thought of turning back now had put them all in a decidedly sour mood.

"I think I know," said Childermass, dusting the snow from his coat. "A thing almost as satisfying as burning it down."

Chapter Forty-Seven: In which Cyrus recalls a half-remembered terror and finds himself a home.

The courtyard was filled with smoking torches, black sooty sticks left to smolder in snow drifts; Houndswick villagers stood beneath stone walls, watching the pigeons scatter across the moody grey sky, the new-risen sun behind a cloud, blearily bright like a moving human eye. Nothing soft touched that dawn, two mornings after Christmas, and the air still held the cold colors of last night's winter storm – broken branches, a chill brush and stir of wind, the sharp stop and slap of a threatening drizzle.

***

They were all waiting for the return of Feversham, Dagworth, and Childermass who had gone inside to ready the Priory for its guests and for the commencement of the masquerade – for the next evening was the Feast of the Holy Innocents.

"What are they doing in there?" Cyrus whispered to Withing.

"Oh, you'll see," the boy said. "They shouldn't be much longer."

And they would not have been much longer at all, were it not that there was a further business to be carried out before the Priory was made wholly safe. A business that kept Childermass standing in the shadows of a hallway, the hallway in which Cyrus slaughtered the Marquis. The chimney sweeper listened to the sound of dripping, moving liquid and drew his coat tighter about his shoulders, not because he was afraid but as proof against the cold, for it was a cruel morning and the wind came through the glassless window of that corridor with choking force.

He had taken to cutting his store of enchanted blood with milk and the effect of it had worn off somewhat; he felt it as no more than a glow somewhere in his brain and heart, much like the effect of a strong spirit save that it had an afterchill rather than a warmth to it. He knew that neither Cyrus, nor anyone else, would ever understand his actions; that they might even hang him if they knew that he still kept his former lord's blood and drank it at his own pleasure. Well, the blood had saved him once from death. Perhaps it would do so again. All the same, Childermass hoped that it would not come to that. The blood could restore and heal, yes; but he was not so certain of how long these effects lasted and he was not eager to test its limits. Better to enjoy the enchantment in secrecy than risk the loss of everything in a moment's imprudence.

A mist was gathering at his feet, rising to the level of his face. Something took him by the shoulders and pushed him back, hard against the wall. But it was only for a moment; a moment of something cold and wet against his flesh and some bodiless, invisible gaze that wanted to finish what it had started with him. It filled him with those images and sensations that he had felt only hours ago when hanging in Sir Robert's awful chamber; those horrors that he had felt when he had first realized what it was that would be done to him. The same faintness that overcame him then now came upon him once more. His vision was now dark, occasionally alight with bursting stars – then a sudden, savage pain ran through him, forcing a hot tear down his cheek. The visions came to him again, but this time they were not memories – they were improvisations made all the more complex and intricate because the mind that devised them had found sufficient time to improve upon their former model. He saw himself standing in a windowless chamber of cold stone, his hands fastened behind his back with chains of silver, his neck held taut and upright by a rough noose of hangman's rope, his mouth held open by a device of iron. The only light within that chamber emanated from the motionless flame of a single cresset that hung above him, that illuminated the flute of glass that fed the blood of his heart down his throat and shone down upon the table that stood close by, upon which stood two bowls of beaten gold, one holding a collection of his teeth floating in a bloody pool of rosewater and the other, the grey curl of his uprooted tongue in a bed of dried petals.

As the brutal vision vanished before his eyes like blown smoke, he felt sick and tried to steady himself against the wall. He knew that this would happen, that there would be this last confrontation to overcome. But it was when he felt himself caught in the arms of the torturer and knew that this was no vision but the actual, coalesced substance of that running flesh, that he finally felt his gorge rise and hung his head, trying to cough out his sickness.

Wet, barely formed fingers seized his hair, drew his head back, whispered mouthless promises into his ear.

"Poor creature, vomit up what I feed you and I shall only make you drink it down again."

Its grasp on him vanished, the whispers ceased, and Childermass found himself stumbling back, shaken but free. The mist had dissipated and resolved itself again into the same swamp-like dew that had been settling upon the stones.

With unsteady fingers, Childermass mopped it all up with the rags that he had brought, soaked it all until the floor was as dry as his mouth. Then, stowing them all in a sack, he returned to Sir Robert's chamber and hurled the sack as far into those charnel depths as he could. He shut the door, but not before he saw those tendrils of wet mist begin to rise again and caught a whisper, a plea: something begging not to be locked away in a windowless world for all eternity, something that wished not to be left alone with all its bloody visions unshared.

He closed the door and turned the key; then put his ear to the door and listened. Somewhere behind that barrier, he fancied that he heard a low sigh or sob, the groan of a soul that cannot leave its own residue because what remains of it still lives, though utterly shapeless.

Childermass licked his lips and left that place. He went to a window, still fingering the key, imagining what would happen if he were to let it cast it down into the dark thickets that bordered the Priory's walls, where vines and insects would wrap their tendrils and dig spiderholes beneath its rusted weight.

With a steady hand, he returned the key to his pocket; returned it, with that red thread of enchanted blood running through him, wrapping him up in its visions, rewarding him for his *appreciation*, showing him what the Priory really was. He licked his lips again, this time with raw, wet desire. As he passed the locked door of Sir Robert's chamber, he thought he heard something plead and whisper behind it. But Childermass only gave a chilling little smile, before continuing on his way.

***

A flock of blackbirds crossed the sky above the Priory, and Cyrus followed them with his eyes and as he did, he saw a dark figure at the edge of the forest. His heart ached familiarly after it, but his attention was suddenly drawn to the door of the Priory as Feversham, Childermass, and Dagworth stepped onto the porch. They were wearing the robes of nobility: Feversham in a robe of oaken green, Dagworth in crimson, and Childermass in black.

Their stations had been utterly reversed, in accordance with the masquerade of the Feast of the Innocents. And with one accord, Withing, Mariah, Clarice, and the rest of the noble assemblage bowed before them.

Dagworth made a backhanded gesture with his hand. It was time for the guests to rise and enter. As they filed past, he looked at Childermass and said, "When the feast is done, who will be our lords then, eh, Master Chimney? The boy Withing?"

"The Priory's head has been sawed off," Feversham said morosely. "Friends, we are finished. Even if the place has been saved from being torched, we are still left with a lord who is only a boy."

"And what of it?" Dagworth said with a gruff laugh. "As though we were ever given any real direction from Sir Robert *or* His Holiness. Lord Withing will come of age in a few years, fear not."

"And until then?" returned Feversham.

"I fear," said Childermass. "I fear that we alone are its stewards."

They both looked at him sharply.

"And I know," Childermass continued. "That we will serve our stewardship with the utmost faithfulness."

"Dear Lord," said Dagworth. "He will give us a sermon." But he said it with a peculiarly soft edge to his voice, like an animal with a cruel temper that at once snaps and fawns. Childermass spat sharply into the snow and said nothing more. There was no need, for they all understood and there was little in what they understood that did not please them.

"A strange thing," said Feversham. "For the three of us to have lived within these walls longer than any other soul…"

"By God's throne, the man will make every one of us sound as old as was Sir Robert," Dagworth cried. "Why not smile, man, and give up this pretended melancholy once and for all? Even Childermass knows a piece of luck when he sees it. Lads, it is finally *our* season."

And Feversham, seeing the congratulatory looks that Dagworth and Childermass exchanged, made an exasperated noise in his throat and said, "Well, I'll be off to see about making preparations for dinner. I hope that your highnesses won't be kept too long."

"Fear not, Your Grace," Dagworth said, with a bow. "Lord Childermass and I will be with you shortly, after we discuss a few affairs of state."

Though only late morning, the sun had already begun to sink behind the mountains so that only a grey trace of it remained along the haggard horizon.

The gusts of wind that blew past stung like summer wasps, yet Cyrus lingered on the porch of the Priory as well, his gaze upon the horizon that he could see past the trees, past the low mist and the black trees. A rain of snow had already begun to fall again; a cloud of ashes from a silver, burning heaven.

The figure that he fancied he saw earlier was there again. Again, that stab of familiarity; he raised his hand in greeting. The figure returned this salute; the next moment he turned away into the forest and vanished. Cyrus did not know who he was, but Childermass did and said nothing, for he was warned in a dream to keep silent. A father, even a tongueless phantom father, would wish a last look at his son, but he would not want his son to chase after ghosts and shadows for his sake. The Priory would see no more of him, nor of Nat. They were gone from this world forever.

Cyrus looked at Childermass and saw that everyone else, even Dagworth, had returned inside, and that they were the last to remain without.

"Where will you go now, Master Plainstaff?" Childermass asked.

"I can find some work in Houndswick," Cyrus replied. "There are a great many shepherds in these parts who would need an extra hand like me. I'll manage, have no fear. But what will become of Withing? He is only an orphan now."

"We are all of us orphans now, Cyrus," said Childermass. "Withing has his cousin Mariah's company, though he trusts my wisdom still more. But what have *we*, Cyrus, save Heaven?" He paused, expelled a misty sigh. "And the Priory."

Cyrus looked up at those grey walls and thought of how they had seemed so haughty and yet so beckoning when he had first looked upon them. It seemed years ago – that morning when Withing had taken him in Squire Toby's coach to this forbidding place. All of a sudden, extraordinarily, Cyrus found himself wishing for that morning in place of the one he found himself in; found himself hating the idea of departing, even if he knew such a departure was inevitable. He put his hand to his face, rubbed the corners of his eyes, and felt very tired.

"It is only a place. A forbidding place, to be sure, but nothing more than stones."

"Haven't you lied enough since you came here, Cyrus?" said Childermass. "And to lie to *me* of all people: I, who have read your heart better than any other. You love this place and you long to stay." He paused. "You feel something here, don't you?"

Cyrus felt a shudder come over him at these words. He thought of the strange dreams that had assailed him ever since his arrival; of the passages within walls, the secret chambers, the odd way that Childermass had often spoken of the Priory's *wanting* them and wishing them to save it.

"What is it, then?" he whispered. "Is it all the dead who have ever lived in the Priory? Is it something else? What could it be?"

Childermass smiled. "I don't know, but I cannot tell you how well it pleases me to hear you speak so."

Cyrus turned away, unable to tell whether he was being made a fool of or not.

"Will you not have one drink before you go, for friendship's sake?" Childermass asked softly and as he spoke, he held out the cup of enchanted blood that he had been drinking.

There was something in Childermass's eye that momentarily unraveled Cyrus's courage. It was that glittering glance that precedes laughter – and something in that intimation of laughter was a horror. In the back of Cyrus's eye, he could see a cunning creature ascending to the highest branches of some dark tree; he could hear the rippling echo of some intelligent madness; but whatever hidden memory this vision intimated was lost to him, locked away in some place within his own mind.

In a moment, the fleeting fear was gone – replaced with all the cautious warmth that he felt before for his companion, though he declined his offer.

"I will leave soon," he told Childermass. "But I cannot leave too hastily, with Withing doubly-orphaned."

"He has his rightful guardians, Cyrus."

"When the snow melts, then? As I said, I could find work with a shepherd in Shrewsfield or Houndswick in the mean time."

"That you could," the chimney sweeper agreed.

Cyrus frowned and looked from Childermass to the cold, grey towers of the Priory above them.

"You don't seem very concerned about my leaving," he said at last.

"Well, Master Plainstaff," Childermass smiled. "Neither do you."

THE END

Printed in Great Britain
by Amazon

83861142R00241